The Desert

Tales of Miurag

BY

A.S. Etaski

Published by Corpus Nexus Press
ISBN: 978-1-949552-23-2

etaski.com
etaski.com/sister-seekers
miurag.etaski.com
www.patreon.com/etaski
www.goodreads.com/etaski
www.bookbub.com/authors/a-s-etaski
www.facebook.com/asetaski
mastodon.online/@etaski

Cover Design by Eris Adderly
Book layout by DocKangey

This book is a work of fiction and intended for adults only. Sexual activities represented in this work are between adults and are fantasies only. Nothing in this book should be interpreted as the author advocating any non-consensual activity.

INTRODUCTION

The Desert IS THE ORIGIN STORY OF THE VALSHARESS ISHUNA, THE DARK ELF Queen in the *Sister Seekers* series. Worth noting, she is *far* from the only antagonist who discovers her path in these pages.

In this story, we catch glimpses of many powerful figures from *Sister Seekers*. Most of them are perhaps more relatable when we see them younger and less sure of their goals.

Originally written at the request of my patrons as two shorter works, *Sisters of V'Gedra (2016)* and *Ishuna (2017)*, this tale has been heavily revised and combined into a whole and continuous novel.

The story begins roughly 3,500 years before the start of Sirana's tale in *No Demons But Us*.

Warning: This book contains mature themes and is intended for a mature audience. The story includes explicit sex and some violence readers may find disturbing. Discretion is advised.

A glossary is available at World Anvil where I keep my series lore.

PART ONE

LIFE & WATER

CHAPTER 1

KOORUL – 401 B.S.E.

THEIR EYES MET, EACH GAZE SLIDING ONCE TOWARD THE CAPTAIN. THE ELDER sister signaled, turned her stallion's head toward the canyon ahead. The younger nodded.

"*Hyah!*" cried the Queen's daughter, digging her boot heels into shining sorrel flanks. Her mount neighed loudly and surged forward, kicking up his hind legs as he sensed her excitement. Innathi just clung on.

"*Hai, you two — !*" Xala called.

Any further words of command were lost in a doubly thunderous gallop. Ishuna's silver-white mare was just behind the copper-red stallion, having already been given her head. The heir kept her focus on her mount, lest he shoulder the mare to a halt so that he could rear up onto her with no concern for the riders present.

"*Hyah!*" she urged the fine *Hilsav* faster, her tight grip on the reins keeping his eyes forward. "*Qee-vaiy!*"

The finish line was that first, multi-colored stone jutting up from the rust-red sand, heralding the trailhead through the canyons of Koorul. The waterfall deep within would be the endpoint of the sisters' journey, where they would allow the horses to drink, rest, and then saunter their way back to the Queen-Mother's city.

A full two weeks out of the Capital this time. ostensibly because the royal daughters had reached acceptable maturity for this anticipated trip. The Queen-Mother always knew how to keep them wanting more, and over the last twelve decades, Alyarra's heirs had come to know the desert they would one day inherit a little at a time.

Ishuna claimed victory by a mere head as the stupid stallion dropped his speed and turned his neck to nip at the mare's bright shoulder at just the wrong moment.

"*Vith!!*" Innathi cursed, slapping his withers with her crop as the charging hooves slowed to a soft canter and then a trot. "Horny beast! Typical! So dumb!"

Ishuna gasped for breath as she laughed, keeping one wary eye on the stallion as he lifted his lip toward her mare. "Rest in that shade here?" she suggested, indicating the tall cliffs forming a narrow entryway into Koorul — the only shelter available this far into the morning as the sun climbed high.

Innathi inhaled to accept.

"*Qu'essanil!* Stay there!"

Innathi and Ishuna turned their horses at the commanding voice, pausing to allow Captain Xala Ja'Prohn to catch up with them.

Trusted by the Valsharess to bring her daughters home each time, Xala displayed legendary patience at times. Perhaps tellingly, the dark gelding upon which she rode responded to the slightest command from his rider without a lash.

The Captain wore a dark red uniform of fine quality, the blouse and pants loose enough to breathe, with supple, earth-red leather armor with matching boots and gloves. Her hood was shade-shaped to not easily be knocked off by a stiff breeze, her pure white hair, the whites of her eyes, and her teeth standing out within it.

Sharp, crimson eyes evaluated the royal *Hilsav* mounts, along with every shadow on those cliffs. A strong jaw and stronger mind worked while Xala formed her next "suggestion," which her two charges knew they dismissed at their peril.

Their relationship had been fairly easy for decades now: the *qu'essan* listened to their bodyguard, and their bodyguard kept them alive while they had their fun and learned about the Queendom.

"The day is hotter than anticipated," she said finally. "The horses will need more water after a race."

"I planned to give Tiuin the rest of mine," Innathi began. "Ishuna and I have some extra."

"I did not hear that," Xala replied with mild amusement. "We will stay low for the day's zenith and travel when the sun is much lower. Before twilight."

Ishuna made a face within her pale, elegant headwrap. "So, we crouch next to a wall for the next several hours, pouring water into our palms while muzzles slobber on them?"

"Just like yesterday," Innathi chuckled.

Xala winked with a smirk. "We'll go farther into Koorul and hope we find the waterfall."

"Hope?" Innathi echoed. "You know the location of *every* oasis, where to overturn every stone to find the smallest well of water. How could you *not* know where the waterfall is?"

The smirk mellowed. "I take it you haven't been listening to the caravan stories about Koorul, *qu'essan*?"

"Pfft. What stories? That the waterfalls never match the maps or seem to be in different places? Or even that there is only *one* waterfall, but sleeping in Koorul steals your memory of where it is?"

"Ah. You *have* been listening."

"Mystic superstition. Surely you recall the Queen-Mother's law about that."

"I do, *qu'essan*. Some stories have deep roots, is all, and we may not be the only ones here."

Ishuna lifted her tan-gloved hand. "Do they not also say one must be open to '*harmonine*' to find it?"

Xala offered a modest bow of her head to the younger sister as Innathi laughed, flipping her hand. "*Harmonine?* Isn't that pretending to predict what hasn't happened?"

Her sister's shoulders hunched. "Not … quite."

"Hm," the Captain grunted, watching the younger until the horses loudly smacked their lips and stamped their feet. "Hm. Let me lead you to some shade while the others catch up. Perhaps they can do some scouting."

"No, I want to stay at the front," Innathi argued. "I want to see Koorul without passing by a pile of fresh road apples."

Xala chuckled. "Very well."

"If we find a waterfall," Ishuna began skeptically, "could we bathe?"

Another bow of her head. "As always, *qu'essanil,* once I deem it safe, you may do as you wish."

The sisters shared a look, imagining the best midday *syvis* yet.

"Let us go, then," Innathi said with a sweep of her arm. "And hope we get 'lucky,' Captain."

KOORUL WAS AN EXTRAORDINARY PLACE.

The bands of rock displayed all shades but green which was claimed by the plants clinging to the many ledges and crevices. The patterns became ever more complex the deeper the travelers went, even as the height of the cliffs rose many times above their heads within the first quarter-league following their break.

Neither Innathi nor Ishuna had seen anything like this in nature, though now saw exactly where some of their best artists and architects might have gotten their inspiration. The vibrant, multilayered rock appeared to have been carved and sculpted by some massive god's hand reaching down from the sky, displaying more variation and nuance than they could take in a fortnight.

The Queen's daughters gawked to imagine how adding a waterfall would alter the brilliant scenery.

"The Zauyr like to say this place was carved by Musanlo, the sun god himself," Xala explained, amused. "As a gift to a mortal Queen of theirs whom he courted for a time."

"I read something like that before," Ishuna said, her voice quiet like the Captain's so as not to echo off the walls while she absorbed the breathtaking canyon. "I never imagined something extraordinary like this."

"Indeed," Innathi said, eyebrow arched. "Sssooo … If there *is* water here, why isn't there a settlement? At least a trading well?"

Xala raised her brow in confusion. "Koorul has been neutral ground for generations, your grace."

"So, we say, but why?" The heir chuckled, not quite hiding her impatience. "I am sorry, but I just imagine that every ruler or general has thought about the advantages here, not to mention the beauty!"

"Ah. Well, you aren't wrong, *qu'essan*. Some have tried to break the Preservation Treaty."

"And? They've somehow kept being pushed out?"

"You could say that."

"By us?"

Xala pursed her lips, and Ishuna shook her head, scoffing softly at her sister. "No one stays for long, Innathi, not Zauyr nor Davrin. Not on purpose."

"Not your fearful *stories* again," the elder growled.

"Well," the Captain ducked in seeing Ishuna's expression. "This *is* a labyrinth in the middle of nowhere, your grace, far off the regular trade routes with nothing else to recommend it except a pilgrimage to say you saw it, plus a little water to give you the strength to go back. We know it's at least sacred to the Human tribes and many travelers, even if the Queen of V'Gedra has paid it less attention these last centuries."

"I have *read* about the sacred places in the southern continent," Innathi responded, squaring her shoulders with a tart look at her sister. "As part of my lessons! These canyons, pretty as they are, were not among them."

The younger sister gazed around. "They should be."

"It still is," Xala replied, "to some."Your Queen-Mother's mother allowed the Zauyrian Realms to claim it as theirs to worship, as long as there wasn't war between us."

Ishuna smiled a bit. "Because she knew they would not stay, and words of Humans change ten times during a single Queen's reign."

"*And* because there's nothing here we want," Innathi countered, smirking on a shrug. "Except maybe a drink and a bath."

Xala nodded. "Though do note the Sorcerer-Kings of the Realms are longer-lived than most. They remember their bargains better than those around the Great Lake, and thus are often our best allies."

"I remember, Xala."

"Just the rulers," Innathi repeated, squinting with suspicion. "I've always wondered how those 'kings' manage this when many Humans have no magic at all!"

"Lots of speculation," said the Captain without sounding like she wanted to get into it.

"About five kings, yes?"

"Exactly five, your grace. Seems a stable number for them."

"And each sorcerer also has one of those, *hm*, corpse mages among his Court?"

"Death guides," Ishuna added, pouting as her sister stuck her tongue out at her.

"Close enough! 'Guiding' each death among Humans would certainly be a lot of work. So many, aging so fast, I see the eldest dying every day!"

"You'd be correct, *qu'essan*," said the Captain. "In that regard, do *not* underestimate how quickly they learn in the short time they have. Their scholars have made ours' heads spin. I've seen it."

"Hah! Perhaps I'll invite some to the archives when I become Valsharess. We can compare records."

"Not unheard of in V'Gedra," Xala mused. "Though you may be waiting on four generations of Zauyrians not yet born to write everything down and bring it to you."

The Queen's daughters looked taken aback by the thought despite the regular presence of Humans in their city.

"Perhaps we need to sit in on more of Mother's audiences with the Realms," Innathi said with a chin rub. "Try to keep track of which leaders change out and when."

"She won't let us into her audience until she says we're ready," Ishuna replied. "We're still too young."

"*Are* we?" The elder tossed her head. "Is three centuries not enough?"

"She waited fifteen hundred before she had us."

Innathi palmed her face, muffling a slight growl. "And ruled for twelve hundred to avoid the risk of an heir growing impatient before the Queen's transition. The fact she bore *us* means she looks ahead to that very moment. We must prepare!"

"Patience, *qu'essan*," Xala said. "I'll mention your interest in those meetings in my report."

"Will you?"

"Sure. Heh. Though, I should warn you, they can be boring."

"So are my tutors, but I do what I must."

"They're not *that* bad," Ishuna muttered, eyes drifting over curls of colored stone.

"They never look at me!" her sister complained. "They never laugh at a single jest I make!"

"If you would jest about anything but how to use a prick, perhaps …"

"Pricks are funny."

Xala cleared her throat. "They're afraid of offending your Queen-Mother, your grace."

"*Pfft*. As if I'd tell on them? Fearful scholars are boring. At least the Guardsvrin will banter for my amusement."

The younger lifted her eyes toward the cliffs. "If banter and gossip are the same."

"Oh, be quiet, sister. As I've said, better to know what happens in the Palace and around the city, and they only speak if you make them laugh. Now we must expand the view!"

"I'd rather just enjoy this one."

"Well, so be it. That waterfall can show itself anytime."

ALTHOUGH THE SUN WAS STILL HIGH IN MIDAFTERNOON, THE DEEP SHADE within Koorul made the atmosphere seem closer to dusk, especially whenever the mind wandered. More than one in the company had asked another about the time of day.

The royal sisters had fallen quiet as well while their *Hilsav* grew thirstier with no water to be found. The liveliness of the day had dimmed and grown sober as concerns grew. Even Innathi let the scouts make their reports to Xala without interruption.

"Should we turn around?" she asked quietly after they'd left, leaning on her antsy stallion. "We might make the oasis by midnight."

Xala had been observing Ishuna in the corner of her eye for the last league, watching how her light red eyes drifted in wonder. She weighed how to answer the Queen's heir now.

"This ... may be the best course of action," she began, watching Ishuna's shoulders sag slightly. "But I want to try one thing, first."

"What thing?"

"Will you remain with Lead Baetae while I go farther ahead with Ishuna?"

"What?" Innathi was confused and miffed. "Why her? Why not me?"

Xala exhaled softly. "A promise I made to your Queen-Mother, your grace. Please, trust me. It won't take long. Then we'll turn around and head home."

Reluctantly, Innathi agreed to stay behind as the Captain led the younger royal daughter up the next gradual incline. Ishuna questioned with her face rather than her tongue but appeared less put out by the separation.

"Have you been ... feeling odd, *qu'essan*?" the mature Davrin asked with care. "While we've been here?"

Ishuna swallowed. "You mean, unwell?"

"Not necessarily. Just anything different."

The horses' hooves clopped over the stone and sand. The royal daughter's breath wavered as she pulled air in and let it out. She hesitated to answer, but the answer was yes.

"Nix it, I never asked," Xala murmured, not for the first time. "Just walk with me."

Perhaps it was only their history that this helped at all. Xala could not have said *she* felt any change, and perhaps the truth was that her long, sensitive ears had picked up the sound of water spattering over rock by chance, an echo like the already rare rainfall in the desert being sequestered to one small spot.

There. She breathed in, detecting the faintest hint of vapor across her tongue. *Just around the bend.*

She didn't dare return to her company until she'd laid eyes upon it. For the sake of her charges, she *must* be certain they'd found the waterfall of Koorul.

"I hear voices," Ishuna said, trying not to sound afraid.

The next moment, Xala heard them as well.

Men.

Beco's Balls …

CHAPTER 2

"LOOKS LIKE WE CAUGHT THEM IN SOME RITE OF PASSAGE," XALA EXPLAINED once she and Ishuna had crept back to their entourage, the rush of the waterfall still touching their ears. "If the Zauyrians bother coming all the way out here, these gatherings can last a few days. We will have to negotiate for the water. Shouldn't be difficult, though, if you let me do the talking."

The royal sisters nodded, and Innathi said, "What about the bath?"

"I can't say yet, your grace. Depends where they are in their rituals."

"I want the bath," she repeated. "Include it in your negotiations."

Xala's face settled into focus. "We risk a conflict if they won't all leave to grant privacy, *qu'essan*."

"Then they can watch," Innathi stated.

"What?" Ishuna asked with alarm, looking down at her with a frown.

"That could be dangerous, your grace," said Xala.

"Why? They're just buas."

"Not the best comparison, *qu'essan*. The men tend to make all the decisions about politics and defense."

"So more like you and me? Very well. And hasn't my beauty been part of fertility parades back home? I've stood showing the public as much in those sheer costumes."

"Well —"

"Wouldn't that be a tempting privilege they could claim in their stories back home? Surely you can protect me, Captain." The Queen's heir barely waited for that pause of indecision. "Might I suggest you also get the best-looking of them to bathe as well, so they have someone to risk."

Xala blinked and smirked when she spotted the pathway. "Get naked, you mean?"

The elder sister grinned. "I've never seen a Human man nude. We can make this fun. Wouldn't you agree, Ishuna?"

"I don't care about the bathing," the younger said. "I'll pass."

Innathi sighed. "Whatever."

Ishuna scowled but looked to her protector. "What do we have to negotiate for the water?"

"Not sure yet," Xala admitted. "I'll have to talk to them, but they *will* negotiate if they want to keep the treaty, though they wouldn't risk insulting the Valsharess by suggesting something demeaning involving you two."

"How do you know?" the younger asked bluntly, for that very thought apparently had crossed her mind.

"Because one of them is wearing the firebird symbol on his clothes, so he's at least *related* to the ruling sorcerer of the Third Realm."

Ishuna nodded, but Innathi narrowed her eyes. "Only one? And not the ruler himself?" she asked.

Xala shook her head. "The Sorcerer-King wears a firebird ring no one can remove but himself. It's too far to see if he wears that ring." She paused. "Plus, he looks young."

"Young? Hm." Innathi cleared her throat, straightened her back and gestured to Xala as her stallion pranced sideways. "Well. Negotiate on our behalf, Captain. Whatever is necessary. Our horses are thirsty."

"And lusty," one of the Guardsvrin behind them said as the red stallion sidestepped and again fought his mistress's control to sniff the white mare's haunches, tossing his head excitedly and lifting his upper lip. "Bad time to go into heat."

"As if the mare times it that way," Xala commented with eyebrow raised.

"No insult, Captain, just my wager. Another day out here and not even a *qu'essan* can hold him back."

Ishuna pursed her lips, moving her pale, shimmering mount farther from her sister's red sorrel. Soon they had to sleep, which meant that her current favorite would be pregnant with a foal before long.

Preoccupied by Innathi's teasing stallion and what the evening would be like being so close to the Zauyrians, Ishuna almost missed the cue from the Captain to ride forward into view.

"Time to show ourselves," Innathi murmured to her. "Keep your back straight. We're representing Mother and V'Gedra."

Ishuna yanked herself back to the present and nodded. With a gentle kick, she moved forward with the rest.

They kept plenty of distance between the two groups while Xala stood in the middle with a Human man wearing a uniform of his own, bearing less red and more blues and golds. They had dismounted and stood on even ground; Xala's gelding was even the first allowed to wander over to the stream and start to drink in loud slurps. The men had started grinning and pointing, looking amused but also admiring the brilliant sheen of the dark *Hilsav* coat.

That must be a good sign, Ishuna thought, wondering why she felt so anxious about being here. The Captain spoke smoothly in the Zauyrian language, a growling, rolling sound much faster than Davrin speech, but she didn't know if it conveyed any more nuance.

The younger *qu'essan* flicked her eyes toward the others lined up on either side of the stream closer to the waterfall. The Zauyrians were *all* male, no females among them, which was a strange sight to see. She granted that it appeared as though the Davrin company had interrupted a ceremony, as all kinds of items — bowls, daggers, pouches — appeared deliberately placed and far too ornate to have been brought to use at a mere campsite.

How could Xala be so sure they were safe here if the men were offended at all? What if their short-lived pride dismissed that an all-female Davrin troupe could be more dangerous than them? The *qu'essan* knew they would win, but she was still afraid of a fight breaking out.

More gestures, more strange words. Ishuna could not make them out, so she tried to read Xala's body language instead.

The Captain was confident, at ease; she even laughed, keeping her best humor, and had the Zauyrian man smiling at her. It seemed genuine, even admiring.

Does he … know her from before?

What about the rest?

She peered carefully for the one wearing the firebird symbol on his clothes, but she could not see him right away. What she glimpsed instead was the subtle pulse of a young mage trying to hide his aura when he wasn't accustomed. Perhaps a Davrin child born twenty summers ago might not see it, but that aura was *very* plain to her.

Eventually Xala broke off with the man; they each returned to their group with the proposed terms. The Captain was smiling, her hands resting on her hips as she began to speak.

"So, good news, your graces. They haven't yet started the important part of their rite and can delay it up to one day. They have men available if any of my Guardsvrin need stress relief, and no obstacles to access to the water up to the time limit, which means we *can* bathe if desired." She looked up and swept eyes over her company. "All of us."

Ishuna's mouth sagged a bit, but Innathi spoke first.

"Wait, do you mean you bargained with 'stress relief' as if they are serving *you*?" the *qu'essan* asked, astonished but with a touch of glee.

Xala shrugged and gave her a wink, shifting her weight. It was a slow, graceful sway that some of the men were watching as they listened to their leader. "I've met this man recently, your grace. Akil Safiya, Head of the Guard for his Sorcerer-King's property closest to our borders. He paid tribute at V'Gedra to share training and exchange enforcers. And … well, we've fucked before, your graces."

Innathi laughed in delight, pressing her palms together, though Ishuna licked her lips before speaking. "Mm. How often do your Guardsvrin rut with Humans, Xala?"

"Fairly regularly, your grace."

"H … How regularly, Captain?"

"Either when there are no Davrin buas around, or we don't want to risk catching a baby." She shrugged. "Or both. As in this circumstance."

The younger sister nodded reluctantly, extrapolating what this must mean: *They're willing.*

She had even heard the gossip around the palace that Elves and Humans could not breed. A few infamous squads of soldiers bragged about having done Zauyrians so often that, if true, they would practically prove the theory by themselves.

"I wouldn't recommend you two indulge, however," added Xala, "unless you want a separate bargain."

"Wait, I still wish to bathe," Innathi said, dismayed but trying not to sound petulant.

"If you wish. And you don't mind their eyes on you."

"I do not." She harrumphed. "But why *not* indulge?"

"Innathi," her sister hissed.

"Men have been known to misinterpret its importance," said their Captain. "Remember, their women don't live long but catch even easier than we do. Plenty die giving birth, so they choose who they allow between their thighs with care. The less experienced *can* take coupling as a promise, especially if she's wealthy or higher status, which would be an annoyance to your Queen-Mother."

Before she had him executed, Xala did not say, though both daughters knew the truth.

Innathi and Ishuna made eye contact. They knew all about buas trying to bed themselves into a higher status. Such games back home had been light thus far, but everyone at Court knew the royal *qu'essanil* had "indulged" a few times each.

Suddenly the younger sister straightened up as she realized, "So what have they bargained for? You told us what they would give us. What do they want in return?"

The Captain chuckled. "Well, Zauyrian men can be extremely promiscuous given the right situation. They'll take sex alone as payment here. As long as we use each one for our 'relief,' I can guarantee there won't be a fight and you may watch if you wish."

Innathi hid obvious giggling behind her hand, scarlet eyes sparkling, while Ishuna quickly counted the men.

"Uh …" began the younger. "Some of you might have to … mount two."

"Then so be it, your grace." Now Xala winked at her. "Trust me. My caits don't tire easily, especially when it's the best way to protect the royal sisters."

An orgy beside the stream didn't break out right away, to Innathi's amused chagrin. But then, the Queen's heir didn't know exactly what to expect. She watched Xala and Akil introduce the two groups and clearly stated the terms in both languages.

Upon witnessing a wave of interested smiles on heavy, brown faces, Innathi tucked away the hint of possibility in leaving before dusk. The Davrin would be here at least until nightfall and would rest after the "payment." If her troupe was too tired to travel at midnight, at least it was welcome at the waterfall. They'd probably leave at dawn.

Well with me.

This was the most exciting thing to happen on any of their trips so far. If only her sister would relax a little.

"We're untouchable," Innathi whispered to Ishuna as they tugged their exhausted horses to the stream to drink. "You heard it. Don't be so tense."

"I-I sense something strange here," she murmured with a touch of her hand to the Hilsav's withers as the mare ducked her head. "I can't explain it, but … it's like something in a dream."

Oh, no, not this again.

"What, is our sire speaking through dunes again?" Innathi teased.

Ishuna took that as well as she ever had. "Shut up! I was just a child, and it was a *horrid* Reverie!"

"Glad to hear you say that."

Her mouth popped open to form a hole. "Horrid doesn't mean it wasn't real — !"

"Ishuna, *please*. You *said* Reverie. It wasn't real."

"*You* weren't there. *He* was."

"How *could* I be there with you? *Argh* …" Innathi flipped her hand. "Never mind what I said. I'm sure this has nothing to do with him."

Ishuna bit her lip to force herself to take a breath. "Perhaps. But there is *still* strange magic here —"

"Of course, there is. Third Realm royalty is here." She tried looking for him again, recognizable by that barely suppressed aura, but Ishuna was tugging on her sleeve at the same time her stallion wrenched her arm.

"No, not him, I mean —"

"*AIEE!*"

The red stallion had finally waited long enough. His thirst slaked, the spirited animal jerked free from his rider's distracted hand and nearly kicked her sister trying to clamber up onto the neighing mare's white back, a long, mottled erection hanging underneath his belly.

"Move, Shuna!" Innathi cried, reaching for her as she dodged low but stumbled over a stone. "Get out of the way — !"

The elder sister tried for a shield spell for them both, her magic disrupted when Xala was suddenly there. Raising a magic shield of her own with little effort, their Captain pulled them back from the stream and behind her as the horses got to coupling before any of the Guardsvrin.

Stepping around her own shield, Xala gave a hard slap to the stallion's rump with the flat of her sword. The beast hardly noticed as he thrust his hips, seeking relief in the source which had made him so hard to handle the last two days.

"Idiot *we'ha*," Xala groused. "Couldn't wait until the saddles came off and save me a mending spell?! *Shuaknen!*"

Chuckling from the Zauyrians bounced gently off the cliff walls. Shaking her head with a smirk on her lips, Xala sheathed her blade and took her two young charges by an arm. "Come on. Better just to let them finish already. Hopefully the foal gets her mother's smarts."

Innathi glanced back, fascinated by the forceful, demanding rut in a way she hadn't been until recently. How much of that long prick had disappeared into the mare's quim as he mated, so desperate to breed her while she took the breeding stance to hold them up.

The Zauyrian men even seemed to like what they saw; a few whooped and clapped, laughing alongside the Guardsvrin at the spectacle. If Innathi understood their accents better, she would have thought there had been a couple of innuendo jests about what was coming as well.

Her face flushed, quite warm — surely, she needed water — when she turned and found herself placed before the tiny pool at the base of the spattering waterfall. The flow was not as abundant as what she'd heard about in the green lands, but this precious flow was more than enough for all of them.

Four or five could even bathe beneath the water at once.

Innathi was free to step right beneath that stream and let the water beat on her head. She wanted little else right then and, feeling bold with the palatable anticipation surrounding her — not to mention backed by the trills and squeals of mating horses — the Valsharess's eldest Daughter loosened her belt, willing herself to be the first to strip from her dusty traveling clothes.

"Innathi!" Ishuna whispered, unaccountably shaken.

"I *asked* for this, and I *shall* do it," she replied with her Mother's elegance. "Only fitting that our eve of rest and play begin with me."

Xala didn't protest but stayed close. With a hand on the hilt of her sword, eyes up, and her flanking officers on alert, the heir to the throne effectively stunned every male there, not only with her Elven beauty but the confidence with which she revealed it.

Innathi's first thought had been to act, show no hesitation once she'd decided — something she learned from her Mother. She knew what she wanted, after all — *A bath in the falls!* — but she could not have imagined the looks on the tanned faces of these dark-haired Humans as they watched her shed her clothing and show them … well, everything.

One might think they are about to drop to their knees.

Either to worship her or hide immediate erections.

She smiled a little. Then a lot more. She *liked* this.

Oh, I can enjoy this.

With a brilliant grin, Innathi tossed her clothing toward Ishuna hiding behind Xala and stepped into the shallow pool. *So cool.* Delicately licking at her ankles as the spray prepared her skin for the falls.

Or so she believed.

Innathi gasped at the unexpected chill but then shivered with delight, wetting down her gritty hair. Her nipples grew painfully hard as the cool water glided down her back and over her hips; she hummed.

Xala was right. A bit of paradise in the middle of nowhere.

Innathi's attention was drawn briefly from the shower of water to her Captain when the older Davrin cleared her throat expectantly. But the experienced fighter wasn't looking at Innathi or Ishuna but rather Akil Safiya, one eyebrow quirked and a wry smirk on her face.

"Of course, Captain," the Human captain managed to speak in acceptable Davrin.

Of course, what?

Bowing his head to Xala then to Innathi and Ishuna, Akil stepped briskly to another Human wearing a familiar robe. The Head of the Guard said something brief in Zauyrian, nodding toward the falls, and bowing his head one last time.

Innathi's heart picked up once she recognized the poorly hidden aura and glimpsed the firebird emblem on his sleeve. Upon removing his hood, this younger man revealed dark hair, bronzed skin, and a white grin. His lower face was smooth and free of hair.

When the man reached for his own belt, her body stilled within the downpouring water, eyes watching with more than curiosity. Like her, he acted as though he'd never done anything so brazen in public during his, no doubt, short life.

And he *was* young, even for a Human, confirmed as he shed his robe and loose bottoms, dropping both to the ground.

"Xala?" Innathi asked over the droplets landing on her ears.

Some of the men, including the young one removing his sandals, fell still upon hearing her voice.

"Your command honored, your grace," said the Captain, sounding pleased. "The handsomest among the men is to strip for your pleasure while you bathe."

Xala beckoned to the young man; Akil reassured him as he discarded the final shoe.

"This is the second son of Begir al-phon, Third Sorcerer of the Realms."

A direct descendant of the Sorcerer-Kings of Zauyr.

Mm. Excellent.

If she was first nude among the Davrin, then only appropriate that the first Human man she saw naked should be of similar royalty.

Xala must have known th— … Oh.

The Queen's daughter knew she was staring as the lean, masculine form approached the pool. He wasn't as bulky as the ones who possessed a little grey in their hair, but he might become so with time.

His hands and feet were larger than the average Davrin bua, his eyes smaller and not angled upward as she was used to. At first glance, his ears seemed stubby being so round, but then she saw they were in proportion to his skull. Even better, his skin was perfectly even in tone, a rich, golden-brown hue. Though only lightly haired on his chest and legs, he presented thick, dark patches at his armpits and …

… his crotch.

His penis had lengthened even in this short time, stiff and bobbing just like her *Hilsav* horse, thickness matching the larger frame. Ah, but could he lose control like her mount? Was he a beast to try and seize her, to touch her … even try to mount her like a stallion teased for days?

She shivered at the view in her mind's eyes, at the grappling thoughts.

H-he had better not!

Xala was watching. She would run him through, King's son or no!

All of this ...

So intriguing, so primal and daring. Especially so far away from Court.

Where Mother cannot speak a word.

Innathi lifted her bare, dripping arms and ran fingers through long, white hair, waving her hips a little side-to-side. The young man's steel grey eyes practically shimmered in their appreciation of her beauty, and he took this as a sign to step carefully into the water. Stopping just short of his arm's length, the Sorcerer's son gave her a close look without joining her directly under the stream.

Very nice.

A moment later, he tested her tolerance. His hand took hold of the rigid appendage at the junction of his thighs, intense eyes watching for any sign of disapproval. When she smiled and gave him a little nod, he tugged a few times.

And grew bigger and redder still.

Oh, my. And I must abstain while Xala claims a servicing stallion of her own?

"Your name?" Innathi asked, keeping the question simple in case he didn't understand Davrin.

"I am Cris-ri-phon, your grace."

Ooo. His pronunciation was good. Educated; careful, not sloppy. His voice bore a lower timber than she expected.

"What are your people doing here, Cris-ri-phon?"

He had to think about it, possibly translate it in his head, first. His tongue wasn't fluent. "At my twenty summers, we come here. It is our custom."

A rite of passage, like Xala said. She supposed she had no need to know the details. They hadn't brought women, so this wasn't a fertility ritual.

Innathi forced herself to look away from him, glancing at her surroundings. Both groups on either side of the stream witnessed how the two of them interacted. Ishuna had curled herself next to a rock with her knees drawn up, still the only one so disconcerted she seemed to expect some fire-breathing Dragon to come out of the sky above them.

The rest of them ... ?

The rest just waited for a signal from someone.

Xala waited for a signal from her.

Innathi appraised and admired Cris-ri-phon again, from his big feet to glossy-black hair atop his head, lingering broad shoulders, long arms, and noting a mage's well-kept hands. His belly was taut, his waist trim and ...

Sweet Sisters, that Human stiff-stalk.

The Sorcerer-King's son also no longer suppressed his aura. She made herself blink lest she stare at its delicious complexity all afternoon.

"You are beautiful, Cris-ri-phon," she said. "I accept the head guard's trade. Stay. Let me look at you while I bathe."

Xala chuckled and gave a hand signal.

The Guardsvrin of V'Gedra became all white smiles in dark faces as they boldly crossed the stream. Each eagerly took hold of a man of her choice, often surprising him with a light stroke between his legs before his belt came off. Most recovered quickly, helping her to strip him before getting to her own uniform.

By then, Xala had pulled Akil into a lusty kiss, biting his lip and cupping his jaw before dropping one hand to his crotch. He seized her ass in a firm squeeze.

Just as the Captain had said, the Zauyrians could be easy rutters. They would share a sacred water source and put a custom on hold in exchange for some dark *raza*.

Fine for me.

Innathi enjoyed knowing her Guardsvrin would have such fun after weeks being on alert, returning to scrubbing her body with her hands as she focused on the young sorcerer before her. She bit her bottom lip in amusement before she spoke her thoughts.

"Stroke it again, Cris."

He shook his head once, his expression letting her know he didn't comprehend something, so she added the gesture. "Stroke. For me."

Now he understood.

Cris-ri-phon rubbed quickly, his cock growing harder and turning a familiar purplish color. He hadn't blinked, and she motioned for him to slow down so she could enjoy it a little longer. Her fingers searched for her cleft at the same time, dragging the tips across her hidden nub. She shuddered and did not take her eyes away, either.

"Turn around," she breathed, twirling a finger with her free hand. "Stroke, but I want to see your back."

And your backside.

Goddess, for a Human, he was impeccably well-balanced.

Gorgeous. And I must abstain? she whined privately.

The aura of this Sorcerer's son flared alongside his excitement, both in performing for her and watching his people taken balls-deep in hers. This intangible show of strength for a mage showed her unknowable shades of red and orange tracing complex patterns of icy blue and dark silver.

"Mm. Back to me, Cris-ri-phon."

He obeyed. The head of his cock was so swollen she expected it to explode at any time.

Or on my time.

At last, the Queen's heir stepped out of the waterfall and approached the man. Xala was busy protecting in her own way and couldn't fence her in.

Innathi bent on one knee as his beautiful, grey eyes grew impossibly wide. She reached to cover his hand with hers, stilling it, and smiled up at him.

So disbelieving. He doesn't think I'll do it. Hmph.

She captured the head of his penis between her dark lips without hesitation, licking and swirling her tongue around, tasting his strange, salty flavor. *Wow, that's different—*

"*Lihan—!*" he cried in a started jump.

Instantly a hot, tangy mess spurted to the back of her throat.

"*Auogh*—!" she uttered, pulling back, swallowing to avoid choking.

Cris-ri-phon's knees nearly collapsed, though he caught himself and stayed upright as he seized his cock and desperately pulled the rest of his cream out. It splattered all over her chest.

Innathi stared at it, at him, unable or unwilling to move until it finally stopped. The King's son sagged down onto his knees into the water with her, gasping for breath. Somehow, he looked a little afraid of her. Or of his reaction to her.

His semen stayed moist in the misting spray, enough to drip down her tits as Innathi trembled. So close to him, she could *feel* his powerful aura. His sweat, the scent of his magic, the clear instinct that threads of energy might spark off him to her fingers if she so much as touched him again …

He wasn't Davrin, but he was strong. And *open*.

Their auras *had* merged, just a little. Right now.

Oh … oh Sisters … what will Mother say?

Probably something dry and layered. *As usual.*

Innathi touched the mess on her breasts, tasting it on her fingertips as Cris-ri-phon watched her with awe. She ran the fingers of her other hand along her slit, attempting to soothe the ache. It only grew when her partner's mage aura intensified again.

She quickly forgot about what her Mother would say.

Or Xala, for that matter.

Whimpering, Innathi rolled onto her back upon the worn, smooth stones. The pool was so shallow, it lapped at her puckered netherhole and cooled her buttocks. She opened legs wide, capturing the gaze of the kneeling man when her fingers parted dark lips to reveal bright, oozing pink.

"Mouth here," she demanded, gasping. "Suck."

Cris-ri-phon opted not to question her, or himself. He lowered himself down, seizing her thighs and latching lips onto her sex.

"Yes! Oh!"

He groaned to hear her, relishing that first taste before nothing could hold him back from eating *raza* to her peak. Innathi writhed under his attention, turning her head to look at the shore to check if her bodyguard had noticed.

Xala hadn't; she was riding her chosen captain as hard as if he was her gelding in a race. The man couldn't decide where he liked his hands best: grabbing at her jiggling tits or spanking and squeezing her shiny ass.

Some of the excess men hadn't waited, either.

On the Human side of the stream, three of her Guardsvrin had been penetrated by two men at once. The second cock either stretched her pucker as she used her slit on first or he stood before her so she could take him between her lips.

Meanwhile, Cris lapped desperately at her cunt, thirsty enough to ignore the precious liquid surrounding them. Innathi languished in his dedication and focus, allowing his tongue, the groans, and all that slapping skin to overwhelm her.

"Ohhh, goddess —"

Suddenly, Cris pushed two thick fingers into her swollen slit.

His aura flared out of his control when she screamed.

"*Ahhh!* Oh, Cris, *YES!*"

Innathi's body splashed in the water as waves of energy flooded her, rolled over her, held her helpless. She stared for an eternity at the late day sky, the fever pitch of her pleasure hardly slowing enough to blink. The young sorcerer leaned above her, perhaps concerned or—

Wait ...

His erection was back.

He was pressing that large head right in between her slippery nether-lips. And she was yielding. Sucking him in.

"Goddess," she squeaked, hearing a very small, frightened voice. *No, no, wait, too fast —*

Too quiet to pay any mind over the howling turmoil between splayed legs.

He lunged in.

"Oh, *Goddess!*" she shrieked.

His cock felt even wider than it looked! Innathi felt her cunt strain to adjust as he stretched her open, gasping as he went deep, deeper than anyone had dared on the first stroke. Her hands flew around him to clutch his back, her fingernails digging in. He growled.

"Slow … !" she peeped.

He paused, quivering to hold still as her sheath spasmed around him, not yet able to relax. "I-Innathi … .?"

"Cris … Cris-ri-phon," she gasped, biting his shoulder as a fierce heat swept her belly. "Ohhh, gods …"

He withdrew more slowly before pressing his cock in again with a grunt.

"Yesss," she hissed.

He pulled out all but his tip and plunged in again. And again. By the third stroke, he was easier to take. She nodded, approving, willing to receive his thrusts until she came again.

"Yes! Rut me, my stallion!"

He braced himself and his hips started pounding against her, each lunge filling her up.

"*Innathi!* What's he doing to you?!"

Ishuna.

"F-fuck!" she stuttered. "G-go away!"

"No! This is different! Something's wrong with you! You must make him stop!"

Oh, but she couldn't. She *couldn't* make him stop, and she didn't want him to!

Small, black hands shoved hard at his tan shoulders.

"Get off her! Stop!"

"*N-niakten bideshu!*" he barked, swatting at her younger sister, his cock still buried to the hilt between the legs of the Queen's heir.

"Get off her before I blast you off!"

A bluff.

Since when did the little scroll-reader learn combat spells?

The young Human wouldn't be intimidated. When Ishuna went for his face, he ducked down, an incredibly fast arm reaching out to seize Ishuna's leg.

"No — !"

He jerked it out from under her. She fell next to them in the water.

"S-stop!" she yelled, kicking at Cris with her boots. His cock was still hard as stone when his arm went around her, trapping both of hers down at her sides.

Cris hauled Ishuna next to Innathi where he gained the leverage to clamp his arms down and hold them both in place while he thrust to finish inside her.

The fire hadn't lessened.

"Oh, Goddess, faster!" Innathi cried above Ishuna's pitiful wailing as she struggled. against her constraints. "Cris, more!"

"Innathi ..."

She opened her eyes, and their gazes locked. The young sorcerer looked so desperate, so overwhelmed.

"W-want ... you," he gasped. "You. Only."

He looked at her like a goddess.

"Finish," she wheezed. "Inside me, give it to me!"

He grimaced in response, roaring louder as he thrust harder, getting closer—

"No! Stop!" Ishuna screamed.

"*Ugh! Ugh!*"

"Ohhh, god — !"

"Release me!"

Cris shouted in his ultimate release, spilling his seed, the spike of his aura penetrating her even deeper. His power carried her up with him, ever higher, as she shrieked to the skies.

"Goddess, Cris, *yes!*"

Innathi came down in small, arresting drops, her mind and body too dazed to think. Her sex felt bruised, throbbing as Cris-ri-phon finally withdrew. His body was shaking, trembling uncontrollably. He could barely climb to his knuckles above her.

"Innathi ..." he whispered.

Ishuna had finally gotten loose, but her body struggled to make her way back to dry land. Glazing at her, Innathi wondered, confused, if her sister had climaxed, too?

"F-fuck … gods *damn* you!" the second-born Daughter seethed, crawling on elbows and knees, trailing water behind her. "Wh-why wouldn't you *listen?!*"

Cris slumped onto his side in the shallow pool, next to Innathi. He was barely conscious enough to take a drink before falling limp, his sweat-soaked head resting on his arm. He looked as exhausted as she felt.

Sex had never felt so good before … Never so wild.

Not even so frightening.

She was three centuries old and had yet to discover things like this?

Even now she found it hard to look away from him.

But he was Human.

What happened … ?

CHAPTER 3

THE TWO CAPTAINS, JOLTED OUT OF THE INTENSE FERVOR SWEEPING THE canyon, finally noticed their young charges sprawled in the pool. Hurriedly, they scrambled off each other and hustled into the pool.

"What happened?" Xala asked urgently, slipping a hand carefully beneath Innathi's head, checking for injury. "Are you alright, your grace?"

Her eyes were open and focused on her, but she didn't answer at once. Her mouth hung open, lips hinting at forming words.

"Sorkin gishi aru'yr?" Akil asked the Sorcerer's son, shaking his shoulder. He remained unresponsive, his eyes closed; the head guard reached to make sure his nose and mouth stayed above water. "Captain Ja'Prohn? Is the *qu'essan* well?"

"Better than the second son," Xala muttered. "Let's get them on dry land."

Sitting Innathi up, she pulled one arm across her shoulders before reaching beneath the heir's back and knees to lift her up. Turning toward the shore, she began, "Ishuna, did you see anything — ?"

The Captain froze, barefoot, nude, and carrying the elder sister when she finally noticed that Ishuna was completely soaked.

She's been in the pool.

"Ishuna — ?"

The young Davrin had her hands clasped to her long ears; she shook her head urgently. "Get him away from her. He is strange, he is so strange … ! Living and dying!"

"Dying?" Xala asked, concerned enough to take another look at the young man whom Akil was struggling to get to respond. She asked in Zauyrian, *"Akil, how is the boy's pulse? His breathing?"*

"They are both good, Xala," he answered back in his native tongue, his eyes and expression matching his words.

With an exhale, the Captain finished the last few steps onto dry land, laying Innathi down near Ishuna. *"So, he is not dying?"*

"No. Though I heard what she said."

Akil was still in the water with Cris-ri-phon. The sex among the guards on the other side of the stream was slowing down as more of them reached climax and slowly noticed that something else was going on.

The Human head of his guard chose his next words with care. *"Is your … younger royal a seer?"*

Xala frowned, kneeling beside Innathi, who took a deep breath and started to move on her own. Glancing at the sisters, she answered with equal care. *"Not according to the Queen."*

Akil was an intelligent man. *"Ah. I see. My apologies."*

"Oh but, I'm curious," she continued. *"Why would you ask this?"*

He pursed his lips. *"There is a reason that our rite for Cris-ri-phon has not yet begun. We await the Maiden Deathwalker. She is the only one until today who has described Cris in such a way, both living and dying. And* she *most definitely is a seer."*

For once, Xala was glad that Ishuna was not fluent in his language or his accent. Her Queen-Mother would not be pleased with even the suggestion that her Daughter was "strange."

Even if the Zauyrians would never see her as such.

Their exchange ended as two men came to Akil and assisted him, moving the naked, young sorcerer out of the water and onto the far side of the stream. He was far away from Innathi and Ishuna now, which was probably a good idea.

Lead Baetae had gone to her horse and brought a blanket to Xala, who used it to dry off the Queen's heir and cover her up just as Innathi regained her wits. The Captain was too experienced not to notice that Innathi's cunt had been fucked hard. The boy had even creamed her.

She had no idea how many guards had seen it.

Fuck.

"Akil?" she asked across the way, mostly to distract herself from a possibly grim fate.

Akil lifted his head to look at her. "Ai, Captain?"

"*What is a Maiden Deathwalker? Someone at your King's Court?*"

"*Well …*"

He hesitated, then something drew his attention further downstream. The head guard nodded that way, looking back and raising his arm to point into the deepening shadows of evening.

"*She comes now, Captain. You may ask her to explain.*"

Ishuna could not stop shivering as she pressed her side to the boulder. Captain Xala concerned herself with her sister and talked with that Zauyr Man to the point of ignoring her.

Bitter as that tasted in the back of her mouth, it was just as well. The Captain would want facts, first. Hard details on what had happened seen with her eyes or heard with her ears, but those would *not* help anyone to truly *grasp* what she'd witnessed. The younger Queen's Daughter was not sure she could explain it to herself, even, but she *would* understand it.

One day. I will understand. She whimpered, tears leaking out. *I'm so afraid …*

She held her middle with her hands, applied pressure as if she had been stabbed, although there was no visible wound, not even a tear in her clothing. She squeezed thighs again the echoing throb between her legs, just a taste of what it had been like for Innathi, and the lingering body heat from the Human sorcerer where he had held her tight, motionless and frightened as he raped her own sister beside her.

Ishuna muttered, beseeching the Sisters that Innathi's mage gift had answered the living magic in the man ... Not the death magic, as she herself had felt.

Like a dagger piercing her, drawing out part of her very essence, letting it float away.

He is Death for an Elf. He could become —

Ishuna blurted a short scream when someone kneeled in front of her.

It wasn't Xala but a Zauyrian woman wearing a hooded, grey robe and gloves, her body protected completely from the sun. The woman's face was not just homely, with rough, ashen-brown skin, but Ishuna could not miss the scars on her face and neck, leading down into her clothes.

The marks were too ... *clean*. And straight, showing distinct patterns, circular and angular, too deliberate to be the result of accident or torture. The younger sister also couldn't tell how old this woman might be in Human years; though not grey-haired, she was not young.

The hooded woman peered straight through the *qu'essan* with those black, void-like eyes. The whites had disappeared beneath the inky spread.

Ishuna yelped again, beginning to scuttle back.

"Easy, Ishuna, easy." Xala knelt as well, placing a comforting hand on the trembling shoulder. "This is Houda, the Third Sorcerer's Deathwalker, and she has a few questions she'd like to ask."

"D-Deathwalker?" Ishuna squeaked, shrinking away from the odd chill flowing off of the woman.

"Every Zauyrian Sorcerer has at least one," Xala explained, though not as though she understood it. "Akil says they are mystic teachers."

Ishuna shook her head. *Mother doesn't allow those ...*

"Houda is one of Cris-ri-phon's mage instructors as well," the Captain continued. "Will you answer her questions?"

So . . .

Xala wasn't going to interrogate her first?

Hesitantly, the young Davrin nodded, though she still could not look directly at Houda for long. Xala spoke to her instead in Zauyrian and received a reply. The woman's voice was hoarse, almost whispering . . . a bit like the voices in some of Ishuna's worse Reveries.

"Your clothes are wet," Xala translated. "Were you in the pool with them?"

Ishuna nodded. "I tried to push him off of her."

Xala translated, and Houda nodded, speaking again through an interpreter. "How did he resist your attempt to stop him?"

"He pulled my leg out from under me and grabbed me, too. Still . . . still rutting my sister."

Houda frowned, and Xala translated. "When did he release you?"

Ishuna shuddered. "After. . . . after he was finished."

The next question the Deathwalker asked had Xala screwing her face up in confusion. Akil was nearby, and Ishuna could at least read that he encouraged the Captain to ask the question anyway, even if she didn't understand it.

"May Houda see where you are hurt?" Xala said.

"N-no!" Ishuna cried, looking at the grey mage. "Don't touch me! I'm not hurt, just shaken!"

Another exchange which had the Captain baffled. "She says you *are* hurt, Ishuna. She can 'see' it. Your . . . hm, fuck, I don't know that word."

Houda made a motion with her gloved hand, tracing a finger from shoulder to shoulder a steady distance from her physical body, before touching her forehead, lips, the hollow of her throat, and her chest. Ishuna watched every movement, oddly fascinated.

The woman's long, covered fingers paused at the heart then moved down to her middle.

She knows. Ishuna's mouth tightened unconsciously. "Aura."

Xala squinted. "Hurt in your aura? But that always heals after some sleep, right? What does she mean?"

"I-I don't know!" the young Davrin answered defensively. "Wh-what about Innathi? How is her aura?"

Xala just stared at her.

"Ask her!" Ishuna demanded, pointing at Houda. "Is Innathi hurt, too?"

The Captain translated, sounding more nervous now, and Houda answered readily with barely another glance at her sister, though it wasn't a short response.

"Her aura is strong," Xala said. "The Sorcerer's son did not hurt her. He hurt you." The Captain licked her lips. "Though he likely did not mean to. His magic is very strong and he is only just beginning to understand it."

Houda said something else that had Xala shaking her head in protest. The words sounded like they were spinning out of control, even though it was just normal speech to a Zauyrian.

"What?" Ishuna asked, then louder. "What did she say?"

"She ... offers to come with us to help explain to your Queen-Mother, to make amends for any insult or injury done to the Davrin Queendom."

Mother will execute her ...

"She wasn't even here," Ishuna spat, hating how pathetic her voice sounded to her own ears. "She didn't *see* anything; she can't even speak Davrin. And she *can't* help me. Her magic of the same silver that *he* is, which hurt me in the first place!"

Instead of arguing further after Xala repeated this, Houda stood up, slow and nonthreatening, with the statement that Ishuna could change her mind and accept the offer, "if she wished."

Then the Deathwalker excused herself to cross the stream, heading to kneel next to the Sorcerer's son. Cris-ri-phon now struggled into his clothing, which was a recovery far faster than Innathi, but his limbs were shaking.

While Xala checked again on her sister, Ishuna watched the interaction between the Deathwalker and the man in the firebird robe. He looked just like Ishuna had a moment ago: shaking his head, trembling, trying to explain the unexplainable to her. The difference was that he allowed Houda to touch him.

Houda tugged off one glove and carefully laid a cool hand upon his sweating brow. This seemed to calm him down. His aura roiled less, even as it burned hot still, with all the colors of flame. The dark, silver base brought the fires under control.

The Deathwalker could help him, Human to Human. Ishuna didn't have another Davrin who could help her. She didn't even really know what her aura looked like right now …

"Oh …" Innathi breathed, clutching Xala's blanket as she sat up with the Captain's help. Her hair was tousled, already half dry, and her eyes were …

Luminous.

Just as her aura was, blue and gold and now mingled with red and orange.

Like his.

Her elder sister even smiled, looking around, searching for the Zauyrian and finding him. Innathi didn't notice how small her sister tried to make herself.

What has he done to you?

"YOUR GRACE," XALA BEGAN INCREDULOUSLY, "WILL YOU PLEASE SAY THAT again?"

Innathi dipped her chin with confidence "No harm done, Captain. I touched him first. He only did *exactly* as I commanded him, every moment. He can hardly be punished for wanting to please me, can he?"

And he couldn't help himself.

The Queen's heir still remembered the look on his face, how desperately he held her. She remembered every hard thrust of his cock. She didn't even mind that she'd be sore riding a horse again; she was privately proud of it.

"Well," the Captain said slowly, "he did something to Ishuna. To … her aura."

Innathi grimaced in sympathy. "Well … she got in the way. Any mage knows you don't disrupt another mage's concentration. She could have harmed us both. She can take the consequences and learn from them. Such a lesson makes a mage's senses stronger with time."

Xala was cautiously relieved, Innathi could tell. The two of them would be allies in explaining this to the Queen-Mother. The heir to the throne wouldn't be rushing back to the capital, crying for war against one of the Zauyr Sorcerer's over an unexpected, public coupling.

Innathi had more pride and respect for herself than that. In fact, she could take this and make it work for her, for her entire Queendom. She would gain power from this, not display weakness on account of it.

Like Ishuna. Sulking over there by the rock.

Why had the fool interfered in such powerful magic, anyway? She knew better.

Probably jealous.

Be that as it may, not a chance would Innathi allow her little sister to ruin what must be the most intriguing connection between their two peoples in centuries. Their magic had been so strong together, hers and Cris's, that it had affected everyone here at Koorul's waterfall.

I can see it.

That was why Xala had been late.

The Queen-Mother had said to Innathi before that She regretted losing power and influence over the Humans of the desert at the same time the Deathwalkers had grown more prevalent. This wasn't something She spoke of often, certainly never in public, and her firstborn had always wanted to learn more.

Ishuna never heard our Mother's wish, that's obvious, or she wouldn't be pouting right now.

Innathi had a chance to show the Queen-Mother, V'Gedra, and all the Queendom that she could look ahead. She could plan as a matter of course and would be a worthy successor. *She* would define this amazing, confusing incident, not let it define *her*.

Cris-ri-phon was Human. He would live a fraction of her lifetime. *I must act on this now, while he is still young.*

CHAPTER 4

V'GEDRA – TWO WEEKS LATER

"INTERESTING."

Just the one word from the Queen-Mother.

Not a great sign.

Her aging, copper eyes gazed at each one of them with the precision of a scalpel. A languid finger rested against her temple as she reclined in the most comfortable chair of the room. Innathi and Ishuna stood with Captain Xala before Her, alone without witnesses.

All of them were still dirty from their hustled trek home. It was early evening and they had only just arrived. Innathi acted nearly normal now, although her eyes held a certain intensity which suggested she had not stopped thinking about the young sorcerer and had more to say to her Queen-Mother on the topic.

Ishuna, however, was withdrawn, often staring into vacant space, acting startled if touched. Sometimes she placed her hand over her middle, as if checking for a scar or blemish that she never found but could not well leave alone, although that motion was happening less and less since leaving the canyon.

Maybe it was getting better since she slept?

The Captain was worried for them both but could not truly know if she would still be around to see how they fared through this. She could, quite soon, be facing some serious consequences of her own — anything from reassignment to exile to execution — depending on how this meeting went.

Innathi was doing a good job presenting those chaotic moments at Koorul in the most politically advantageous view possible.

"I would like to send an invitation to the Third Sorcerer-King, Begir-al-phon," Innathi suggested as her finish. "To include his two eldest sons and Houda, the Maiden Deathwalker."

The Valsharess sat still for some time, Her only movement a subtle tap of her finger against her temple.

Then, "We will consider this carefully, Daughter."

As that was all the Davrin Queen would say, her heir merely bowed in acceptance and waited.

Then elegant, crimson eyes shifted smoothly to Xala. "Captain Ja'Prohn. Report."

Xala was prepared to do so and did not waste Her Majesty's time with uncertainty. She presented each highlight to the entire journey, all four weeks they had been gone. Though it took a while to recount, the Queen did not stop her or ask for anything to be repeated.

She had only a few additional questions for the incident inside Koorul at the end.

"And you did not hear Our Daughters cry out."

"Not at first, Your Highness. Sound can be distorted in the canyons, but we stopped the moment we became aware."

"Would you say all, some, or few participants had become as deaf beyond the rut?"

Xala swallowed. "All or most, Valsharess. Including me."

The Valsharess smiled. "Had it become a ritual by that point? As Innathi has suggested."

"I, uh …" The Captain inhaled to calm her heart rate. "If it was, it seemed spontaneous. Magic gone wild."

"What magic, Captain Ja'Prohn?"

She exhaled. "Head Guard Akil Safiya stated his people were there for the second son's initiation to begin study as a Deathwalker. His

… teacher, the Court Deathwalker of the Sorcerer-King, had not yet arrived."

"Why not?"

"I can only repeat what the Zauyrians claimed, Your Highness."

"Noted. Do so."

"They say Cris-ri-phon bears mage-line power in two conflicting affinities. Fertility and healing, and decay and death."

The Valsharess wrinkled her nose. "Hm. So. We hear that the boy arrived with his entourage to cleanse himself of one and embrace the other."

"As I understand it, Your Highness."

"And Our Daughter instead brought him flush against the choice he'd thought to discard."

Innathi lifted her chin, shoulders square, with a small smile on her lips. Her Mother noted it but maintained Her usual stoicism.

"Did they speak on what's next for this second son?"

"No, my Valsharess." Xala hesitated. "The Sorcerer-King's Deathwalker, called Houda, offered us her service for any insult unintended, if Your Highness should desire to hear more from their expert on this subject."

The Captain left the final interpretation of her own competence and trustworthiness to the Valsharess and did not try to excuse herself further.

The Valsharess nodded and repositioned herself in her chair, at last looking to her younger Daughter. "Ishuna."

The cait jumped, blinking rapidly. "Yes, Mother?"

"What was your experience in Koorul?"

The young Davrin's lower lip trembled, and it was clear that she knew what she wanted to say but was terrified to do so.

"Speak," the Queen-Mother ordered. "You have not made eye contact with Us, or anyone, since arriving. You look like prey caught in a trap. That is not acceptable behavior for a royal Daughter. You make Us look weak."

Ishuna flinched but made herself straighten up, forcing her mouth to move. She could not meet her Mother's steady gaze for long, however. "I had a … vision of the Sorcerer's son, Mother."

"A vision," the Valsharess repeated with narrowed eyes.

"Like my sire, I-I believe."

Her displeasure rolled over them like an earth tremor. Xala's stomach dropped with dread.

"Cris-ri-phon should be kept away from us," the second Daughter pushed forward. "He will bring us to ruin."

"Ishuna!" Innathi hissed, vastly irritated after spending an entire trip cajoling her sister not to say that again.

"We do not rule by visions, Daughter," said the Queen, her upper lip curling with a subtle snarl. "Many a time have We been told of 'ruin this' and 'warning that' by manipulative counselors, yet *all* these events have a solution in the awake and the material. We did not ask about visions. Tell us your experience, for this is the only thing that can show us where we stand at all points in time."

Ishuna trembled, something only the Queen's lower vassals tended to do. "Koorul is sacred, a sacred site. Magic is en … enhanced there. You knew this, didn't you?"

The Queen-Mother lifted chin slightly. "Sacred to them. Less so to us."

"Is … is that why the Deathwalker seemed most … *aligned* with the place?"

"An interesting observation, Daughter." Queen Alyarra tilted her head slightly. "What was her name again?"

Ishuna swallowed, licked her lips. "Uh … H-Houda. The Maiden Deathwalker."

"We doubt she is a 'maiden' in the sense of *their* term. Most likely referring to the Grey Lady." Their matriarch lowered her finger from her temple, balancing her posture with both elbows on the arms of her chair. "The young sorcerer bears conflicting potential, but may it be presumed that his aura did *not* match the older grey mage you saw?"

The second daughter nodded her head. "True, Queen-Mother. Not yet. A-and when he touched Innathi …"

Her voice quivered to a halt when she noticed her sister's look, at her fist tightening.

"Speak," her Mother demanded, low and penetrating.

Ishuna's throat seemed to hurt as she tried. "I s-saw a vision of —"

"No. Your experience, Ishuna. Now."

"M-my vision *was* my experie —"

"Then why do you hold your middle as though someone struck you with a dagger?"

"Because he did!" she blurted, voice rising. "He used something unseen —"

The Queen-Mother's eyes flicked to her left, seizing Xala in their gaze. "Captain, you checked them both for injuries, correct?"

"I did, Your Majesty." Xala worked to keep her breath steady. "I found no physical injuries, though Houda claimed another wound I couldn't see, even with my own mage's eyes."

"Did she suggest how to tend it?"

"No, Majesty, but we also didn't give her much opportunity to say it. She asked to look, but Ishuna refused to be touched. We left that evening."

The Valsharess's mouth pressed in obvious disappointment as she looked at her younger Daughter with a quiet sigh. Xala held her tongue; she wasn't sure what this was about now that the Deathwalker seemed of interest.

The Queen-Mother stared at her "injured" Daughter, frowning in thought. "There is much we don't understand about Zauyrian death magic. Perhaps We shall take her up on this offer."

Innathi glanced at Ishuna and back, looking a little more concerned. "Do you believe she has a … a 'death' injury, Queen-Mother?"

"Time will tell."

"But … he did not *feel* that way. Not to me. He was a match for my own strength, my fertility magic, and in a Human, no less!"

"This is unusual," the Valsharess granted. "And the Captain did say the Third Realm is aware of the divergent focus. But you are clever and learn well, my Daughter. This is an opportunity we should consider before it slips from our hands."

The Queen-Mother's gaze slid to the side in patient contemplation. Before too long she spoke again.

"You are dismissed, Innathi and Ishuna, until I summon you again. Captain Ja'Prohn, you will stay and hear your sentence."

"Yes, Valsharess," they said in unison.

The days passed one after the other, and Xala was gone. The populace continued their daily trade and bickering politics in blissful ignorance of the sandstorm coming.

Ishuna grew to hate coming out of Reverie. She hated being in it almost as much, but the process of coming awake – and convincing herself that she *was* awake – was an ordeal which seemed to have no end.

Sometimes the way out was a deliberate dive down to the bottom of quicksand, or the path lay within the shadow of the doorway as opposed to the door itself. Abstraction and symbols became routine even as voices nibbled at the edge of the wound in her belly.

"Ishuna, well met. How do you feel today?"

"I am well, Mother, thank you."

"You look like you need more rest."

The Valsharess would not yet speak on Innathi's idea of extending an invitation to the Third Realm Court, to include the second son and the Deathwalker.

Ishuna started seeing the hole in her gut clearly in Reverie, whenever she had the courage to lift her dress or her shirt and expose it. Ordinarily, her aura was purple and gold. But now, a horrid, dark silver stain branched through a small part of it, as though someone had thrown a hard object and struck a silver mirror, transforming it into slow-burning lightning.

The webbed design wasn't growing bigger, or smaller, but it always burned and itched, somehow preventing her from feeling wholly connected to her body. Whether awake or in Reverie, Ishuna hesitated before casting a spell, *any* spell, feeling a twinge of pain or a spin to her head, fooling her into thinking she'd fallen when she had not.

"Concentrate, Ishuna! A mage's concentration is the backbone of her ability."

"Of course, instructor."

The worst Reverie came with a vision so revolting and terrifying in every aspect that Ishuna knew, even as it happened, that it *must* be a dream. She must wake from it sooner or later, though the torment was slow and vivid … and endless.

Xala would have come into her room before the *qu'essan* had screamed her throat raw.

She would have heard me.

Now, her guardian was gone, and whoever arrived to check on her was always somebody different.

Ishuna awoke screaming once more when no one came to her door. As in her childhood, this had grown tiresome for her Mother to hear the reports from her Guardsvrin of the royal daughter's disturbed sleep, and Innathi was now too far away in the Palace for it to interrupt her own rest.

This would pass, like it had then.

Even Ishuna waited for it to pass.

The only image she dared to recall and make note, absently scratching oversimplified lines on parchment, was a big-belly Davrin sitting on her Mother's throne. She was giving birth to a child-sized scorpion, preparing to take her own life with a dagger.

No. I've got to save her.

Ishuna burned the parchment over a candle flame a few moments later.

CHAPTER 5

V'GEDRA – 400 B.S.E.

NEARLY A YEAR IT HAD TAKEN TO ARRANGE FOR VISITORS WHO WOULD BE THE Valsharess's guests. Now, the streets buzzed in preparation for the day it would come to be.

Voices murmured that more than *twenty* Humans would stay inside the Palace for at least a month, including the Third Zauyrian Sorcerer-King and his two eldest sons. Begir-al-phon had more children, so others said, but the Queen-Mother would not have invited even the eldest son if it weren't an insult and blatantly lacking forethought.

The Valsharess had grown accustomed to this King now in his second century. Negotiations had been mutually beneficial, their borders quieter than most. The Zauyrian sorcerer, however, was clearly aging. Planned for his death, Begir had taken a dedicated interest in two of his younger sons: Cris-ri-phon a mere twenty-one years of age, while his older brother Leur-en-phon — the true heir of the Third Realm — held thirty-five.

"These are the two who inherited enough of their father's magic to become sorcerers of the Long Life," an advisor had explained more thoroughly to the Queen's Daughters. "There are and have been older sons and daughters with far less of a gift, and some of *them* are old and preparing to die as well. Only in the last forty years has Begir-al-phon cared to seek out a young woman of powerful heritage and convince her to bear his heirs."

"Which took all of her strength to do so, I take it," the Valsharess commented wryly.

"Correct, my Queen. The mother is no longer among them. It is a House of men."

"Typical Zauyrian."

That evening, the Valsharess dined alone with her Daughters, settling her goals.

"You are ... certain about the pull being enough?" Ishuna murmured as the topic came up again.

"He is young and malleable," Innathi said, spearing a green rod on her plate and acting as though she were not the same when it came to their Mother's wishes. "I will have him as my formal Consort. For a time, he will live here."

No.

"You mean, if his Father agrees."

"He will be convinced." Innathi shrugged, looking at their Mother, who observed with fingers laced. "I won't be having children for centuries yet, and this is a perfect balance."

"But —" Ishuna began.

"He is not the heir of his lands," Innathi continued, "so he must still work for a legacy of *any* kind. His people do not know what to do with his mixed magic; they haven't the history or the teachers. He will be motivated to learn from *us* and shall have the needs of the Queendom always in mind." She grinned at her younger sister. "We may enjoy his connections to the next ruler of the Third Realm and learn more of the Deathwalkers, but what we can offer him will assure his devotion to me and V'Gedra, while he cannot claim blood or heritage through offspring."

Ishuna had no doubt her sister could accomplish this, especially as she'd set her mind to it.

Meanwhile, the Valsharess seemed amused, possibly impressed. She was certainly pleased with the plan to poach Begir-al-phon's doubly gifted son. She focused on Ishuna after a moment. "We may also find among these newer mages what will help you rest again, Daughter."

The younger *qu'essan* was stunned. She hadn't anticipated that Queen-Mother had even considered her daughter was still unsettled by what happened at Koorul, by her "visions" coming back with such force, much less plotting to do anything about it. They had all waited for Ishuna's dreams to pass and, for how little the Queen had been bothered by it lately, most had assumed they had.

The Valsharess looked at Innathi. "And this is truly how you wish to spend your third century, Daughter of mine? Rutting with a Human Consort?"

Innathi chuckled. "It shall be my pleasure, and my service, Queen-Mother. I have already claimed him in public anyway, and I expect I have much I could learn of newer magic. Why would I let some lesser woman hold his attention? I'm only sorry the Sorcerer and his son cannot get away from their people sooner than they've said. But I can wait. The alliance will be for the Queendom and our future, Mother."

Ishuna said nothing else through supper, listening and eating with one hand in her lap, though tasting very little of the fine food. Her mother and sister had stopped listening to her plea to reconsider, that Cris-ri-phon should stay away. Even now her vision seemed faded, and she wasn't sure how well she could justify her opposition.

Especially now that she had heard her Mother acknowledge seers at all, however obliquely.

Find among these what will help you rest again.

Daughter.

Standing at her mirror that very night, Ishuna frowned as the surface seemed to shimmer a moment. In the lower right quadrant formed a web-shaped crack, its legs reaching through the brittle glass until it obscured her belly over her purple dress. The young Davrin reached out to touch the mirror, tracing her finger along the lines. She could not feel the breaks, nor fine splinters of glass to threaten the perfection of her skin.

Am I awake? Or not?

She hadn't laid down, hadn't shut her eyes. She *must* be awake.

Ishuna rushed to her door and threw it open. "Guardsvrin! *Guardsvrin!* Come here and take this mirror away. I need a replacement."

She heard a sigh, oddly resigned. "Yes, *qu'essan.*"

The Guardsvrin stepped in with a bow and approached her mirror. She watched their face, their eyes — did they see the crack? Did they *not* understand why the royal daughter needed a new one?

The Guardsvrin simply detached the mirror from the wall and took it out of the room, promising a new one within the hour.

"Make sure it doesn't get damaged," she said at the door.

"Of course, *qu'essan.*"

Her new mirror did arrive, and it didn't have a crack in it.

Though it seemed familiar.

"Have I had this mirror before?" Ishuna asked, quietly, and more to herself, but the Guardsvrin took it that they were being spoken to.

"Yes, *qu'essan.* We have had it repaired for you. It is just as it was last month."

A reassuring smile, a graceful bow.

The Guardsvrin had responded well, had done everything right, but they weren't telling the whole truth.

Ishuna's stomach felt cold. She listened with her ear pressed to the door after it had closed in case anyone was talking about her. It seemed quiet. Eventually she left the door and sat back down on her bed.

***I am** seeing what I'm seeing.*

Am I not?

At last, the Sorcerer's son stood before her.

Here in our courtyard, the Palace of V'Gedra.

"Welcome, Cris-ri-phon," said Innathi after his family had been announced.

Such hunger in his eyes. Such stark naked relief that she recognized him, as if her presence and gracing him with a smile had set everything right. He bowed before the Valsharess more like a vassal and less like a guest from a neighboring kingdom.

A good sign.

Innathi managed to pay attention to the formalities and properly greet the Zauyrian ruler and his eldest son, as well as the Deathwalker. As elegant as her Mother, she was a little surprised with the twinkle in the white-beard's hazel eyes.

And his words which followed.

"Shall Your Majesty, myself, and Houda take refreshment in a place of your choosing, Great Queen? We may discuss the boring politics while the young decide whether they can even tolerate each other."

Brazen suggestion. The old Zauyrian wanted to cut down the time it took to find balance between their families, which came as no surprise. One had only to imagine mortality staring him in the face.

Begir-al-phon did not seem afraid or in denial, however, and was less interested in controlling every interaction his offspring might have but rather in removing obstacles. Given what happened at Koorul, perhaps it was just as well.

Innathi almost thought her Queen-Mother could yet learn a thing or two from the frail old man before he died.

The eldest Daughter looked to her Mother with lightly raised eyebrows and a subtle, enticing smile for the rest of them. Both brothers were affected, staring at her a bit too long for a public greeting.

The Valsharess exhaled with equal subtlety. "My Daughters shall give your sons a tour of the Palace and its grounds, Begir, since you've already had that. Let us retire out of the sun. Musanlo's Eye is strong today."

The Deathwalker Houda did not speak, her head covered by a hood in the same drab robe as before. She offered a slight nod to eldest son which could have been a farewell, but for his response: closing his fingers into a fist while leaving his thumb extended. Innathi wondered what it meant but was more than content when Leur-en-phon approached Ishuna with a deep, respectful bow.

"Will you and your sister lead my brother and me through the splendor of V'Gedra's Jewel, *Qu'essan* Ishuna?"

His words were nearly perfect. The heir of the Third Realm was far more fluent in Davrin than his younger brother.

Stiffly, Ishuna bowed back to the deeply tanned, lightly bearded man, glancing at Innathi to make sure she and Cris-ri-phon would follow before they excused themselves from their parents.

"This way," she said.

The main courtyard containing the central well was massive and busy, packed with temporary carts, tents, and Davrin whose posts lay just outside the curved walls. The sandy streets were lively, the noise leading away in a gentle decline from the Palace.

"It's mostly empty past midnight," Ishuna began, "with space enough, they like to say, for a Dragon to land within if he wishes. Taking to this place under cover of night is assumed subversion, one should have no cause, so do not explore before dawn without a Davrin escort."

"Most certainly not, *qu'essan*," Leur said with more charm and gentle amusement than Innathi would have given to a Human so young. "Our hosts honor us too much to risk such trespass."

In contrast, Cris was hardly listening, glancing at Innathi often in the hopes that she would look back — and she waited just a little longer before giving him that. In fact, Leur acted as if he wasn't the same age at all, even though Elves born a mere fifteen years apart were nearly considered twins.

Yet still, I must not forget these Humans wouldn't be of an age to mate had they been born Elves.

Innathi's cheeks flushed recalling how Cris-ri-phon *could* indeed mate. He was endowed with quite a sword, one which she intended to claim. She nearly looked at him but forced herself to keep away, amusing herself with then thought. She, too, was barely listening to Ishuna as her gaze drifted over Leur's body, reading his unspoken language.

He is not the same as Cris at all ...

Leur even had hair on his face.

She and Ishuna were often treated as the same age. The royal sisters were only two decades apart, after all, conceived while their Queen-Mother had a special Consort available to her for only a short time — a wizard who lived deep in the desert as a hermit.

The strange, faceless Ilharn chosen by the Valsharess was said to be gifted enough to speak with Dragons. Queen Alyarra had wanted two Daughters, and she *got* two Daughters before the wizard vanished back into the dunes and away from the public view.

Their Queen-Mother never talked about him and, this early in their lives, would not even give them his name. Perhaps when they were older, just before the Valsharess passed her way into legend. Innathi sort of savored the mystery, even if Ishuna claimed to have encountered him in a dream.

Thoughts flew from her mind when Cris-ri-phon reached out and touched his fingers to her wrist. She felt the shock of the contact far more than she had with other young buas.

He's touching me.

For a moment, this was all there was. Their auras answered the other, a small, magical trilling tremor just beneath her skin.

Finally, Innathi looked at him, her face warm and her ears starting to burn. He smiled — no, he *grinned*. She could smell his distinct musk and figured his loose, silk trousers hadn't tented because he had another garment underneath to hold an inconvenient erection flush against his belly.

Because he most certainly had one.

Oh, Sisters …

She didn't want to wait. Koorul had been a full year already! Surely that was a good enough test of patience for Mother—

Leur said something to her and Innathi jumped, looking away from Cris as he blessedly released her wrist.

"I-I'm sorry, what was that, First Son?"

Leur smiled kindly at her, bowing his head, and gave his younger brother a gently judging glance. "I asked if he is too bold with you, *qu'essan*. He has been enchanted by your beauty for the last year, and now with your presence, of course. We've said before, we are honored to be here." The older man gave a small shake of his head, showing his amusement since she wasn't scowling. "But my little brother hasn't earned all his wisdom yet. Humans his age face great tests of impulse control. As you have seen."

As if he needed to remind me!

But … impulse control. Suggesting Leur-en-phon considered himself better than that?

Cris-ri-phon was glaring at his brother and hissed something in their native tongue. Leur only chuckled, slowly folding arms which were more muscular and filled out more of his pale-yellow shirt. The two men taken om side-by-side, Cris may still have some growth to do.

I need to learn Zauyrian.

The Humans always spoke Davrin when dealing with the Valsharess; only certain officers with regular contact with the settlements, like former Captain Xala, became fluent in the desert Humans' ever-shifting language. The dialects changed so quickly, many in the Queendom couldn't keep pace with the Five Realms.

"I appreciate knowing that a year hasn't cooled his fire," Innathi said to Leur but with a smile for Cris, who forgot that he glared at anything at all. "I understand circumstances change quickly for your race. I might have wondered if I had missed my window."

"Never, *qu'essan*," Cris-ri-phon said, then blinked. "Um … window for what, if I may ask?"

Innathi grinned her pleasure at him. His spoken Davrin had become *much* better. He must have worked at it since Koorul. The young sorcerer wanted very much to impress her.

The royal heir chuckled and could not resist brushing the tip of her finger beneath his chin. She felt just a little stubble, and his grey eyes widened. "My window? I mean, simple, when the time is open to ask you a question."

He swallowed. "What question?"

She blinked at him. "If you are interested in being my Consort for a time, Cris-ri-phon?"

The young sorcerer was about to say something — probably some form of agreement — but Leur-en-phon suddenly reached out and gripped his brother's shoulder. His grip was so hard it caused pain and prevented Cris from speaking more than a blurt of surprised discomfort before he rather violently shook Leur off.

"We are most grateful for your forthrightness, *qu'essan*," Leus spoke quickly, overriding his brother, "as we've wondered what purposes we are meant to discuss during our stay. However, we do not know what this entails. Such an arrangement does not exist in our land. May we ask you and your Queen-Mother for more understanding before he gives you his answer?"

Once again, Cris looked furious with Leur but upon hearing his words, his expression changed. The second son brought his obvious desire under control with effort.

Innathi tilted her head, watching them. *This is becoming interesting.*

The younger agreed with the older, and the elder actually spoke for him in some regard.

"Of course," she answered with a bow of her own head. "We wouldn't wish the young Sorcerers of Third Zauyr to make any alliance they would regret. Peace between our peoples keep the Red Desert prosperous; indeed, keeps it habitable!"

Leur bowed, deep and elegant, giving his thanks while Cris seemed a bit disappointed with her answer. Perhaps what she'd said was more a Queen's answer considering the greater good rather than being solely about him.

*Well, I **will** be Queen one day. He should always bear that in mind.*

She wanted him; she would not deny that to anyone, but they would couple on *her* terms this time. He had had her eyes and lips touch him first; he had tasted her as few others would; and he was certainly the first and only Human given the chance to seat his cock inside her!

If she had to court him a little to please his older brother, who would very soon also be a ruler she would have to make deals with …

Well, I can do a little courting.

ISHUNA STOOD AWKWARDLY, WATCHING UNHAPPILY WHILE HER SISTER BANtered and spoke double meanings with Leur-en-phon, displaying their courtly manners in plain view just off the main courtyard in the shade.

Others were watching them, be they staked out in a stall or shuffling by, and she personally wanted to get into one of the gardens where it wasn't so loud and public.

"If we've agreed on that," the First Zauyrian Son closed, "then let us move on with your sister's tour."

Ishuna turned on her heel and started walking, almost not caring if they caught up with her. No *her* idea to be the guide; she did only as Mother had instructed.

And as the tall, *polite* Sorcerer's son had requested.

The way Cris-ri-phon gaped at her sister was as disgusting and unsettling now as it had been a year ago. Those piercing, steel eyes beneath a shock of black hair, his brown, smooth face so intense and hungry. She didn't care if Leur-en-phon made excuses for the boy in being young and having problems with "impulse control."

That is no *excuse for what he did! He should be castrated!*

If Innathi had been even the *smallest* bit visibly upset with the attack, Ishuna would not be so worried. *Maybe*. But no, now her older sister was always smiling, talking like a diplomat, setting up a future advantage with far too small a focus.

She wants a Human bua to be her servicing stud for the next twenty or so years, while he is still virile and while his sire-King is considering his inheritance. Bah!

There could be no long, Elven courtship as they learned all his flaws and strengths. She had to lead by the cock while it was still plump.

Peh! How quickly they shrivel!

"I'm sorry, I missed that, *qu'essan*."

Ishuna had made an audible scoffing sound. *Oops*.

"Here are Her Majesty's Sunset Gardens," she said aloud, ignoring Leur's statement and presenting the ornate, carefully cultivated desert landscape containing some of the oldest and rarest plants to be found anywhere in the Red Desert.

"And you likely know the name of each glorious survivor I see before me?" said the First Son gallantly, drawing her attention despite herself.

Survivor.

Glorious survivor. That *was* how Ishuna thought of them. How did he know?

"I do," she said stiffly.

"Introduce me, *qu'essan*." He made a gentle, Davrin gesture for her to lead the way. "Please. I have never seen many of these."

She did, speaking more than she was accustomed to, letting her thoughts play farther as she indulged the Sorcerer's heir. Before long, Leur was pretending he did not see Innathi and Cris trying to get away with light touches when they thought his sibling wasn't looking.

Observing his calm, amused smirk, Ishuna decided to take Leur's lead on that, or she would be glaring at Cris every step of the way. It was very tiring.

Leur-en-phon was clearly the smart one. More educated, too, and physically larger. His hair was lighter than Cris's, a curious dark red-brown glinting with honeyed streaks, though his eyes were dark like a classic Zauyrian. The brothers' skin colors were about the same, and they appeared related the same way Innathi and Ishuna looked like sisters, despite the hair.

Ishuna did not let herself be more generous than this. Leur was clearly trying to woo her about something, to coax her into letting down her guard, or soften her up to agree on some proposal he intended to make.

Probably more to benefit him and his sire, or even Mother and Innathi, than the 'weak' Second Daughter.

The group eventually made their way to the small fountain provided beneath a grandly generous shade made of bright red sandstone columns and a tough silk framework. Innathi sat down to dip her fingers in the water with a sigh.

"May we rest here a moment, sister?" she teased her, blinking bright, red eyes. "I was not under the impression we had to cover all four gardens in an hour!"

Ishuna shrugged and took one of the stone benches farthest away. "As you wish."

The two men glanced at each other, but Innathi beckoned Cris to sit next to her, which left Leur standing alone. He looked her way and stepped forward boldly.

"May I sit, *qu'essan*?" he asked.

"Have you purpose or just rest?" she returned with narrowed eyes.

He nodded. "I have purpose."

Ishuna blinked. When he made no move to sit, she eventually scooted to the side to make room and gestured to him.

"What do you want?" she grumped as a vivacious Innathi leaned to whisper something private to a flush-faced Cris-ri-phon. Ishuna couldn't even guess what it was, for the sound of the fountain helped to mask it;, but the youth's eyes sparkled.

Leur looked down at his big hands, carefully considering his words. "I wish to help you, *qu'essan*."

Ishuna tore her gaze from the other two. Leur waited for a response.

She stared. "What."

"I wish to help you," he repeated, holding her eyes. "Houda says she can still see the damage caused by my brother last summer. My Father and I are both distressed to see nothing has been done, but we hope it is because of a lack of knowledge about death magic and not punishment to you for what happened. It wasn't your fault, *qu'essan*."

Ishuna was speechless. She did not expect the lump in her throat or the sudden rise of tears to blur her vision.

She looked away.

Leur leaned toward her, keeping his voice quiet. "You would not know it to look at him right this moment, but Cris *is* sorry. He has agreed to apologize to your Mother and you, and to learn from Houda what he must do to heal the wound while we are here. Until then, I will not allow him to answer any offer from your elder sister."

Tremors spread through her. His fault, it was that *boy's* fault — exactly what she had been saying these last months! Did that mean the Third Sorcerer-King himself agreed he'd been reckless? That Cris-ri-phon had been too violent with her sister and her?

She whispered, "That ... that would require him to touch me again?"

"Yes, but with Houda's guidance."

"Not yours?"

"I have none of the grey magic in me, *qu'essan*. I cannot help that way. I am sorry."

She barely withheld a scoff at the presumption. She hadn't been asking Leur to touch her instead of his little brother. She didn't want *any* of them to touch her again. Not the younger brother, not the ugly woman. She wanted to go inside, to leave them out there, even though that would be unbecoming rudeness from her Mother's Daughter to much-anticipated guests.

Don't touch me.

"I do not need your help," she murmured.

"Yes, you do." His tone was serious. "Your magic will become harder to focus with each passing year, the results less predictable. You may start to see unsettling things, if you haven't begun to already."

Ishuna blinked. In that instant of darkness, she saw again the pregnant Queen preparing to stab herself for what was coming out of her womb.

She hadn't intended her face to be so easy to read, but Leur reached for Ishuna's hand without asking. Closing it in both of his, he pressed a sincere kiss of apology in the manner of the Davrin.

"Let us help you, Ishuna. We can mend it. Make it balanced again."

She said nothing for quite some time. Innathi never noticed.

"H-how ... how did you know?"

"I didn't. Houda is wise for her age. Please, at least speak with her, *qu'essan*. We would help you, not leave you to face these obstacles alone when it was *my* blood who set them before you."

She turned her head. "Why? Because you'll be a ruler one day and peace is best between our peoples?"

The Sorcerer's heir nodded agreement. "I cannot deny that truth, but that is not my only concern. You've a strong gift as a mage and a seer, do you not?"

She swallowed.

"It should not be left to fester and scar. We have the knowledge and the means to help a mage we hurt, and so it is our obligation to do so."

Ishuna glanced at Innathi, who was still teasing and talking with her would-be Consort, teaching him new Davrin words already as if he was moving in tomorrow.

Her Mother and sister had left her alone to suffer, hadn't they? They wouldn't even acknowledge her nightmares.

"I will speak with Houda," Ishuna agreed, watching the large, brown hands withdraw at her answer.

Leur smiled with a slow, deep nod. "Thank you, *qu'essan*."

THE ROYAL SIBLINGS MANAGED TO MAKE IT BACK TO THE COOLER, DARKER AND more private wings their Mother often used for negotiations and discussions. They did so *without* Innathi slipping away for long with Cris, but there had been a few moments when Leur had to stop walking and call out for his little brother in a strong, magic-tinged command which he ultimately answered.

Ishuna had a near-permanent scowl on her face from the tiresome game, her sister playing against the Sorcerer's elder son in a flirtatious rebellion. Innathi's delight in splitting the youth's attention and loyalty from his elder brother was obvious, as was her certainty that Leur fought a losing battle against undeniable attraction.

Every time Ishuna thought she was getting somewhere interesting in conversation with the elder heir, Leur would have to stop and make sure his young brother was not rutting between her sister's legs on a table somewhere.

Innathi's being a selfish slit.

For bragging about being ever aware of how her choices affect the Queendom, the heir was certainly missing something damned important within her own family thanks to her burning loins. For that reason alone, Ishuna asked Leur if she could speak to Houda first and *without* Cris-ri-phon present.

"I must still interpret for Houda while keeping watch on him," Leur voiced his concern with some attempt at humor. "Make sure he doesn't promise the entire Desert and all its peoples to your sister for a kiss."

"Let your sire do that for an hour or so!" Ishuna pressed.

"I believe he's still meeting with the Valsharess. As is Houda."

Ishuna threw up her hands. "Then let them couple and break the tension. This is exhausting, Leur. Gag him to keep the promises out, if you must. I'm sure he can still figure out how to hump her with a root stuffed in his mouth. I can't stand them like this!"

Leur chuckled helplessly at her words, his face flushing with embarrassment. Innathi was both close enough and taking a break in teasing Cris to actually hear Ishuna's last comment.

"I admit I like *that* idea, sister," Innathi said, stepping toward them with her hips swaying, her grace hypnotic and likely magically enhanced.

They watched as she pulled free a length of silk attached to the waist of her royal purple gown. Ordinarily it would be used as a light wrap and sun shield over her head and shoulders while out walking, but now she made a small show of tying two knots on top of each other dead center, holding it up for Cris's inspection.

"Would you bite down on this for everyone's contentment, my handsome mage?"

Cris glanced at his older brother for permission to play and, after the last few hours, Leur was finally worn down enough to consider it.

Ishuna leaned up to whisper, her frustration leading to a plea. "You think he'll be able to focus on Houda's instruction to help me before my sister gets what she wants? She *always* gets what she wants!"

"I see, yes," Leur granted, his shoulders slumping a little.

He'd finally accepted he lacked a position with the Queen's Daughter where he could command more than he had. His first time coming head-on against a Davrin's will — even a very young one choosing a mate — and level heads and reason like his wouldn't prevail in the end.

Innathi put the silk knot up against Cris's mouth. His lips parted willingly as she giggled and tied it snugly behind his head. Smiling, he bit down, showing his teeth. She stared into his eyes the entire time as she gagged him. Much as she disliked the display, Ishuna noticed her sister's hands were trembling.

"There," Innathi breathed, taking his hand and reaching for a door handle. She paused, glancing at the two, her eyes burning. "Will you wait out here, dear siblings, or will you step inside to make sure we don't burn the Palace down with our passion?"

She chuckled in her own jest, but Leur nodded, accepting. "I will step just inside, *qu'essan*. Thank you."

Both sisters' eyes widened, and the tall Man nodded, confirming his choice.

Damn you both.

Ishuna felt she had no choice but to go along with it or be left out. Not two hours ago she had been set on just this — left out and leaving the idiots to their dealings. Now, she'd changed her mind. If the older brother wasn't ready to give up, neither was she.

Overcoming her surprise, Innathi just shrugged and pulled Cris into an unused meeting room not three down from where their parents were. She left the door open for Leur and Ishuna to follow.

"You'll be safe this time, *qu'essan*," Leur whispered as he touched her waist. "I promise."

I'm not afraid of him, she thought as she frowned at the elder son.

But she didn't speak it aloud as Leur stayed beside her the entire time.

CRIS FUMBLED TO OPEN THE FRONT OF HER ROYAL GOWN, DESPERATE TO TOUCH soft breasts as Innathi leaned up against the nearest, sturdy table. As at the waterfall of Koorul, she enjoyed keeping in the back of her mind the knowledge that others were watching her pleasure and her beauty at once.

The Queen's Daughter once again allowed the Zauyrian between her thighs — this time with clothing still between them — and willed the extraordinary merging of their auras to wash over them, into them. Her future Consort had been on the edge so long, the sorcerer leaped to answer her call.

Oh, Goddess! she thought as he finally got his large, hot hand into her dress to squeeze a breast, pinching the stiff, purple nipple. Simultaneously he pressed his blatant, hard staff against her groin, and she wished the clothes would simply vanish into thin air!

She planted small, hungry kisses along the edge of Cris's gagged mouth, his back teeth set hard and grinding on her silk knot as he trembled in her arms. He pulled harder on her dress, a bit roughly, tugging it farther down off her shoulders.

He put his nose to her skin and inhale with a groan.

"You'll not last long this first time, will you?" she whispered in his ear. "I've teased you too much."

He groaned, then growled with a small nod.

"But you'll rise again, won't you? You won't need to pull out before you'll plough me and plant your seed a second time …"

He grunted, wordless, cramming his erection against her with a nod. His grimace bordered on desperation as he gritted his teeth around her silk. She yanked up her skirts on one side, and he took that as permission to pull them up the rest of the way, exposing her bare legs. He stared down with elation, seeing the proof at what she'd whispered to him by the fountain:

"I wore no underclothes, knowing you were going to arrive today."

The *qu'essan* lay open, available. Glistening. He could just slide right in.

Innathi giggled and worked impatiently to loosen his waistband and push the loose, blue trousers down over his hips and ass before attacking the undergarment which kept his erection restrained. The hidden garment was an interesting, banded wrap not unlike what the Davrin buas wore, meant to keep the groin dry and lightly swaddled while leaving most of the buttocks exposed.

She liked it — it looked good on him — but it had to go.

His penis was leaking when she finally got the stiff, hot spear into her palm. She nearly jerked it but they both knew he'd probably spurt all over her mound and thighs. She pulled him toward her slit instead. This time, her own hand guided his flared, engorged head to her slippery cleft.

"Now," she whispered.

Cris rammed inside in one stroke, and she cried out, as shocked as he was by the rush of sensation and magic. They held still for a moment, adjusting to the new equilibrium after the surge. Innathi managed a glance over toward Leur and Ishuna …

And grinned when she saw the elder brother's arms wrapped lightly around her younger sister, his face flushed just like his brother's. He kept his eyes upon the top of Ishuna's white head as she, too, tried to pretend she wasn't looking at them.

Just relax, sister. Maybe a good rut with a Human sorcerer is what you need to sleep.

The silk knot in Cris's mouth was completely sodden, and he murmured something unintelligible, grunting and stroking again. She groaned to feel him stretch her. They would probably drip their mixed juices down the underside of her dress, but she didn't care.

"Faster," she gasped. "Twice before you're finished, remember?"

The young sorcerer's pace quickened until he pummeled her for a glorious, brief recurrence of their first time under the waterfall. Her pleasure arose with his thanks to their entwined auras, effortlessly carried upon his efforts.

Squealing more than a little, Innathi clasped her hands behind his neck, dark shoulders bare, lush breasts free of her gown and jiggling with every impact from his hips. Suddenly Cris was groaning louder, grunting, his cock jerking inside her though he kept thrusting.

"Yes!"

Her cunt, already soaked, wallowed in pure, sloppy, sexual noises as he filled her up.

Ohh, how can this so good?!

Thoughts clustered to answer, about how she needn't worry about becoming pregnant, that he was tall and *thick*, and she could mount him as many times as he was capable of … or have him mount her. She rather enjoyed his show of such ardor and aggression.

With his fertility magic enhancing her own, she felt so starkly alive every moment. She was truly blessed by some deity to have found this so early in her life!

I cannot wait *for the agreement to be met, for Leur and his Sire-King to leave and let Cris stay here. With me …*

Cris rested his sweaty forehead on her shoulder. He kept his cock inside her as she'd commanded. She helped him stay hard by massaging him with her sex, by murmuring her desire for him. She licked her fingers and played with his dark brown nipples, pinching them as he had hers.

"Ohhh, Cris, you were made for this."

"Mnngh," he garbled through his gag, pressing his turgid penis in a bit deeper, pulling out, feeling her body squeeze hot and wet around him again.

"You bring such pleasure, breeding a worthy female. I love it. I don't want to share you with anyone else! You are mine!"

He put his arms around her, whiffing at the scent of her throat and mumbling his own pleasure. She kissed his round, blunt ear, purring in satisfaction even knowing she wasn't finished.

"You might have tasted some Human girls after we met," she whispered, "but they weren't enough. Were they? You couldn't forget me, could you? Now we both know why."

Light, magical shocks crossed over his clothed back from her fingertips, and Cris bit down harder on his gag with a loud groan. He drew out farther, his prick harder than he had been shortly before, and Innathi encouraged him to plunge inside her.

She felt — and imagined — his creamy, white seed pushed out and dripping down her crack, coating her dark, purple netherhole before landing on the inside of her dress. Soon he would give her more to replace it.

So brazen, this rut in her Mother's office. So primal and powerful, it had to be god driven. Not even her Mother could deny that this bond would have to see itself through.

Being parted without exploring this would drive me insane!

Their siblings would simply have to wait a little longer to leave the room.

ISHUNA BURIED HER FACE IN LEUR'S CHEST. SHE COULD HEAR EVERY SOUND, every thrust and grunt and chirp of delight from her horny sister. She could smell his musk, feel the humidity rising in the room. But she did not have to watch.

Not again.

Leur had already apologized to her. He had an erection, admitted it, and occasionally it would brush against her stomach, unlikely to go down for some time. He was male, it couldn't be helped.

However, the Sorcerer's heir took no other action but to allow her to remain where she was — protected, as he'd promised — where Cris's aura couldn't strike her again.

"Not even Houda expected it to be this way," he murmured.

Cris and Innathi clearly weren't listening, but Ishuna hesitated to respond to the leading statement.

She decided to bite. "What way?"

"Cris is special. A rare birth. Born under Musanlo's power omen on *Yuern Amalti*," he said low in his chest.

"On what?"

"Our Day of the Dead. The Deathwalker predicted he would make allies with the Elves somehow. Just ... maybe not like this."

Ishuna snorted. "Omens. Mother doesn't hear about those. Best not say this to her, or you won't get whatever treaty you're after. She doesn't govern by visions and dreams."

"Of course," Leur murmured. He paused. "Is … that why you haven't been healed, Ishuna? Does the Queen not acknowledge you as a seer?"

"I'm *not* a seer," she replied, clutching at his shirt. "I have strange dreams sometimes. They mean nothing."

"I don't believe you —"

"How dare — ?"

" — because *you* don't believe your own words."

She should strike him for saying something so insolent to her. As if she hadn't tried and *tried* to explain. Tried to have her own family even consider that she must be like her sire!

Ishuna fisted one hand but … took it no farther.

She was just so tired.

Again, the lump returned to her throat.

SOON, INNATHI AND CRIS-RI-PHON WERE BACK WITH THE VALSHARESS AND Begir-al-phon, momentarily sated and on their best behavior with their eyes twinkling.

The Deathwalker Houda moved her chair to make room for Leur and Ishuna at the table. The youngest Davrin accidentally made eye contact with her. Unlike the solid black eyes of before, the whites of Houda's eyes had returned, and her irises were so light blue they appeared almost clear. It was unsettling.

"Our honored Begir and his Deathwalker have described a bit of what Our Daughters interrupted last year," the Valsharess said with formality, peering at Innathi. "You should understand more about this, *wun'ilye*."

"Understand more about what, Queen-Mother?" Innathi answered, leaning forward. "I *do* wish to understand."

"*Yuern Amalti*," the Valsharess enunciated in the Zauyrian tongue, and quite well. "Not a ritual performed at Koorul every year, but only rarely. In times when a young grey mage may step forward for apprenticeship. Though in this case, it also happened to be the very day of a Firebird-son's birth, on his twentieth year, when many Zauyrian mages publicly embrace their greatest strength and discipline in magic."

The elderly Sorcerer chuckled. "You well understand the needs of our people to claim control of the fates now and again, Valsharess, if only for a motivating performance."

"Indeed." The Valsharess looked amused, her finger again placed at her temple again, though she seemed contemplative. She held a delicate glass of pink-tinted wine in her other hand. "Ours are very much the same. So, We understand these two Zauyrian moments were to be combined: a rustic, solitary ritual without other Firebird children around to sway his self-discovery, though a Deathwalker must still be present at the start of *Yuern Amalti*."

The Davrin Queen tilted her head coyly at Houda and finished, "It only seems she arrived a little late for her stated purpose."

The Deathwalker did not react to the jab, didn't even blink her strange, blue eyes. Begir continued next.

"After the chance meeting of our two children under those falls, I assure you all who were there have told my people it *wasn't* by chance. They are open to greater trade and mutual defense with the Elves more than they've ever been, but they will not accept my young Cris-ri-phon as a grey mage now any more than he believes he could be one after that day. He's embraced a different magical strength in him thanks to the challenge of the Firstborn Daughter of the Davrin, and now we request the attention of the Valsharess to come to understand it."

"He is no death guide, Sorcerer Begir," Innathi said with a nod. "He is clearly a Consort."

"And what service is that, *qu'essan*?" Leur-en-phon prompted.

"Among the Davrin, it is a male of high fertility and focused, sexual magic," the Valsharess explained. "They are valued for their pleasure services, sharing their sensitivity to magic with their mistress, and their ability to quicken children on command." She smirked. "Clearly, We do not require him for that last bit."

"If you'll consider, Valsharess," Leur spoke. "I would say that my brother has far more capability than that." He nodded to Innathi next. "As honored as we are for any insight into this strong connection we've never seen before, Cris would be wasted as a bed servant."

Innathi frowned, turning her gaze directly on her lover. "What else can you do, Cris?"

"Indeed, tell us," the Valsharess said.

The young Man glanced between Innathi and the Valsharess, then between Leur and his sire. He exhaled softly and straightened up, speaking clear Davrin words for the first time in hours. "I have training in strategy, defense, leadership of numbers of fighting men. I am well instructed in survival in the desert. I know spells related to all these things and shall learn more."

"Hm," the Valsharess hummed with a short nod. She wasn't impressed with the youth's claims but was humoring him.

"He can learn anything needed of him," Leur spoke up in his favor. "He has shown strengths in spells of the elements — fire, earth, air especially — he still shows talent for the sights and spells of the Grey Mists, thanks to Houda. And now you tell us he has a focus of fertility and pleasure, of the magic life itself —"

"But only with me," Innathi interrupted, "thus far. This Elven magic has more to do with the specific auras involved than it does a pure 'life magic.' There is no 'life magic' discipline such as we provide for the arcane elements or healing, or even a more mystic divine, as you claim. One discovers this compatibility with another mage, or one does not. It's *quite* straight forward, nothing mysterious about it. Like a … recognition."

Leur listened to her and nodded slowly, absorbing this.

"Such as the 'Grey Mists,' " the Valsharess mused curiously, looking again to the still and quiet Deathwalker.

Houda lifted her chin in response, her grey cowl remaining in place. She was the only one here with her head covered.

"Did We hear correctly a bit ago that this one can make predictions beyond what can be deduced with enough eyes and ears and insight of Elves, Dwarves, and Humans?"

Ishuna had been watching and listening — she was unimportant to this conversation — but gripped her hands beneath the table when she heard that tone come into her Mother's voice. *Not now, don't start talking about it …*

But her Queen-Mother did.

"The Naulor — you have heard of them, yes, young man? The Pale Elves."

"Yes, Valsharess," Leur answered politely.

"They have a new Queen, much younger than Ourselves."

"Queen Yivon," Leur matched her. "Yes, Queen-Mother, the news has spread."

The Valsharess smiled a bit at his courage, sipping from her glass. "The Naulor have turned almost completely to governance by signs and portents. Sounds chaotic, does it not? Easy enough to do when water and shelter are abundant on your land, perhaps. Well?"

Leur appeared a little confused as to her point. "I suppose so, Queen-Mother, but I have never been outside the desert."

Their Mother waved her free hand, discarding that. "We understand the people's need for a spiritual life. What is it now, eight deities are honored in V'Gedra?"

"Ten, Mother," Ishuna murmured.

"Oh, yes. With priestesses spread out like this and all speaking their prayers a little at a time but with no decision-making power, the spirit is always there and yet it doesn't interfere with necessary living." The Valsharess winked at Houda. "But then little Yivon might find her ways of refusing to live in the present as having more in common with you, dear Deathwalker."

The grey Woman bowed her head respectfully, acknowledging the statement — or perhaps the insult — but still said nothing. Ishuna began to wonder if her Mother had been trying to get Houda to speak all this time, or … ?

"She can't speak Davrin, Mother," she said.

"Oh, but she understands it." The Valsharess flicked her piercing eyes at her younger Daughter. "Her Lord would not leave the poor creature at such a disadvantage sitting at Our table. Might it be that piece of obsidian around her neck which translates for her, Begir? Or perhaps one of her rings?"

The Third Sorcerer chuckled. "If you have not figured it out yet, my wonderful, beautiful, Queenly neighbor, then Houda masks her aura quite well. She does it for the comfort of all here."

"Indeed, and more skilled than I expected for one so young. I assume you gave her that instruction?"

"I have yet to see a Davrin completely at ease with the full aura of a trained death mage." The Sorcerer leaned back easily in his chair, looking pleased with himself for some reason. "There seems to be an antithesis between the Elfish 'life magics' — however you would choose to describe them — and the Human 'death guides'."

"We have magics which cause and use death," Innathi said.

"But not any which call or control the energy released beyond the natural transition, *qu'essan*," Begir returned immediately with a wink. "And your Queen-Mother is curious to know more."

The Valsharess tilted her chin up. "Perhaps."

"Well. We seem to be in a rare position to trade our children's skills with each other. For a time, at least."

Her Mother frowned a bit but nodded. "We are still not convinced."

"We've accepted your generous hospitality for one month, Valsharess. We shall have time to explore our options, shall we not?"

"Indeed. We shall."

CHAPTER 6

THE PALACE OF V'GEDRA – 400 B.S.E.

AFTER THE LONG MEETING WHICH HAD TURNED INTO EVENING-LENGTH DINING, their guests were sent to their new resting quarters. Ishuna sighed to have a moment to herself but could not, of course, stop thinking about many parts of that conversation.

Trade our children's skills.

The Realms would certainly benefit from that more than the Queendom, and Innathi hadn't even flinched to hear it. Perhaps her sister was not at all concerned about the implication that she might be as much of a pleasure servant for Cris-ri-phon as he was for her.

How could Mother not see that?

The second daughter shuddered and started dressing for bed. She was pondering which book she might take off her shelf when a knock sounded at her door. She had an immediate guess who it was.

"Leur," she growled, opening the door a crack.

"Good eve to you, *qu'essan*. You asked to speak with Houda in a private moment. She requested this attempt before you slept with some urgency."

Ishuna squinted. *Right now?*

She spotted the shorter, robed Woman just behind him. The nearest Guardsvrin stood out of earshot but could certainly see everything.

Many others about the Palace would have seen Ishuna walking with Leur all day and, unlike Innathi and Cris, it at least appeared like the elder son wasn't trying to corner her alone.

"Um. Very well."

Just get it over with.

Ishuna allowed the two Humans into her quarters and closed the door behind them, both the lock and silence spells a thoughtless addition since her third decade. Looking around, she realized she only had a total of two chairs, each of them intended for her: set at a small writing desk and a smaller vanity stand.

Nothing inviting for guests.

Swiftly, Ishuna moved them closer to the bed — upon which she would sit — so that she could see all three of them in her new mirror. In case she saw something strange.

"You said earlier that you must interpret for her," Ishuna prompted, indicating they should sit. She crawled onto her bed barefoot, tucking them beneath her deep blue sleeping pants. "But Mother said she has a trinket which allows her to understand me. This is so?"

"It is, *qu'essan.*" Leur tested his greater weight carefully in one seat; it creaked but held. "If you have similar magic which allows the same in return, do you want me to wait outside?"

She frowned, glancing at the Deathwalker. In contrast to the sorcerer son, Houda was tiny — like most Zauyrian women. Perhaps she was even lighter than Ishuna, so she had no similar undertaking in a seat intended for Davrin. "Mm. No. Nothing I care to delve into right now. I would miss Zauyrian nuance, yes?"

"Probably." Leur smiled. "Houda had questions after our supper about what she heard. I agreed to be the interpreter. This has not changed."

A pause, and Houda said something.

"Whenever you are ready," Leur said.

Ishuna sighed, massaging one tense shoulder as she focused on the Mist Woman with the same dark silver within her aura as Cris-ri-phon. "What did he do to me?"

Houda did not look to Leur but kept clear, pale blue irises on the Queen's daughter, scanning over her as she had at Koorul. She spoke in her same quiet, gravelly voice, moving her hands now and then to pantomime something as Leur translated.

"The simplest way to describe it, he 'ripped loose' one of your anchors grounding you within your unique space in the world."

Ishuna's frown shifted toward a scowl. Leur continued translating.

"Elves possess many more anchors than Humans. These are responsible for your long life and are very difficult to set adrift, especially by force. But, should it happen, a loose anchor can allow others within your space to … interact with you through the flow which exists in-between."

No one within the Valsharess's Palace spoke like this.

"That is the 'simplest' way to explain?" she remarked incredulously.

Houda smiled ruefully. Not at all beautiful. The ash-brown skin of her face was still strangely pale and ritually scarred. Her teeth were on the yellow side and not entirely straight, yet the change in expression — a smile — was welcome.

At least she can show emotion.

"Can Deathwalkers 'rip loose' the 'anchors' of the living at a whim?" Ishuna asked directly.

Houda shook her head, speaking again through Leur.

"Deathwalkers never loosen the anchors by force. Only when the essence is willing, during a natural transition into death."

She jerked with horror and insult. "I *wasn't* willing!"

Houda nodded in urgent agreement, clarifying something Leur strove to pass on quickly.

"She reminds us that Cris-ri-phon is not a Deathwalker. After what happened at Koorul, he decided not to continue training with Houda and focus on fertility magic and healing."

He did?

"Raw *power* jolted you and your sister at once, *qu'essan,*" Leur explained, "All his lust to create was focused on your sister, and his … impulse to destroy was targeted at you. This is how the magic manifested. He will never do it again if he focuses his talents on one or the other."

Talents. Such "talents" were dangerous in such an ignorant mage. Ishuna suppressed the urge to weep. "But you … or rather, Leur claimed he could heal it? And … apologize."

Houda nodded, paused, then reconsidered something.

"She will be guiding him," Leur spoke for her. "She has been helping his fevers in similar ways since he was a child."

Fevers.

"I would do it for you, *qu'essan*, if only I had my younger brother's strength to either damage or heal Elves in this manner. But … I do not. Neither does our father."

"I don't understand how 'death magic' could heal at all," Ishuna said flatly.

Houda nodded, speaking in her native tongue for a long spell as Leur kept up with a rhythmic pace.

"First, think of death as the opposite, balancing force to life. The aura defines all Human life, and yet it can shift in death. Transform. And from what Houda has confirmed here in V'Gedra, the aura also defines all living Elves, but in much more complex ways, and we have never seen a death to know how the transition may be different.

"But *you* have been pushed too far to one side, too quickly. The instability caused by this damage will either accelerate or stifle your own talents, for your aura has reached farther into the 'in-between' than most."

"How could one boy do that?" Ishuna asked, teeth clenched.

Leur paused as the Deathwalker adding something, and he looked at Houda as if to ask her to repeat something. He nodded. "Because … by your life patterns compared to other Elves, she theorizes that you have reached into the in-between even *before* you met Cris-ri-phon. He pushed you farther."

Something cold trickled through her ribcage.

How does this woman know?

Ishuna blurted, "Why?!"

Houda narrowed her eyes as if trying to guess the question.

"Why will it affect my talents?" she clarified.

Deathwalker glanced at Leur, who waited patiently for her to speak.

"Because ..." he began, "there *are* other places beyond our world. And there is space between those places, within our Red Desert itself. Such as Koorul. All of it determines *our* world's balance in relation with the rest of existence."

The heir licked his lips, his translations seeming to grow more difficult. Ishuna certainly thought so.

"From these other places, entities, big and small, could scent an open wound like this, and may feed upon it once they find it. Like any healer trying to cleanse an injury gained in the wilderness of the sand and pus ground into it, this ... this humble Deathwalker would do the same for any weakened *soul* she finds along her path."

"*Soul*?" repeated the *qu'essan* with a squint.

"The ... the parts of the whole, which *allow* you to realize your identity, and which can be transformed when a Human dies."

Soul.

Such an odd word.

Humans are so strange.

Ishuna did not speak for a long time. All she could think at first was how few spoke like this in V'Gedra. How few seemed to even glimpse what troubled her.

Even among the priests and priestesses serving various gods and goddesses, none dared to speak of the abstract as if it had been *observed* if they had anything to lose. Thanks to her Mother's rigid, thousand-year rule, only the poorest and unrecognized Davrin babbled unchecked in the Queen's Desert, and never for long.

Plenty of grifters in the City took advantage of weak moments when some circumstance made one want to believe the seers' visions were true and reliable. These deceivers often filled their prisons, a punitive punishment for sowing selfish fields of illusion at the expense of the Queendom.

Wiser worshippers explored and spoke of practical things: safe travel, enough water, a successful harvest or hunt or trade, greater spells or skill, even the misfortunate of a rival. This was how one asked for favor in the Davrin-dominated Desert without falling into a spider's trap.

Yet, Ishuna had found mentions of Davrin mystics in the oldest archives, a few passages in various tomes which described and reflected upon them without contempt. They were the ones who, despite all risks, claimed to see what lay unseen by normal eyes, see beyond their own borders. Even their own lifetime.

According to rumor, such Davrin were still out there somewhere.

Including my own sire.

Even now, her Mother's voice in her head warned her to caution against believing such stories, yet why did the Queen never talk about Her Consort? A mage of Ja'Prohn powerful enough to be chosen by the Valsharess to quicken Her Heirs.

Why would he live in exile?

And how else had Ishuna been born this way?

Houda isn't a Davrin, but she seems … real.

"If you can make this … 'unanchored' feeling go away," Ishuna murmured, covering her stomach and glancing in the mirror, spying the edge of the spider-webbed hole again, "then I shall find some way to repay you."

CRIS ATE AN ENORMOUS PORTION OF FOOD THE NEXT MORNING.

Innathi couldn't help but smile with pride as she filled her own empty belly. Her maids would have some fresh gossip while changing her bedding and cleaning up her chambers, not to mention finding that lost couch cushion somewhere in the garden below her balcony.

Sweet goddess, she was sore!

She felt distinctly jealous when Leur called his brother away just after the meal to talk in private with their father. She had grown accustomed to having the young Zauyrian nearby — his warmth, his scent, his adoring smile. She already thought of him as belonging at the Palace. If someone wanted to speak with him alone, it should be by her leave.

Ah, but Cris is still a guest.

He was still beholden to his Firebird family, reaffirmed when the brothers did not return, even when it was time for the midday meal. They were busy with her Mother, Innathi was told, and she had not been summoned. She'd be required to entertain herself for the time being.

She was also told Ishuna was hiding in the library.

"Come, sister," Innathi said to her soon after. "Come riding with me. You hardly ever do any —"

The elder Daughter stopped and almost gasped when the Deathwalker Houda drifted out from behind a freestanding bookcase. She covered her surprise at seeing the silent and eerie woman. "Ah. Good morning, Houda. I did not realize you were here."

Houda bowed formally. "*Qu'essan.*"

The woman could speak this word, at least.

The Deathwalker was ugly even among Humans, possessing scars darkened with charcoal on her sickly-tan skin, obvious designs and intentionally inflicted on her face and her hands, probably the rest of her body if she could see it, though Innathi was grateful she could not. She wondered whether the Humans had filed down her teeth to make them slightly sharp or if she had been born that way?

Cris-ri-phon truly been considered becoming like her? What a waste!

When Innathi got her way, she would see that his perfect skin was *never* marked so coarsely.

Houda still couldn't speak their language but, thanks to her Lord's trinket, had understood Innathi's suggestion and nodded to Ishuna, gesturing with her hand toward the door.

"I don't feel like riding," her sister mumbled.

"The sunlight will help," Innathi insisted. "You just need to make the effort."

Houda nodded agreement again, stepping over in her ragged robes to reach out and gently close the book into which Ishuna was staring.

"Ishentu begran," the Deathwalker murmured, perhaps trying to sound soothing but only being creepy.

"Fine," Ishuna groused, likely not understanding the words any better than her older sister, but she was a Court Daughter. She could read tone and body language just as well when she tried.

Ishuna stood up to join her, and Houda followed them out of the room. While Ishuna brightened, Innathi felt dismayed.

"I don't recall inviting you, Deathwalker," she began.

"I want her to go," Ishuna cut in, looking at Houda. "Ride with us?"

"Abi," Houda answered, nodding yes.

In a stubborn mood, are you?

Innathi rolled her eyes where neither could see. Nothing was going her way this morning. Resigned, she passed on the orders to have the usual gathered: their mounts, honor guard, water, and food, noting they'd have a wrinkled, hooded woman in tow.

Later, Ishuna stood for a moment next to her new mare, since her favorite one was nursing her foal. She stared into nothingness for a few moments then asked, "Innathi?"

"Hm?"

"Do you miss Xala?"

... Where did that come from?

And why ask questions like that in front of the Guardsvrin and this strange, grey mage?

"Captain Ja'Prohn is where she is meant to be," Innathi answered stonily as they mounted up. She winced upon landing in the saddle. Her crotch was still tender. Maybe riding all afternoon wasn't a good idea.

Bother. I'll get some healing salve after we get back and be ready for tonight.

She certainly planned to sequester Cris from his overprotective brother again tonight but, until then, she had to find something to do. She could deal with the rub.

"Houda must be blindfolded for this next part," Innathi said, grinning sweetly and gesturing to the Guardsvrin.

The Deathwalker looked at Ishuna, who nodded, and the woman reluctantly allowed her eyes to be bound tight.

They took the shortcut out at the back of the Palace, a heavily warded underground passage with a climb steep on each end. Allowing two horses abreast, it took them underground just long enough to leave the city and exit among the Edonil foothills.

Not too far from the exit was a protected ravine which nearly always contained at least a trickle of water and green plants. Within this ravine, the Queen-Mother's Daughters first learned to ride.

"Behold!" Innathi exclaimed happily as they removed Houda's blindfold.

Unsurprisingly, the Deathwalker bore an understated reaction: interested and curious, with a nod of approval, but with no inspired awe that Innathi could read.

Boring crone.

The sisters talked less with the Deathwalker's presence, but they avoided the late afternoon heat deep in the shade of the ravine. No doubt they were both reminiscing about their caits' adventures together, outside of V'Gedra and their Mother's watchful eye, holding that freedom to test the boundaries a little.

Ishuna soon proved her wrong.

"Mother said we might find something to help me among the Deathwalkers."

Her sister's voice was very quiet, the Guardsvrin far enough back not to hear over the clopping hooves, but Houda could. Once upon a time, Captain Xala might have heard it, too, but …

No longer.

"I remember," Innathi said stiffly.

"Houda says the mage power lies in your would-be Consort." Ishuna licked her lips, as if nervous. "He must apologize for what he's done and help mend it."

"Apologize for … ?" The heir laughed to hide her confusion. "He did no harm."

"To you," Ishuna retorted. "He did to me. The young mage doesn't know his own strength."

Innathi believed that. The thought of that made her shiver. And he would dedicate all that strength to her with the right persuasion.

"Is that what Houda has told you?" Innathi asked, narrowing her eyes a bit. "He only must 'apologize,' and you will be well again?"

"And help mend it. So, I'm not left so … exposed. In m-my Reverie."

Sigh.

"You were hearing voices years *before* you ever met him," Innathi said testily. "I don't appreciate her encouraging this if —"

"It's real!" the younger sister blurted, a little too loudly.

Innathi flicked her eyes back toward the guards in warning, suggesting, ⋆In hand sign, then.⋆

Ishuna shook her head, refusing. "Houda doesn't understand sign. She should hear."

"Why?" Innathi challenged. "Frankly, I think you're trusting her far too quickly —"

"And *you* aren't trusting Cris-ri-phon to be alone with you, despite *all* good sense?!"

"Shhh!"

They glared at each other but finally Innathi sighed, looking at the woman staring down at her gloved hands as if she wasn't listening to every magically translated word.

"What makes you think you know what to do for my sister, Deathwalker?" she asked bluntly.

Houda lifted her head to look out from within the shadow of her hood, nodding acknowledgment without speaking. She pulled back on her reins to stop her horse, forcing the rest of them to do the same, and made a motion with her hand as if they should stay where they were.

Hmm.

Gently, Houda kicked her gelding to move closer to the stream and into direct sunlight before turning in place to face them. Next, she slipped off her gloves and rolled up her sleeves before lowering her hood.

What in the — ?

Innathi gaped when the Deathwalker's skin changed color like she'd been doused in paint, darkening from a paler Zauyrian brown to the very shade of a Davrin. With her hair already black with only a few traces of white, Houda appeared like a living shadow with piercing, crystal-blue eyes.

Or like some demon coming out of the tales of old.

"Mage's illusion," Innathi snapped, loudly enough to calm her nervous Guardsvrin.

Houda tilted her head but proceeded to unhook her cloak, laying it over the haunches of her horse as she opened her robe next.

What are you — ?

The Deathwalker revealed her bare shoulders, arms, and breasts, her torso down to her belly. Her scarred, oddly pale skin shifted dark, perfectly in time with its exposure to the sun, presenting a bizarre reversal to the Davrin which Innathi had presented to the Zauyrian at Koorul.

Nude from the waist down, her breasts sagging and her gaunt body all-too-Human, Houda nudged her horse closer without leaving the sun and held out her hand. Innathi stared at it, rough and wrinkled like a Human, yet its color almost identical to her own.

The Deathwalker silently invited the *qu'essan* to test for illusion.

Fine. I'm not afraid.

Innathi kicked her mount forward to join her, first holding her hand above Houda's extended arm as a block to the sun. The Deathwalker's skin lightened where the shade touched it. Though not as pale as when the shadows were deeper, the response was instant, following no matter where Innathi hovered her hand.

The Queen's daughter knew more than enough magic by now to test for the presence of any active spell or magical item. She also tried her own counters and reveals — which *should* have worked by just knowing the strange female was a mage as well. The *qu'essan* detected nothing active except the translator ring she already knew about.

Houda was not drawing upon her aura; in fact, she still suppressed it. The sun-shifting quality of her skin was a make-up of the Deathwalker's existence as opposed to anything deliberate Houda was doing to look this way.

How? … Why?

Ishuna approached now as well, sensing her sister's uncertainty. "You recognize Houda has knowledge we do not?"

"Of course. Mother said as much."

"And she is not faking this."

Innathi expelled air through her nostrils. "I suppose not."

"Then …" She dropped to a whisper. "I need Cris tonight."

She jolted from her stare and turned her head. "No!"

"I need him to listen to Houda and do what she says!" Ishuna hissed, tears leaping to her eyes. "Please!"

Oh! Oh …

Ishuna *wasn't* suggesting that they share him in bed.

That's good.

Ishuna continued with her voice low. "Leur will be there. He can translate for Houda even if Cris is concentrating."

Her mind's image grew clearer.

"And you expect this to work somehow?" Innathi squinted, murmuring secretively. "Is it a spell?"

Ishuna sounded cagey. "I … I don't know. W-we need Leur to explain. It might be a … a ritual."

Ritual!

Innathi's eyes widened. "Mother does *not* allow those in her Palace."

"Or she just doesn't want to know about it," Ishuna replied, her face stubborn and pinched. "She gave tacit permission before they ever arrived, remember? To find something 'among them' to help me sleep. So long as we don't flaunt it out in front of her, that's what we're doing. Please, Innathi, I need your Consort tonight. Just for a while. After this, he's yours. I shall never ask again."

Your Consort. He's yours.

Though soothed, Innathi chewed the inside of her cheek. She had been annoyed with her day, but it looked as though the evening wouldn't be much better.

Regardless of any healing salve for my nethers.

"You may have him, but *I* shall be there, too," Innathi said, looking at Houda directly.

The Deathwalker nodded. No protest.

"Good. Now for the Queen's sake, put your robe and hood back on, Deathwalker."

CHAPTER 7

THE WAITING SEEMED ABNORMALLY LONG TO REACH LATE EVENING.

When all were certain that the Queen-Mother was done with her guests and it was time to retire, they each went to their separate quarters at first. Closer to midnight and with all subtlety and redirected guards they could manage, four siblings left their rooms and collected in the first garden Ishuna had shown the brothers the day of their arrival.

"The fountain has water we will need," Leur explained as he warded the little pavilion from prying eyes, wanderers, and nighttime guards. "And some of the plants may need to give up their leaves. No one will *want* to approach from the feeling they will receive. Yet from the outside, it will look empty."

"Also," Cris added, "my brother's magic has less familiar taste to natives."

"True," his older brother agreed. "Plenty of powerful mages live in V'Gedra but few will be drawn in the middle of the night to this specific place. We shall be small and quiet."

Small and quiet.

Ishuna wanted to shrivel and be just that when Houda suggested that she sit on Leur's lap, so that he could hold her up if she began to slip and fall.

"Slip and fall?" asked Innathi. "Why?"

"Your sister will be in a trance for part of it if we do it right. We do not want her to hit her head."

Her sister winked at her. "Oh, then, by all means! Sit in his lap and let him hold you, Ishuna."

The teasing made her stomach turn that much tighter and more sour. Ishuna glared but gingerly sat down in the older brother's lap. Only Houda could have encouraged her to lean back against him, giving clear instruction to bring her legs forward and together in between his.

Now, he cradled her, and the Deathwalker crouched by their feet, removing the lid from a small jar and using her fingers to dip into something fluid. Houda began drawing markings around them, smearing something sticky and soot-black upon the bright red sandstone.

Then, dabbing more goop with her little finger, Houda stood up and turned to Cris, creating smaller versions of the same markings upon his cheeks and the backs of his hands.

Ishuna's heart picked up observing her. *Ritual . . .*

"So, my lover," Innathi began, startling her, "I understand you aren't even *allowed* to accept my proposal without first apologizing to my sister for what happened at Koorul, here and now?"

Cris's face darkened in embarrassment at her tone, but he looked at Leur and Houda. Each nodded calmly to him, his brother making some encouraging hand motion. The second son exhaled softly. "Yes, *qu'essan*."

"Innathi," she said firmly. "Say my name."

He cleared his throat, distracted from whatever instruction Houda was giving him in his native tongue. Ishuna glared at her sister from Leur's lap, trying not to feel foolish for her spiking annoyance.

"No sex games now, if you please," Ishuna snapped. "Surely you can hold onto your slit long enough."

Innathi looked like she'd been slapped and gaped at her. Cris frowned and was about to say something to the younger sister on his brother's lap.

"Prehuda reu!" Houda barked loudly, clapping her hands, fixing

Cris's steel grey eyes solely on her. "*Initigaf,* Cris-ri-phon."

"*Abi*, Houda," he replied.

Leur did not miss Innathi's lifted nostril when the Deathwalker cut in between them. "Ah … Would you feel more comfortable waiting elsewhere, *qu'essan*?"

"Absolutely not!" she barked irritably.

His tone hardened. "If you insist, your grace. But for your sister's sake, you *must* be quiet and still. Do not draw attention to yourself or talk directly to Cris. He needs to concentrate, or he may just hurt her again."

Of course, her elder sister wasn't used to being commanded by anyone except her Mother. Innathi narrowed her eyes at the Sorcerer's heir but then glanced at Ishuna sulking and shrugged. Finally sitting down, she leaned back alone on her bench and crossed her arms.

Now perhaps they could get started.

The ritual itself wasn't *too* different from a magic spell, at least at the start. Water, fire, plant, air, dirt, blood … plenty of components they were already familiar with. Where it differed was in longer preparation, the repetitive chant, and the … prayers?

"To Musanlo and the Grey Lady," Leur whispered.

Its cadence was unlike anything Ishuna had ever heard before. Warm song and cool whispers intoned with harmony, distinctly different from the arcane rules of command and will.

Leur was right; she *did* fall into a trance. It wasn't a first time, but it was odd that she felt aware of herself — fully aware — as some part of her touched one of those "other" places, directed by a calm, guiding hand.

She was floating; they all were.

Where am I?

⋆*You are here. Open up, let us see the wound.*⋆

Unbidden, Ishuna relived some of Innathi's pleasure at the waterfall as Cris obeyed instruction, tentatively touched the front of her dress, and began to undo it.

Highly inappropriate but necessary.

The young sorcerer grew more confident when she did not fight or scream. Without the rough, heavy jerking he'd used on Innathi's dress, Cris-ri-phon carefully exposed her shoulders, breasts, and belly.

Until they could plainly see the festering wound that he had created. The young man flinched, grey eyes flashing. ⋆*Oh ... Ah, Ishuna. I ... I **am** sorry. I did not mean to hurt. I only ... meant to hold you still.*⋆

Ishuna sensed Houda's approval but did not hear her voice the way she heard Cris's. They waited for her response.

I hear you, she responded reluctantly. *Just ... h-heal it like Houda says you c-can.*

The youth nodded and placed his large hands on her. She instantly disliked how it felt ... because the magic felt too strong. *Far* too strong for any male to wield on a Davrin. Especially a Human.

Cris was healing her, as Houda instructed, pressing his palm against the hole in her gut with a comforting weight and heat. Slowly, she saw the hole was stitching itself up, the webbed cracks melting, beginning to fade into nothing before ...

Resistance.

Something fought back. Harsh hissing filled her mind. The clacking like a giant creature consuming a corpse, bound and trapped, made her cry out with icy fear.

Get it out! Oh, Goddess-Queen, get it out!

"Shhhh," Leur whispered, arms holding her tightly. "You are well, all shall be well. Houda says we must go deeper."

D-Deeper?

"Um. H-Houda asks that you open your leg. Just a little."

My legs?!

"Please, trust us. The wound has grown deep."

Cris's free hand slipped between her thighs, encouraging them to part. Ishuna resisted, clamping them together.

Is that truly *what Houda is saying?!*

Ishuna felt the answer, indistinct but affirmative, coming from all three around her.

Growling with continued reluctance, Cris nudged her open and moved between her legs, pushing her gown up with one hand, one side at a time, keeping his hand on her naked belly. Unlike her sister the other day, Ishuna was wearing small clothes, but Cris simply wormed his thick fingers past the edge and nudged at her core.

She gasped. *J-just like Mother said!*

These "rituals" were tricks to steal something from her!

No tricks. Only truth.

**Ishuna. This midway point is dangerous. Please focus — **

She squirmed, trying to keep his probing digits out, but she gasped in horrified delight when the Sorcerer's son pushed two fingers into her slit and somehow closed a loop, his aura rushing through her to flow between his hands.

Magic and pleasure surged through her guts; the healing accelerated. The dark shrieks and skittering feet fled to hidden shadows, their noise overtaken with her own.

Ohhh, nooo! Please, please, I'm drowning!

**You're not drowning. You are rising up. Do no fear — **

Fighting yet helplessness, afraid to forget herself in the sandstorm power, Ishuna struggled to reach her surface thoughts — any of them! —to grasp hold and resist becoming that floundering, mindless *thing* her sister was while feeling his magic!

What is he?!

The shadows hissed at her, taunted her that she had *no* idea what he was. She was being tricked.

We all *are.*

He will bring us to ruin …

Ishuna reached out to him, demanding, *What do you* want *from her?!*

Want from her? He sounded confused. **I only …* want *her. Only her.**

A bitter laugh leaked into the healing space between his hands.

She plans to use you for what you're worth, you know, until you're too old to pleasure her. Long before you're ugly to her like Houda. Then she'll choose another. You must *know this.*

He looked shocked. **No. No, I love her. I will prove it — **

How?! Ishuna groaned and writhed in Leur's arms, Cris's fingers still up her cunt. *How?! You're Human! She will be an Elf Queen! She will live for a thousand years and you barely two hundred* ***if*** *you can manage that, Sorcerer!*

There's more to this bond than age! he cried. **I know it!**

Ha! She'll not follow you. She'll never need a death guide, be that you or your rejected teacher! she sneered, pounding a fist against his fears and insecurities, seizing them, trying to shred them.

Denying him *and* herself that oncoming, healing climax.

You won't be able to keep up with her. Sooner or later she will need her own heir, which will be long after you're dead. She must choose a Davrin to make children when she's much older and has proven herself a Queen, just like our Mother has done.

She laughed. With hysteria.

Stay, and accept her proposal if you wish. But it is a lark only, and sidewise for whatever information and contacts you're willing to give her. You can't be so foolish as to think it is anything else!

Cris stared into her with horror and disbelief, revolted by whatever he saw. His face broke, any vision he had been dreaming up until this moment pierced clean through.

Just as he'd pierced *her* at Koorul.

You're right, he whispered, and his fingers slipped out of her, leaving her empty and on the edge. **I must find another way.**

"Cris!" Leur pleaded. "Focus!"

In a dead space, the moment snapped.

Another cry inside as Houda groped for any action to retrieve the slipping ritual, to bring them to completion.

The First Son tried to help as well, reaching down to crush Cris's hand to Ishuna's belly, holding it there as Leur himself moved her small clothes aside and penetrated the *qu'essan* again with his own fingers. He moved them knowledgeably, stroked her hard and caused her body to jerk in shocked surprise as he added his own mage's power, forcing her to peak.

Ishuna screeched in shock, surprised by the pleasure felt every moment as she drew enough power from her assailant to finally close the wound down upon the hissing protests. It went on and on, the hole shrinking by infinite measures, and her thrashing body nearly slipped and fell from the older brother's lap.

Leur held on to her stubbornly, every moment, and did not let her fall.

Finally, Ishuna passed out and lay still.

INNATHI HATED THIS.

She hated watching *every* moment as she had her own fingers crammed between her legs, using part of her dress to cover it from Houda's occasional glance her way.

That should be me in between them!

She wanted to be there in Leur's lap with Cris partly undressing her, lifting her skirts and having his way in her slippery sex without even removing her underclothes.

All that attention. Unshakeable.

Disliking it as much as she relished watching, Innathi had never seen Ishuna more sensual than when she was like this: held helpless in this ritual, knowing she did something explicitly forbidden in the Valsharess City of V'Gedra.

Her little sister had the same hot and randy side Innathi did, she *knew* it. No matter how rarely she indulged, no matter how she denied it with faces of disgust! Ishuna had just been jealous of her older sister at Koorul. Maybe all this had just been to get such attention.

Clever, clever cunt, if it was.

When that final surge hit, however … even Innathi could not deny that something more had just happened. The bitter, covetous thoughts vanished in a breeze.

"Cris," she gasped, her heart pounding in her chest. She beckoned. "Cris, step away. You're finished. Come to me, now, before it fades …"

Shaking her head, Houda gestured silently for Cris to go. The crone had finally given up. She looked exhausted, and Cris looked dazed as well but did not resist answering her invitation.

Innathi felt exalted. Finally! Even Leur and Houda together couldn't compete with her!

Within moments, the sorcerer's lips were on hers, hot and hungry as he kissed her. She let him taste her tongue and tasted his in return. His right hand wet from her sister, he partly dried it when he pulled her dress up and he fumbled to free the erection within his pants. She let him mount her again, again not wearing small clothes, and chirped in utter satisfaction, biting his shoulder as his wide cock buried itself inside her again.

So good . . .

Cris held her tightly around her waist and fucked her on his knees as she sat splayed on the bench. His strokes grew more determined than ever, pleasuring her so much, she couldn't imagine even conception with a properly magical Davrin centuries later being so intense.

Sooner or later, though, this was what any Mother's Daughter had to do.

"LEUR . . . L-LEUR —" ISHUNA MOANED AS THE AUBURN-HAIRED MAN CARRIED her, praying they weren't seen as he managed to get the *qu'essan* and Houda back inside. Innathi had already taken Cris to her quarters and the three now stood at Ishuna's bed.

She wouldn't let go of his shirt. She was barely conscious.

"*Shh*. Ishuna, Ishuna," he whispered. "You must rest now."

"This is stronger than we imagined," Houda murmured in Zauyrian.

"We managed to heal her," Leur said, trying to pull down the covers for the Davrin princess. "Right?"

"Yes," Houda granted, but the way she said it sounded ominous.

Leur took as deep a breath as he dared when he finally settled Ishuna in bed and peeled his wrinkled shirt free of her grip. He looked at his father's Deathwalker. "What troubles you?"

Houda shrugged slightly. "Cris will find it harder to hear the song meant for him in this place. But I fear we cannot make him leave it."

Leur's shoulders sagged as he imagined leaving at the end of the month without his little brother. That seemed … very likely now. He watched Houda's subtle expressions, which he knew how to read from the time he was a young child.

"What else, wise woman?"

Houda watched Ishuna sleep. "This princess hears a song as well, yet we've confirmed she cannot make out its meaning, either. While our young Cris may learn to flourish amid Elvish magic, even if it delays his calling, the young *qu'essan* seems smothered here. Perhaps your father is right."

"Right about what?"

"About trading the skills of the children. If the Queen-Mother would have Cris-ri-phon for a given time, then perhaps the Third Sorcerer of the Realms may have Ishuna for the same time. They have been discussing it, he tells me."

Leur frowned. "I … didn't believe he could even get the Queen-Mother to listen to such a trade."

"It seems there is a real chance." Houda tilted her head at him, watching him with that eerie yet familiar gaze. "I will leave now. Stay with her a little longer, Leur. See if she is open to having you as a companion for some decades over her smitten sister."

The Deathwalker tilted her head in the other direction when he didn't reply.

"You do want her, do you not?" Houda said. "A seer *and* Queen's daughter together is more valuable to your rule than Cris shall be to a princess who will not rule for some time."

The Sorcerer's heir sighed quietly and nodded. "You will help me with her talent, won't you, Houda? Guide us?"

"Of course. This one has touched dangerous skeins in her sleep. I would rather not leave her entirely without guidance. I told you I saw this in the Mist."

Leur-en-phon nodded, grappling with his nerves about back then, about now, and whatever was yet to be. "Then … I will stay a little longer. Good night, Houda."

It was dark as pitch. She couldn't see anything.

She could feel, though.

What was she doing, still fully clothed in her bed?

Ishuna struggled to get out of the hot, restricting clothing …

"Here, allow me."

His touch wasn't so heavy and intense as the other one, though he undressed her in a similar way. She quivered, waiting until her arms were free before shoving and pushing at the unwelcome silk around, moving it over her hips and down her legs.

Leur tugged it from beneath the covers, and she heard it tossed over a chair. She sighed, the fine sheets shushing against her bare body but for her small clothes, she reached out blindly.

"Leur … ?"

"Here."

She gasped at the hot skin, touching light hair upon a broad expanse. His shirt was off. She supposed he was too warm in her room as well. From the sound of his sitting next to her, he still wore his trousers.

He rubbed her arm gently and she could smell his familiar scent. Her middle was still tight from the …

The ritual.

And she struggled to remember the details.

Such strange magic. It had felt like she'd been wrapped in a cocoon, suspended above the floor, yet hands touched her directly. Their touch directed the flow, able to dive *deep* inside her, and …

And they had burned all the cobwebs off.

Leaving her raw and sensitive and …

Yearning.

She could feel the evidence dampening her small clothes.

"Leur?"

"Yes, Ishuna?"

"Lie down next to me."

"Are you certain?"

"Lie down and remove your trousers."

"*Qu'essan,* you are dizzy —"

She reached out boldly and cupped his crotch in her hand. He was already half-erect and quickly became stiffer in her hand. She smirked. He was as male as the rest; it couldn't be helped.

"Take down your pants, sorcerer," she said. "Take it all off."

Such delight when he obeyed. She came to her knees to pull down the light fabric around her pelvis. The room was still dark; they slipped out of their clothes without speaking, or looking, and came together again by feel, by scent, and sound, all of it more intense for not depending upon the eyes.

She rolled him onto his back and got to her knees to straddle him, gently dropping her underpants onto his face.

"Mmm," he said, inhaling long and slow.

She chuckled quietly, exploring his arms and chest, following the trail of fur down his belly to the musky patch at the base of his hard pole, so hot and smooth. He groaned when she caressed him, leaving her damp, scented bit of silk on his face until she removed it — if she chose to. He didn't once reach up his hands to touch her; not without her asking him to.

She rather enjoyed knowing that.

Soon the young Davrin was rocked against him, rubbing her crotch back and forth along his length, murmuring in pleasure as she smeared her lubricant all over him. He tensed and moaned with her, and still he didn't reach with his hands to grope her, to maul or seize her as his younger brother had. Leur didn't try to press her down, get on top, and rut his way.

He'd let her have *her* way with him.

She trembled with the anticipation of allowing him in, of feeling his larger size stretch her. It had been a long time for her already, and even then, she hadn't been so eager to sit on *that* cock like she anticipated claiming *this* one.

Kneeling up a little higher, Ishuna used her hand to position him properly, testing her own aim by squatting down a bit, until just the head was inside. Leur sucked in his breath. She pulled up, tried again, took him a little deeper.

"Oh, Goddess," he whispered.

Still he did not touch her thoughtlessly; he kept his hands up by his head unless she said otherwise.

"Ohhh, yesss," Ishuna crooned as she rose up and squatted down still farther, pressing him deep, deep inside.

Yet she wasn't sure she had all of him yet.

Up again, then down; he was slickened up now. She could move easier. She reached forward to take his wrists, finding them near his head.

Pleased, she whispered, "I'm going to rut you, Sorcerer. I'll do it hard until I climax again. You'll wait until *after* me to peak. Understand?"

She stroked up. Held still.

"Ohhh … yes, your grace," he whispered through her small pants. "I understand." He slipped into Zauyrian. "*Fuck me, princess.*"

She rewarded him by squatting down. *Yes.*

His staff was wide, thick, as it had felt in her hands. Again, she stroked, moved faster, reaching for her rhythm, and using her grip on his wrists as leverage. He strained beneath her; his hips jerked up once in desire, but he didn't steal the pace from her.

That one slip could be forgiven. *After more teasing.*

"Do not move your hands," she demanded, releasing him to lean back and squeeze his shaft with her inner muscles. She swirled her hips slowly, barely even bouncing.

He was clenching his hands into fists, open and closed, but they remained by his head. Eventually, after a good, long tease, he asked, "Your grace … please …"

She giggled again, panting. "Ready to *'fuck'* some more?"

He was gasping; sweat dotted his chest. "Yes, *qu'essan*. At your pleasure."

Her cunt fluttered around him, hearing his voice. Oh, sweet Mother, she wanted him. She would get her climax, and he would get his.

Never had anyone let go so easily with her before. He feared nothing she might try and, in his confidence, even as an heir to rule with her wet panties on his face, he placed himself underneath her and treated her like a Queen.

He wasn't so needy and pathetic as his little brother, so "impulsive" or overbearing. She never would have guessed the next ruler of the Third would be so surprising at every turn.

A month was not long enough to understand him completely.

CHAPTER 8

THE RED DESERT – 400-390 B.S.E.

AT THE END OF THAT FIRST VISIT, THE RULERS OF V'GEDRA AND THE THIRD Realm had determined they would have new residents. The greatest shock came to Innathi, who evidently thought she could keep both the sister of her childhood and her new lusty playmate together at once.

"Mother, why are you *really* sending Ishuna away?" she asked, keeping her voice low even in one of their rare private moments. "You can't think she will do well away from here. She needs to be taken care of."

The Valsharess nodded once, slowly. "And she will be. Leur is quite taken with her, though we are not discussing a true mage match between them as you know for yourself, Daughter. She shall also be in a position to witness far more of the Deathwalkers and Our old friend Begir, not to mention the next-ruling son, than anything Cris-ri-phon will see of Us while living here as a Consort."

"But —"

"Enjoy your lover, my dear. His time will pass soon enough. Ishuna will *always* be your sister, and when I am gone, you may depend upon what she has learned in her time more than what you might from that boy."

Innathi just avoided scowling at her Mother for this; the Queen didn't like to be glared at. "Everyone — his father, his brother, his people, even Ishuna knows how much potential he has as a powerful sorcerer."

Her Mother nodded, looking bored. "And we shall use it for what it is worth, should he bloom beyond this strange compulsion he has around you." The Valsharess raised an elegant, sardonic eyebrow. "Have you done something … *specific* to make him act thusly?"

"What? No!" Innathi denied, genuinely aghast. "It … It's natural! A pure discovery, Mother."

"Very well. I envy your youth, Innathi. Do not waste it."

"HOW ARE YOU ADJUSTING TO YOUR NEW HOME, YOUR GRACE?"

Ishuna spun away from the view from the Sorcerer's Tower with her heart in her throat. Once the shock of hearing a *native* Davrin tongue passed through her, she recognized—

"Xala!"

Forgetting herself, she rushed to embrace her former bodyguard.

The older Davrin accepted, wrapping arms around her shoulders as if she were fragile. "Good to see you, *qu'essan*."

Ishuna responded with a tighter hold fueled by another surge of emotion. When the exiled Captain hissed in pain, she jumped and released her immediately, worried confusion scrawled on her face.

"Apologies," Xala grimaced. "My back still has sore spots."

What an understatement for a detail Ishuna was ashamed to have forgotten. Her voice was stuck in her throat at first, she uttered, "I-I didn't know if you'd survived …"

"I made it through," Xala replied, her face carefully neutral. "Lucky to have had the option of exile after all that, honestly."

After all that.

"And … you are here?" Ishuna asked, shaking her head. "I didn't know you would be here."

Xala smiled. "I asked Begir not to show that coin to the Queen after he took me on. Didn't take much persuasion to keep it back for a bit." She shrugged. "Figure you'll have to tell your Mother about seeing me, sooner or later, so I wanted to reintroduce myself."

Reintroduce ... ? It hasn't been long.

Why did the Captain sound like she'd been gone for *longer* than a year?

Ishuna swallowed, noticing the lingering, purple streaks on Xala's hands and face, more of them disappearing down beneath her Firebird uniform. The *qu'essan* shook her head. "I ... don't have to tell Mother you are here. I won't."

"As you like, your grace. That's between your Mother and you." Xala looked her over. "You seem better from last year. Are you?"

Ishuna nodded. "It didn't get better until Leur and Houda helped me."

Suddenly, Xala grinned. Proved she still could. "Did they? So you let yourself listen to a cryptic sage?"

She fidgeted. "Y-yeah."

"Yeah. Me, too." Xala turned her head toward the daylit window. "At least enough to encourage them to try talking to you despite your Mother." She looked back. "Glad they got farther than I did."

Xala had *sent* them to her? To help?

"It worked, and Mother's *wrong*." The young Davrin's voice grew stubborn against the impulse not to speak it. "I *am* a seer. I'm here to learn from Houda. Since it's allowed here."

The former Captain of V'Gedra reached out and squeezed her shoulder, her smile still in place. "Very good, then. Sounds like you're adjusting already."

"My Mother will outlive you, Cris, despite how she looks. You'd best get used to her dining room remarks."

"I can do more than pleasure the royal daughter in bed, Innathi, if only she'd let me focus on something else."

"Oh? What, something else?"

He shrugged. "Swordplay, sorcery, survival …" He began ticking off on his fingers. "Drilling, strategy, even magic crafting. Do I really need to tell you all this again, my love?"

"You don't need to, no." She smirked. "I was just curious if any specific 'teacher' called to you besides me."

He winced at her teasing. "You mean that? Or are you tired of me already and want me out of the Palace doing something else?"

Innathi chuckled indulgently and slinked off her bed to walk toward him fully nude. She lifted her arms and placed them around him; he'd gotten even a little taller *still* in his time here, shoulders broader and arms bulking out. His Davrin speech was almost flawless, as were his manners in public.

He was still a bit of a brute in private.

"I am not tired of you, Cris. And you seemed bored with the magic I'm studying. It's hard for two mages to get anything done studying the same thing anyway, right?"

She waggled her eyebrows suggestively. Cris leaned to kiss her; there seemed a touch of sadness and uncertainty to it. He hesitated a moment before he said it.

"Maybe I need to be away for a while, *before* you tire of me."

Her eyes widened. "What?"

"I will return," he assured her. "But some time apart might hone the edge of our passion, would it not?"

Her body flared with anger. "Our passion has dulled so much for you already, has it?"

"Innathi —"

"Do you think I have even a month to waste with you being away from me?" she demanded. "Before you'll be away forever?"

He scowled. "Yes, I'm quite the swift-spoiling fruit, aren't I? Neither you nor your Mother can help but *always* bring that up!"

She lifted her chin. "It's Queen-Mother to you."

He grunted in frustration, barely holding his tongue on that. "Why couldn't I learn some of the Elvish sword fighting, at least? The Blade Song. You must be a mage to learn that, right?"

"She won't allow you to start because the training takes longer than you'll be alive."

"*Like a sidewinder's ass*," he muttered in Zauyrian, turning around.

"I heard that!"

"Good of you to learn *something* of my kin," he said bitterly. "I can expect double the expected life of a regular Zauyrian. My own sire lived to be a hundred and eighty — he only just *died!* — and that still isn't good enough. For you *or* for her!"

She looked irritated. "Good enough for *what?*"

"To teach me *more* of anything at all! I could be doing much more than I am for the Queendom! I could be earning respect among the Realms on your behalf."

"Is that why you want to leave? Cris! You accepted my proposal to be my Consort. I chose *you* above all others. Do you know how much Davrin buas *envy* you?"

"Yes, only to imagine you riding a colt for all you're worth until he gets too old and breaks a leg falling off the balcony. Which all the 'jealous buas' are just waiting for me to do! They'd push me if they could."

She chuckled at the mental image. "Perhaps, but they'd not get away with it." She sighed. "Why are you so focused on this, Cris? Why have you changed your thinking so suddenly?"

He glared at her. "It's not sudden, *qu'essan*. I'm Human. Ten years is a long time when his queen has hardly changed her thinking at all."

ISHUNA WAS INCREDULOUS, HER EYES WIDENING IN HORROR. "WHAT DO YOU mean 'he left'?"

Leur shrugged helplessly, looking worried as he rubbed his auburn beard. "Just that. News has come that Cris has left V'Gedra."

"Is he coming back here?" she asked nervously. "To your home?"

"He left in the opposite direction, I'm told, to the north and west. He might circle around, eventually. I am not sure, he hasn't contacted me."

"Did ... did he leave with the permission of the Valsharess?"

Leur nodded. "He received that, at least, or he wouldn't have made it over many dunes before being shot down. Though ... Innathi was furious with both him and the Queen-Mother. She couldn't hide it."

"Hm," Ishuna said, noncommittal. "Barely a decade."

Neither Leur nor Houda had seemed to change so much in that time as Cris had, even as they gained grey in their hair. Ishuna was beginning to understand this about Humans, that the fastest change happened between the first decade and the third.

And Innathi doesn't have the exposure had to figure it out.

The younger sister had only to understand more about herself and her "inward" magic as well, but at least her Human tutors were patient. She had more time to live, and the visions did not come at her bidding.

Houda would ask her now and again.

"Have the dreams of shattered crystal and spiderwebs returned, Ishuna? What of the scorpions?"

And she could shake her head no.

"They have not returned. Thank you, Deathwalker."

Other things had come to her, though, which Houda had helped tremendously to interpret, such as signs of a betrayal to Leur during the Ruler's Transition or of finding a new source of water.

With the Deathwalker's insights, her dreams had even revealed a criminal who needed to be pardoned, or one that must be executed immediately. Never were these Zauyrians Ishuna knew personally, but someone close to Leur, Houda, or even Xala always did.

The visions had arrived mostly in the direction she wanted to look at the time. What made the most difference was the Third Sorcerer-King always listening to her, the same as he would listen to Houda.

Leur made his own decision despite what people would say, but always after weighing the words of his two mystics with his magicless sergeants and ministers working on ground level, he would deal with the consequences, come as they may.

His people said he was a good ruler.

Watching this, Ishuna allowed her visions to come without fear because she *wanted* to help the Zauyrian Realms. After all, she still looked for a way to repay Leur and Houda, although both had told her that she already had.

Chapter 9

The Red Desert — 254-241 B.S.E.

When the Valsharess Alyarra passed after more than sixteen centuries of rule, the Queen's Throne coming at last to the First Daughter, Ishuna wondered why she suddenly missed the Deathwalker Houda.

The old woman walked into the Grey a century ago.

The Sorcerer-King Leur-en-phon looked just like his father Begir-al-phon on the first day that she had met them both. The Davrin Seer didn't couple with the King anymore — that had stopped some time ago, and he was too old regardless — but their companionship had not diminished in the last century while his mind was still sharp and his magic strong and admirable.

During that later time, the Third Realm had been involved in a few skirmishes where new conflicts or competitors had arisen, alongside visions and dreams their new Deathwalkers after Houda weren't so comfortable interpreting. Most of those had to do with the Naulor Queen, Yivon.

Out of nowhere, it seemed, the pale-skinned Elves wished to cause trouble along their southern coast. Queen Alyarra wasn't having it.

Leur and Ishuna had travelled to V'Gedra about every twenty years for treaties and bargaining, and the second daughter would give her "intelligence" to her Queen-Mother and Innathi at once. Afterward, she would state her desire to return to the Third Realm.

Ishuna had stopped mentioning Cris-ri-phon on any of her visits, and Leur had long ago grieved and admitted the possibility that his younger brother had been killed somewhere out in the wilderness.

"More than a hundred years," the old ruler wept, "and he's never returned home. Eyes everywhere, and no one has seen him."

Ishuna's Mother had been in no hurry for her to divulge everything about the Deathwalkers at once, and the Seer was careful to give only a little at a time, with the assumption she would continue to do so for Innathi in the future.

"Good," She said. "We are glad you are comfortable there."

Now, the Queen-Mother Alyarra was dead. Long live Innathi Au'renthia, the Virgin Queen, for she would be tested long before she gave birth to her own heir.

All Five Sorcerers of the Realms arrived with their families as honored guests to witness the funeral of the Thousand Year Queen, the coronation of the Virgin Queen, and to pay tribute to the Everlasting Davrin of V'Gedra. Ishuna was there as part of her first official ceremony since leaving for the Third Realm, though she felt almost out of her depths being around such a large Court again.

She would loathe this day and yet be glad for it, because if she had *not* been there to see it, she would not have known that the danger she once dreamed of a hundred years ago was *not* gone.

The threat had only been sleeping.

In the perfectly planned manner of any wielder of power intent on making a grand entrance, a Sixth Sorcerer wearing a Firebird ring and with a scorpion on his coat arrived with his caravan to pay tribute.

Leur's eyes had teared up, and he began one of his coughing fits. Ishuna could barely move in her shock.

Innathi stood regal and unreadable, the perfect image of a Queen as a man who looked like Cris-ri-phon strode up the steps to bow low before her. He appeared only a little older than when he'd left, and not one strand of grey or white marked either his black hair or neatly trimmed beard. He was tall and strong.

And young.

If it was Leur's brother, he would be one hundred and thirty-six years old.

"Great Highness Au'renthia V'Gedra," he said, pronouncing it as perfectly as a Davrin would. "Forgive my lack of a formal invitation on this most auspicious of days for Your Queendom. I am here to pay all my respects, long overdue, and must call upon an old promise in begging your mercy, Virgin Queen."

That old "promise" was probably the only reason Innathi didn't have him killed immediately. His formal and public plea forestalled her decision just long enough for her natural curiosity to kick in.

As he must have planned.

Ishuna's hand tightened into a fist, hidden from general view when Innathi allowed the Scorpion Caravan to remain in V'Gedra.

She had watched the Court like a hawk in the days that followed, listening to all the gossip. Far too many Davrin remembered who this Human was. Or had been.

And according to Leur, it truly was him.

Somehow.

Ishuna, like many others, tried to determine whether Innathi had allowed Cris back into her bedroom during the coronation week. Those others would have liked to say so, but her older sister was careful, and few were ready to lie. She always had witnesses, and she made far more public appearances than originally planned.

Thus, Innathi made it through her celebration and her Mother's remembrance without the rumors sticking to her new cloak.

Cris-ri-phon didn't push for this, either, or make any blatant mistakes. He tended his own affairs and spent more with Leur than with anyone else, which Ishuna resented, for she was asked to leave their presence on more than one occasion.

She knew Cris would also be meeting Leur's own young son, Shal-al-thon — brought out by a woman as small and short-lived as any Zauyrian — and the Sorcerer of Scorpions was generally a perfect guest at V'Gedra. He even left with his entourage before anyone else.

The last to arrive and the first to leave, with the new Queen's blessing.

Before he did, Cris-ri-phon promised to bring "an unknown wealth" back to the Queen of the Red Desert but refused to be clear on what that meant.

While trying to rest in her childhood quarters, Ishuna began having *those* dreams again. The ones of Innathi giving birth to scorpions and choking the life from one before stabbing herself in despair …

And this time, the Seer didn't have Houda to soothe her.

Leur also could not refuse Cris's request to visit his boyhood home before returning to wherever he had come from. The man who looked far more like Leur's son than his brother came back with them, and Ishuna could only grind her teeth, ignoring him as much as she might.

Sooner or later, Cris cornered her in his brother's Tower to talk.

"Leave her alone," Ishuna hissed, hardly listening to his explanation. "Just leave my sister alone!"

"I have," he said earnestly. "For a *very* long time. But in my recent travels I have learned about those eager to test this new Daughter following the Thousand Year Queen, to see how well she can defend her Queendom. I am here to help her. Tell her this, Ishuna. Counsel her to ask for me. I will be her ally in this first war and see her through it. She will be triumphant."

"No," Ishuna flatly refused, feeling her throat tighten. "Hidden viper. You could have arranged such a threat yourself."

"I could have, but I did not." The man in his prime smiled grimly. "Queen Yivon seems to prefer her walking trees."

"What?!" she cried, fingers hooking into claws as she went stiff, confusion roiling. "H-how are you even here? How do you appear like *this* when your brother is *dying*?"

"I've searched long and learned much about both gifts I possess," he said. "Of life and death, of growth and withering. I did it to prove myself. And I have, as far as I can. Now my true quest begins."

"What *quest*?"

His intensity frightened her, as it always had, but his newfound charisma was impossible to ignore. "I am surprised you haven't seen it yet in Reverie, Ishuna. Perhaps we diverted the flow of your gift too far in one direction, as yours did mine? Or perhaps you became too accustomed to the Grey numbing your touch to the outside, so you can sleep."

Numbing?

She stared into his layered grey eyes, taking poorly that disrespect of her talents, her middle shifting like boiling oil. Cris didn't seem to realize it; perhaps she had become unreadable to him in her time among Humans.

That's good.

She had *needed* to learn to be mysterious since Houda passed, becoming Leur's primary Seer.

The mature yet youthful Sorcerer kept speaking as if he hadn't insulted her. "Suggest to your Queen that she summon me if she needs war counsel, Second Daughter. War *is* coming, and your home jewel behind the Edonil ridge is the ultimate target. Do it because it's the right path for your people. I still love her. Tell her that for me, too."

Ishuna stubbornly refused, and Cris was much more patient than she remembered him to be, choosing his time to leave Leur's Tower. She thought about their exchange, tried to see a vision of her own on an upcoming war, vowing to spite Cris no matter what …

But …

After visiting Innathi again and seeing her worry at her inexperience; after sensing her birth city at its most tense she could ever recall; and witnessing the fragile balance of the Desert tilt, only to realize Leur was not up for righting it again …

Nor is there another Sorcerer-King we can trust …

Then, after *finally* getting that vision of her own, in which she'd seen the Naulor Queen far in the distance of her dream.

Ishuna reconsidered.

"The Sorcerer of Scorpions would aid you," she murmured quietly in private with Innathi. "As he will the Third Realm. He … ah … . He still loves you."

For speaking the last, Innathi had slapped Ishuna across the cheek.

In time, just as with her younger sister, the Virgin Queen reconsidered and invited the Sorcerer of Scorpions back to V'Gedra to discuss the possibility of war.

FOR THAT FIRST YEAR, HER ZAUYRIAN SORCERER SEEMED CONTENT JUST BEING in the same city with her, seeing her face only when she had cause to summon him. This gradually became more frequent.

Innathi could still see the young bua Cris had once been when he looked at her, but only if she watched carefully. He had become someone else in his time away. The only thing he could *not* change, even had he wanted to, was when their bodies got too close. Their auras would pulse, one as a call, the other in answer.

Always a surprise who would call the other first.

Quickly, the Queen grew comfortable around her mysterious former Consort, becoming both a trusted advisor and engaging presence when he wasn't riding out to check on her borders.

Within the year, Cris-ri-phon became a formal part of the Court and Counsel, as much as he could be, for he acted more Elf-like than any Human who lived within their borders. He had no lingering loyalty to the Third Realm that anyone could prove, and the Queen had yet to be convinced he was a spy.

With his return came stories of his travels to other places, around the Lake and south of it, describing conflicts where he'd done something extraordinary to shift the balance in favor of one or the other. He was a "godblood," touched by the divine, so the mundane people had said.

This held only in the "middling" decades of his sojourn, however. No one had any credible stories from that time just after he'd left her or in those years just before he appeared at her coronation.

In both slivers of time, the Zauyrian Godblood had simply seemed to vanish.

Now living once again in V'Gedra, Cris-ri-phon acted like a Sorcerer of the Realms without a Realm of his own. Called the Sorcerer of Scorpions now. A long-lived, experienced mage-warrior offering that unseen Realm he'd brought back with him to the Davrin Queendom.

For *her* benefit. This grew ever clearer.

"The Scorpion understands the tactics of Human mercenary and raiding groups we've confronted this last year, my Queen," said Captain Shorlu said in a private debriefing. "Those coming from the West Raguruos, the Great Lake, and the Northern Steppes. None of the Dwarves have yet gotten involved, though hostilities with the Orcs stir up once again, disrupting supplies and safe trade passage."

"Wonderful timing, as always," the Davrin Queen sighed. "May this be for the last time. But tell me more about his knowledge. Has he yet said how he's come to have it?"

"He has not. We've confirmed these groups have more magical help from faraway lands, all of which supports his on-scene appraisals. None of it is enough yet to accuse the Naulor Queen directly."

And what would I do if I could? Hmph.

"Nonetheless," Shorlu continued, "Cris-ri-phon's knowledge from his travels has proven crucial to swift counterattacks to defend your border settlements, most of which cost the mercenaries more than they can recover in the field. We keep watch for the sources of their reinforcements."

A pause as several sets of red eyes exchanged glances.

Innathi frowned. "Speak."

Finally, the Captain said it.

"Your Highness, the regiments spread over the border settlements have also reported … um. Wild Elves. Aiding them in their defense."

The Queen narrowed her eyes. " 'Wild' Elves?"

"Yes. And being quite effective in sabotage and stealth tactics."

"Where did they come from?"

"The Wild Elves claim to live there."

"What? Since when?"

"For at least five decades."

"And no one has mentioned this *before* now? Or captured one to bring to me?"

Her officer shook her head. "These Elves only became known when their homes and families were attacked. They disappear when they do not want to be found. The Davrin troops have attempted to retain one but have not held them for long."

"How is that?"

"They always escape."

Innathi straightened up. "Wait, wait, what do these Wild Elves look like? And why are they 'wild'?"

"They have brown skin, lighter than ours but not Naulor, though often with much variance in their hair and eye color. They always claim to have Davrin blood, however, and the border settlements speak for that unanimously." The Captain shrugged. "The Wild Elves are … family members."

The Queen rubbed her temple against an ache. "And with *whom* could my 'border subjects' have been rutting? Naulor?"

The officer cleared her throat. "It seems so. The brown ones' magic is strongest with the Desert plants and animals, much like the Druids of the West. They can even take the form of a beast and retain their wits. Part of what has made them so difficult to capture or hold."

That cleared up the image in her mind.

"Druids," she echoed, shaking her head. "In my Desert?"

How? When?

Moreover, that was certainly a magic they could use …

The Captain dropped the final surprise in her lap. "Most of the Wild Elves recognized Cris-ri-phon, Your Highness, or at least knew who he was. Perhaps you should ask him for more insight."

Her stomach clenched.

"Perhaps I shall."

No doubt he waited patiently for this opportunity, too.

IN THE NEXT QUIET PERIOD BETWEEN CONFLICTS, INNATHI MET PRIVATELY with Cris-ri-phon for the first time to learn better who he had truly become. He didn't hesitate to show her, answering her first question with significant poise and mature charm.

"The Wild Elves are a gift to your Queendom, my Valsharess. Not all Naulor agreed with restarting hostilities across their borders once again. I met some of those exiles in my travels. The Nalari Druids."

"Where? *Where* did you find them? And why bring them here?"

"They followed me," he answered, forthright. "From Manalar, across the Raguruos Spine."

"Manalar," she echoed, trying to place the familiar name in a report.

"A new city built upon a well-protected spring, Valsharess." He smiled. "Not unlike V'Gedra."

Innathi squinted. "And Naulor settled there? So close to my border?"

The Queen was assuming a hostile move her former lover had somehow gotten involved with before Cris shook his head.

"Not anymore. Mostly Humans and Dwarves live there, now." He paused. "But I was there long enough, I watched it grow and change … and the children of those Druids came with me to the Desert because they had no place to go to find peace."

"Peace," she repeated, voice flat.

"Your outer settlements saw the mutual gain, my Valsharess. Enough that they had children together. I hope that you might as well, and not try to expel them as the Naulor Queen would. The Wilder have bonded with the Red Desert, nowhere else."

Innathi still chewed upon the part about her people mating successfully with the pale-skinned ones. She blinked, trying to juggle the rest as well. "How do you know, Cris?"

He leaned in, eyes briefly dipping to her lips. "I have said, over and over, I have learned so much. I can help prepare the Queendom to anticipate any method, magic or base, that the Naulor might weaponize, directly or no. I can help bridge negotiation with the Wild Elves, too. But it would help if you granted me more authority to do so, be I working with an army of Davrin, Wilder, Zauyrian, or a mix. There are strengths among us all to protect our home."

Our home.

He was home at last, wasn't he?

"Hm. I shall consider." She paused then leaned forward as well, wondering if she dared kiss him. "But I have another question."

"Ask it, my Queen."

She spoke it in a bare whisper. "Can you still pleasure a Davrin cait?"

Cris blinked, staring in her eyes. He chuckled low. "I am still virile, Valsharess, if that's what you mean."

"Ah."

Excellent.

She nodded. "Might you … *want* to pleasure *me*?"

His own nod was slow; his smile lessened. "Not 'might.' I … *do* want that."

'Want you. Only you.'

She shuddered in memories from long ago, a burst of excitement flooding her middle. "Will you, Cris? Tonight?"

The sorcerer swallowed once; his aura had heated up, as had his desire. "I will not, my Queen. Forgive me."

His rejection struck like a cold bucket of water.

"Wh … why?" she barked.

He neither flinched nor grimaced. "I have heard about a few others in Court. I cannot be one bua among many with you. I am sorry. I hope I may serve in other ways."

"What do you mean? Those others do not matter to me."

"And others have not mattered to me," he replied.

Innathi stared. She had never seen him with another cait. She had never *imagined* him atop another.

Doing so now scalded her stomach until she felt sick.

"Being near you? Alone?" he continued, watching her. "It is as I expected." His expression darkened. "If I accepted your touch again, Innathi, I would kill any competitors for your attentions, no matter who they were. I would *not* stand by and share you with scheming courtesans or the occasional vassal's son. I know this."

Her stomach fluttered unexpectedly. Few others might have *hinted* at such a fierce response to other males, but she'd never believed any of them could back it up.

Until now.

"Best we not to even begin, my Queen," Cris finished, his sun-bronzed face under stoic control. "Lest your Court be mired down in challenges for your pleasure, and our focus is fractured away from where it should be: on the threatening opposition to your Queendom."

It had taken her an embarrassing pause to come through her shock and formally dismiss the Godblood for the night with any grace at all.

Intensely flustered and bitterly disappointed, Innathi had sulked in private afterward, thinking all manner of contemptuous names for the stubborn Sorcerer. How could he have such high requirements to bed him now? This was so different from before!

Only later did she realize she was still pleased with his answer.

He must have known he could get away with refusing the Queen.

He might be the only one.

The next time they were alone, she tried reasoning with him. The desire had come up too strong for her not to try.

"I would honor you above all others, in public, but I cannot keep to just *one* favored male, Cris-ri-phon. Certainly not just one Zauyrian man. It would send the wrong impression to the Realms. Unless you mean we are exclusive until you die, which we may discuss."

"Ah, just as it was before, then?" he challenged, dark eyebrow arched. "Except ... you do not know *when* I will die now. Do you?"

Again, that unexpected flutter. She looked him over, and his aura.

No, she didn't know.

"I've been curious. How long will it be, Cris?"

He smiled. "I will not tell you, Innathi."

And so, the game went on for three more years.

More than once, he'd asked, "Why must you wait until you are old to bear children, my Queen? Other Davrin have children while much younger."

"That is the best way for the Davrin as a people, sorcerer. Your own sire and brother learned it from us! An experienced and wise Queen, who is undoubtedly the *elder*, is the best teacher for the next ruler. Not one that will eventually become like a sister or have time to become impatient to rule and attempt a coup. *This* is how Davrin rulers must think. How the Queendom keeps the Red Desert stable for the younger races."

Cris had shaken his head, no longer accepting all of that. "Perhaps this is best while little changes, as in the time of the Thousand Year Queen. But a time of upheaval has come, Innathi. I know you've not seen as much of it, but it is already here, and I believe even the Davrin will have to change their ways."

Her lips tightened as she listened, and he paused, watching her expression.

"Have you listened to Ishuna and Leur?" he asked. "They know."

Innathi exhaled deeply. "Ishuna has been having these 'feelings' since she was a child. It has been over four *centuries*. While I am glad she is happier away from V'Gedra, where mystics and signs are more accepted, I —"

"This isn't your Mother's Queendom anymore, Innathi," he interrupted. "Have you been *listening* to your people since Ishuna's been away?"

She bristled. "Perhaps. What have *you* heard, *counsel*?"

Cris took the opening for what it was. "They have been talking about your sister as a true oracle. They've been hearing word from Xala Ja'Prohn and other Davrin who've traveled, and they want to hear *more* of what she has seen."

Xala. Sometimes I wonder if she should have died in exile.

Cris nudged past her thoughts. "Perhaps you should consider bringing your sister back."

Innathi felt a different yearning then. *Bring her back … ?*

He pursued her in reflection. "Leur will pass soon and Shal doesn't want to 'inherit' his father's lover as there is little affection between them. Your sister is less happy now, my Queen, though she has not told you.

Wouldn't it be better to have the Davrin Seer back as an advisor to the Davrin Queen rather than let her wander the sands or risk capture for ransom after Leur dies?"

Wander the sands.

Cris had meant it figuratively, of course, but Innathi pushed the unnerving thought aside to focus on the more practical.

Having a Court Seer in V'Gedra, like the Five Realms?

And a close relative, as well.

On one hand, it suggested a strange favoritism the Court would love to gossip about. On the other hand, it might add to her reputation and expand the rule of her bloodline, offering more options should upheaval come.

This would change everything from how Innathi had learned to rule from her Queen-Mother, yet her Zauyrian Sorcerer may be right. Would Innathi prefer that Ishuna find a different place on her own once Leur passed away? Or be used as a pawn against the Virgin Queen of V'Gedra? In any case, would Innathi be better off having no true knowledge of what her sister was doing within her borders?

No. Not a good idea.

Ishuna had always needed more care than that, anyway.

"I shall take this into consideration, Cris."

Never could a Queen be more glad in taking a former consort at his word, THOUGHT Innathi.

The next year, following the death of Leur-en-phon and celebration of the Ruler's Transition, the Valsharess received her sister back, though Ishuna's presence proved tumultuous at first. She had changed much in her time with the Third Realm and still grieved for the past Sorcerer-King with his people, even after she left their lands.

What is wrong with her?

What had *always* been wrong with her?

But with the arrival of the next conflict that very year, Innathi discovered the counsel of *both* her new General and her Seer to be invaluable. Cris was her stalwart ally and educated warrior, and Ishuna …

She predicts things.

The Court Seer really did seem to *see* aspects of time others could not.

After a stressful five-year conflict, the Davrin Queen had won again. They'd done so by anticipating and pushing the traitors, mercenaries, and barbarians back until they broke their supply lines and forced a retreat.

Success because of the knowledge, insights, and loyalty of these two serving her.

Perhaps … perhaps Mother was wrong?

"Please, Cris, you were nearly *killed* this time," she implored in her private office, trying to sound queenly. "Let us celebrate being alive and together!"

Let me have you, for goddess's sake!

"You know my condition, Innathi."

He refused once again. She was starting to lose count of the insults.

"Long as you may live now, as extraordinary as you are," she argued, "I cannot make that promise to you."

"But you would still take from my remaining time without giving something of equal value, my Queen?"

"Equal value! Bold, Zauyrian. Very bold!"

That smile again. "Or perhaps my measure of worth has increased with age. Tends to happen among 'typical Zauyrians,' I'm afraid."

"*Pfeh!* And this has nothing to do with wandering the world for over a century."

The smile broadened. "I still have stories to tell about that. And no grey hair."

"That may be, but you're still a brute as before."

"So you imagine to this day."

Innathi flushed. She had had a little too much wine at dinner, she thought. She was exasperated, and so *aroused*; her aura relaxed and reached out to him, again and again.

How does he resist?

"You're being unreasonable, you foul-playing man."

"And *you* are magnificent, my Queen. I admire your willingness to rule beyond your Mother's limits in this time of change —"

"Pfeh!"

" — and so do your people."

"*Hmph.*" She smirked with satisfaction. "I know."

The intensity between them only grew in that final year after victory, and with it, Cris's moments of melancholy.

"What is truly on your mind, sorcerer?" she asked.

She would not be deterred, no matter how he tried to change the subject. Finally, he sighed in defeat.

"I … want children, Innathi."

The words were a punch in her gut.

What?

He was going to split his attention to the Queendom *now*? He would choose some Zauyrian weakling to bear *maybe* two offspring before giving up and dying, leaving him to raise them alone?

Knowing him, how would those kids force the Queen of V'Gedra to negotiate, even to fight for his service should she need him again?

No! You can't leave! You're mine!

Yet it brought to light at last the most painful thing about their answering magic. They could not breed, even if Innathi had the desire to change her Queendom *that* much. To have her heirs so early in her reign would be disruptive as she became like an older sister to them, perhaps even tempting a coup.

And imagine, to cut their lives so short by choosing a Human father, if that were possible …

Cris-ri-phon began courting that very year, doing what he could not to shove it in her nose as she tried not to do with an occasional dalliance in her bed. Somehow, she still heard about him and the Zauyrian women, how he was roaming, visiting many strongholds and keeps now that he wasn't distracted by an upheaval in her lands.

He was already distracted from her.

It had taken a false message of urgency to bring him back to Court, but Innathi had good reason to lie.

"I will take you as my sole Consort, Cris," she told him, figuring she had nothing more to lose at this point. "My Sorcerer, my General, if you will accept. There shall be no other buas while you live, no matter how long."

Innathi saw a light in his eyes, like that moment long ago when a twenty-year-old man had nearly jumped at the chance if Leur hadn't gripped his shoulder and hauled him back to think again.

This time, Cris gripped and held himself back as he considered very carefully.

"I admit I did not count on ever hearing such a promise from you, my Queen … Innathi." He sounded choked. "Now … Now that I have, I must ask you something before I give you my answer."

She sat down slowly next to him, a weakness in her middle making her afraid of what he was about to say.

"If it were possible for you and me to have children —"

She blinked. "But it … is not."

"It could be," he replied, looking at her eyes. "Imagine that it is. If we joined, and it happened, would you keep them? Would you carry them for me, my love? They … need not be the heirs of the Queendom. They would be mine. My heirs. To keep your people happy, you *should* indeed have your true heirs when you are older, with the Davrin blood of your choice after I'm gone. Until then, would you trust me to father them, to love and serve you as I do? The way the Wild Elves have come to do above the Naulor Queen, as I promised."

Innathi hadn't spent even one moment in her years of yearning and plotting and speculation on a request like this. In a moment of panic, she had begged more time; she was the one to walk away from a proposal between them.

Cris didn't sulk. For the moment, he made it known he'd stopped looking for a wife. Once again, he served his best as her General, even if there was no war.

He waited with renewed hope and patience.

The Scorpion and his people worked with the Davrin to keep their borders strong. After all these years, she felt they still did not truly *know* what the Naulor Queen meant to gain in these attempts to harry the massive borders of the Red Desert.

She's so far away, and I've not seen one hint of installing a proxy within these sections of dirt the mercenaries claim.

Perhaps Innathi was missing something important. Perhaps she could only accept that Cris-ri-phon and Ishuna were right; they were still living in a time of great change which hasn't passed yet.

We're only in a lull.

So .... why not another such change from her Mother's time? One for which Innathi would *always* be remembered. The Virgin Queen, distinctly different from her Queen-Mother in so many ways.

Bold, courageous, daring ...

Bringing together the ways of the unknown mystics and the known arcane, the Davrin and the Wild Elves together with the Realms of Zauyr, with all of it working with her own loyal family at the core. Never so distant from each other as her time growing up.

Who else would do so much for her?

What would she do for them?

"What do you think, Ishuna?" she had asked, unable to keep it to herself after several months of thinking. She must pass this idea of Cris's by someone, and the only one she could tell was her sister.

Ishuna had stared in shock — which was fine, her own face had looked just like this when Cris asked for this. Her sister didn't speak for a long time, her tawny eyes lighter than they had been in her youth, staring at the floor. For a moment Innathi wondered whether another vision had come upon her.

At last, Ishuna blinked, and a tear landed on her cheek. "I-I ... uhm. I would worry for you. What if such a thing sapped your health as it did Mother?"

"She was old when she had us," Innathi said. "By custom. That is what happens to the Queens. I am young. You've seen Davrin our age bear children, they are fine. Even without the fertility magic he and I bear within us."

Ishuna trembled with clear anxiety. "Even if they don't want the throne when they grow up, they … the change will be so far-reaching. It will mix Elves and Humans as they have children, too. We will become one race."

Innathi sighed. "Or they will not be able to breed as well, and it is merely an extraordinary gift I grant to the Zauyrian General for his service. Long-lived heirs who shall eventually vanish."

Her sister looked away. Saying nothing.

"Consider the Wilder whom Cris has brought to us," the Queen tried again. "We've already seen new children from *them* since they received formal acknowledgment and welcome to enter the City. Don't you see? Our people are *already* changing, Ishuna, and perhaps it is time to get out ahead of it. Mother didn't want *anything* to change, but … I am less afraid. Especially if the Naulor continue to represent a threat. Perhaps they will grow blatant, more extreme. My reputation *before* that happens will play a lot into morale and readiness."

"Less … afraid," Ishuna echoed softly, watching her.

Innathi shrugged. "You are still afraid of your dreams at times, aren't you, little sister? You still push forward. For Leur."

"And Houda," she murmured.

And who … ? Oh.

Once Innathi remembered, she held her tongue as, again, the Seer stared for some time without speaking. She swallowed, blinked. "Has … Has he given you a gift?"

"Has who given me a gift?" she checked.

"Cris-ri-phon."

Innathi smiled a little. "It depends what you count as a gift."

Another swallow. "Like … a dagger? Ornamental, or special?"

Interesting.

"Mm, no, he hasn't. Why do you ask?"

The Seer was nervous; even a little sweat popped out on her forehead as if the interpretation of her abstract "sight" took great effort. "Give him his heirs if that is what you wish, my Queen … but if the Scorpion offers you the gift of a magical blade, please … Refuse it."

Innathi absorbed that, first hearing that her only family would support her choice and her greatest desire. She had never felt more gratitude toward Ishuna in her life.

But with it comes a warning.

Cris even said Ishuna acted how he remembered Houda did sometimes.

"Of course, Ishuna," Innathi said with a smile. "I promise."

CHAPTER 10

V'GEDRA – 241 B.S.E.

"THERE WILL BE A FORMAL CEREMONY LATER."

They agreed on this much, barely having the concentration to make certain the intended couple agreed to read from the same scroll before falling into her private quarters.

He'd become so *strong* in the field, in his body, his magic, in every way! He lifted her so easily, encouraged her legs and arms about him, and carried her to the bed as if prepared to carry her halfway across the Queendom.

And still he had no grey in his hair.

Desperately, they kissed, stripping each other, reaching to touch long-hidden skin. Nude, they pressed as close as possible.

The first time that night would be like Koorul all over again. More so, for Innathi hadn't the presence of mind to lick the head of his penis first. Thus, he didn't spurt so suddenly, and there was no need for him to eat her slit until she came next.

That could wait until later.

Next time.

He gripped her hips, lifted them up, and sank deep inside with a beast's growl. She screamed in delight and shock, having truly forgotten his size. A mere decade with him at first, and more than two centuries without. She'd taken no other Humans to bed, either.

Which made this moment as new as his mage's aura could be.

Their magic merged almost at once; she heard once again the song from long ago as he lay on top of her, moving powerfully. Then suddenly, he brought her up with him. Kneeling on her bed with her impaled in his lap, his broad hands gripped her ass and her back.

"Innathi ..."

He lifted her to nuzzle her breasts, caught her on the way down with cock stroking up into her again. The Zauyrian sweating yet far from exhausted, kissing her, the thrust of his hips suddenly speeding up ...

"*Aia*, Innathi!" he cried as he filled her with his cream.

The flare of his aura overwhelmed; the magical surge struck them with the power of a sandstorm.

"Yes!" she answered, breathless.

"*Gru lo'wicova!*"

"*Yes!*" She quaked just before the long ride down. "Yes ..."

Afterward he'd fallen over with a bounce, taking her with him. Innathi was on top of him now, with him clutching her and holding his stiff erection in place as if pausing to catch his breath before the next go.

They were both dizzy.

She chuckled softly against his shoulder. "I love you as well, my Godblood."

ISHUNA WENT TO HER CHAMBERS EARLY IN THE EVENING, PLANNING NOT TO leave them — perhaps would not even leave her bed — until dawn. Her sister would finally consummate the yearning, frayed bond with the Godblood. Recognizing familiar signs, the Queen's sister wanted to be asleep before she might hear sounds of passion drifting down the hall.

Instead of remaining in her rooms that night, the Seer walked in her sleep. This was something she was known for occasionally but had not become truly troublesome to either Leur's or Innathi's homes. The most unsettling thing about it was when she frightened the Guardsvrin, seeming to come out of nowhere.

When Ishuna became aware, seeing through her mundane eyes again, she felt so sick she could barely stand. The high-pitch of an aura-song was loud in her ears, filling her head, and tears dripped down her cheeks when she recognized it.

"No, please, not yet," she whispered, her voice quivering.

A sensation like being struck in the gut, an old scar tearing as she fell to her knees with a grunt. Vomiting part of her evening meal onto the fine carpet, Ishuna held her middle and shivered without control, breaking into a cold sweat.

It was only a matter of time before this would draw them here again.

The voice was in her head, calm and matter of fact.

Like Houda had always been.

Ishuna had started crawling toward her personal wing when a Guardsvrin found her at last. The young Davrin helped the Seer back to her quarters and called for a healer to attend to her.

Innathi wasn't to be disturbed; they said she was "quite engaged."

I know, Ishuna thought miserably.

"I don't see anything, your grace," said the Davrin healer, trying to hide her nerves. "Why do you hold your middle this way?"

"I retched too hard. My stomach aches. That's all."

Cris could still be Death to an Elf.

The Seer bid them to find Xala.

"Send her here."

We must return to Koorul. Soon.

"SO," XALA SAID QUIETLY, HOLDING THEIR HORSES, LOOKING UP AND AROUND. "This is where it all started."

Ishuna nodded absently, scanning the layers of brightly colored stone which formed the winding paths leading to the heart of the sacred site. The waterfall was still there, they'd found it almost immediately as it "came to her," although tonight it was more of a trickle.

The feeling of long ago wasn't as strong, but now that she knew what it was, recalled how Houda had described it — *A thinner spot between this world and the next allowing a subtle, cool draft in from the Grey.* — the Davrin *qu'essan* could still confirm its presence.

She had felt it before when she was very young.

"Wait here," Ishuna instructed her bodyguard. "Keep watch for me."

"Of course, Seer."

Ishuna wandered around for quite some time, touching both smooth and rough stone in places, dismayed as no other feelings or images came to her. No ideas, no visions, no intuitive insight.

Instead, she saw Innathi's face — lower lip quivering in excitement and fear — as the Queen told her that she was pregnant already by her General-Consort.

It worked, as Cris said it could. "How" didn't truly matter anymore.

Innathi was willing, and pregnant with a half-Human child.

"If it's a bua, we'll name him after Leur," Innathi had said just before Ishuna's trip to Koorul. She looked radiant. "But it shall be a proper Elvish name."

Leuren'qo.

"If a cait?" Ishuna asked because that was expected.

"We can name her after you —"

"*No,*" she replied immediately. "No, ah … That's not … not necessary, sister. Name her after out Mother, perhaps."

Innathi had covered her dismay with teasing. "Oh, but Shunraeki is a *lovely* name, isn't it?"

"Perhaps."

If there never was a child with that name, perhaps her mother would survive to bear the true heir.

In the canyon of Koorul, Ishuna blinked her eyes to her present again. *Don't let her die. Not that way. Please.*

"We'll stay here the night, Captain Ja'Prohn," the Seer said somberly to her close, pardoned guardian. "I wish to see …"

Just. See.

"Of course, Ishuna. I'll be waiting here."

You always have been.

The Sun lowered on the horizon, seeming to set the red stone ablaze like the hottest of forges. Despite the appearance, the air shifted and cooled rapidly, however, as the stars began to appear in a narrow river of sky above their heads. The water spattered against the rock and sturdy plants rustled in the breeze as their eyes adjusted to the dim.

The night began as a moonless one, starting in full darkness but for the stars. Soon it would be too difficult to see at all.

Houda? Can you hear me?

A whistle of wind streaked overhead. Her heart beat faster as she looked up at the pinpoints of light.

I'm afraid, Houda. The Scorpion never healed me as he should have. He's forgotten everything you taught him, and I can't touch him without feeling … violated. I cannot let him try again … even if he knew what to do without you. And Leur.

I need your help again.

When no answer came, Ishuna shook her head, squeezing her eyes shut against the tears. Then, a small desert creature crawled near her hand, brushed it, she gasped, startled. At first, she couldn't make out what it was.

"*Qu'essan?*" Xala asked quietly, testing if she was in another trance.

The Seer attempted to answer but found herself paralyzed. Perhaps she *was* in a trance? Her body felt heavy as it did in that state, yet she was awake. Alert but silent.

The creature … Was it a black scorpion? Was there to be yet another warning about the General-Consort? It crawled onto her hand. She shivered, managing then to lift her hand to look closer.

No.

It was a spider.

Go away, she commanded in, setting her hand back down for it to crawl off.

The night hunter obeyed for the most part, but the way it stopped periodically, deliberately turning around to look at her with its multitude of eyes before turning again and continuing its way …

Made her think this was no ordinary spider.

Perhaps the sign she waited for.

The Big Sister Moon was rising now, and the spider sped its pace, disappearing into a shadow which resembled a robe. Eventually, after a long period of staring, the moonlight touched it. Coloring it grey.

Ishuna's tawny eyes brightened. *Houda?*

The Seer stood up to follow where the spider had gone, leaving her resting body behind. In this state, she was more willing to approach the eerie apparition. They stood not far apart, but Ishuna's eyes could not make out the face in the shadows.

You seek healing, child? said the figure.

She sounded like Houda, and that was always a jest, that the Davrin of three centuries had been like a child to the forty-year-old wise woman.

Yes. Houda, please help me.

The apparition shook her head. *We cannot leave here. We cannot attend you back at V'Gedra. We do not have what We need. We are sorry.*

Her heart felt pierced. She trembled in fear.

Why not? she cried. *What do you need?*

The figure became less distinct, almost vanishing from view. Barely there, and so quiet.

No! Come back!

But she faded away.

The spider remained, skittering abruptly as if startled, diving into deeper shadows. In its haste moving the dirt, something … metal … shifted into the moonlight.

Ishuna stared. The object was heavy; she could not touch it until she woke up.

As when she was a child, the mystic stood paralyzed.

The sun was soon to rise, and the moons were setting when the Seer finally shifted within her heavy body. She forced it forward, stumbling weakly over dry stone to where she had seen the messenger the night before. Searching upon the dark ground, she was mostly blind and used her fingertips.

"What is it you seek, your grace?" Xala asked quietly.

"White metal," she slurred, dizzy.

"You mean this?"

Her guardian brushed dirt away and lifted the chain holding a pendant. It was a jeweled spider, the abdomen formed from a dark amethyst, eight eyes made of the tiniest rubies, the rest of it framed by the brightest silver. The Captain held it up, frowning in confusion before looking at her charge in awe.

As she had many times before.

"How did you know it was there, Seer? You didn't move from your spot all night."

"I saw it," Ishuna replied. "I … I had a vision. Please, give it to me?"

Xala paused for another moment to study the jewelry but handed it over. It felt comforting in her hands. A gift from the Grey.

Ishuna slipped the necklace over her head and felt an answering warmth in her injured aura.

Yes.

This would help see her through Innathi's time of change.

Thank you, Houda.

Part Two

Birth & Darkness

CHAPTER 1

THE PALACE OF V'GEDRA – 240 B.S.E.

DAWN HAD ARRIVED, BUT THE MORNING WAS STILL EARLY.

Preparations and activities filled the open-air courtyard, having continued through the cool of the night until the sky moved beyond purple and pink to hint at the best time: when the night chill was chased away with the sun not yet scorching.

Walls and columns which had appeared muddy in silvery-blue moonlight now brightened into natural shades of reds and orange stone, further chasing dimness or shadows from around the figures bustling in the public space.

Ishuna stood within the courtyard wearing a gown as blue as the sky would be by midmorning. The neckline was wide enough to display her favorite pendant, a silver spider with its abdomen formed from a dark amethyst, eight tiny eyes made of ruby.

Her presence complimented the grace and beauty of the tapestries, platforms, and columns intended to honor the Valsharess and her General-Consort this day. As the Queen's sister and Court Seer, Ishuna and all others were dressed in vibrant color for this occasion.

Ishuna frowned a bit, her gaze pausing. *All but one.*

A scarred man of Zauyr stood as the exception, a Deathwalker wearing the drab grey robes of his study as a mage.

Taib was new to the Court at V'Gedra, only recently invited by Cris-ri-phon to be a resident. Thus far, he had kept his distance from others unless called by the Queen's Consort. Even now, the grey mage stood still and apart from the crowd, as if pretending he was not there but a trick of the eye.

What was *not* a trick, Ishuna knew, was the skin of his hands and face changing color. As the sun rose, they gradually turned from a pale brown to black, as dark as her own skin.

Old memories flickered watching this Deathwalker finish his mystical change. He was a fraction of her age, yet she'd once been close to another Deathwalker. Houda was long dead, passed into the Greylands, as she once claimed.

Fighting the distressing rise of emptiness, Ishuna looked first for Xala Ja'Prohn, her personal Captain and bodyguard. She spotted the Davrin mage-warrior where she was supposed to be: standing apart and observing all within the courtyard. Xala's firm and solid presence, her head moving on a swivel, cancelled out Taib's eerie stillness.

Ishuna breathed out and tried to relax as the "groom" and his guest of honor joined the guests in the Grand Courtyard.

"Thank you for being here today, Lord Rousse," Cris-ri-phon said, briefly making eye contact with Ishuna as they passed on the main platform. The Sorcerer-General acknowledged her, nodding his head, but continued speaking to the extraordinary arrival. "Your presence and that of Jennyn, each standing with us will send a strong signal of unity to Queen Yivon when we need it most."

He could have spoken in Zauyrian, not Davrin, Ishuna noted.

Cris wanted certain ears to hear that.

Her heart thudded harder beneath the spider pendant as the ethereal Ice Lord glanced at her as well, but it slowed again as he continued his way.

Ishuna stared at the masculine backs as they moved toward the throne, wondering how many guests here knew a single whisper about the new arrivals, and whether it would send any signal at all.

If the people here know anything, it's precious little, she thought with a hint of resentment at the secrets Innathi had been keeping for well over two centuries, ever since their Queen-Mother had died and Ishuna had gone to the Third Realm.

Lord Rousse and Jennyn.

Two Elven elders whose names were already ancient when Ishuna's Mother was a child. They arrived yesterday at sundown. Ishuna hadn't been told they were coming, because Innathi hadn't been sure they would.

But she knew enough from Mother to invite them. Somehow.

The Ice Lord from the Dargevold North had arrived quietly and without pomp, with very few servants. The Valsharess and her Zauyrian Godblood had dropped what they'd been doing and swiftly led the small entourage elsewhere.

"We'll get them settled personally," Cris-ri-phon had with a smile, sending the attendants away.

Ishuna hadn't been close enough to be invited then, but she had followed long enough to witness the encounter with the second ancient in one of the Palace Gardens. She overheard the exclamations that Jennyn had arrived on the grounds unbeknownst to anyone, entirely alone and not seeking attention.

Except for a red sorrel horse who follows them around without lead or tack.

Jennyn *and* the red horse had joined the Ice Lord and the promised royal couple, the group drifting inside the private wing of the Palace.

Ishuna waited until much later into the night to be summoned. Before that surreal moment, she had known of the existence of such auspicious guests, but only as references in her Mother's archives, for they'd never appeared here in her lifetime.

Now, it seemed they were here to bless Innathi's marriage to a Human who *should* be dead by now.

ISHUNA HAD BEEN CALLED IN THE MIDDLE OF THE NIGHT TO A PRIVATE MEETING chamber and formally introduced to their honored guests.

The Ice Lord Indrath Rousse had come from the Dragon Coast, north and east.

"Jennyn," no title, had traveled from Break Water on the Twin Peninsulas, south and west.

The two were from opposite ends of the continent, according to the maps, and with the sparse details on their appearances from Palace records, Ishuna had also not accurately imagined what they looked like.

Neither presented as Davrin, Naulor, *or* Wilder, yet they *were* Elves which the previous Queen had welcomed precious few times during her reign as well. All Elf-bloods in the room had in common the long, tapered ears, the large, uptilted eyes, an unconscious grace, and creaseless beauty displayed in a body with an incredibly long life compared to the younger races.

But that was almost where the likenesses ended.

"A pleasure to meet you, Royal Seer Ishuna, the Queen's Sister." Lord Rousse offered an elegant bow though a cunning gaze seemed to read her in a moment. "I shall be the master of ceremony who will conduct the Human marriage ritual for the General-Consort and your Queen."

The Lord's manner of speech *should* have been strange to her ears, but it was not. No one translated for Indrath Rousse, and she understood what he said but somehow also had the sense he was not truly "speaking" in Davrin, as Cris-ri-phon could.

Their communication held its proper context without cultural stumbles, though she could not sense a use of blatant translation spells, so she did not understand where his words came from.

Perhaps there was a relic or brooch somewhere which provides that understanding when one is near him.

Her reply to her own thought was a little less prudent than it should have been as her eyes covered him from head to toe.

If there is, there aren't many places for him to hide it.

Other than being intensely beautiful like Innathi, Indrath did not look like a ruler. This Lord from the North wore no jewelry or adornment which might hint at someone of great status. Instead, he displayed all his enticing form from the waist up, bare and unconcerned.

And truly, why be concerned?

The skin was flawless bronze, framed by long, thick hair of deep, auburn red reaching to his waist. His eyes were like emeralds, the distant beauty of his Elven face exotic enough not to assume he was one of the Wilder Elves of V'Gedra.

His blood could be nothing so recent as the Desert's border-bred children of a band of displaced Naulor Druids.

Conversely, Lord Rousse covered everything from his waist down with a heavy, leather sarong, cut and draped to make the viewer want to see just a little more, as if he lay on a bed with the silk sheets slipping to expose him as he turned over. One could not even glimpse Indrath's feet, and his steps were unnaturally quiet.

Ishuna wetted her mouth and placed her eyes on Cris-ri-phon. "Lord Rousse will conduct the ceremony? Why not a shaman of Zauyr, as it is a Human ritual?"

"Because Lord Rousse is willing," the Sorcerer-General replied with a respectful bow to the Northern Elf. "And I believe it is good for Innathi's people to witness this crossover of our cultures."

Ishuna glanced down at Innathi's middle and back up. The Seer's tawny eyes met her Sister-Queen's bold, scarlet crimson. Innathi subtly shook her head. They had still not formally announced to the city that the Queen was pregnant; only the three of them knew.

"I see," the younger sister said. "Less doubt of the legitimacy of the oath?"

"Indeed," the Ice Lord agreed with a warm smile that set her heart racing, much to her surprise. "Less concern over property and heirs when acknowledged by the right allies to be legitimate."

Oddly, Queen Innathi smiled at him and inclined her head. "Exactly, my Lord."

Has she told him?

With a swallow, Ishuna turned to the other strange Elf in the room. "Jennyn of Break Water? Welcome. Why have you graced us on the eve of my sister's wedding?"

The powerful aura of this Elf gave off no ploy or allure like the Ice Lord, yet Jennyn was still unnerving to Ishuna, more so even than the Deathwalker Taib. Hazel-green irises shifted within her eyes, always moving, suggesting that the colors could turn in either direction at any time.

The ancient Elf could have been male or female but was at least clearly Elven in shape, if completely hairless. The ancient's head was fully bald, enhancing the sight of the longest ears Ishuna had ever seen, more so than any Davrin, Naulor, or Wilder. Even longer than the ears of the Ice Lord.

The head, face, and full arms were bare, the rest covered with extremely simple, undecorated robes of earthen beige. The rough cloth was cut in such a way to the presence of breasts or hips which might answer the true sex.

Finally, though Ishuna tried not to stare even now, she was certain of the subtle, swirling colors glimpsed *within* the muted, drab skin. Ever more colors, shifting subtly from blue to green to yellow … and red … ?

What are you? Are you an Elf or do you wear a mask?

With the slow, subtle tilt of the head as Jennyn looked at her, studied her and then the Ice Lord, the young Seer was strongly reminded of her Mother. She would think of Jennyn from that point as female.

"I offer blessed witness to all my children in time of need," Jennyn said, her voice abnormally low as she bowed first to Innathi, then to Ishuna. "In honor of your Mother and Father who could not be here."

Her voice struck them all deeply, even the only Human here. All sound seemed open as Jennyn spoke in a language certainly not Davrin yet, as with the Ice Lord, Ishuna could understand it. As if Jennyn's very words contained small threads of the bald Elf's aura, which in turn demonstrated an unlimited patience to convey meaning.

In honor of your Mother and Father who could not be here.

These words landed upon her ears, and Ishuna could not help but listen with a peace that made the Desert Seer envious on some deep level.

And perhaps her sister, too ...

"Yes," Innathi said, her back straightened and she reached to hook her arm in Cris's, "our Queendom shall remember our late Mother Alyarra for all time. Thank you, Jennyn."

"And what of your Father?" Lord Rousse asked curiously, arching a brow at the two Queen's Daughters. "Will the Queendom remember his name?"

"I-I do not know his name," Ishuna admitted before seeing Innathi's expression. She read it, and expressed her dismay, blurting her thought. "*You* know his name! Mother told you, and you never told me?"

"He wishes to be forgotten," Innathi replied, both to her *and* the prodding Ice Lord. "Mother said he never wanted to return to V'Gedra, and that you and I would never be enough reason to change his mind. So be it. They are both gone in this case."

Jennyn had looked between Ishuna and Innathi, considering before she chose to speak her last words for the night.

"Wruzdiin is not gone from his body yet. He has been banished into the deep Desert by your Mother."

"How did you know that?" Innathi asked accusingly.

"What?" Ishuna rounded on her. "She's right? *Banished?*"

Lord Rousse leveled a look at Cris-ri-phon, amused sympathy touching his lips as the sisters began to fight on the eve of the Sorcerer-General's wedding.

CHAPTER 2

AFTER WAITING THROUGH THE FIRST FLARE-UP, THE ICE LORD AND THE SORCERER-General had somehow convinced the deadlocked sisters that resolution on this topic could wait for another time.

"It's not as if there is time to find him to be present," Lord Rousse said, more to Jennyn than the Davrin sisters. "That is why *we* have come, yes?"

The hairless Elf bowed her head in silent acceptance.

"We must get ready," Cris-ri-phon implored. "It is almost time. The courtyard is prepared, the guests will be arriving soon."

Innathi exhaled in relief, a hard look returned to Ishuna as she disengaged from the hurtful argument. "Of course, my love." She turned to the bald Elf. "Jennyn, is the … ?"

"The horse is still yours, Valsharess," the ancient replied.

The dawn arrived far too quickly for Ishuna. She had excused herself from the private chambers and left for the public courtyard to watch the sunrise, where she'd gazed at Taib the Deathwalker changing skin color.

By now, Innathi would be outside the Palace.

As the guests arrived, they would witness their Queen riding Jennyn's red horse upon sand mounds and streets alike. All would see how she needed no bridle, reins, or lashes to guide her mount. A reminder the Virgin Queen still ruled on her own grace and will, despite what she was about to do.

The horse had been a gift of protection offered from the elder Peninsulan Elf before Ishuna arrived. The Davrin Queen had accepted with glee, and Ishuna knew how Innathi would enjoy being surrounded and admired by her people, showing herself in her most beautiful scarlet gown and matching veil.

"I shall present the gift of longevity during the ceremony," Lord Rousse had explained, eyes gliding between Cris and Innathi. "As my blessing to you both."

"We thank you, Lord," said the Godblood.

Why did Cris-ri-phon sound so ... *comfortable*, perhaps even familiar, with the Ice Lord when the Zauyrian's bearing toward Jennyn grew reticent?

What have they been planning? For how long, where I could not see?

There was little Ishuna could do now without destroying the delicate balance the Virgin Queen had been building for her new reign.

Less than two decades old, and already with too many challenges to her borders. Ishuna hadn't been home long enough to say what was different or what her Sister-Queen was planning. *I just ... worry.*

She always had.

Meanwhile, the nobility and wealthiest merchant guests of V'Gedra awaited their Queen in the cool of dawn at the Grand Courtyard, along with her Seer and Sorcerer-General.

The Ice Lord from Dargevold stood ready on the head platform, and the drifting Elf from Break Water bore peaceful witness, as did members of all Five Realms of Zauyr.

The Naulor Queen had sent no emissaries or diplomats, which was noted. In a way, the Wilder children of the Nalari exiles stood in for them.

The tension and anticipation seemed to rise — especially from Cris-ri-phon — and Ishuna felt her stomach upset after watching his active, churning aura for too long.

Ohhh, no. No. Careful.

Ishuna stepped quickly into the shadow of one pillar of the courtyard, out of direct sight of the guests and making eye contact with no one. One hand covered her middle as she held her breath and checked yet again for that deep feeling of hollowed injury, that broken essence leaking out. Her anchor somehow "ripped loose," as Houda had once described it.

Hands trembled with fear, and within it, the recent resentment burned through her chest again, pushed to the surface like a hot spring by the fight of last night.

Most of my lifetime I have suffered. Deemed fragile and weak, left untrained and stumbling because of Mother's willful ignorance of my talents. She knew. And she still banished my sire.

And even after Alyarra died, Innathi didn't tell her.

I am too much like him, I know it. Why Mother could never accept me. My dreams were dismissed because of it, leaving me helpless and vulnerable to that boorish attack from a young Human unable to control himself!

That Zauyrian Sorcerer was not so young now. He should be dead of old age like all Humans, even the heirs of the Sorcerer-Kings. Yet there he was, standing by her throne as he waited to marry the elder sister!

He still doesn't understand. He ***never*** *understood what he had truly done to me, for which he has never made amends! He can't have done it again just now, no. I am not so weak anymore.*

Not since speaking with Houda again at Koorul.

Strengthened by her thought, clasping the spider pendant hung around her neck, Ishuna breathed out in relief. With her free hand, she nudged her middle a few times with her fingers.

Yes. The hole is gone.

No nausea, no terror. No intangible *bleeding* to allow the infection of nightmares and waking illusions which blurred her reality, disrupting the True visions which protected the Red Desert through these uncertain times.

Ever since Ishuna had meditated all night at Koorul praying for Houda's aid, the injury was gone and had not returned. Ishuna had never felt stronger, even though enough minds within the Queendom still thought her delicate from those past whispers.

Just as well.

The younger sister would need all her strength to watch this public symbolic joining, happening now only after a true joining of the unknown had occurred.

Two incompatible races, soon to be joined by blood.

Innathi is still a young Queen, not meant to have heirs for centuries yet, according to tradition. Now she is pregnant by a Human man, a Sorcerer who keeps his own secret from her. Why is he still alive? How long will he exist?

One day, she would See this answer in a vision. Innathi said that she will need her.

She does not yet understand how much so.

Exhaling, patting the amethyst pendant at her throat, she murmured aloud, "I can do this. I will be well. No one can reach into me."

Not again.

I am strong.

Ishuna had gathered enough of that strength to step out of the pillar's shadow and be visible to the crowd.

To her left and closer to the main archway was Jennyn, standing upon the same elevated pathway as Ishuna. Standing almost opposite the hairless, long-eared Elf was Taib with his scarred face. They both seemed to be watching her just then.

Ishuna frowned. *I'm not the one who needs watching. I am a mystic like both of you. Try watching the too-bold ones like—*

Her thoughts were interrupted as she heard the distant cheers of crowds loitering outside the Palace. The gallop of a horse approaching the ramp leading to the archway soon followed. Swelling noise moved like a wave from the gate leading to the streets into the Grand Courtyard itself among the royal guests.

Charging hoofbeats slowed to a loping cantor and then a trot as the Guardsvrin straightened and stood at attention to welcome their Queen.

"The Virgin Queen Au'renthia!" they called.

Innathi entered the Archway to eager applause, resplendent in flowing red gown and veils as she sat sideways upon the fine, shining mount from the Peninsulas.

Her hair was done up in a complex design with only a few strands out of place from the ride. This only made her look better if Cris's reaction was any indication. Ishuna wondered if Lord Indrath would have to reach out and steady the man.

Their Queen did not appear pregnant yet, and her smile glowed even more than the modest spot low in her abdomen, a recent hint for those with the knowledge and focus enough to see it.

Ishuna wagered the Deathwalker almost certainly could, better than anyone who had to rely solely on seeing magic with their gaze. If Taib possessed even a fraction of the gift as Houda in his insights of life both growing and fading, the new glint in the Davrin Queen's belly might be the first thing he'd notice about her.

Seeing no change in his expression, however, Ishuna thought snidely, *Perhaps none of you are as gifted as Houda.*

Cris-ri-phon stood dressed in his General's dress uniform, a distinct and formal design made up of the colors of Innathi's Queendom — stark black, white, and red — with orange trim harkening to the Third Realm of his Father's bloodline before adding a sash displaying the black and gold scorpion that had become his symbol.

She saw him mouth an endearment with her name: "*Aia, Innathi.*"

The dark-haired man with eyes the color of steel strode quickly down the stairs opposite of Ishuna. The crowd parted for him so he could help lift his Queen down from her new mount using his strong hands, exaltation naked on his face, clear for all to see.

At last, he could touch her so familiarly in public, and she welcomed him. Accepted him.

"Your Grace, we've been waiting," he said in a rich baritone accustomed to public speech," and to my heart's joy, you have come. Our allies have gathered to give their blessing and bear witness to our official union this day. Your people and mine, wedded together as surely as you and I shall be."

Subtle, Ishuna thought, noting how Lord Rousse had started smiling.

Cris leaned to whisper something else in her ear, private and playful, and he leaned back with a young glint in his eye as she responded in kind, much to his elation. His worship of her Sister-Queen still made the Seer uncomfortable after all these years.

Yet he had better reason than ever before to adore her, for she had truly *joined* with him to catch a child when it *should* have been impossible.

No Human has ever achieved such a thing in these lands, much less expected to receive his first born of a Virgin Queen's womb! Who does he think he is?

Ishuna stared at the couple, and before she recognized it, peered next into the near future. Her magic snatched at new glimpses as her spider pendant seemed to writhe on her chest.

She will bear him a male heir of his own ... who will outlive all living Zauyrian Sorcerers of the Realms, though he will not rule them.

Frowning, the Royal Seer found herself back just in time, reluctantly pushing her thoughts from personal dismay to the broader reach of action or anticipated reaction.

Their son will live to adulthood. How will it change our Desert and its borders? I cannot imagine it will be as Cris says. That there shall be no challenge at all to our pureblood Heir later. Unless the half-Elf dies first, when Innathi bears her own daughter, surely it will cross some male mind to protest, to use her first son to cause trouble ...

Whether Ishuna liked it or not, Cris's status in the Davrin military and their city had increased with his victories in battle. Even more with this public "wedding."

It will increase again when they announce the coming of that child in her belly.

With success always came jealousy and enemies. Ishuna along with the rest of the Queendom would have to deal with a half-Human relative to the throne, and whatever his powerful father became.

Sister. What have you done? To be so desperate for his bed, to agree to this?

Innathi had invited it, embracing this with clear eyes. Many Davrin would be nervous, knowing the type of sway a Human man now held in their Queen, in their very bloodline. Ishuna felt *she* must be the one to See every possible bit of treachery coming their way if their Queen was to maintain the line of Her Matriarchy past this ill-granted choice.

The wedding ritual had already begun without added talk, something Ishuna could at least be grateful for.

Cris bent to one knee and kissed the hand of his Queen, standing up once again to offer his arm and lead her to the platform where Lord Rousse awaited them.

Innathi looked over her shoulder, searching for and finding her younger sister standing back but above the crowd of guests and servants. She smiled and winked, perhaps trying to reassure her after their fight last night.

Still weighing these things too lightly. Pay attention.

Oh, but Innathi's attention was blade-sharp, despite her overconfident air. This was a Human ritual, not one of the Davrin, with more Humans present by a small margin. The sheer distance some of their Elven guests had traveled to attend lent more weight to it, certainly the most to Cris-ri-phon himself.

"Of course, it will," Innathi told her when Ishuna raised the concern. "This is what he truly needs to repay me for this child."

"What? Repay you? I don't understand."

Her Queen appeared so confident and regal as she placed her hand over her abdomen. "I have already made my promise, Ishuna. It is here inside me, and I will see it through. The words of any Human ritual do not matter to me, now that I've decided. However, in engaging in this public 'marriage,' I shall see to it he will not be able to break his vow to me. Ever again."

The Seer had blinked, surprised within the depths of her worries. "H-how?"

"I will tell you as soon as I have confirmed it. But please, no matter what happens, do not interfere. I know what is best for the Queendom."

Did she?

Ah, but that was an ungenerous thought.

The ceremony in full motion, Ishuna realized she had forgotten to follow up with Innathi about what she'd said hinted at. Had Innathi "confirmed" it or hadn't she, and what was it?

Was it that the two sisters had fought over the whereabouts of their mystic sire last night that Innathi had not had the chance to say? Or had she abandoned her idea of securing Cris to her somehow?

The Seer sensed deep foreboding, as if she had missed some critical moment despite standing now to watch this historic marriage take place.

Ishuna did not have to wait long to understand the feeling, unfortunately. After speeches and vows and translation spells allowed all witnesses present to understand their nature without repeating into five or more languages, Ishuna saw what she had missed.

Despite having already Seen in coming in a different form. Long, long ago.

Cris-ri-phon moved his red sash at Lord Rousse's motion and revealed a black dagger with red runes at his side. He loosened the blade from his belt — sheath and all — to hold up in both hands, flat across his palms.

Terror stunned Ishuna's insides, and her mouth opened in shock. *That blade ...*

"My gift of longevity," said Lord Rousse. "That this bond may overcome *all* obstacles. You may speak your vows, Sorcerer-General."

No.

"And so, I promise to honor and protect my Queen and all that is hers," Cris-ri-phon spoke for all to hear as her sister accepted the gift into her own hands. "My oath sealed with this gift I give unto you, Innathi."

No!

"Not a mere symbol but a promise forged in the most powerful magic to swear to you and assure all your subjects. Even as I am not Elf in birth, I shall be in action, and I pledge myself to the Desert Queendom and V'Gedra until I pass for the final time into the Grey."

Ishuna was about to charge forward, to throw herself at her sister and disrupt the ceremony. She had to—

Indrath Rousse lifted one graceful arm high, drawing the attention of all for an instant, yet no one seemed to notice the Lord Elf gaze directly at the Queen's Seer.

His green eyes burned into her very essence. Unwillingly, she froze.

⋆*You are not invited, Ishuna. It is done. This is a formality.*⋆

Helpless, trembling, she remained where she was, forcing her eyes over to the Deathwalker then to Jennyn of Break Water. They were still watching her, watching the throne, their attention helping to muffle the Ice Lord's echoing thoughts in her mind.

Only they seemed as sorrowful as she in the sea of well-wishers and eager onlookers.

Cris-ri-phon tugged open the front of his uniform, ruining the crisp lines and exposing his chest enough to present the hollow of his throat and the dark hair growing in the center of his chest. He let the crowd satisfy their eyes to see no additional armor in place before facing her again.

"I have led many battles, survived many challenges," he said, "yet you, my Queen, do not need anything so grand to stop my heart. This enchanted blade *can* kill me. Against it I have no defense, but one. Let me show you. Place the tip of this dagger to my chest and push."

The crowd laughed softly at the instruction, touched with skepticism — partly for the theatrics, but also because anyone with connections to the army had seen or heard of this same trick with many other blades. This was a favorite display of the Sorcerer-General, and no blade had ever worked.

In every way, the Scorpion was difficult to kill, as his magic was simply that powerful.

The crowd quieted the moment Lord Rousse lifted one hand, nodding for the ritual to continue. At the General's added encouragement, Innathi drew the blade from its sheath.

Just as in Ishuna's dreams, it shone like black glass, its markings carved in like blood forever fresh. The Seer waited for the Hellish shrieking to begin, for the screams and the struggle she had witnessed happening many, many times before as Innathi stabbed herself just above her pregnant belly ...

No.

The dagger was silent, still. Inanimate. No surge of chaotic rage, no voice, nothing.

The Courtyard was quiet.

With the rest of the crowd, Ishuna watched, still and without protest, though against her will. She could still not move toward Innathi when she placed the point of the dagger against her General's naked chest. He did not flinch but kept his back straight and chin up, staring at her in open trust as his hands held open his uniform.

The point of the dagger was truly sharp, and proof that Cris did not have any magic shield in place arose in a welling of blood. The black edge *did* cut him, but Innathi had pushed harder, in response to Cris's urging. She struck its pommel with her full arm, and the crowd gasped as he winced.

The tip failed to go deeper. Blood trickled slowly.

Cris-ri-phon's voice rose, continuing his oath.

"For as long as my loyalty holds to none but you, my Queen, this magic blade will *not* take me. Only when I know with this beating heart that I *have* betrayed you will Soul Drinker draw out my very life.

"This Elven relic of the North is to keep, *lo'wicova*, always at your side to do with as you see fit as ruler of V'Gedra and all its holdings. You shall always have the tool of my execution ready should I break my oath to protect the Queendom of V'Gedra, or to be faithful to you."

Voices murmured.

"The Queen can harm him. She carries the power ..."

"He swears himself. He is of the Davrin for as long as the Queen will have him."

"No challenger to the Sorcerer-Kings of Zauyr, but a strong liaison ..."

There were many ways this could be a trick for the crowd, Ishuna knew, yet most — perhaps nearly all — seemed to believe it exactly as stated.

Given his history, most would take Cris-ri-phon at his word. He had never been known to lie for self-gain or shrug off promises lightly, and many had long known his deep devotion to the Virgin Queen. This ritual performed to impress upon all how seriously he took it himself.

He would never leave Innathi again.

Ishuna felt cold. *Sick.* Her visions, her worst fears neglected. Dismissed. Again.

This was what she meant, what she did not tell me. She ... told me she *wouldn't take it. She **promised** me not a year ago that she would refuse a magical blade from Cris!*

How could she do this?

After sheathing the red rune dagger and attaching it around her waist, Innathi helped to wipe the blood from Cris's chest and heal it with a mutual touch. The couple kissed passionately, revealing to anyone with eyes that they were lovers, and the Sorcerer-General boldly splayed his hand over her womb.

The Grand Courtyard was growing loud and active when the Ice Lord looked at Ishuna again. Though they were separated by a jubilant crowd raising early toasts, the Elf Lord still seemed to know her thoughts.

And she heard his voice answer.

This is the less harmful path, my child. Rejoice in their happiness, embrace your new family, and rest well knowing this Godblood cannot betray you. The Queendom will endure the strife and change, and you need do nothing, Ishuna, but live your life and pass into the next.

Ishuna shook her head in denial. *No. No ... I hear a different song. I always have! Absolutely not. This cannot be!*

The Ice Lord was lying. He must be.

As the newlyweds now stepped down to receive congratulations from the guests, Ishuna hurried over to Jennyn. The ancient Elf sat in quiet and peace, lightly touching the soft nose of the sorrel-red steed who stood patiently in the Courtyard, ears flicking.

"Jennyn," Ishuna said. "Do you ... .do you approve? Of what Lord Rousse did?"

Subtle colors still swirled and shifted underneath her skin, her eyes having changed from earth and leaf to sun and fire. Jennyn nodded slowly, looking back at the calm and faithful mount. "We understand our son takes a step of his own. We do not desire to see where it will lead, but yes, we approve."

What?

"Your *son*," she asked, aghast. "Who is 'we?' "

"We are your elders, daughter. Those who love all our children."

Son … daughter …

How Jennyn just tossed that claim around!

The Seer's hands clasped tightly as frustration swelled inside her chest. "If you 'love' us, even living so far away, wh-why did you *come* here if you would not *stop* him? Or help *me* stop them?"

Jennyn and the horse looked at her then, their eyes such strange, deep wells of feeling. "I am not the singer of your song, Ishuna. You must seek who is. Seek what you miss most."

The Royal Seer spun away from the honored guest with a growl and moved away from her. From her *and* Taib, who had just taken down his hood, thus letting guests eating *food* see the scars on his grey-brown face. The Deathwalker bowed to Cris-ri-phon and Innathi as they moved through the crowd.

Rejoice, indeed!

Leaving the Break Water Elf behind, Ishuna found herself moving in Lord Rousse's direction. She hesitated, too late for him not to notice.

Fuck.

When Captain Xala moved to intercept, Ishuna decided to keep her path while the Ice Lord remained in his place. He smiled as she drew closer, and suddenly seemed less … *parental* as he tilted his head, allowing his hair to shift over his bare shoulders, his intense eyes flicking over her blue gown with subtle flirtation.

"Yes, Ishuna? What can I do for you?"

She caught her breath when he spoke her name, then shook her head. "Stop! Whatever you're doing. I want you to take back that magic dagger from my sister."

"That I cannot do," Lord Rousse admitted readily with a small, elegant shrug. "Even had I changed my mind in granting it as a wedding gift."

"It's going to destroy her! Is that your intent?"

"On the contrary," he said, smile never faltering, "Soul Drinker will protect her and her unborn child. The blade is as bound to serve her as Cris-ri-phon now is. Without it, her reign won't last another two decades once the child is born. This is what they asked for, Ishuna.

Protection from enemies they cannot see for their child. And I *always* protect innocent children."

"How dare you?" she seethed, glaring as the Ice Lord smirked. "I will protect her! I can See what they cannot! We do not need that horrid, foul thing you've placed in her hands!"

A disturbing shiver took Ishuna then, as the Ruler of the North relaxed the restraint on his aura. He'd been holding back.

A frightening desire to strip off her gown and present herself for his inspection swept through her, and she stiffened up completely, gritting her teeth, as her only means to combat it.

The crowd nearest to the throne thoughtlessly grew more familiar in their touches to each other as a seeming side effect; all more easily aroused as they laughed, talked, and watched the newly wedded Queen and her Husband.

"Do not look upon me to take the blame, my dear," Lord Rousse cooed, his eyes locking on hers. "You shall have much to reflect upon in your own choices. Soul Drinker is here as much to protect your sister from *you* as from the Godblood and the Naulor Queen. Although ... the Valsharess of the Red Sands doesn't know this, and perhaps you shouldn't tell her?"

The Ice Lord languidly lifted one hand, stunning her with a rush of realization that she might weep and scream if he touched her ... Even in a light graze. She did not know if it would be pain or pleasure.

⋆*A little of both,*⋆ he promised in a mental whisper, a touch of menace slithering in as his fingers hovered over her spider pendant. ⋆*You would like it, my child, I promise. But that 'foul' thing of your own that you carry would most certainly* ***not.***⋆

Ishuna watched herself straighten her back, pushing out her chest, offering her breasts and getting them closer to his fingers. Her nipples had hardened beneath the sky-blue silk and her middle grew hot. Abruptly she recalled — *vividly* — her first night with Leur.

Cris's older brother, buried not even a decade ago.

She remembered pinning his wrists on her mattress and impaling her sweating body on his. She lived again in that moment, riding him all the while with her damp, fragrant small clothes draped over his face …

"Stop it," she whispered, wondering why no one in this crowded courtyard seemed to see her distress. Why wasn't Xala coming to drag her away? Why hadn't Innathi summoned her?

Once again, neither of them even knew Ishuna was in trouble!

★*Are you certain you do not want me instead?*★ Lord Rousse offered, moving one finger to lightly trace around one nipple over her dress, now so sensitive it was painful. ★*Perhaps we could rip that wound in your aura open again, just one more time, and I can heal it properly. Once and for all. It would take some suffering on your part, but there would be pleasure, too. It may be worth it to save the rest of the Queendom, Ishuna. Something to consider.*★

The Elf Lord was right. There *was* pleasure, but … something …

Something inside is screaming.

And it simply would … not … *Stop!*

The Ice Lord terrified her.

He knew, knew so much about her, and he terrified her!

Seeing this, he only continued to press his case.

★*You must submit, Ishuna. You know you aren't strong enough to mend this on your own. We may avoid quite a lot of fallout if you will sacrifice yourself for them. Right now. Tonight. Begin by sitting on my lap and lifting your skirts, just as you did with Leur and Cris by the fountain.*★

Not again.

★*Only a select few ever receive this offer, Seer, but I promise … it will feel right. You shall feel right again once you release control.*★

Never. Never again.

The corners of his mouth softened, his lips opening in suggestion of something intimate yet to be released.

★*Shall we not sit, you and I? Shall I not learn you and help you feel mended on the deepest level, the best way I know how?*★ He paused. ★*It's the only way to save your sister* without *Soul Drinker.*★

Curse him to the Depths!

*I will **not** do what you say!* she shouted inside, her body trembling and pleading with her to run. *Y-You … are **not** my Lord! You are worse than anything I've seen! No wonder Cris-ri-phon admires you and takes your 'gifts'!*

That overbearing phallus wants to be just like you!

Lord Rousse chuckled inside her head; neither of them had blinked and her eyes were drying out in the bright morning.

Why would I accept solutions to the very problems caused by males like you?! she snarled. *None of you have the wisdom to see past your own erection, so you will always abuse your power!*

⋆Hmm. What can I say, qu'essan? At least your Sister-Queen recognizes her match when she meets him. In my time, I have found little weight in such accusations of the body, given enough power and drive. Some I know quite well are not male or female at all. But you are still young. If you change your mind, the offer shall remain open. For a time.⋆

At last, he blinked; Ishuna could breathe. She could *move.*

The Seer hurried away out of the courtyard with Xala following her, while Innathi and Cris enjoyed their celebration before the sun would soon grow too hot for continued play outdoors.

CHAPTER 3

"ISHUNA?"

The Queen's sister shook her head without answering her bodyguard. Glad as she was that *someone* was following her, that someone *cared*—

"Ishuna!"

Her vision blurred with tears. Her skin felt it singed with a persistent, alchemical fire. Even after leaving the Ice Lord's presence and placing multiple walls between them, the arousal and desire she felt did not fade.

But not for Lord Rousse of the North did she yearn.

Memories of Leur as a young man, fresh as a bleeding cut in her mind. Her body flushed as if he had accepted her and given such pleasure only last night.

The callous, invasive Ice Lord had stirred them up — *intentionally!* —in the hope that the grief and the loneliness which came with them would convince her to submit!

Ruling males, she seethed. *Self-absorbed, conceited, arrogant, overbearing* ...

And now they conspired together to take Innathi!

How dare they? Power hungry ... trying to control everything they can fuck!

Except Leur.

How in the Great Sands had he been so *different* from his brother?

He should have been the one given an Elf's longevity. Cris-ri-phon should be the one long aged to death and turned to dust!

A Davrin Guardsvrin moved at first to prevent her from entering her own wing of the Palace. The insult flared in her gut as she glared at the bua, who clearly hadn't been expecting her and realized his mistake.

Stepping back to take to one knee, his dark fingers touched the floor with appropriate humility.

"Royal Seer," he murmured. "Welcome back."

Ishuna trembled with the impulse to strike him, more than once, even knowing it was the Ice Lord she truly wanted to hit. The rage at being held powerless beneath his bright green gaze roiled and writhed inside her like a living thing.

How dare he threaten me? How dare he make me remember?

Captain Xala had caught up by now, looking splendid in her dress uniform which also covered the permanent scars the Thousand Year Queen had given her. The betrayal of her loyalty and the harsh punishment never seemed to leave her eyes, however, and the former Captain of House Ja'Prohn was ill-at-ease living in the Palace.

Meanwhile, this young Guardsvrin knew nothing of such hardship, or of her worry for the future of the realms. His innocence was another insult, blind and ignorant as he was to the forces seeping into V'Gedra on this day, grasping and grappling for dominance.

Long past the point of no return …

"Bring him," Ishuna ordered Xala, her face contorted in rage. "Follow me."

"*Qu'essan?*" the bua said with alarm as Xala took his arm and brought him to his feet. "Wh-what have I … ? I-I beg your forgiveness, I did not intend to block you from your own quarters —"

"Next time, look a little farther forward, novice," Xala said gruffly, though without hostility, and her commander's voice seemed to calm him a bit. "Come with me."

Ishuna didn't speak as she stalked toward her room, waiting until all three were inside before setting her own locking spell on the doors and windows. She wouldn't be interrupted.

Turning away from them, the Seer lifted her bright blue skirts, cursing the Elf Lord for her burning loins as she reached for her sticky small clothes to pull them down her legs.

You'll never see this yourself, you infernal cunt tease. I'll never let you anywhere near these netherlips. You think you can heal me? Well, you're too late! I already am. I don't need you, and never will!

The hapless Guardsvrin was staring at her, his eyes impossibly wide as it only just dawned on him why he might have been brought here. His expression was entertaining in a way, and exactly what a bua's should be when in the presence of a powerful cait.

And I am powerful. I am not injured. There's nothing to heal.

Not anymore.

"Put him on my bed," she ordered her bodyguard. "Hold his arms upon my pillow."

Xala knew better than to question her in front of a male guard, but Ishuna saw the elder's concerned, bewildered expression from behind the young bua. Slowly, as if to give her time to change her orders, her Captain removed his weapons-belt and then pushed him forward gently, her hand on his back.

Ishuna ignored the look for now; she liked better noticing how the Guardsvrin was trembling.

Better. Much better.

As soon as the bua lay on his back upon her mattress, Xala took hold of his forearms above his head. Ishuna climbed onto the bed herself and plopped the damp silk which had been cradling her crotch all morning straight down onto his face.

He stiffened, eyes closed, mouth pursed tight. She could not see the outline of his cock growing within his trousers; he remained flaccid.

Disappointing.

She reached out and smeared the silk across his mouth and cheeks with the palm of her hand. "Stick your tongue out. Taste me in it, smell it, relish it! Few ever receive this offer, enjoy it!"

He obeyed, but it was thoughtless, far more confused than relishing.

He didn't know how to even pretend to please her.

How dare he not even try?

Xala cleared her throat, drawing Ishuna's attention from her rising temper, and asked calmly, "What is your name, soldier?"

His eyes were closed tight, his heart pounding in his chest. He needed to speak through Ishuna's intimate clothes. "I-I am Szoroan of House D'Shauranti, *viirclad*."

Xala nodded, satisfied with the honorific — he'd acknowledged her the dominant warrior without challenge — and although she still held him by his forearms, looked up and spoke to her quivering charge. "Szoroan of House D'Shauranti, my *qu'essan*. He is the son of Lizabet's cousin, Ruthrea."

Ishuna heard the quiet chiding, understanding the importance of Xala recognizing his name in that House's vast lineage. The Queen's sister exhaled in exasperation, yanking her panties back off the bua's face as the raging hunger inside her protested.

He is just a little too "important" for what I really want to do to him. Very well, get him out of my face! He'll be sorry!

"The Royal Seer desires your services, Szoroan," Xala continued before Ishuna could pitch the fit in her mind. The Captain kept her voice level, making what sense she could on the spot. "She enjoys dominance games. Have you any experience?"

"No, *viirclad*," he murmured, glancing up at the Seer fearfully then back down, visibly collecting himself at last. "But I have sworn to serve the royal family. I-I'd not embarrass my Mother by failing. I'll do anything you wish, Seer, though I beg forgiveness of my ignorance. I have had no instructor in this realm of service."

Ishuna frowned, although she felt placated by the humility.

He was well-spoken, clearly a Noble Guardsvrin serving his time before his Mother would place him somewhere else. Perhaps he was much younger than he looked.

"No 'instructor' at all?" she asked skeptically.

He swallowed, crimson eyes vibrant and uncertain as he lifted his gaze for a moment. "As the young play. Nothing more. I-If you will grant patience to teach me ... ?"

*I don't want to **teach** you! I want you to **know!!***

Ishuna growled without speaking, gathering up her skirts to straddle his head while facing Xala. She didn't sit down right away but let her blue dress drop, covering Szoroan from view from his chest up. She could feel his quickened puffs of breath on her moist snatch and smirked.

Must be pitch black under there now. The room dark and hot ...

The Guardsvrin's hands remained lax, fingers lightly curled as Xala held him. He was trying to remain calm.

The *qu'essan* reached for his trousers to open them, pushing impatiently at his hips to expose his soft genitals, an average, dark penis resting on a patch of white fur. Ishuna cupped his balls with one hand, rolling them and tugging the sack, once making him squeal and jump.

There.

She chuckled as she leaned down to feed the flaccid member into her mouth, tasting his musk and realizing how long it had been since she had done this.

Szoroan gasped with surprise beneath her skirts as she sucked hungrily, using her tongue on every finger-width of him. Finally, his member began to plump up, to stiffen and give her more length to work with. His hot breath flowed along her inner thighs, unable to evade her scent from heated loins.

The bua lay as if stunned, held down as the Royal Seer molested him, but he would understand soon what he was to do. She would not attempt to smother him until he *asked* for it.

Like he should. Soon.

Meanwhile Ishuna edged him, stopping and pinching the head of his prick each time he was close to spurting in her mouth. Though Leur had enjoyed this for whole segments of the night, Szoroan groaned in dismay as if it was some confounding torture. He writhed against Xala's hold, and Ishuna laughed at him the more times it took him to understand what he was supposed to do.

*Selfish, clueless bua. Is it not directly above you? Is it not right in your Goddess-damned **face?!***

Her frustration grew, as did his, and she became rougher with him, on the clear verge of hurting him just as Xala spoke up.

"*Qu'essan*, this Guardsvrin is properly disciplined," she whispered urgently. "He will *not* touch you without your command. You know this! Tell him. You are in control."

I am in control ... Yes. I am.

She ached. She *ached* to be touched, but why did *she* have to tell him every little thing she wanted? She felt so ...

So alone. As she thought it.

Ishuna growled, lowering her hips closer so that her cunt was within reach. "Kiss me, Szoroan. Now."

She felt it as the bua lifted his head to meet her, to kiss her dripping center without hesitation. He did not wait before he next licked, sucked gently, then kissed her again.

"Ohhh," Ishuna breathed.

The violent urgency was receding as it became clear he *wanted* to please her and had the proper instincts to do so. He was neither stupid nor antagonizing her.

He had been waiting. Obeying.

She had confounded him for nothing.

I am such a fool ...

Soon Ishuna encouraged Szoroan to settle back his head onto the mattress to leisurely ride his face, rocking her hips forward and back, spider pendant swinging between her breasts.

Wordlessly they worked out a rhythm for him to breathe, to anticipate her, to nudge her sweetly in those intimate places.

"Xala, release ... his arms," she ordered, her voice wavering.

Her bodyguard nodded and gladly did so, withdrawing from being so close to Ishuna's mouth and the Noble son's stiff, leaking rod. Xala stood at attention a few paces away, watching.

"Szoroan. Touch me with your hands."

He lifted his arms, slid his hands beneath her skirts and slid them up her thighs to cup her buttocks. The Seer groaned, grinding her crotch harder against him. His erection had softened some as he concentrated harder, as she got closer and closer to the edge.

"Wet one finger," she commanded. "Slip it in my netherhole."

The bua was surprised — possibly a first for him — but he did not hesitate. He used the slick spit and lubricant all over his mouth to coat his finger and then penetrated her with it, requiring one correction in his aim before he pushed in deep.

Ishuna squealed softly in joy as she closed her eyes and imagined it was Leur. *Yes!*

"Suck me!"

He did, and she rubbed her slick juices all over him; every part of his face from hairline to chin, from cheeks to ears, was damp with her arousal, her scent, their sweat, from his face burning hot from between her thighs.

Sometimes he made desperate gasps for breath but knew better than to ruin her final climb. When she reached her peak, the waves began, and Ishuna grunted and groaned in that ultimate, private indignity.

Her sweet release oozed out to coat him anew as she mashed herself to his face, clutching his naked hips. Arching her back, she finally, *finally* completed her climax, dropping forward, and lifting her slit from his mouth.

She heard even more desperate gasps beneath her skirt. Eyes hazy, she saw his prick in front of her, saw how insultingly soft it was. He should be *more* than ready …

Before the glow could recede, the Seer lifted herself up and swallowed him fully again. The bua cried out in shock, and no doubt gratitude, his hips jerking just once in pure reflex. Ishuna sucked and sucked him hard, until he quickly exploded into her mouth.

Augh!

Swallowing some by accident, drooling out a bit more, Ishuna shook her head. Coming abruptly back to herself.

Very well, so he's not so disciplined in some things.

So, I'll teach him. As he asked.

Swift to lift herself off his face, drawing back her skirt as though she drew back a curtain, Ishuna was briefly baffled to see the face was so dark-skinned, the hair so white, and with ears just like hers …

But she smirked and rumbled low in her throat as she claimed his mouth with hers, forcing it open and making him taste himself as she tasted some of herself. He didn't fight her. He most seemed to want to catch his breath and just let her finish.

There. There, now I am strong again. I can be among the guests.

Ishuna flopped back from that kiss only long enough to catch her wind as well, turning her head to spy Xala watching the room at large without much expression on her face at all.

What? What is she thinking?

As soon as the Royal Seer caught Szoroan out of the corner of her eye, tentatively reaching to tug up his pants, that was her excuse. Ishuna got up on her elbow and waved her hand.

"Go," she commanded. "Get cleaned up and make sure your uniform is presentable should the guests see you. You will speak to no one of this, or I'll be sure your Mother hears my version the instant after the servants hear yours."

"Y-yes, Seer."

The young Davrin got up, carefully tucking his spent genitals back in as he got himself sorted. His face was not only an absolute *mess* but his expression a mixture of puzzled exhaustion and uncertainty.

Szoroan bowed to Ishuna, then saluted Xala in proper fashion. Her bodyguard saluted back and nodded to Ishuna, who released the magical lock long enough to allow him out without another word or command.

Ishuna sighed, relaxing upon her rumpled bed, slowly stroking her middle. She searched for that weak spot and once again satisfied it was not there.

She smirked at Xala. "That was fun. I suppose it is time I clean myself up as well. Innathi will wonder where I've been."

Xala nodded in agreement, watching her carefully as the royal rolled up and to her feet. "*Qu'essan?*"

"Hm?"

"Why did you force the first Guardsvrin you saw into your bedroom to smother him between your thighs?"

The afterglow vanished all too soon, and Ishuna found herself scowling at her most trusted ally. "What do you mean 'why'?"

"That is not your temperament, *qu'essan*. This was unusual for you."

"How would *you* know, Xala?" she snapped. "And you were the one holding him down!"

"As you commanded me, *qu'essan*," the Captain replied, "and to stop you if you hurt him. You were not acting yourself, and I've known you since you were a young cait."

Her mood cooled even more as Ishuna straightened in defense. "Well, if you've noticed, Xala, I'm no longer a cait. I 'smothered' him because that's how I *enjoy* taking my buas now. Although, I suppose this speaks well for you not spying on me and Leur when we lived at the Third Realm."

Xala blinked, drawing back in modest surprise.

"But these *are* my tastes, and Leur loved being treated so, I'll thank you to not judge either of us for them."

Her elder straightened and bowed again in respect. "Ah. Be that as it may. What I mean is that I saw you run from the courtyard after a strange interaction with the Ice Lord. And I followed you only to find you seeking any youth with a cock to slap upon your bed. Ishuna, you and I know *that* is not your habit."

That was true.

The Seer swallowed, trying to make herself listen to her childhood guardian. If there was ever anyone from her Queen-Mother's Court who had cared about her well-being, even after punishment and exile …

It was hard. There was so much noise in her head. She wanted to deny she'd done anything wrong. She didn't want to admit she might be vulnerable again …

"I was missing Leur," she murmured, pouring water in a basin to prepare to wash her face. "Badly."

"Leur? But … you grieved, *qu'essan*. He's been dead for over a decade and I imagine you weren't, ah, this close in the last fifty years —"

"Yes, I know!" she snapped, tears coming to her eyes. "Th-that …

is what he did. The Ice Lord made me *remember*, as if I'd just found him yesterday. Only to lose him again the same day …"

Her guardian frowned in genuine displeasure. "Why would the Valsharess's guest of honor do such a thing?"

Ishuna's face became a mask of hatred. "He wanted to seduce me. He wanted … I …"

She paused, afraid of saying more. She swallowed. "He is a powerful being, Xala, and a callous ruler. Perhaps he is bored, bereft of challenge. I-I … may not have been able to resist my own yearning he brought forward, but at least I did not make a fool of myself with him in front of the entire Court."

CHAPTER 4

SZOROAN LEFT THE SEER'S QUARTERS NAUSEATED AND LIGHT-HEADED, BUT confused why he was so. He checked the halls carefully before making his way to the nearest washroom.

It was meant for guests, not guards, but those guests would be occupied for a little longer. He couldn't go to the servants' area and *not* be asked many awkward questions with the Seer's feminine marks quickly drying on his face.

Her callous voice still repeated in his mind.

You will speak to no one of this.

He was a horrible liar.

Szoroan found the guest washroom and quickly gathered water, soap, towel, and cloth while his thoughts spun.

Was it over? Just the one time, or would she call him again? To "teach" him. Though he would not have thought to refuse the Royal Seer had she been clearer in what she wanted, she had taken him roughly. She had done things to him he had not known any cait desired, and he'd nearly passed out several times.

He shuddered with an exhale, feeling used and wrung out, diminished as if she had been feeding on his blood, and dazed by how quickly he'd fallen beneath her powerful force of will.

Szoroan wondered whether he could avoid this in the future when he heard the voice behind him.

"Beautiful child. Do not wash it off yet."

Szoroan spun around, glimpsing one of the brown-skinned guests standing in the doorway. An apology was on the tip of his tongue but did not leave his stunned mouth. He'd at least heard about this one before now.

The Ice Lord of the North.

"M-my Lord?"

"Just wait."

The bronze Elf was shirtless, masculine. His presence dominated the small space, as intimidating as the Seer had been. Neither Ishuna nor this unnerving Lord were Szoroan's usual desires at all, but …

As it had been with her, the youth couldn't leave, couldn't deny.

Not only might anybody disbelieve him, but he would harm his Mother's standing as well by insulting such a guest.

He was trapped. Again.

Szoroan held still as the Elf Lord pushed him up against the wash basin. A powerful aura and seductive scent wrapped him, gripping hold as sure as Xala's strong hands had, and giving him an erection he did not want.

H-he wants me as well?

It seemed to be a day of firsts for him.

The young Guardsvrin knew he had been fortunate in managing to evade eye contact with this Lord, staring at the sculpted chest until he got closer. So close, they'd touch if he tried to shift away.

Szoroan turned his head all the way to the side, closing his eyes tightly as when the Seer had smeared her panties over his face.

Maybe if I just wait, don't fight, the Lord will be finished quickly and just leave. I will speak to no one of this …

⋆*Well. I am glad to hear that, Szoroan. But you are so afraid.*⋆ The voice caressed his mind gently. ⋆*You expect I will simply strip you and push you down? That I will mount you like some entitled animal with no care for your consent?*⋆

Szoroan saw that in full, lurid detail, as if the Ice Lord had simply held up a mirror of what the youth expected to happen in this washroom. His humiliation spiked hot as his erection hardened further against his will, enough to weaken his knees.

He thought for one horrifying instant to lift his eyes, to look at the Lord's ethereal face and tell him: *Yes, it was what I want.*

Szoroan shook his head, desperate to keep his eyes closed and his lips pursed. He was unsure how much longer he could hold himself upright.

No, please. I do not want it. I don't.

The Lord's voice was filled with compassion. **Then I shan't force it, Szoroan. I promise. I have much more respect for you than that, and you have already been ravaged once today, haven't you?**

An elegant hand reached up to caress one side of his tacky, slit-smeared face. Szoroan still wasn't looking but he *felt* claws …

Sharp tips on the Lord's fingers.

They did not cut him but lightly scraped the surface before tilting so the pads caressed his night-dark skin.

The Elf Lord was amused.

Yes, she tried to drown you, I think.

The ruler exhaled slowly, his breath unnaturally moist and fragrant, like an underground pool of water resisting evaporation. It had the effect of reviving Ishuna's smears, making them fresh and slick on Szoroan's skin once again, as if she had only lifted her cunt off his face a scant moment before.

Suddenly, the Guardsvrin was again desperate to catch his breath. He was suffocating, smelling her so strongly again, remembering the infinite textures and moist, smothering heat as he did his best to service the Queen's sister under duress.

Beautiful, Lord Indrath commented.

A claw scraped a sample of the Seer's juices and gently prodded Szoroan's lips, the Ice Lord encouraging him to taste her again. The bua opened his mouth rather than have the claw cut him, and the bronze-skinned Elf was very careful, sliding in and pressing down on his tongue.

Suck, Szoroan.

He closed his lips around the Lord's finger, the claw barely avoiding a spot that would have made him gag. The Ice Lord leaned in then, hovering so impossibly close without touching. Szoroan was certain the ruler could feel the heat of his own uncooperative erection so close to that taut, bare abdomen.

His captor withdrew the finger from his mouth, collected more of Ishuna's slickness and fed it to him again, at the same time inhaling the dampness in Szoroan's matted white hair. As his finger pulled out for a second time and tucked itself beneath his chin, perfect lips moved next to the youth's ear.

"Open your eyes, Szoroan. Look at me. This is important."

The urging held all the promise of a desirable secret. Somehow, the breath of that whisper spoken aloud seemed to break the tension.

Someone else knew what had happened, yet the Guardsvrin hadn't broken his order; he hadn't spoken of it. Szoroan did not know why, but that felt … better.

The Lord did not blame him for what happened. Instead, he held the young Guardsvrin like something precious, or someone treasured.

"Look at me, Szoroan."

The Davrin bua opened his eyes and looked upon the face of the most beautiful, brown-skinned Elf he had ever seen in his life. His bottom lip trembled, and that made the Lord smile. It felt good.

Szoroan's mind opened to listen to the voice in his head, the fear numbed for now.

You've just had your first encounter with one touched by the Abyss. It will get worse, Szoroan, and the Abyss will take something most precious from the Royal Seer, something the Elves all need. Yet if I were to attack now, while it is weak, it would destroy that precious thing all the same, and retribution would come to me instead of the Pit where it belongs.

He was not afraid but … *I-I … don't understand.*

The Ice Lord's sigh of regret was tangible. Musical. **I shall return to my domain soon, but I would charge you with convincing her, Szoroan. Convince her, as she cannot hear me or the Godblood. But you …* * Indrath placed his clawed finger at the hollow of the youth's throat. **Her defense to protect it* *against you can be weakened, thanks to her own actions. I can teach you how to make you stronger, so that you alone shall get beneath her skin.**

Weakened defense? To protect ... what?

**You must learn to be stronger before you can understand, my son. Will you? Can you prove you are more than you seem? If yes, you may salvage for the Seer, indeed, salvage for the entire Queendom what should not be lost.*

His heart pounded as he felt only the vague hint of what that meant. His eyes widened as he stared at that future. This Lord cared more about him, about the Davrin, than the Seer did.

.... Yes, Lord Indrath. I will.

Good. You shall make your Mother and your House proud, Szoroan. Most proud. Finish your service here at the Palace, and then ask your Mother Ruthrea once again for training in Blade Song with Lizabet D'Shauranti. She will listen this time. Trust me.

Fiery-warm lips kissed his cheek at last, tender and loving. Szoroan eyes fluttered shut in blissful response.

His whole being felt buoyed up. All fear drained away to be held in the other Elf's arms. His face, neck and ears, everything farther down which had been slick and wet, marked by the *qu'essan*, now drawn into him, leaving his skin supple and smooth without cloth or water.

Indrath kissed his forehead before releasing him, leaving the young Davrin to stand on his own two feet, prepared to return to the celebration.

"Return to your post, Szoroan, and fear not the darkness. The day shall come when the darkness will fear you much more."

CHAPTER 5

THE PALACE OF V'GEDRA – 239 B.S.E.

THE QUEEN'S LABOR BEGAN ON A RARE EVENING WHEN SHE AND HER HUSBAND shared the same bed within her private quarters.

"The cramps aren't stopping," Innathi whispered as she tried to hide her fear behind her excitement, attempting to control both with breathing. "I-I think it's time!"

Cris-ri-phon promised Musanlo immediate praise at dawn, no matter what. He would be here for her, for them, to see the miracle. Though he could have been out in a tent surrounded by manure, or a guest at a House's stronghold far across the dunes, talking and planning late into the night … he was not.

He was here. Right where he needed to be.

It's happening.

Just about every Davrin in V'Gedra would be surprised on the morrow; in any other Davrin Mother — no matter her age, no matter a Noble or a peasant — this moment was far too soon for her to be giving birth to a healthy infant.

And yet, for Cris and all the Zauyrians cohabitating with the Elves, a Human woman carrying this long would have died. They had all been waiting far too long to see the General's newborn son.

A son.

He knew because Ishuna had told him what she'd Seen on his wedding day. She had also told him the bua would survive his birth, as would his Queen-Mother, and Cris had never felt more grateful for Ishuna's gift.

They shall both live!

Yet even having the far-seeing eyes of his sister-in-law to reassure him, Cris battled fear more than he ever had in his life as he gathered Innathi up into his arms and carried her to where she wanted to be.

His own mother had died birthing him. Many more among his people's small, Zauyrian wives would be lucky to survive two births and live on to raise them herself. Few Desert women would risk a third child. If a family had four or more, the wife was always an outlander.

So many complications, so widespread that a persistent legend told how the very first Kings of the Five Realms had done something to earn the wrath of a god, or they had made a bargain with a curse attached to it.

Zauyrian men were large, strong, and healthy on the whole, while the women were delicate and slim, their health less sure or if a girl grew up full of fight, all it took was a pregnancy to sap it away, more if the baby was a boy.

Because the boys become men who live on, far beyond their mothers.

And thus felt the strong urge to protect everyone around them, to take care of what they could on their behalf. Or in their memory.

"Put me down," Innathi whispered again, smiling despite the light sweat breaking out on her face. "Come, get in with me."

They had reached the coolest place they could find on a warm desert night: the pool room connected to another meant for high-rank sparring.

Built as a stepping-stone depression into the floor and filled with precious water from below, a dozen Davrin could fit in at once. The intent was not to swim but to sit, letting the heat bleed out and the sand slide off itchy skin.

Where the weight of the world could lift for a few moments.

Innathi and Cris were here alone, the Sorcerer's spells masking their presence in sight or sound, until such a time as they wished to reveal it. They had decided together, thanks to Ishuna's prediction, they were confident they could try this. No would-be assassin would be tipped to a vulnerable moment which belonged to nobody but the married couple themselves.

Cris stripped his own robe and helped his Queen remove hers, stealing a soft kiss at the junction of her neck and shoulder despite knowing that her large, rounded belly cramped uncomfortably.

"Mother would say this was foolish," Innathi whispered, gazing at the moonlight reflecting off the water through a tall window.

Next, she looked at him with eyes that blazed even in the night.

His heart pounded in his chest. "The moment you wish for your servants, beloved, they shall be called. For now, I am grateful that I am enough."

They rested in the pool together, his Queen's nude back lined up against his front, two sets of contrasting hands resting upon her stomach as each contraction passed. Squeezing deep in her gut grew stronger, and Innathi gripped one of his broad hands; she moaned, and his heartbeat surged in his ears before he could slow it, breathing deeper.

She can squeeze as hard as she likes.

Nothing was too much pain for him compared to what she felt now, her glorious and perfect body trying to bring his son forth into the world to take his first breath.

He prayed the boy was not too large for her to pass.

"*Aia,* Innathi," he murmured. Her groans and gasps had begun to wrench the heart in his chest. "I am here ... Breathe."

He whispered spells to relieve her pain enough to keep her talking, though not to numb her in case she could not feel if something was wrong. They could not stay inside the pool for the entire time, as his Queen would become chilled, or their skin wrinkled and water-logged.

Sometimes he helped her stand and climb out, he would towel her off and they would relax on a chaise, and he would massage her tired back. If Innathi grew too hot again — as she frequently had during this pregnancy — he would undress her and slide with her back into the pool.

Half of the night had passed in this way, and the time seemed both too fast and too slow for the new father. His wife had told him her water had broken in the pool this last time, knowing they crept ever closer to the birth.

"The urge to push him out," Innathi whispered, her voice trembling, with a hint of awe like his own. " … Strong! Unrelenting!"

"Then push is what you must do, my Queen," he answered, kissing her ear. "Wail your strength and your victory if you must. None shall hear you."

She wanted to stay in the water to do this, but she needed his help. Innathi scooted off his lap and sat on the bench not far below the surface, the water playing at the bottoms of her milk-heavy breasts. Cris came around to kneel in front, using her eyes and her face to direct him as he became familiar with the feel of her bulging vulva each time his son came a little closer to surfacing.

Innathi stared at him, shocked by some thought then laughed, shaking her head when her contractions were at their peak.

"What is it? What's wrong?"

"Oh … My dagger. I forgot it. Not a very —" She winced. " — good plan to block an assassin, hm?"

"None can hold the relic but you, Innathi. It will still be there when we get back. Tell me when you are ready to push again."

She giggled amid her efforts. "Are your … hands tremoring like your voice, my husband?"

Cris blinked back tears as he stared beneath the surface of the water. "Yes, my wife … I … I can see him now. His head is crowning."

Leuren'qo.

They had already decided he would be named for Cris's older brother. A strong and kicking half-Davrin babe who did not even weaken, much less kill, his vital Queen-Mother as she pushed.

The newborn slid out and into his father's hands.

Still hours before the dawn, but Cris would make the time to pray as the sky lightened in the east.

My eternal thanks for your mercy and bounty, Musanlo.

ISHUNA WAS AS SURPRISED AS THE REST OF THE QUEENDOM WHEN SHE HEARD, though at least she was first to be called to her sister's quarters to see the new infant.

Leuren'qo would be either suckling, sleeping, or complaining while she was there. Once he wasn't doing at least the first, Innathi offered to hand him to her.

"Come, hold your first nephew!" the Queen ordered playfully, laughing at Ishuna's uncertainty, though the Seer wondered if she detected an uncertainty of her own in her Sister-Queen.

Ishuna took the bua in both hands, a bit surprised at his density. "He's heavy …"

Innathi chose to preen with a mark of pride. "Zauyrian buas usually are. Imagine carrying him around in your gut for more than a year! My back … *hmf!* I am glad it didn't last as it would if the sire had been Davrin."

No one could deny the fact that the sire *was* not an Elf. Leuren'qo had lighter skin than his Mother, but it was still a true night-shade compared to his father the General. The hair might not come in pure white, either. *Perhaps a strange blond or muted, ashen-grey?*

At least his ears were pointed at the tip, though they looked stubby. He wouldn't live as long as a Davrin naturally, but he may live much longer than the average Human.

"What about his magic?" Ishuna found herself asking. "Did you have any dreams about it?"

Innathi lifted herself straighter against the pillows propping her up. "I told you what I dreamed. He and his father will cross blades figuring this out but, as I told you then, I did not sense them as enemies or competitors."

"So, he'll choose the Human path of magic?"

Innathi shook her head. "Surely not! In fact, I … was thinking. Um …"

Ishuna cocked one eyebrow at the unusual stumble. "What were you thinking?"

Innathi shrugged, pretending it didn't happen. "That I'd like House D'Shauranti to train him as he gets older. Cris can participate to continue refining his own Blade Song as he trains his heir. That is what makes the most sense to me, for what I dreamed about for this child."

Ishuna stared down at the tiny, unfamiliar face, her thoughts shifting in an odd direction. "Did … Did Mother ever mention anything … ? What she saw for either of us while she carried?"

The Queen exhaled with a bit of irritation. "Ishuna, I promise, she did *not* tell me as much of her private life as you believe."

"She told you our sire is still alive."

"But I do not know where he is," Innathi stated flatly, holding her little sister's eyes without blinking. "I swear to you, Ishuna. Wruzdiin Ja'Prohn has not been found because he does not *want* to be found. Exiled or not, he did not go unwillingly. Chances are better that exile was just an official story for Mother to save face at the time. Everyone at V'Gedra forgot him quickly enough."

Ishuna was beginning to question whether that was true.

The separation of the knowledge between the mystics and the arcane had been softening ever since the Seer's return to stand by her Sister-Queen's side.

Mystics are persistent creatures, if nothing else.

One such example was out in the hall, just parting ways with Cris-riphon when Ishuna had been excused and stepped out. The Deathwalker Taib had turned away with his hood up as the Seer came into view. When the Sorcerer-General's face brightened to see her exiting the Queen's quarters.

"She's asking for you," Ishuna said, both the truth and what he most wanted to hear.

"Thank you, sister."

Ishuna pursed her lips after he'd walked past and entered the room behind her. She wondered yet again how such unguarded joy could *still* show in a Human who'd been through countless battles already, and who no longer had any living relatives of his own race that he knew well?

Humans were not meant to live this long.

Ishuna wasn't convinced Cris-ri-phon was prepared in his outlook. To force both himself and his new son to live like Elves, to pin all his hopes of future contentment on Innathi was something Ishuna had never liked. It was too unbalanced, had always been, and one of Houda's deepest concerns for her former pupil.

He's probably long forgotten about his Deathwalker tutor, just as he has forgotten about his failure when she called upon him to help me.

... No matter. I have tapped into my own strength.

Ishuna acted on the unusual impulse to hurry after Taib before he got too far ahead. As much as the Deathwalker wasn't what she expected to see in one with that title, he still filled an official capacity at V'Gedra.

To provide proper ritual and clean transitions for the deaths among Humans serving the General in V'Gedra.

The gossip among Davrin suggested most thought this to be the vaguest and most questionable presence at the Palace. Yet the Zauyrians said they would have more "ghosts" around if not for a Court Deathwalker.

I wonder sometimes if Humans make up stories to make their brief lives seem loftier when compared to an Elf. It works simply because Cris-ri-phon has the royal ear and placement to continue a story in a place where it does not fit.

That was her own Queen-Mother talking.

Ishuna knew better on a deeper level, having lived in the Third Realm and away from Court for a quarter of her life thus far. Innathi herself sometimes hinted — subtly and vaguely — that she wondered how their Mother would approve or disapprove of her rulership so far.

This is one decision of which Mother would have stoutly disapproved and even have fought against were she alive to do so. Having a Human mystic as a permanent part of the Queen's Court?

Therefore, a Daughter cannot begin her reign until the Mother was truly dead and gone.

So. Do you fit somehow, Grey Man? Let us see.

"Taib! Hold a moment!"

The Deathwalker paused as he was bid but lacked the courtesy to turn around and pull down his hood. Ishuna swore this one had even worse manners than most Deathwalkers she had glimpsed in her time. She might have thought it a calculated insult here if the Seer had not known Houda and others could be like this at times — particularly when they had been meditating more than usual or had been a long time alone walking the Desert.

Rather than distract them both with formalities, Ishuna simply positioned herself in front of him. She was close enough to smell the strange mustiness of his scarred flesh and dress, to see a long, homely face with thin lips and deep, black eyes with purplish bruises underneath.

Is beauty a disqualifying trait in becoming a Deathwalker, or does the training make the comely look wasted?

Would Cris-ri-phon have been an exception had he continued his teachings with Houda?

Taib did not speak first, but at least he looked directly at her and bowed his head, proving she had his attention.

"Taib," she commanded, "speak privately with me."

Wordlessly, he followed her to a double stairwell where they would not be glimpsed no matter which direction the servants came from. Ishuna congratulated herself on her courage in being in such a small and close place with the eerie man.

She was about to speak when Taib slowly removed an odd, polished stone from his pocket. Holding it out on a flat, pale palm, he showed her the dark green shot through with streaks of red. She blinked.

"Bloodstone," Taib said in Davrin, his voice raspy and hoarse, as if someone had stuffed thistle weed down his throat as a child. "If one of us holds this, our words will not stray, and you may listen to them again later, one more time."

Ishuna stared, her middle coiling down tight in suspicion. "Why would anything we say be something to hide or listen to again?"

"You asked me here, Seer, yet you have not spoken with me since I arrived. You tell me."

The Grey mage had learned her language very well.

"I don't have time to test your truthfulness about that stone," she snapped. "Put it away and keep your aura muted."

He obeyed and waited. She exhaled, clearing her head, and leaning out to listen for anyone close by. Some servants moved through with new sheets, chatting happily about the royal baby, but then all was quiet.

"You were speaking with the Sorcerer-General just now," she said.

He bowed slightly. "I report from time to time."

"On what?"

"The health of his army, and those citizens living in the poorer quarters. Even some of the merchant class, when they do not see me as a death mage coming to rob their soul." Taib smiled just a little, then it vanished. "I can see a rise in illness before it becomes overwhelming. The General wishes to know of such invisible threats while V'Gedra enjoys its trade deals from farther afield, or if hints of another conflict arise."

Ishuna blinked in surprise. "You aren't just here to stand over dying Humans?"

"I may do that as well, but no. Not just."

"You do the work of a city healer?"

"I cannot heal, but I see in ways many Davrin healers cannot, especially the Human auras among them. I can direct them to prevent silent plague from taking hold in worse conditions than this."

Ishuna touched her lips, still astonished to hear of this first use of a Deathwalker to fill a Court position created especially for him, it seemed. "I would never have thought to use a death mage so."

"Cris-ri-phon has allowed Deathwalkers and death mages among his army for decades, Seer, and his Queen approves. It was only recently, I understand, the General convinced enough Davrin officials to allow one of us a stay here as an advisor."

Another thing Innathi didn't tell me. Why is she being so secretive of her plans for the Queendom? Somehow, they all seem to surround ways which would benefit her new husband ... and now her child.

"I had expected Queen Innathi to have informed you of the reason for my presence." Taib read her with unblinking eyes, his tone neutral and without a hint of mocking. "Indeed, I thought the Sorcerer-General had told me he said as such to you, and you had disagreed. That is why you do not approach me."

Until now.

Ishuna shook her head, doubting for just a moment. *Had* she been told? How could she have forgotten? No, they simply had not told her ... And there could be a legitimate reason for that. There had been times when Ishuna herself had agreed with the two lovers, that they should *not* speak to her of their broader plans, because ...

Because it made my Visions more convincing, more accurate, if I was kept ignorant on certain security matters. There was less clutter for me to worry about. I would speak what I saw, and they would know its Truth ...

They had worked with this balance for years until the marriage. But now? Innathi always kept that black dagger with her on her belt, offered to her and accepted in *exactly* the way Ishuna had warned her against.

Why? Because she said it was bound to her, obligated to protect her and her son when Cris-ri-phon could not.

Just as Lord Rousse claimed. As Cris-ri-phon had asked.

Or bargained.

How else could this sorcerer have gained such lengthy youth and vitality? The figure behind that dagger was menacing and powerful. A plot to undermine a long-lived Queendom sinisterly possible during a time of uncertainty, as Innathi broke with tradition in more and more ways.

How can Innathi not see the Ice Lord's manipulation of her Queenship? He wanted to make her his puppet, and he's blocked my Visions that would prove it to her!

Ishuna swallowed, momentarily forgetting that Taib was still there, watching her, perhaps waiting for a response or perhaps not. The Seer grappled to recall what they had been discussing.

"I might have disagreed to your presence?" she managed to pick up the thread. "Yes, I may have at that. There aren't any Humans in official status within V'Gedra's Court except for Cris. And now you. I see more protest should this trend continue. In fact, what purpose have you to stay in the Palace if you always leave to be among the Human sick? I'd think that could threaten us all here with plague, especially as my Sister-Queen's new son is half-Human."

Taib bowed. "I acknowledge that concern. I cannot be a carrier —"

"Because you are a Deathwalker?"

"Yes." He barely paused, offering no further explanation. "Also because I am required to purify my skin and robes upon return, without fail, and provide proof to the Sorcerer-General. This is as we do in the army as well. The methodology is established and effective for Humans, and Elves do not get sick quite as we do. Your race can suffer from malnourishment and dehydration and over-exposure, as with all living creatures. An open wound can fester if not kept clean. But you do not seem to become ill in the way of plague very easily."

Ishuna felt goosebumps rise from the way he was looking at her before he continued. Like a butcher studying how the muscles of an ox were connected before choosing to make the next slice.

"The knowledge we've gained from living among you and practicing new methods has improved the overall health of the Zauyrian population," Taib said, "and over this century, their closest Davrin neighbors have finally begun to notice."

Is this true?

Ishuna had not heard of anything like this living inside the Palace or riding occasionally out among the populace of the Capital, nor among those religious groups who welcomed her as an honored guest.

Humans had long seemed susceptible to more strange attacks on their health leading to temporary periods of grotesque weakness — another reason plenty at Court would have liked to see less Humans ingratiating their government with that of the Dark Elves.

Regularly, someone would stir fears that, one day, a virulent sickness would jump from Human to Elf from which they had no defense, and it would wipe them all out without enough mage healers to combat it. The Queen had responded by opening a second healer's school for Davrin.

Meanwhile, Cris-ri-phon had already been exploring ways to temper and relieve these concerns with the two races living together, using both healers and death mages.

For how many years now?

He had seen success in his fighters at the border settlements where the most contact with the Realms of Zauyr and more distant peoples occurred. Why wasn't he crowing those victories in the face of his opposition, as if the first hundred years were not enough to speak of it?

So many details he simply does not share. Or maybe he shared them with Innathi and that is why she acts as she does around me … Why not more with me?

Again, her visions.

Perhaps they saw her as not needing help to understand, and she was not in the habit of attending every political daily session or meeting; it exhausted her. She preferred to spend her time in the library studying or out riding, or …

No. No, that was before I met Houda. That was me as a child and a youth. I am much more now. I keep tabs on all the Elvish mystic groups of the capital. I collect scrolls and histories from afar, I scribe some of them myself to make copies, to translate … . I represent my Sister-Queen to vassals, and I help keep the Queendom safe when there is conflict … .

Yet, disturbingly, she had not had another true vision to share ever since the wedding day when she had seen Leuren'qo born. Memories of these past two years without open conflict were … dimmer, as if she were waiting, or meditating somewhere far away like in Koorul.

And yet ready to focus ahead.

Now the firstborn son was here, and the Royal Seer was blind as to the next leg of the Queendom's fate. This had been worrying her more and more, yet she could not force herself to *see*. She already knew this.

"Were these plans displayed before the councilors during the last conflict?" she asked.

Taib frowned a bit in confusion. "I would not know, Seer, I am a newcomer here, not present at that time."

"Of course, of course," she said with a wave of her hand. "I should be asking the General."

"Mm. But you are better impressed how Humans work this much to solve long-standing problems?"

She thought perhaps he had not blinked for this entire conversation.

"A little," she admitted. "You care about my being impressed?"

Taib bowed his head with respect, if not grace. "I do. Your Queen will push for change we have not seen yet in the name of her half-blood son. You fear this as much as any of her councilors, but you are listening, as a fellow mystic."

Was she?

The Deathwalker continued. "Believe that the General wants to raise his people up closer to the Dark Elves, not drag you down to dwell among us. Cris-ri-phon seeks enlightenment of Human purpose next to yours. He believes this is the source of longevity and wisdom, but he does not want to usurp it from you as if it is something he can take. It is not. The Queendom and the Five Realms of the Red Sands will always come first to him, but he has believed for much of his life he is on a higher path which will heal a greater part of the world than we can imagine."

What?

This was a first.

Delusional. And lying, for he just usurped our longevity in Innathi's womb . . .

Ishuna stared down at the paler, long-fingered hands rather than reveal her first thoughts. A wall slammed into place somewhere inside her before she could have been tempted to look farther out, and she felt a welcome calm come over her.

The Seer nodded. "Interesting. Well. While I continue to envision the General doing nothing to harm us, I will have no reason to speak out."

CHAPTER 6

HOUSE D'SHAURANTI – 229 B.S.E.

SZOROAN FOUGHT TO CATCH HIS BREATH, SMILING UP AT THE SKY FROM DOWN on the ground. He put his hands forward, palms up, sword lying in the dust to the side.

"Yield! I yield to the General!"

Cris-ri-phon was grinning as he stood above him, winded as he reached out a hand to help the Davrin to stand up. Szoroan accepted, clasping firm, nearly springing to his feet before letting go to retrieve his sword and bow to his Matron following the exercise.

"An excellent decision to train this one, Matron," complimented the Queen's Husband despite the defeat. "Szoroan is moving quickly through the skill sets and may yet surpass me!"

Lizabet D'Shauranti smirked then chuckled softly with a nod. "Our bua has been persistent, that is certain. We've seen many mage-fighters more gifted than him but few as stubborn. Not a wonder you like him, General. Does he strike you as familiar?"

Cris laughed at the good-natured comparison, as accurate as it could be for the only Human alive learning the secrets from House D'Shauranti, whose Warrior-Matron provided the elite of the Davrin side of his army for the last two centuries.

Recently, the Sorcerer-General had even opened discussion for mutual defense agreements between the Matron Lizabet and the Sorcerers of the Five Realms, as greater unrest than ever seemed to always be threatening from the coasts, the Steppes, and the West.

The tactics and strategies of previous battles led by Cris-ri-phon, the tales of blending the strength of each while shielding the weaknesses could not be denied. At last, the elder Matron was willing to listen to the younger Sorcerer-Kings wishing to discover whether these Elven skills could be refined and perpetuated into its own version among the Zauyrian Realms.

Cris would visit the newest recruits or those climbing the ranks of sorcerous blade fighting. Occasionally he would accept a challenge from one to spar. Today it had been Szoroan, the second son of Lizabet's cousin, Lady Ruthrea, who managed a significant portion of the Queendom which provided supplies to his soldiers.

Now this Lady of D'Shauranti offered up her own blood as well. Cris would be sure to put a good word in Innathi's ear for her.

"I must admit, I do see something of myself in him," the General said with a small salute to the young fighter. "Keep it up, Szoroan, you're doing something right."

"Thank you, General!" Szoroan bowed. "Fear not the Darkness, for the day shall come when the Darkness will fear you more."

The General returned the bow, if not the unusual blessing.

Soon, the trainers saw the small crowd which had gathered off to their duties while Lizabet signaled to Cris that she would like to walk. He nodded acceptance, the usual protections soon in place for them to have a slow-moving, private conversation in her desert garden.

"I hear Leuren'qo grows more swiftly than the Court is accustomed to," the Matron said. "He is only ten years old, yes?"

Cris nodded, years of old anxieties returning in an instant as he remembered various threats and crises which had cropped up back at the Capital surrounding the security of his son. He hated being away even now. Somehow, as promised, his wedding gift to her had warned Innathi of each threat, and all of the aggressors had been executed without mercy.

His Queen was at her most vicious when protecting her blood, surprising even her husband. Sometimes he wondered if he should have been looking for a place away from Court sooner, but his Mother had been insistent about keeping the bua close to her.

"Leuren's energy and fearlessness exhaust his governors," Cris said, both in sympathy and pride, "and our Queen cannot stop her meetings to chase after him when he leaves the protections of the Palace."

"Especially now," Lizabet agreed. "She is pregnant again?"

The Queen's Husband closed his eyes briefly. His gut flashed hot from vivid memories of just last month.

He had been away on a long trip to address a matter of fair distribution that threatened to erupt into violence. The General's direct involvement proved the Queen was paying attention and reminded all of her great power supporting the Desert.

As they'd hoped, his presence forced negotiations to the table, and he'd helped hammer out an imperfect but tolerable compromise that would not require one side of the water-users to die.

The Queendom needed it this way. Open fighting and raiding would disrupt the trade of imbuement gems which saved so many of his fighters in battles and force the Queen to pay exorbitant prices to have Dwarves bring them from farther afield.

When Cris returned successful, Innathi had gotten them alone as soon as she could divest herself of her councilors. Before her General could finish his water, his cock was deep inside her.

He fucked her atop one of her office desks, each of them still half-dressed. She smelled of no one else on her dark skin or gown. Her arousal seemed so pure as to scald him as she writhed, nails scraping his scalp as she finger-combed thick, dark hair, her teeth biting and nibbling on his lower lip.

"Take off your shirt!" Innathi demanded, gripping, and pulling at what remained of his uniform as if she would rip it if he didn't obey.

Her cunt clutched eagerly around him as he paused to strip to the waist, where his Queen's smooth, dark legs wrapped around him, her ankles locking together. Lifting her stunning eyes, full, purple and pink lips offered up to him, they kissed.

She was the one who pushed her aura out at him first. "Now."

He gasped, thrust in three more times, whispering her name, getting ready to come —

And found the point of the black dagger pressed to his chest.

He froze, and she shoved the blade hard enough to cut him. He bled, almost exactly like their wedding day, but did not die.

"Hmm." Innathi smiled wickedly. "Still no betrayal?"

"Not this day," Cris said, taking her wrist and twisting it before pinning it to the desk. She groaned in modest pain. "Not ever!"

Innathi had arched her back, laughing and squeezing her hungry body around him, releasing the dagger and letting it fall to the floor, a note like glass striking stone ringing into the air.

"Then fuck me harder, husband," she cooed, her aura opening to entwine itself around his own. "Feel your surge and give your Queen another baby."

Aia, Innathi …

Lizabet was patient as Cris took a deep breath and nodded. "She is with child, yes, but it's not been announced. Please tell me, Matron, how did you hear?"

The Matron shrugged, touching her own abdomen. Any possible bulge was well-hidden beneath her armor. "I did not. There was no leak, General. You confirmed a … Well, a moment in Reverie concerning my own unborn when I knew I had conceived."

Cris quieted in his astonishment. Beyond the announcement of Lizabet's conception, to hear a Matron speak aloud, and so peacefully, of something mystical …

It truly isn't the Queendom of Innathi's Mother anymore.

"Though, if you are the sire —"

"I am the child's father, yes," he cut in, his irritation plain.

"I apologize, General, of course. Then with you as Ilharn once more, I suspect Innathi will give birth before I do. Though, we may have conceived at roughly the same time."

Cris's dark eyebrows lifted in astonishment, his defensiveness evaporating at the news. "Truly! Congratulations, Matron. Who is the sire?"

Lizabet showed her white, straight teeth in a beautiful smile. "Oh, you'll think me strange for this, perhaps, but I am not certain. The sire could be one of three. They all spilled in the right hole, sooner or later."

Another quiet, understated chuckle as he blushed in the sun.

"It was a long and intense evening," she explained. "But all that truly matters among Davrin for honor and property is who bears the child, Cris. Do remember that, even though you have a strange arrangement with our Queen which reflects more of your own culture."

"I remember," he answered. "And no insult intended, Matron. It is a common question to ask among Humans."

"So it is."

The elegant Matron-Warrior smiled peacefully at him, though any fighter worth his or her water would be able to see the ever-sharp focus of this Davrin. She had already raised three elite Blade Singers, and all knew she was hardest on her own children to excel. No doubt there was a future-fourth within her belly.

"She has not chosen a name?" Lizabet asked then, more as if to confirm this was the case, not a demand.

Cris shook his head. "We do not yet know if we have a daughter or another son."

Lizabet nodded. "Well. Let me know when she has. I would like to give mine a title linking the two. Having a name-twin between us will remind other Houses that D'Shauranti shall always stand with the Valsharess Au'renthia."

A deep flush filled his chest, rising to bring an instant of dizziness in his head. If the centuries of work he had done on behalf of V'Gedra had earned him this moment, with no aggrandizing and no manipulation, then Musanlo had truly rewarded him well.

A Davrin name-twin, in his bloodline, for two children conceived together! Rare among Davrin regardless, not only the timing but for two matas to want to be bound in such a way.

And here, in honor of what was to be his own second-born …

"Thank you, Warrior-Matron. May you live long and forever wise as you are now."

Lizabet smiled with more amusement than ever. "Your fast-blooming, energetic little half-blood may not wish me so after enough guidance. I've been waiting for you to ask me about beginning training for Leuren'qo."

CHAPTER 7

THE PALACE OF V'GEDRA – 190 B.S.E.

ISHUNA STOOD IN FRONT OF HER MIRROR, HER FAVORITE PENDANT GLINTING silver and purple in the candlelight. She had spent far too much time contemplating the laces supporting her breasts and wishing someone other than herself would tug at them, loosen her dress, and slip it down and off her body.

Dark and hot.

Her netherlips would be dewy inside her small silks. She could feel the heat, the tightness from secretly teasing herself beneath the royal dinner table all through the afternoon meal.

Why?

Perhaps it has just been too long for me, yet again.

A pity she had made no arrangements for a male servant to already be here, presenting himself to be ridden. Then again, even if it was her right and her usual method to relieve this feeling, the scenario didn't appeal to her right now.

She wanted something else but wasn't sure what.

The mirror in front of her shimmered as it had in her youth when she thought she saw spiderwebs that weren't truly there. The mystery cracks which had made the guards talk about her.

Tensing, she leaned forward to look closer. Being reminded of her darkest time following Koorul, before Houda had arrived to help, strengthened Ishuna's resolve to peer unflinchingly at the void.

Denying my visions is not required of me anymore.

The flash of events was abrupt and violent, as her visions sometimes were, as she had long accepted.

Still, she was shocked.

Ishuna stared at her own face: wide-eyed, tear-streaked and open-mouthed. Naked and kneeling. Bracing herself.

Gripping Desert stone which scrapes my palms and knees.

Something black, amorphous, clung to her hips and squatted between her open legs. Based on her own movements, particularly her jarred, swinging breasts, because she could not identify the shape behind her, Ishuna must think that it was ...

Rutting me.

It humped her in a way Innathi had hinted before, in how she allowed Cris to mount her from behind like the breeding stallion he was. Sometimes, with her permission, the Zauyrian bred the wrong hole, stretching her purple pucker instead of her netherlips.

Which she assures is worth it.

In the mirror, it appeared Ishuna had granted similar permission.

With ecstasy.

I've ... I've never done that before ... Will I soon?

A phantom tongue tickled in between her cheeks. Beneath her dress. Probing.

Testing.

The Royal Seer leaned back, and the vision vanished.

She stood alone in the room *and* in the mirror, fully dressed and breathing harder. That sight had not thrown a cold pitcher of water on her persistent arousal, to her surprise. She remained hot between her thighs and ready for an opportunity to strike.

That was the problem, however. Opportunities to her liking had always come rarely, and none had ever matched the late Ruler of the Third Realm. Ishuna did not seek out lovers at the Palace of V'Gedra. By now, everyone knew that.

Nor had she ever taken such a submissive position beneath a male.

To take his staff up my … ? Disgusting.

With a sigh, Ishuna turned around, meeting the rest of her chambers with her own eyes rather than a reflection.

Even if she might get a Noble suitor naked and flat on his back, the Queen's Sister trusted that none of these buas professed "affections" were genuine. They only wanted to get near her to get nearer to the Queen's ear …

Or to the Queen's children, for a number of reasons.

Leuren'qo was safer now from Palace intrigue because he was gone much of the time. So strange how the First Son was nearly grown when he should still be a child playing, but Leur's namesake would not be still.

Already he had pushed hard to stay in longer and longer training missions with the D'Shauranti fighting force. The half-blood bua was exactly as proud and as hot-headed as his Father. Ishuna felt she hardly knew the bua, despite him being the first out of the womb.

Hmph. At least Leuren'qo possesses visible sign of his Mother's grace.

Less could be said for Matalai and Phaere, the next two siblings, who moved more like Humans. In the third birth, Innathi had finally received her daughter.

Except that shouldn't matter.

Phaere would never be the accepted Heir of the Queendom.

This constant thought of children wouldn't stop any time soon, however. Now, earlier this afternoon, Innathi had confided in her yet again. *Yet again.*

Another child was growing in her womb.

The fourth in only five decades.

This is far too fast, it would sap her sister's strength! Just how many children did the Queen and her General intend to have? Was it happening by accident, beyond her control? Do they try nothing to prevent offspring from coming so close together?

If it's a cait, I must persuade Innathi again, to ***not*** *name her after me.*

This was part of her arousal and loneliness tonight, she knew. Ishuna *still* overheard Innathi with Cris coupling on occasion, or sometimes she spied on them when they weren't careful enough.

As happened this afternoon.

The Sorcerer-General had serviced Innathi again not even an hour after the Queen had told her about the new child. Ishuna gone to search for them, for they were late for the family meal, and had caught them fucking like their passion was undiminished despite decades. Her older sister seemed to get so much pleasure from the Human sorcerer's rough and desperate rutting.

That had never changed.

Ishuna had known exactly what that secretive little smirk on Innathi's face at dinner had been about when she had winked at her husband. The Queen would not have had time to clean up, so her cunt would still be full of his seed.

Or her netherhole, perhaps.

The Seer growled at herself as thoughts blended together to leave her aching — spying on her sister with herself kneeling to be plundered anew by some dark shadow. Her own slit's wetness seeped a little more into her small clothes.

A good thing Innathi's presence had grown so powerful in public before the Court. They had watched her belly swell three times now, and she had ruled even stricter than her Thousand-Year Mother at times to suppress the growing protest.

Regularly, she drew out the black blade, Soul Drinker, more often now than at the start of her marriage, to execute troublemakers in public. That weapon — alongside the screams of agonized terror it pulled from its victims for a blade so small — was gaining a fabled reputation of its own.

Ishuna had helped pull a few of those conspirators into the light by using her visions, but she didn't feel as exalted as Innathi in their success.

Perhaps because they don't seem as clear as before.

The Royal Seer hadn't been as *sure* in her accusations. Not that she dared to show doubt when an example must be made to the public regardless. On that account, Ishuna hadn't demanded the attention for her part in the peacekeeping; fewer spoke about her in the hushed gossip than before.

Soul Drinker and Innathi seemed content to capture the imagination and the respect, and Ishuna let them have it. Innathi would need it, with her belly about to swell a fourth time.

Turning back to the mirror, Ishuna pulled impatiently at her own dress, spreading her feet a bit apart as she anticipated bending over her vanity. Soon she would be watching her hand thrust against her sex, her naked, jiggling breasts in the reflection.

Yes.

Her chest only just exposed to the warm summer air, the Seer breathed in relief and excitement, smoothing her fingers down her flat, childless belly to slip beneath the silk covering her mound—

"Aunt Ishuna!"

Cursing, the Seer jumped straight again and yanked her dress closed, listening to Xala try to physically block the insolent child from simply diving between her legs for the door handle.

"No. You can't go in unannounced, Phaere."

"Let me see her, you old witch! Aunt Ishuna, can you hear me?"

"Lower your voice, child, your Mother wouldn't approve."

"So what?! This is important! Aunt Ishuna! You can hear me, I know you're in there!"

Dear Goddesses, she's just like Innathi at that age.

Just *which* age that was, however, was a bit harder to determine in the half-breed. Phaere was growing just as fast as her brothers.

Ishuna sighed, tightening up her laces and resentfully adjusting her skirts. The damp spot in her undersilk was going to be unpleasant for a while.

The Royal Seer opened the door and stood in the doorway, staring down at her dirty blonde-haired niece, who at least stopped harassing Xala and stared up at her with odd, orange eyes and an excited grin.

"You've got to come and see, Aunt Ishuna! The Blade Singers of Deesheraunty are giving a show! Mother wanted me to come get you since you left dinner too early."

There was a reason. But she forced a smile. "Very well. Go back and tell her I shall be coming soon."

"No! I'm supposed to come with you. Mother knows you're just going to hide in here. She says you're in that mood again."

Braqth damn …

"Fine." Ishuna stepped out with the other two making room and closed and locked her door behind her. She gestured irritably to both subordinates. "Let's go watch a show."

ISHUNA COULD SEE WHY SHE'D BEEN REQUIRED TO COME SIT WITH INNATHI, Cris-ri-phon, the children, and the councilors. She even spied the Court Deathwalker present as well. Not Taib, as he had grown older or moved on, as his kind tended to do.

A female this time. Ishuna half-recalled her name was …

Gresha, I think? Bah.

An array of Nobles had come to the Grand Courtyard from around V'Gedra and the surrounding Houses. Everything was set for a party that would last through the dark of the night.

Rather like Cris-ri-phon's wedding to Innathi.

Did I miss something?

Obviously, she had.

"Happy Fiftieth Anniversary, my Wife," Cris-ri-phon announced, surprising many Elves but pleasing just as many Humans to applaud. "It has been my honor and my joy to serve and grow your Queendom's power. Here's to the next half of the century and our union!"

Fifty. Ishuna tried to think why that number was important to a Zauyrian man, because it certainly wasn't to the Davrin, but she let it go to watch events unfolding.

The Valsharess sat proudly, accepting the kiss and further ceremony before getting to the surprise her Sorcerer-General had prepared with astonishing secrecy. Apparently, it had involved Matron Lizabet D'Shauranti and even a contingent of House Ja'Prohn.

Knowing some of what the Blade Singers could do even when they *weren't* attacking an enemy, Ishuna could guess it a good choice to wait until full dark beneath the stars, after the moons had begun to set. She began to anticipate something beautiful indeed as she was handed a fermented drink, tested by Xala, which she sipped to relax and enjoy.

The massive salute not only to the Queen but to the entire Court began a practiced display of V'Gedra's magical and military might.

The colorful lights, the flashing arcs of blades, and the song of the warriors' magic harmonized to fill the night. The demonstration held her and the entire Court in awe of their skill and admiration for their discipline and devotion to a difficult art.

This was one reason Queen Yivon's hostile little tricks and hidden plays wouldn't work. Because no one would break this army with elites like these to inspire them on the field!

The mood of the Grand Courtyard readily swept out into broader celebration, the guest eager for the release of daytime worries. After the final blade had been put away, after the gracious thanks and grand words of power exchanged, after children had been collected to be put away for the night, Ishuna breathed out and became aware of the fact that her crotch was *still* damp.

The performance and the strong, tangy beverages had done nothing to cool her down this warm night, but at last, all the pure Davrin, all the Wilder blend-skins, and the smattering of Human guests were formally encouraged by their Queen to enjoy the festivities, food, and drink for the rest of the night.

They were all invited, including the Blade Singers themselves.

Hm. I wonder if any present would be submissive before the Seer? she wondered with a smirk. *Maybe I could persuade a warrior to come to my room … or Xala could find one. She knows some of them …*

Such tactics had worked well enough before, including the original eve this "anniversary" was supposed to commemorate.

Ishuna shuddered first to recall how shaken she'd been after confronting Lord Indrath Rousse, squirming a little to remember how Xala had described her.

"You aren't acting yourself."

Hadn't she? After she'd nearly smothered that guard ...

That bua from House D'Shauranti.

She couldn't remember his name now; her memory was too fuzzy with drink. She and Xala hadn't talked about that night in years, but at least Ishuna had gotten better about not snagging random Guardsvrin in the hall who turned out to be a Matron's cousin.

Still. The solitary Seer knew she had a reputation among the servants for being — *Well ...*

Forceful. Frightening.

Demanding. Needy.

Callous.

All those things she had hated about Cris-ri-phon back at Koorul. All those words she'd flung at the Lord of the North on Innathi's wedding day. All those words the servants had whispered about her, sooner or later.

When had that changed? Why had it become her habit to force others to take after Leur?

Perhaps because of her habit of waiting too long between spells, until she simply *needed* to touch someone, to send herself high, to keep herself *sane* and there was no time to seduce.

Yet the idea of coaxing them slowly, of keeping them around to annoy her when they were required to obey her anyway ... She had no yearning, no patience for that. She didn't see the point of trying unless the object of her desires was of higher status.

Ishuna had slid down into her chair, on the border of a sulk, but blinked at movement getting closer. She looked again.

A Blade Singer approached her.

No. No, he's ...

Xala straightened and took a step closer. He was indeed approaching, and he bowed to them.

"Royal Seer. Good eve, *viirclad.*"

Ishuna stared at him. He was younger than her, but not *too* young. He was in fine shape with an attractive form, clearly a warrior who had worked hard for decades. He possessed the signature blades of his trade as well as the dress uniform, and … he …

He seems familiar.

The Blade Singer grinned broadly, chuckling with a shake of his head. "You do not remember me, do you, Seer?" He glanced up at her bodyguard. "She does, though. Right, Captain?"

"*Qobor*," Xala responded, calling out a mid-ranked Blade Singer for Ishuna's muddled brain to filter through. "Yes. I remember you, *Qobor* Szoroan. How is your Mother, Lady Ruthrea?"

Ishuna's elbow slipped from the arm of her chair as she felt that icy cold splash clearing her fuzzy memory. Her eyes seized on his face.

*Oh yes, his **face** … !*

She had covered that young face with her slippery snatch, hardly allowing him to breathe as she made herself climax on his nose and tongue. Xala had held him down on her bed at first; later Ishuna had played with his cock until he came in her mouth.

Fifty years ago, tonight. I was just thinking of this.

"Yes, how is your Mother?" Ishuna straightened in her chair and tried to inject some bit of confidence, so abruptly confronted by the first servant she'd mishandled.

Although, it was clear Szoroan was no Palace servant now. He could be called to duty by his Queen, his Matron, and the Sorcerer-General, or any of his ranking officers and instructors, but that was not the same as before. *Nowhere near.*

Even as the Queen's Sister, Ishuna ironically had no authority over him without risking much more insult to his connections than she had the first time. The young fighter knew this, it was obvious, because the brat in him clearly *enjoyed* the horridly awkward conversation which followed.

He made it stretch on for a subjectively lengthy half an hour … .

"Look, Szoroan," Ishuna sighed finally, glancing around to see if anyone paid attention. No one obvious. She looked back at him. "Can I do something for you?"

The young mage shrugged. "You seemed lonely sitting here, Ishuna.

I thought I would alleviate some of your embarrassm[...] pretending to be interested in spending time with you."

The Seer frowned at him. "Careful, *Qobor*. You may h[...] too much, if you speak too freely."

"I haven't imbibed at all, Seer. I know what I say." He s[...] they flirt, it's to get close to the Queen or the General, isn't it? [...] because they genuinely want to be around you, strange *qu'essan*[...] understand better than most why they're right."

Ishuna shot to her feet hearing her own thoughts echoed back her, but she found her own sharp words caught in her throat. Abruptl[...] dizzy, she needed Xala to reach out and steady her.

"Enough," her bodyguard warned in her level voice. "Go elsewher[...] Blade Singer."

The bua didn't appear at all afraid of upsetting them, not as he *shou*[...] be. "I speak the truth as she knows it, Captain. And I've decided y[...] could have acted with better honor."

Xala smirked. "Exiles learn to bend a bit outside those formal limi[...] *Qobor*. What do you want, other than to give the Royal Seer a right[...] piece of your mind?"

"Rightful?"

"I'll give you that I agree with all you just said. It changes nothi[...] in the past, but it did not happen again."

His eyebrows lifted.

"Is that it?" asked Xala. "Are you finished?"

Szoroan shook his head in the negative. "I am not. Thank y[...] Captain, but there is one more thing. I said I was pretending to[...] interested, but I was lying."

He paused to let that sink in.

"I can smell her small clothes again. She's soaked through the sil[...]

What? Ishuna tensed as he focused on her.

"I can help scratch the itch, Seer, if you'd like." Slowly, he smirk[...] "But with a few different rules than last time."

She sensed her bodyguard's disapproval before she'd quite made[...] her mind how insulted she should be.

"I think you should refuse, *qu'essan*," Xala said with her arms crossed. "He's got his apology. He wants something else."

Her childhood guard was right, of course, and it was refreshing how the two of them spoke so plainly to each other around her. The manipulation was even obvious to her. Ishuna *should* refuse him and return to her quarters, this moment. The party would run by itself.

She was just about to say and do exactly this when Szoroan smiled at her as no bua or man ever really had — a bit like Cris smiled at Innathi. He inhaled deeply to remind her that he "knew" her scent. With his hands open and at his sides, the Blade Singer shifted his stance enough to draw her eyes down to the crotch of his dark blue dress pants. She could see his erection outlined beneath them.

Well. He either wants a revenge fuck for half a century ago, or he genuinely wants ***me*** *to fuck* ***him*** *another time.*

Either way, it wasn't *just* a trick. He was hard.

So, he doesn't find me … ?

Disgusting.

Her arousal was there, and it wasn't fading away. It had been hours Ishuna had been waiting, distracted, and her only choices tonight were to force another resentful servant, or …

Or take a significant risk with this Blade Singer.

I cannot believe what you're going to say.

"What different rules from last time?" she asked him.

CHAPTER 8

XALA WAS DEEPLY UNHAPPY WITH THE ARRANGEMENT, SHOWING IT IN HER aura as it pushed out and popped in her beautiful, powerful spread of reds, blues, and yellows.

She scowled at Szoroan, her arms crossed once more over her chest. "You go back on your word, Blade Singer, and I will kill you. Painfully."

"You need not worry, *viirclad.* I shall abide by the rules agreed. This is to make them clear to Ishuna, so she won't have a chance to back on them."

"You dare say that about the Queen's Sister?"

He sighed, testing the strength of his knot. "Come on, Xala, you've seen even more of her in how she takes from others than I have. And she's intoxicated. Stop lying to yourself that she plays above the table."

"Someone needs to knock you down a few notches, bua."

"If you can wait until *after* Ishuna gets what she needs, you're welcome to try, exile."

"What are you up to?"

"Exactly what I've said. I'm going to free up a few dams inside the *qu'essan* at her request."

Ishuna listened to them bickering, but she was staring at the newly tightened ropes around her wrists. With hands now bound together, she lay stretched lengthwise and belly-down along a horse's hitching post inside the royal stables. The height was just low enough to keep the toes of her slippers touching the hard-packed dirt, but only one side or the other at a time.

At least the post was wide enough for most of her torso.

I cannot believe I'm doing this ...

The unusual confidence of this bua whom she'd molested decades ago intrigued her despite herself and her preferences.

Szoroan had caught her at just the right moment, when she was bored with her usual methods, tired of being alone in her room, left to touch herself. Perhaps he had cared to find out more about her or had cast a spell that gave him insight into her drunken thoughts just then, and he jumped on the opportunity.

An opportunity she hadn't expected to have tonight.

Yet still, here she was, tied down and bent over in ready willingness to allow this young Blade Singer a rut on her haunches like a stallion on a mare in heat.

Szoroan hadn't made her strip, however, and she wouldn't have agreed to *that* level of humiliation. She was still dressed as she lay along the level, wooden post with her spider pendant hanging off her neck in front of her. The stable smelled of more horses than usual with the heavier guest list of tonight, and the beasts whickered and burred softly, reassuringly calm as Ishuna stepped well outside of her most comfortable habits.

How had he so quickly gotten under my skin? He can say anything and I ... I ... don't strike him back into his place.

The fear wasn't chilling her, nor was rage simmering, nor the rigid urge to seize control. Xala was here to protect her, and Szoroan had told her, once they were away from the party, what he wanted. Without the usual Court speak or hinting understatements. Straight and simple.

He wanted his control back.

"It'll get this weight off my chest," he'd said in private before coaxing her to the stables. "I don't *want* to resent you, Ishuna, it takes too much energy, and I need that for Blade Song. I'm tired of thinking I can plan anything subtle or surprising that would get through all your barriers and wouldn't only end up worse for me."

"So, you … want to fuck me back," she slurred.

"Correct, *qu'essan*. I don't want to kill you, I don't want to wound you, poison you, nothing. You're the Royal Seer, the Queen's Sister, you're untouchable, and you'll keep doing what you want to servants. You'll keep living. But … I *do* want to fuck your cunt in exchange for using it to nearly suffocate me, then just throwing me out like a used towel."

They had stared at each other, silent for long moments, when Ishuna touched the familiar spot in her middle. It felt … softer. Not broken, just softer.

She quivered.

Penance. Give back what you've taken. Let me heal, and you'll not lose something equally precious while you have the opportunity.

Between them, Ishuna blinked first. She wasn't sure who had spoken, if it was him or just more random thoughts passing through her strange head.

You aren't that powerful, she sneered.

He blinked normally, like he hadn't heard her.

Such opportunities were rare enough as it was, and so she had agreed. Then, Xala and Szoroan had agreed on terms to assure her personal safety.

The *Qobor* promised, "I will do nothing she won't fully heal from after a natural sleep. I want to fuck her, and she'll get that good, hard rut she wants. But it must be done my way, to assure I won't be used like before."

So be it.

Xala stood aside, having sworn to Ishuna not to interfere if there were no weapons near and no threat of marks laid on her *qu'essan*.

With that matter settled, and once Ishuna was tied down and in position, Szoroan did not hesitate to begin. Ishuna felt his palms sliding up from her ankles over her calves, caressing the backs of her thighs as he lifted her dark purple dress at the same time to expose her.

His hands squeezed her buttocks through her small silks and tugged the sheer, pale blue material up tight against her crotch, the seat sliding and bunching into the crack of her ass. Ishuna grunted as Szoroan touched her pouty, oozing lips through the tight fabric, felt her face flush hot to know how it must look.

"I can see your cleft through this," he snickered. "Clear as day. You've made it that sodden!"

He could taunt her for quite some time, given the position in which she'd placed herself.

"Will you play until someone interrupts?" Ishuna muttered in familiar derision, frowning at the floor. "They might take away your 'revenge,' Szoroan."

"Good point. Although I'd think that would be much more humiliating for you since your bodyguard is just standing there allowing this. But yes, let's move on."

The young Blade Singer clawed at the edge of her small clothes and started dragging them down. She felt the sodden silk peeling off her crotch, but their descent stopped at mid-thigh, where he squeezed her with his hands, humming with surprising eagerness.

Is he crouching — ?

Ishuna gasped when his tongue lapped gently at her naked netherlips, the tip nudging between them to taste her cunt directly. She sucked in her breath as relief spread through her groin and abdomen.

"Ohhh," she moaned, pulling against the ropes as she shifted her hips back toward him—

But he pulled back.

"No," she whined.

"Shhh," Szoroan hushed with another snicker, prying her buttocks apart with his thumbs. "Someone will hear you."

Oh, goddess, is he — ?!

His tongue darted between her cheeks, teasing her puckered back hole as the deft tip swirled it around.

"AH!" Ishuna cried loudly.

The Blade Singer stopped immediately, pulling her small clothes off her feet and stepping up to her head.

"I'd think no one ever rimmed your well before," he remarked, enjoying her pathetic attempt to dodge as he pressed her cunt-smeared silks up against her nose and mouth, rubbing it in. "Come on, lick it, enjoy it, then open that mouth. You're being too loud."

"MMmmm!" she protested, but the fighter pinched the side of her breast, stuffing the fragrant wad in the moment she yelped, then covering her mouth with his hand so she couldn't spit them out.

He was grinning as he had been when she first saw him tonight in the Courtyard, enjoying her awkwardness and humiliation. "You still can't control yourself, Ishuna. But I can, now."

Xala took a step forward at the threatening tone, and Szoroan lifted a finger from his free hand toward her. His voice was firm.

"No weapons, no marks. Penetration only, and no more than an hour while you keep watch. Sound familiar? We agreed, Xala. 'Weapons' includes my hands striking her, or a rider's whip I'd *like* to use, though you could agree she deserves both and could handle a lot more."

Ishuna noted that Xala stepped back without a word. Certainly, without dissent. Szoroan's hand still covered her lips, keeping her mouth full of female-stained silk. After he was certain they could continue, the bua tugged off her own decorative sash from around her waist and used it to tie across the wad in her mouth, securing it behind her head and assuring she couldn't spit out the gag.

"There. Much quieter."

As he stepped around behind her, Ishuna heard him shifting his own clothing, no doubt preparing to expose himself. She looked down at the wood, eyes going blank for a second as she stared at her necklace, recalling the strange glimpse in her mirror earlier.

Of herself on all fours, naked, being urgently rutted by something inky black behind her ... impaling her in between her cheeks.

Is this it? Is it now?

Oh, I'm afraid not, Ishuna. This will be much more pleasant by comparison.

Who — ?!

Two fingers instead of a penis pushed inside her. She groaned through her gag as Szoroan explored a bit, wetting himself up. He found the hard spot behind her bladder as easily as if he was a trained consort now, quite a difference from the first time. He started rubbing firmly without more foreplay, but Ishuna didn't care as sensations bloomed at once.

Oh, she was ready! *Beyond ready!*

The pleasure grew even better as the Blade Singer added light rubbing on her turgid, external nub as well.

Ohhh, Goddess!

Hard and firm with one hand, delicate and light with the other. Only a Blade Singer would grasp that kind of training.

Szoroan chuckled as she parted her legs for him in response but focused solely on making her climax.

As she'd wanted to do all evening.

It didn't take long.

"*MMM*mmmrff … ! Mmf-mf! *Mmf!*"

The Seer grunted and thrashed, fortunately didn't upend herself and spill off the side of the post. Her dark legs trembled, extended and quivering, as no doubt Szoroan had just won a couple of extra tolerances from Xala for making sure her *qu'essan* came first.

Ishuna breathed desperately through her nose, drool soaking into her gag as she enjoyed the afterglow. The next moment, Szoroan stepped up close behind her, wet fingers gripping her hips tightly.

Good Seer. Now uphold your end of the bargain.

Without tease or ceremony, the Blade Singer pushed the blunt tip of his erection in between her netherlips. In two short thrusts, he had his cock hilted.

Yes!

Szoroan held still then; he didn't move or speak.

Looking at Xala didn't give Ishuna any hint what the young fighter was doing, if anything. She could only become aware of how her soggy cunt settled down welcomingly around the bua's staff, inviting more movement with small, regular clutches and little wriggles.

Her cunt was meekly, silently begging him to rut her. Her cheeks flushed as she heard another voice, different from the first.

Thiss issn't your temperament, Qu'essan.

Derisive. Disappointed.

This iss unussual for you . . . .

Yes. She knew it was wrong. *Unfamiliar ...*

"My Lord, this feels good," Szoroan whispered in awe, drawing himself out smooth and straight before plunging in once again. "Oh, yes! *Uh!*"

Ishuna whimpered as a tiny, fluttering climax crackled through her. *Oh! Oh ... !*

"I wouldn't have thought you'd have such a yielding, juicy cunt, Seer. She who won't trust *anyone* to truly *touch* her ..."

He rammed in, and her sex fluttered, caressing him as, once again, he withdrew and pushed in full length, fucking her thrice before holding flush against her, watching her body jerk in a series of small, continuous orgasms. She sprayed spittle from her gag.

Something'sss wrong.

What was happening to her?

He leaned down to whisper in her ear. "Well, Seer, *I* will truly touch you. I've been shown how. And you *will* open to me. You agreed. Penance for what you've done."

Noooo! You're in dannngerrr. Fffight! Ffffight baaack!

Ishuna shook her head, growing dizzy but trying to clear it, her muffled noises barely carrying. She turned her head toward Xala, moaning and shaking her head, trying to communicate.

Help! Xala, stop him!

Szoroan fucked her too gently to alarm her bodyguard, especially as she kept achieving her own pleasure, toes curling as her sex squished wetly around her own impalement. The bua savored her slick grip on his rod, pulling out all the way before gliding effortlessly back in. He squeezed her ass appreciatively, played with her asshole, pushing a finger in, and made her squirm.

It must look like they were playing.

Soon, he added a second finger and held her open as his cock enjoyed her royal slit, drooling and engorged, welcoming him despite the fear crushing her chest.

Xala couldn't tell; she wouldn't interfere! Ishuna herself could barely justify why her own heart raced inside her!

Sssomething'sss wwwrong … !

Sh-she doesn't realize! Help! Someone!

Szoroan's aura had long since found that soft spot within her own; she'd shown it to him. As she had allowed him to play physically deep inside her body, now … Now he penetrated her *aura.*

L-like Cris-ri-phon at Koorul!

He was forcing his essence inside!

Wrong, Szoroan answered, sounding in a trance, not entirely himself. **Not like the Godblood. Not forcing. We are Elves, Ishuna. We are* meant *to merge with each other. And, for all of our sakes, I have worked to make myself merge with yours, despite my past revulsion.**

He touchesss it!

Now … Feel me, qu'essan … Feel me.

No!

Goddess, she was afraid!

He touchesss it! Nooo, it'sss oursss!

Long familiar voices were screaming at her inside her head, telling her how foolish and *stupid* she was to have allowed herself to get in this position.

All the while Ishuna moaned with ecstatic dismay as she felt her reopened wound truly meld within Szoroan's aura. This meant she was truly *open.* At the height of her fertility …

Waiting to catch when the Blade Singer climaxed inside her.

As he most certainly would.

"Aaahhh, Ishuna … yes. Oh, yes!"

Oh, Goddess, don't!

Szoroan did not pound her viciously the way Cris would Innathi just before he came. The Davrin bua took her sopping, mewling cunt as deep and full as he could. Then he held still, cock pressed in to the root, two fingers still buried in her ass.

She twitched, coming yet again, rippling around him as he released his seed in a flourish of blissful release. Ishuna endured a swarm of colors and sensation, unsure how long it may take for him to pull out, for his semen to drip shamefully out from between her netherlips.

When he stopped grunting, she waited for him to taunt her, to disentangle from her now that he'd gotten his revenge.

No, she realized with a chill. *He's not pulling out.*

Because he was not done.

Szoroan remained merged with her, in body and in magic, and once she stopped screaming in denial, she felt him ... She could *hear* the tenor of his mood, and it wasn't as hateful as she expected. Not as loathsome as she deserved.

There was pleasure, satisfaction. Sadism ... but with belief.

He believed.

I must. I must make sure, Ishuna ... This will save you. It will save all of us in the end.

Szoroan retained his erection through his rebound period without withdrawing. Slowly, he added a third finger into her resisting pucker to share with the other two, and she whimpered as the intensity began to rise again. She had no choice but to yield to that, too.

He started fucking her again as if he had only taken a breather the first time. Xala might not have been impressed by that, but he'd already deposited his first offering inside Ishuna, and was stirring it around as her wet slit sucked and slopped around him.

She writhed, unintentionally giving him a tighter fit as his aura stayed clamped around hers, seeking to coax a powerful surge together, one more time.

To anyone looking — certainly to her bodyguard — Ishuna was participating. She was enjoying it.

Yet something *else* howled and shrieked inside her, pushing back at the way the bua sought to flood her, to overwhelm the other voices.

Filling both her holes, pressing on her lower back with his free hand, Szoroan even somehow fit a fourth finger. The intense, deliberate pressure stretching her netherhole made her wail against her gag. Part of her realized he focused his magic between three points, in a similar way that Leur had two centuries ago, seeking to overwhelm her shrieking aura-pain with pleasure.

Except this conspiring Blade Singer wasn't trying to heal her. He couldn't, she was too strong now.

He only wanted something very, very specific.

It'll work this time, she sensed in a panic. *It will happen! You'll leave me pregnant! Th-that wasn't in the agreement!*

★It was. You just didn't notice it … ★

Szoroan groaned then, announcing his second climax. As his will pulled hers taut and close to listen to him, he forced his voice through the maelstrom of denial and Abyssal curses, insisting that she hear that *one, last* moment of the Elves' deepest, mystical connection.

Ishuna heard him when she climaxed with him.

And they conceived.

★Survival is always in the rules, Ishuna. It's either this now, or what you saw in the mirror during your sister's fourth birthing. We give you more time to hear your song and turn the storm.★

For now, the shrieks had calmed. Ishuna caught her breath, on the verge of weeping.

★Remember what Jennyn told you fifty years ago.★

She nodded as Szoroan pulled his spent cock from her body.

Seek …

Seek what you miss most.

CHAPTER 9

THE MORNING AFTER THE QUEEN'S ANNIVERSARY, ISHUNA HAD KEPT HER room dark and lay in her bed, speaking only to Xala. Her excuse was that she had drunk too much and felt ill, and her bodyguard was able to reassure everyone it was not poison.

Even though, in a way, it had been.

"He's gone, *qu'essan,*" Xala informed her when she asked. "I cannot find him."

"No one knows you were looking?"

"No, *qu'essan.*" She paused. "Did he hurt you, then? I thought … you seemed to be feeling pleasure, Seer."

She had been. So *much* pleasure, and her face burned with shame recalling it. The gag had prevented an impulsive cry to stop, but now she couldn't follow either event beyond this for long enough to decide which way she had wanted it to go.

Szoroan might not have been the only male present.

He *was there … wasn't he?*

But if he had been, no one would believe her now.

Xala's tentative probe ended with a strange, resigned reassurance.

Later, they learned the Blade Singer had done the smart thing and left House D'Shauranti the next morning, probably with part of the army. At least his impertinence and arrogance would not be on public display here at Court. Whatever game he'd started, he was done and would not hang around to engage again.

At the same time, there was no assurance he would not speak to others later of what happened in the stable.

"If he does, you can have him stand before Innathi for slander," Xala reassured her.

Ishuna scoffed. *Slander.*

As if that would help when her belly began to show. Quite reasonably, she should have been trying to quietly get an expulsion vial into her hands as soon as possible.

How dare he? How dare he force such a thing on me?! It's wrong, I shouldn't have to deal with this!

The law was clear as well, and she was in the right.

Though some bua mages, like Szoroan, understood how to use their auras to override a matron's desire *not* to breed, few ever risked it. The punishment was death if a confirmed carrying mata wished to make it public, and she'd just shed his efforts anyway. The mere accusation and a statement that she did not want the pregnancy was enough.

The law always favored the wronged female. *Always.*

But sometimes the hard part was "making it public."

A normal and sane bua would be certain of her consent to conceive; he *had* to be. His own life depended on it! Given how few times this ever "came out" as having happened ... could the Queen's sister admit to such a thing?

No. For a female of such rank to accuse a middling Noble who had earned skill as a competent Blade Singer, the gap in their social status made it much worse for Ishuna in V'Gedra.

Szoroan would die but she would still live, and then she would be asked, "Will you keep the child, Royal Seer?"

I don't know.

This was where she was stuck. Frozen in place, sinking in the sand.

Especially if that Lord was behind it.

Females near her rank probably just aborted and pretended it never occurred. Easier to have the offending bua killed by an assassin outside of the public eye and be done with it.

But if she rejected all of it, handled this on her own, would *he* just try again later with a different bua?

The Lord of the north had already waited fifty years to trap her.

And her sister was too busy to notice.

Ishuna could never open up like that again. Not for *anyone*. She knew better than to take a risk and be so seduced again.

Never again! I cannot stand it!!

All males were unworthy beasts, and when they gained enough power, turned into arrogant abusers like Lord Rousse and Cris-ri-phon.

If that was so, she may never become pregnant again.

This could be my one chance.

This fear of their bloodline being corrupted before her eyes, backed by the haunting warning in the moment she conceived, as Szoroan's aura and magic had invaded her, held her *and* her body open and exposed.

We give you more time to hear your song and turn the storm.

Either this now, or what I saw in the mirror at Innathi's next birthing … ?

Ishuna was still curled up on her bed the next morning. Over and over, she smothered whimpers of terror.

What if Innathi bears nothing but half-breeds? What if she dies early before having a pureblood heir? She is making so many enemies … I-I s-saw something like this … the scorpion in the dreams, the General's war symbol! He's still not done with us!

If Innathi died in such a way — and she very well may, the consequence of ignoring Ishuna's most earnest warning — then this brand-new unborn inside her could be the *only* true royal Heir to survive the fall of the Virgin Queen Innathi.

Szoroan was a monstrous traitor, but he was at least Davrin.

And a Blade Singer.

In V'Gedra, only the Mother truly mattered.

If it is a daughter … For the sake of the entire Queendom, I can't end her.

Instead, Ishuna could make plans for the Queendom after her vision came to pass …

For when we lose Innathi to that dagger, when it turns on her, I shall truly be needed then.

Ishuna exhaled at a point on that second day when her niece and her sister were asking after her at the door.

Saying they were becoming worried.

I must get up now. I must show myself.

And … if I am to keep this heir, I cannot stay in the Capital for long.

"ISHUNA? TELL ME TRUE. WHY NOW?"

Innathi had her arms crossed. She was frowning at her sister in the library. "Why go searching for him now?"

"I have found clues over the years," Ishuna explained. "Have you not heard of this 'Spire of Flame' somewhere in the deep Desert?"

"Mirages," Innathi insisted. "It's always on a different place on any map, and on none of the vetted ones. You would go chasing after rumors in the deep Desert? That is dangerous, Ishuna!"

"I will have Xala's expertise."

"But what if we need you here? We'll be without your visions."

The Royal Seer pursed her lips. "I haven't seen anything truly useful to you in years, my Queen. Not such as what aided us in your earliest reign. You've been gracious sparing my reputation any close analysis, but it is dwindling. We both know this. I … I believe something is blocking those visions now. My … quest is as much for me as a mystic as it is for a daughter."

Her Sister-Queen scowled even harder — clear resentment and jealousy passing across her face — and Ishuna looked away first. She glanced down at Innathi's middle, still flat for the moment but she could see the new magical aura.

Then she looked at the black dagger always at the Queen's side, reminding herself why she had to do this.

"I forbid it, Seer," Innathi said. "You may not leave on such a foolhardy 'quest.' "

Ishuna sighed and prepared herself for another long fight.

It proved of the kind they hadn't had since the night before Innathi's wedding.

I will not stay.

ISHUNA AND XALA MADE IT OUT OF V'GEDRA AND SURROUNDING HOLDINGS before Innathi could find some way to cage them. Dressed plainly and riding in the dark, the two did not speak of anything beyond immediate needs where they could be easily recognized.

Once they were on the outskirts of the capital, her bodyguard looked at the empty horizon, at the moonlit dunes, shrubs, and dry rain beds, picking the subject of their first conversation.

"Cris-ri-phon was helpful," the elder commented.

... *You must be jesting.*

"He wanted me to leave," Ishuna muttered, drawing her hood up to better keep grit from flying against her cheeks.

"I don't think he did," Xala disagreed. "I saw real worry, *qu'essan*. But he *does* support your search for your sire, and persuaded his wife not to do anything rash to keep you. He provided us with a lot of items he could be using within his own forces."

"His forces take up plenty of the treasury's coffers, he could spare a few." Ishuna appraised the three rings on her fingers, the snug band, and the subtle, flat brooch attached to the inside of her right boot.

Xala noticed her taking stock. "All the sorcerous protections and magical assistance a lone searcher could want in the Desert, *qu'essan*. Magic to find and purify water, to resist heat, cold, and sandstorms, to stay true to our direction, to remain unseen, or evade hunters ... He has given us a real chance of success, despite your sister's anger with him. He wants you to live."

That was true.

Perhaps she and the Sorcerer-General had something in common: a strong drive for a pilgrimage, for a personal quest with uncertain outcomes.

They each heard a voice calling … A "song."

Since meeting Cris at Koorul, Innathi's own travels had rarely extended beyond the outer settlements on the fringe V'Gedra. She wouldn't understand. But maybe Xala was right, and the long-lived Human did.

Even if he also helped make things as they were.

Ishuna felt the rings around her fingers again, rubbing them with her thumb. *These items are probably the things he himself had needed or wished for when he was gone from V'Gedra all that time.*

As to where he'd been, he'd never said enough to satisfy her.

Cris-ri-phon must have met Lord Rousse at some point before he and Innathi invited him to conduct their wedding ceremony. Ishuna could only imagine such an opportunity occurring on that quest.

How long has he been waiting? What does he want?

The morning of the wedding had come full circle. She'd been abused in kind, in retribution for abusing the wrong servant.

But it had also spurred her to act.

She'd been hiding in V'Gedra so long, doing nothing, watching her power diminish. Now she felt the drive to change that. *At last.*

Szoroan had at least motivated her, doing what he did.

Perhaps this is what needed to happen.

If little else, she could be grateful the baby would be pure Davrin.

"Xala," she said abruptly. "The … .um. The true reason I left now, of all times … ?"

"Yes, qu'essan?"

Ishuna wrung the reins in her hands, staring at the horse's twitching ears. "I am with child."

Xala kept watch Nodding for her to continue.

"Szoroan," she said aloud.

Her bodyguard was quiet but not for *too* long. "I … thought it possible the next morning. Thank you for trusting me, your grace."

Trusting you … ? She forced a nervous laugh. "You will see her aura soon enough."

Her Captain sounded regretful. "Yes. But I am sorry I did not see what he was doing in time to stop it. Again."

Ishuna shook her head. "No! Do not think that! You did as I ordered you. No marks, no weapons, no interference. I agreed … y-you warned me, but I allowed myself to be bound. I-I was drunk, and I wanted his stupid bua cock, even as it came with his anger. And you *stayed* with me, Xala. As you've always done."

The elder swallowed. "And always will, *qu'essan*, even when I fail … if you'll still have me."

Ishuna's eyes were wide as she turned in her saddle. "I will! That's why you're here! I will *always* need you, Xala!"

Her childhood guardian nodded in thanks. "So, we will be out in the wilderness for two years at least. We will have time to plan."

Her heart pounded as relief flooded her limbs. Such simple acceptance between them. "Yes. Exactly."

"I will help you, *qu'essan*. I agree with your plan. The Queen and her Human Consort should not know about this child for now, and we will not wander aimlessly as your daughter grows."

CHAPTER 10

THE DESERT WILDERNESS – 189 B.S.E

THE FIRST YEAR WAS LONG FOR THE TWO SEARCHERS FROM V'GEDRA. THE pair marched endlessly south through the Red Desert, winding carefully through the Realms after leaving the Queendom. They stopped when necessary for food and supplies, always wearing magical disguises and prodding for more stories to lead the way toward the mystical Spire of Flame.

The scenery changed significantly from red dunes to craggy rock canyons to flat plains before rising to calmer foothills hiding surprising flushes of green around an oasis on occasion. Once-empty land became familiar, filled with birds, reptiles, and insects, with cacti and hearty shrubbery blooming after a brief rain, offering strong scents upon the wind.

Xala's skills and commanding instincts in between the settlements saved them from trouble more than once, as did her lengthy memory and understanding of the Zauyrian Realms as a patchwork of loosely co-operative, swiftly shifting Human "kingdoms" led by largely intellectual sorcerers.

Both understood well the cultures of the Third Realm having lived there for some time, but what works in one place would not necessarily work in another. Xala's mastery of their physical environment, of using all signs at her disposal to find the resources they needed while avoiding the worst threats, convinced the *qu'essan* she needed no one else on this journey with her.

Ishuna herself began dreaming again.

Her wanderings in Reverie flowed more freely out in the Desert than they had in decades sequestered in V'Gedra. Some of her visions were tangible warnings the same day that Xala would spy suspicious tracks or smoke. Others were symbolic imagery which encouraged them in one direction over another in their search for the Spire.

The animals in those latter visions were changing as well, shifting from spiders and scorpions to beetles, wrens, and snakes. Ishuna felt she could trust her own instincts more with each scalding day or chilly night.

"We're getting close," she murmured inside their day shelter, having woken from her Reverie just as the sun set in a maelstrom of colors streaking across the horizon.

"How close?" asked the warrior repairing a hole in a set of cactus harvest gloves.

"Before the next double-full moons. I saw a tall spire vanish as if it would flee but a wren flew around it. I called the bird back to us. It dropped a straw key in my hand. The left side of the moons weren't yet bright like the right."

Xala grunted and nodded. "We have two days' water and food at best and need to find more. I spotted *muekeet* thorns on one bush earlier, so we're entering toe-melting territory."

Thus, it had been like this much of the year. Xala did not tend to question the things Ishuna saw no matter how strange the description, though she always made the physical risks clear to her in return. After Szoroan and the stable, Ishuna did not question her, either.

They worked equally hard to feed and protect her child, and trust was a necessity, as well as a strange source of peace she'd never felt before.

With Xala there to witness it, Ishuna's private excitement had also grown with her small, tight belly and heavier breasts, even as hunger had been a constant irritation which seemed to be reaching a crescendo before leveling off. The Seer had enough of a bump to make it obvious if she disrobed, but Xala had told her it wouldn't grow larger for quite some time.

"Davrin babies are that way," said the Captain with a shrug. "Slow growth with huge hunger for the first year, then some time hovering while the aura strengthens. A mata only gets *really* heavy during the last few months while the infant puts on its final weight."

Ishuna nodded, seeing that in her mind. "Then we have more time."

This was nothing like Queen Innathi's swift, bulging pregnancies. If the sire had been Human, Ishuna would have been waddling at this point, soon ready to drop the child in the middle of nowhere!

Yet her body seemed stronger than ever before from enduring their travel, and it was a relief to hear the hunger would sap less of her strength while her daughter developed her magical gifts ahead of the tiny body.

Most importantly, Xala said it progressed normally. Her Captain had basic army and Palace experience and knew what to look for. She saw a normal, Davrin pregnancy with an ever-strengthening aura shining in her middle whenever she cared to look.

Ishuna felt proud. Sometimes, she would feel these soft, fluttering movements as her baby moved within her.

Perhaps dreaming as well.

Sooner or later, Mother and child would *share* a dream. One that would show something telling, something important about her child's future. Ishuna still waited for that, but she could be patient.

Instead of fretting over it, now was the perfect time for Ishuna to use her gifts to their fullest to find that evasive Spire.

Seek what you miss most.

Within a few weeks, they found a desert valley with a tiny stream trickling a winding path around smooth, nearly flat rocks of orange, pink, and yellow. Taller, green trees provided shade, and the season turned toward the Flowering. No tall spire stared them in the face, and yet Ishuna insisted they keep moving up and down this valley.

"I sense something here." The Seer peered up and around. "I dreamed of this place … This was it. Only the spire is missing."

One of Cris-ri-phon's rings — the one intended to help them hold a true direction — was tested strongly within the valley when it should not have been. Upon the hot salt flats or among the tallest dunes following a storm, it was possible to get turned around, lost until the stars above came out.

A valley, by comparison, should hold true to one path of the sun or moons. The same faces of cliffs and rock should bear witness to the same long shadows growing and retreating with each rise and set of the celestial bodies.

"What the fuck?" Xala muttered on their third night passing up the valley.

By now, they knew it took a night and a half to come to a wider mesa, possibly leading to the coast another week or so forward, and it took another night and a half to return to the entry point where they began.

"Well, at least that's consistent," Xala grumbled.

Without Human competitors to be found anywhere near, there was enough food and water for them and their horses. Pausing to hunt or gather wasn't a worrisome delay. Yet, even as they rested through the hottest part of the day, the sun seemed to be rising in different spots across the horizon, as if the valley turned with the wind, like a needle on an axis.

"It's here, I know it!" Ishuna said again, having started to smile and now unable to stop.

"If it is, it doesn't want to be found." Xala jerked her chin at the round, modest hills. "Those couldn't hide a spire like in the stories if it was bending over and ducking. Unless we're supposed to be looking for something a lot shorter? Or deeper?"

They tested two practical ideas the next night without bearing fruit. All the while, Ishuna pondered her dream.

The discovery had happened at night. The moons had been visible, but … The bird had been a day-song bird, and the shadow of the Spire cut deeper than the soft, diffused light at night.

And what about the 'straw key'?

"Maybe we need to watch the birds," the Seer suggested, keeping her eyes on the lightening sky as dawn grew stronger. "I saw a song bird."

"Only owls at night," her bodyguard noted, nodding agreement. "Maybe that's what we've been doing wrong. You willing to keep moving after sun-up?"

"Yes," the pregnant royal stated.

"We'll go slow."

They and their mounts suffered more under direct and hot daylight, but Ishuna witnessed a familiar rule of prey and predator.

Bird eats beetle, snake eats bird … Or if the bird wasn't grounded somehow, the snake could eat its eggs.

Eggs in a nest. Made of twigs and long, desert grasses … Which looks like straw.

"How would a bird's nest be a key to the Spire?" she murmured to herself.

"Bird's nest?" Xala asked.

The Seer nodded, turning the puzzle over in her distracted thoughts over the hours. Their heads ached from the intense light, and they loathed to leave the trickling stream for long on any search to one side. The direction of the valley still seemed to change, so slowly as to not be able to watch it happen.

As Ishuna sweated and grew dizzy beneath her hood, she was beginning to think she twisted this dream too much.

Xala was watching her, though.

Her and the birds.

"Not very high," the Captain muttered as they neared midday when the light was brightest.

"Hm? What?" Ishuna asked, frustrated and irritable.

She had been thinking more of shelter, and her baby moved as if in agreement. She wasn't sure how much longer she could stay on the horse.

"Not very high up. I've been looking too high, while they're flying, not landing." Xala pointed. "Do you see that?"

"What?"

"A brown snake. Moving slow up that hill base."

Ishuna squinted. *The mage must be using a far-eyes spell ...* "So?"

"A bird carrying straw disappeared before it landed."

"Disappeared?"

"In midair, yeah. And then I saw the snake move. It's going for a nest."

Was it?

Ishuna straightened up. They moved closer while Xala kept her eyes pinned on that snake. She wanted it to be like her dream but worried she was mashing pieces together with her fist ...

But Xala was right.

A struggle erupted; two birds shrieking as they suddenly became visible in the shimmering heat, attacking the snake. If not for the noise, Ishuna might have thought it a mirage.

The brown snake curled itself up, snapped at them, then struck three times at the air above the low curve of the hill. A nest tumbled into view, eggs spilling out as the fight escalated.

The Davrin didn't witness how it ended, because they were staring, mouths open, as their eyes finally began to see through an illusion.

"That hill's not really there," Xala said aloud. "It's ... it's taller."

So it was. Much taller. Ishuna's neck was craned so far back that her hood fell. she was nearly blinded, and her body felt a cold rush of fear and excitement.

We're right beneath it! It ... it practically touches the sky!

The towering stone looked natural, uncut, not the construction of Human, Dwarf, or Elf. An incredible structure, a pinnacle achievement from sheer elemental force.

Shaped like a giant spear with a needle-tip point, the spire was layered almost like Koorul with orange, pink, and red stone reaching for the sky. It clearly did not belong in this valley. Most of the area outside of the streambed itself had drab yellow and brown in its sandy soil.

In the brightest day, the rich colors almost hurt her eyes.

Xala moved her horse in front of her and drew her sword, calling out, "Who goes there?!"

Ishuna gasped and covered her stomach with her arms, hunkering down in her saddle as she cast a ring-spell to shield herself. The sunspot in front of her eyes blinded her to what was closest, yet stubbornly followed her focus on her periphery.

Glimpses suggested a darker spot within the shaded side of the spire which could be an entrance. From there, the suggestions of curving, shallow stairs formed as if by magic, wrapping around the base and into the sunlight of the valley floor.

On those stairs, a plain-robed figure stepped toward them with dark hands visible and a hood covering the head. The figure wore no belt at all and no weapons that they could see; the robe hung without shape. This could have been male or female, Davrin or a very dark Human.

Then the Davrin lowered his hood, confirming his race and the blond hair of an ancient.

Wruzdiin. Alyarra's Consort. *My sire*.

He scowled at them. Though still some distance away, Ishuna could hear his voice as clear as if he stood right in front of them.

"Xala." He knew her but sounded tired. Apathetic. "Why in Fel-Nash'en's Name have you come here?"

A fearful black wave swept over her before she could speak.

To her eternal frustration, Ishuna fainted atop her horse.

WHEN SHE NEXT WOKE UP, SHE FELT WEAK.

Her head and shoulder were sore, her left ankle stiff and swollen. Certain she'd fallen off her horse and landed on the ground, the shield spell must have protected her baby, as she felt no pain anywhere else. She lay indoors and out of the sun, on someone else's bedding.

Inside a cool, circular room listening to heated voices rising.

"You *cannot* stay, Xala. You are not welcome."

"She's your daughter, Consort, and that's your granddaughter in her belly. She has *your* gift of Sight, and it's brought us directly to *you!* She needs your help!"

"I do not care. And you will *never* call me that again, *Captain*. You have no right to drop this burden on my doorstep and destroy my peace. I have earned my solitude at high cost, though *none* of you remember."

"I remember!"

He scoffed. "I do not believe you. Alyarra had a centuries-long penchant for scrubbing her own failures as a Queen, a mother, *and* a companion. She perfected it long before her daughters were born."

His tone was deeply bitter, and it stung as Ishuna understood her older sister had been right. The mere existence of children, important or not, did not tempt their sire to be curious about them.

Though the pregnant female's stomach cramped in hunger, Ishuna was accustomed enough to keep her mouth closed a little longer, even as tears of disappointment filled her eyes. Meanwhile, Xala argued with the blond Davrin elder, her words more direct and body more animated than Ishuna had ever seen before.

It felt … personal. But not on behalf of Ishuna herself.

"Be that as it may, Great Uncle," Xala snarled, tugging her shirt up out of her trousers. "I stayed and suffered, like you. If you refuse to give this daughter anything more than your seed and your 'curse,' then you'll give *me* something in return for going back to the Palace after Alyarra finally died!"

Xala pulled her shirt over her head, stripping to the waist as she unbound her breasts as well. The robed male had no reaction to them, but Ishuna swallowed as the elder warrior turned to show him her muscular back.

"Look familiar?" she asked.

Once again, Ishuna saw the familiar stripes of magical scars ordered as punishment from the Thousand-Year Queen for failing to protect the Royal Heir, visible marks which *still* pained her Captain with periodic flare-ups.

The old male allowed a pause in their mutual barking to study them, nonplussed and academic when he spoke. "These are permanent. You were exiled?"

"The scars are. The exile wasn't." Xala turned back around, scowling. "The Virgin Queen Innathi allowed me to come back to V'Gedra with the new Royal Seer, to protect her."

Xala's Uncle chuckled as if she had spoken a jest. She pushed on, leaving her scars bare.

"I'm an honorific Captain, mostly just a bodyguard, and lately I can't even seem to do *that* right around your daughter. There's something strange going on, Uncle. Alyarra made us forget you, forget all the strongest mystics in V'Gedra. But with Innathi's reign, two powerful mystics were invited to V'Gedra half a century ago."

He sounded interested despite himself. "Who?"

Xala smirked. "In a bit. After that, I've started remembering again. Remembering you, in bits and pieces. I understand now that what the Thousand-Year Queen *did* has left Ishuna open to attack from things I *can't see*. Threats I can't protect her from."

"I *warned* Alyarra," the mystic responded with that same bitterness. "Many times. She never listened. And if what I saw is coming to pass at last from keeping her daughters ignorant of all they are, then so be it."

Xala trembled in anger but managed to keep her hands away from the weapons on her belt. "Ishuna was determined to find you, Wruzdiin. And she *found* you, using her birthright. It's fair game. She earned it. If there's anything left of the Ja'Prohn I remembered, the one I grew up admiring, you'll help her now. I never said we wanted to live here with you, but we did *not* come only to leave with nothing!"

The old mage growled, rubbing his face. "Xala. Listen. I wish to be left alone, especially from family like you, and I will not pretend otherwise. House Ja'Prohn and its leanings are mine no longer. Regardless, that is actually the *lesser* of your concerns."

Xala laughed skeptically. "Oh? How so? Tell me."

"Gladly."

The two stared eye-to-eye as Wruzdiin spoke.

"If you do not plan to leave again very soon," he enunciated, "you will not find a safe place for her to give birth. If *I* allow you to stay long enough to see the baby born *here* of all places, the outcome will be worse for her than in V'Gedra. I cannot even guarantee you will ever leave again. It may be too late."

"Too late for what?" Xala challenged, glancing at her charge staring at them from the bedding. She blinked, then refocused. "Why couldn't we leave when we wanted?"

The resident of the legendary spire straightened his back and turned, looking at Ishuna as well. She stared back in shock.

His face was more wrinkled than she'd ever witnessed on any Davrin bua. Something about him seemed frail — like the Queen-Mother in the moments leading to her passing.

Yet his eyes ...

His eyes were the brightest gold. Molten and metallic.

Ageless and powerful.

"A silent rise to eavesdrop, *qu'essan*?" he asked dryly. "Court instincts, I see."

"You two were shouting," Ishuna muttered, feeling her face warm but refusing to be shamed.

"For good reason." Xala still gripped her shirt in one hand, reaching to take Wruzdiin's shoulder with the other, turning him back to face her. "Answer the fucking question, Uncle. What would be too late if we stayed here?"

The mystic from House Ja'Prohn smirked with a slow shake of his head, as if he saw them both as fools. "The Dragon will be Awakening soon. Simply take my word for it. The outcome is *never* good for an Elf Mother giving birth too close to a Dragon's den."

"A den? Where?"

"Here. The Desert Spire. You are practically on top of it."

Part Three

Spirit & Flame

CHAPTER 1

THE DESERT SPIRE – 189 B.S.E.

XALA HAD TOO MUCH ENERGY. SHE HAD TO GET RID OF IT.

The warrior bound her breasts, left her armor and shirt off since the scars kept itching inside this accursed Spire, and ran up and down the inside stairs leading between the meeting room and the small, open-air platform where the horses burred nervously in their primitive corral.

How Wruzdiin had changed, and not for the better.

Though it appeared he was here alone and without forces to physically remove his unwanted guests, Xala was aware the mystic only had to prepare a few key spells. Ishuna just might suggest tomorrow that they leave the Spire without getting what they came for.

Xala wasn't sure what Ishuna wanted, either. Not exactly. Whatever it was seemed as intangible as a mirage yet as powerful as the sun. The *qu'essan* could not ignore this without suffering severe burns to any part of her exposed. The consequences of doing so were as tangible as anything Xala could detect with her regular senses.

Ishuna's pregnancy, for one. They'd both ignored or missed the warning signs, or perhaps something more had distorted their view for a time, and one of them now carried her first child.

Wruzdiin doesn't care, she thought, pushing herself harder as she worked her body toward ultimate exhaustion. *The only Davrin mage I have ever witnessed disowning his acknowledged progeny.*

Her uncle once told her he had always been warned his "pushiness" would have consequences, as it was unbecoming of a bua to extend his will ahead of his protector.

He'd pushed a Queen too far. What did he *expect* would happen?

On her twentieth pass by the horses, Xala was drawn up short as her Great Uncle now stood in her way, peering at her with eyes which had never been golden before. She was almost sure of it.

"Where did you come from?" she asked, breathing hard.

Wruzdiin tightened one corner of his mouth. His arms were crossed before him, his fingers relaxed on the sleeves of his undyed robe. "I did not 'push' her too hard, Xala. I tried to leave her, for the last time, after Innathi was conceived."

What the fuck ... ?

Was he listening to her thoughts?

"I was foolish," he continued, "and Alyarra lured me back one more time to conceive Ishuna. I will not describe the brutality of that mistake when she broke our agreement, but I'm sure you can imagine."

Xala's heart pounded from her running climb as she stared at him in silence.

After a pause, "Her intent was to murder me, Xala. The Thousand Year Queen did not want me roaming free within her borders or any of the Zauyrian Realms." He ground his teeth. "She nearly killed me, and only failed because she wanted me to suffer, first."

Xala had to lick her lips twice to moisten them enough. She chose and discarded handfuls of thoughts before she picked one that was most like what had helped her after her own trial and sentence.

Something Ishuna had said after listening to her story.

"I'm glad you are alive, Uncle."

Wruzdiin snorted. "At times, I am not. However, I cannot seem to give up for the time being." He shifted their topic as Xala began craving a drink of water. "Will you do what's best and help me convince Ishuna to leave as soon as possible?"

Xala shook her head. "Not without you giving her something any sire should, regardless how much he hated her Mother."

His expression gradually turned cold. "Xala. You were always an intelligent one. You *have* at least suspected, from what I've said so far, that Ishuna was conceived in a rape which almost killed me, yes? Or did I need to make that clearer?"

She swallowed as her middle tightened but refused to flinch. "That's not Ishuna's fault. And her child was conceived unwillingly. Though not … brutally."

"Lucky her."

"Why don't you just use magic to convince her to leave?" she challenged.

"I *could* do that," Wruzdiin said with a frown. "I would have to be as ruthless as Alyarra to make it stick, however. It would not be pleasant for any of us and may prove pointless for she would almost certainly miscarry."

Almost encouraged by that, Xala challenged it. "Not pointless. You'd be alone again. Mission accomplished."

"Alone and proven as horrid as the Queen I left. Quite an accomplishment, I must say."

"So, you do care about Ishuna's baby," she tested. "You want them both to live."

Wruzdiin shook his head, appearing as though he questioned his earlier evaluation about her intelligence. "No, I don't care whether either of them do. I simply will not take up again to be a murderer and controller of your former Queen's ilk. It never suited me and benefits me even less since becoming the caretaker here."

Xala frowned. "Caretaker? Aren't you the master here while the Dragon sleeps?"

Wruzdiin laughed, hoarse and dry and tired. "If you ignore what should be clear before your eyes, Captain, if you do not do what is best for Ishuna now, you are no bodyguard. Let us return upstairs and see if your charge has any better sense."

The Dragon.

Apparently, there really was one in the Red Desert.

He's real?

The stories could have been misleading, exaggerated, or simply false. Too many names, no living witnesses — *Except my sire?* — and no deeds which had left a mark, for benefit or tragedy, on the desert peoples.

It didn't help that Mother suppressed such stories in V'Gedra, Ishuna thought.

After that final statement — that she should not give birth close to a Dragon's den — her sire had refused to speak to her, as if he regretted saying that much.

Xala and he had then erupted into an unproductive argument which skewed quickly to House Ja'Prohn misguided loyalty to the Mother-Queen and Ishuna's Mother herself. The details were so spiteful, shocking, and disrespectful that Ishuna had covered her ears so some of the mental pictures painted by Wruzdiin did not become too vivid.

Her nausea threatened to overwhelm her. They noticed, fortunately for her and the clean floor, and the two elder Davrin abruptly left to cool down in separate corners of the Spire.

If this circular place even *had* any corners.

Ishuna had been left alone on the low pallet with her thoughts, a growling stomach, and a twisted ankle.

The strange qualities of the valley made more sense to Ishuna as she considered the Desert's more mystical legends. Some stories had linked the Spire with the Great Sand Snake, but enough of them didn't that it could seem a fanciful addition.

A lone recluse living within the elusive Spire was the more common story, and her sire had even appeared as one of those mystics long before she'd decided to leave V'Gedra to search.

That story had given her only direction at the start. She'd been right. *I can't leave. I need to stay here, I need to learn, I need to know!*

Her eyes teared up as she imagined being forced to leave, when living pregnant in the Desert this past year had been for nothing! She had found this place when few others ever had, and the master of the Tower was her own sire!

That had to be worth some response beyond, 'Go away.'

Ishuna was embarrassed to be caught weeping when the two Ja'-Prohn returned at last, each calmed down from the last she had seen them. They'd realized all needed water and some food and would eventually sit down with her.

They glanced a bit balefully at each other, but Wruzdiin provided the water and Xala provided the rations. The pregnant *qu'essan* spoke first; she had too many questions churning to wait any longer.

"Did this begin with you?" Ishuna asked her sire, breaking off dense, dry pieces of rations and using water to wash it down. "A mystic living in the Spire? Or — ?"

"I am one of a succession over many centuries," he answered gruffly. "And as soon as you leave, I will see to it that none may retrace your steps here. Tell what stories you like, for the way here is never the same twice." Wruzdiin pinned her with irises of pure gold. "And few will have your gift of Sight to help them."

Xala had replaced her shirt with care, as if it itched with sandfleas, sitting cross-legged. "Why bother answering her questions, then? Or mine?"

Wruzdiin smirked, deep creases forming at his eyes and the corners of his mouth. "Unlike Alyarra, I do not attempt to control what people say after they learn their world is not what it seemed. What was it you said? Fair game? Forcing a denial of the experiences of others only creates blind spots for both the oppressor and the oppressed that delays the eruption at best."

He shrugged. "I prefer the elemental forces perform that task while my essence remains as free flowing as water circling the world. Alyarra would never allow it. She could not stand how it got loose no matter how she tried to direct it."

Ishuna and Xala shared a look, probably unsurprised at the direction.

"Again, with the Queen?" Xala asked, annoyed. "What the fuck does that even mean?"

Ishuna lifted her hand to her. "No, no … I understand, I think. That … that happened to me. I was blind when Mother denied my Visions … but that didn't stop them coming. It only made me afraid to look at them."

Wruzdiin arched an eyebrow. Between that, his hair, and his eyes all being golden or blond, Ishuna felt she could be tricked into thinking he wasn't really Davrin.

Frustratingly, he said nothing more. His scowl was intense, but he'd withdrawn, looking inward. Kind of like Houda.

"And each successor of the Spire," Ishuna began, trying to bring them back around to her questions, "uhm, serves the Dragon in some way?"

Wruzdiin focused on her with an expression saying she had insulted him. He still said nothing.

"Well, then, what is your purpose here?" she continued defensively. "Obviously the Dragon is allowing you to stay near his 'den'!"

The old mystic exhaled irritably. He had been alone for more than enough time to have dropped any pretense of Courtly manners or House protocol. "That is mine. I will not answer that question."

Ishuna sensed his annoyance flow around the question, a bit like water as he described. It would simply leave, and she could not call it back.

"You said you were a caretaker," Xala pushed him.

"You should have been able to figure that out from what I already told you," he rebuked. "I need not repeat myself."

"But you were sorry you said it in the first place."

The old male straightened up and glared more directly at each of them. "If you are both too stupid to hear the clearest reason I can possibly give you for leaving here, I do not know what else I can say on it."

"We're not stupid!" Ishuna said. "Your 'clear reason' clashes with the reason we came!"

"And what is the reason?"

"To ask what can you teach me about our 'Sight,' *Ilharn*."

"Do *not* call me that!" Wruzdiin barked, making her shrink back in her nest. "I am your sire, but I am *not* Ilharn to you. And you must leave sooner than it would do you any good, were I to even *begin* to teach you."

"Not true!" she blurted, pain flaring in her core and her body starting to shake with nerves. "I-I've been learning for years on my own. I helped win the first tests from enemies with my sister, the new Queen! I only need more insight!"

Wruzdiin smirked. "Sounds familiar. But no, we have no time. You must leave, lest your unborn tempt fates you are not prepared to face, Ishuna."

"I haven't been prepared for *any* fate!" she cried, the tears returning. "You and Mother both abandoned me to night terrors and voices crowding the shadows of my Reverie!"

His eyes were molten as they shimmered metallic. "If I *hadn't* 'abandoned' you, Ishuna, I would be dead, and we would not be speaking at all. I'll not apologize for doing what was necessary to salvage my life. It had nothing to do with you. And *you* are much better off back in V'Gedra than I will ever be."

"Horse shit!" Xala interjected. "If you survived a Queen who wanted you dead, what purpose was there to survive at all if not to help Ishuna when she needs you? She's most like you!"

He looked between them, slowly shaking his head in disbelief. "You are not hearing me. I owe *nothing* to any of you, do you understand? Would that all of you demanding, parasitic, controlling cunts *see* what you've done to make your own Hells on Miurag! You have sown it, and now you shall reap it!"

Wruzdiin vanished in a blink of their astonished eyes and left the two alone in his Spire.

For the next two weeks, they'd not glimpse or hear a word from him.

CHAPTER 2

THE CONSTANT, DEEP ACHE WAS TOO MUCH TO BEAR ALONE. XALA SLEPT ON the pallet with her when she needed to try and rest, holding her distended belly as it continued to cramp with her recurring sobs.

One night, as the moons were high and silver light streamed into the Spire from the open-air windows, Ishuna's weakening hope broke down especially hard.

So many days, and Wruzdiin had not shown himself.

The rejection of his blood and the ever-present awareness they were unwanted guests stung worse than anything Ishuna had believed possible.

The constant belittlement from the Queen-Mother was cool and parental disappointment, so consistent it was to be expected. Her sister's teasing? Just frustrating proof of her curiosity. It's what sisters did while growing up.

Ishuna's own envy over Cris-ri-phon's obvious devotion lasting so long while her Leur was long dead? A constant, gnawing irritation that had gotten better with distance.

Her fear of four half-Elves living in the Palace without a vision to tell her what would become of them? More concern for the Queendom than for her niece and nephews. The mixed breeds existed now, allowing any plot to see them murdered and destabilizing the Queendom, risking

Ishuna's future for her pureblood daughter.

But this?

Ishuna hadn't realized how much she had been hoping that her sire would be glad to see her bearing his talent — not until she learned why he hated the very sight of her. Would he have been more open to her presence, despite the private horror of her conception, if she'd been born a bua?

If she had been, she certainly wouldn't be pregnant now.

"Shhh," Xala soothed, her body tense and regretful even as she tried to comfort. "I'm sorry for riling him up to say such things, Ishuna. I did wrong, trying to shame him into helping us."

Ishuna merely nodded, accepting the familiar fingers combing through her hair as her bodyguard patted her back. Pointless to argue, to blame, to want to take anything back. Impossible even if they'd been more civil, as a slower grind leading to an even more disappointing refusal.

The Royal Seer fell asleep from exhaustion, her chest still aching. She let herself drift, wanting the Reverie to last for as long as possible. The noise and stress of the world around her became muted as her dream approached.

A welcome refuge from facing a very big mistake.

She was walking outside the Spire, not going far. She remained in the ever-shifting valley, finding a small spring from which to drink.

She laid herself down on rocks still warm from the heat of the day. Even doing one thing which was needed to continue living, Ishuna thought perhaps no one needed her after all. Not her or her daughter.

Who would need all this contempt. False pride hidden in anger. So much envy, jealousy of those around me …

That was why Szoroan and Lord Indrath punished her.

Why I can't See anything unless I'm right on top of it.

Perhaps she could disappear for good. Perhaps she could die, and things would be better for everyone.

"*Mm-hm.* Let us speak about that, *Ocuirar.*"

Ishuna rolled up quickly into a sitting position, amazed and terrified she hadn't heard such a large creature coming!

A serpent figure with fire-orange scales and sun-gold eyes stood beneath the Twin Moons, watching her.

Goddess …

The face peering at her resembled a sand snake blended with a man, lacking horns or fangs, yet his forked tongue extended out in an inquisitive manner, as if he had caught an interesting scent. He was muscular in the manner of a Zauyrian like Cris, with strong arms crossed in front of him, broad shoulders, and a torso upon which he stood on two legs, yet he also possessed a thick, strong tail, extending impossibly long behind him.

"W-who … ?"

"The Flame."

What … ?

Ishuna was startled by the flexible hood of scaly skin flaring out from the crown of his head and attaching to his shoulders. He wore no clothes at all, but she mercifully wasn't at eye-level with a male member, which seemed like it might be inside of his body.

Or perhaps this form wasn't true to life, simply what she saw in her Reverie.

Not another rape terror while I sleep …

"I am the last about which you need to worry about that."

He'd spoken in a low and quiet voice, clearly able to hear her. Unlike her other dreams, she heard no terrible hissing in his speech.

"You … won't?" she repeated, hesitant.

"No." The Serpent Man shrugged. "I am not even the closest one capable, who shall eventually. She is only waiting."

Bewildered, Ishuna's stomach tightened up. "You aren't accusing Xala?"

He shook his head in the negative and lowered himself to sit across the spring from her. She saw now that his tail must be at least twice the length of his already impressive height. That tail seemed like a separate threat altogether, which could attack her from the flank at any time without the bipedal creature shifting his backside.

"We've reached an impasse, your sire and me," said the Serpent Man without much inflection, and at least no hostility. "You found us, something he thought improbable, and now we are caught in a riddle with no answer. We have questions, but I shall not require Wruzdiin to ask them."

Ishuna thought of the incredibly long, quiet days since the cursing, blond mystic had vanished before her eyes and could be found nowhere they could reach in the Spire. Many floors and most doors couldn't be opened. Xala hadn't even been sure they'd reached the top in how far they'd climbed.

The only spaces where they found what they needed were two platforms they'd seen, the stairs themselves, and a tiny storeroom which only conjured just enough water and raw food for Davrin and horse both — always when they weren't present to witness it.

The *qu'essan* honestly hadn't considered whether Wruzdiin had been consulting with anyone. She'd imagined him sulking and pacing and resolutely putting them out of his mind when he wasn't wishing them dead. She'd imagined he was only waiting for them to give up and leave on their own, but she hardly had the will left to keep herself fed, much less return out into the desert.

"Y-you are the Dragon of the Desert," she whispered, covering her belly, which was never as round in Reverie as it was when she was awake.

"Correct. You may call me Mazdek," he offered. "Shorter to say than some names chosen for me. And you are Ishuna. First, I would like to say that you, your child, and your bodyguard will not be harmed in the Spire, nor any of your possessions confiscated."

A strange feeling came within her chest, a wary warmth as if something cold had loosen up to strangle her less. She hadn't realized she'd been unable to take a full breath since …

Since when? Since I conceived? Before even then?

"Mazdek," she repeated, wiping her palms on her travel pants, as she imagined them being sweaty enough to need it. She hesitated. "No title?"

He shrugged. "*Sargt*, if you wish, *Ocuirar*."

"I do not know what either of those titles mean."

"Then we need not use them."

Ishuna swallowed at his steady gaze. That Mazdek never blinked yet still avoided a comparison of a slithering reptile hypnotizing its prey baffled her. She could only think he must be suppressing everything about his nature, to appear mundane as a Human man despite the scales and hood and tail.

He didn't even have any claws on his hands.

"Y-you have questions, you said," she offered, her signal that she'd finally come to terms with this astonishing meeting.

Mazdek nodded. That was what he'd been waiting for. "My first question is, have you seen your child in your visions yet?"

"No," she answered.

"Has Xala cast any divination on it? Does she know?"

"That is not her talent."

"She does *not* know. Very well. So, she follows your lead as the royal visionary."

A truthful answer forced Ishuna to nod her head in the affirmative.

"Then how do you know it is a daughter?"

Ishuna shuddered in fear. She didn't answer that question.

"It must be."

Mazdek tilted his head and asked a more pointed one. "What will you do if your child is a son?"

"She can't be!" the Seer barked, the fear in her gut spreading out.

Mazdek finally blinked. The action was slow. Deliberate. "Why not?"

"Because that's what they wanted!" she cried. "That's why he did this to me! We need a pureblood heir in case Innathi only produces half-bloods! He said it would 'save us all!' "

The Dragon remained calm. "Who are 'they'?"

Ishuna started shaking, nauseated enough to empty her stomach. If only that would purge the rest of this nightmare with it!

"Ah … A-Ah, Szoroan of House D'Shauranti. And the Ice Lord Rousse taught him how to trick me. I-I am certain. He was there in my mind when it happened!"

Mazdek allowed her to see that he recognized one or both of those names. He nodded once. "I see. But you have had no visions on a trueblood daughter."

The shades seemed so securely drawn within her when it came to her own fate. Hints, warnings, what little she had been able to be sure of these past decades rarely involved her at all, and never her child.

Only that one glimpse in her own mirror as a black shadow clung to her, riding her like a steed pushed to the edge of collapse upon the sands …

And what Szoroan had said.

It's either this now, or what you saw in the mirror at your sister's fourth birthing.

"Ah." Mazdek nodded, his hood contracting partway to his thick neck. "We begin to approach the riddle without an answer."

"Wh-what do you mean?"

"Wruzdiin sees a son for you."

"No!"

"Yes."

"I cannot raise a bua! I hate them!"

Her words echoed in the valley after she covered her mouth with both hands. Mazdek tilted his head, tongue flicking out, until the declaration faded. "Is this the first time that thought has been so clear to you?"

Stunned in an instant which seemed pointlessly cruel — until she realized he was right — Ishuna began to weep in frustration, not wishing to accept *any* of this.

But slowly, she was dragged to do so as the Dragon kept speaking.

"Wruzdiin hates caits just as much, Ishuna, and he has lived with that hate for longer, though I would see him healed from it. Regardless, my *Kiabil* has Seen your lineage continue, but not Innathi's."

Ishuna froze, her weeping silenced as her eyes grew very large. *No, no! No, it can't be!*

This must be what Indrath wanted!

"M-my s-son becomes the Monarch? The Davrin have no Queen

but a King?"

The Serpent Man shook his head slowly, his hood extending to block one moon. "No. Neither your son nor your grandchildren will ever rule V'Gedra. But Wruzdiin says your line will continue nonetheless and live on through him."

A relief somehow even more horrifying.

The Dragon did not speak the unspoken; he may not even know it, as he had said he talked on behalf of Wruzdiin. But Ishuna guessed the other side of the vision. She had used such language at Court.

V'Gedra would fall with Innathi.

Her reign was too short to produce pureblood heirs of her own, and Ishuna's blood would not take the throne in her place.

Because Ishuna would not have a daughter to follow the Sisters of V'Gedra. The child in her belly was a bua. A son.

Not the daughter the Queendom needed to survive.

Braqth damn them a — !

With an abrupt gasp, Ishuna clutched her head in pain as a spike of pure lightning seemed to cut off her curse.

Mazdek smiled just a little bit. "Yes. About that. The riddle."

"What about the fucking riddle?!" she exploded.

Her patience destroyed alongside her hopes, she considered punching herself in the gut repeatedly until she started bleeding. His shoulders tensed, and his long, long tail moved like he might prevent her from doing any such thing, though he said nothing on it.

Instead, he spoke with all the calm and composure he had shown her so far. "Listen to me. If you give birth here, if I allow it, then your son will remain uncorrupted, and the vision which Wruzdiin has Seen shall come to pass. Your lineage will survive. The *Davrin* will survive, he says, but I do not yet understand how."

Uncorrupted?

"If that is the better outcome, then why does my sire only want to kick me out?"

"I know he was trying to scare you, but first let me tell you the riddle."

The riddle!! Argh!

Mazdek smiled slightly, tongue flicking out at her strangled temper. "You see, Ishuna, if you give birth here … your son will become part of my Hoard. As if he was no more than a golden chalice or a handful of coins."

"What?"

"Each piece of my Hoard is bonded to the rest, even a living one. He will never want to leave his 'family,' and forcing him involuntarily … he would not survive to bear children of his own." Mazdek shook his reptilian head. "Yet even to allow a cait to conceive by him while bonded to my own Hoard does not bear the weight of a vision meant to save an entire race from extinction. That is the riddle with no answer."

Her mouth was hanging open. *Ridiculous*.

What was he even rambling about?

"Wh-what of the birthing Mother?" she demanded. "Wruzdiin suggested something similar, that neither Xala nor I would ever leave again."

The Serpent Man shrugged. "He was exaggerating. While difficult, it is possible for you both to leave. But your son never shall if he draws first breath here. He will not possess the strength of spirit to leave, and even should another carry the child away, stealing him from me … ?" He exhaled softly, thinking about it. "The child would cry, and I would hear him. Always find him. And I would not ignore the cry, as I cannot for any piece of my Hoard."

His golden eyes focused tightly on her, his vertical pupils thinning in a suddenly recognizable threat. "Thieves of a Dragon's Hoard are always killed, Ishuna, even if that thief is the Mother. Stealing from a *To'vah* is at least equivalent to the rape by which you conceived. Something is taken from you as you are molested without your consent. I do *not* tolerate any thief to live after that."

Gooseflesh sprang out on her skin, and she hugged her middle protectively. "B-but he's *my* son …"

"I know. That is why Wruzdiin wants you to leave, and why I do not understand this riddle."

"Do *you* not want me to leave?"

"That is irrelevant."

She huffed with frustration. "And if I leave? If I try to find elsewhere to give birth?"

Mazdek nodded. "Wruzdiin has Seen this possibility, too. He is deeply disturbed by it."

"Why? Tell me."

Golden eyes held her captive while he spoke.

"My *Kiabil* sees only blackness, hears only the distant screams of your entire race. It never ends, Ishuna, but the Davrin are no more. He held out in his Vision, waiting to see if it would *ever* go quiet. It never does. This last time he tried to See that far, it almost killed him. You are the caller of that fate, Ishuna. Of this, he is sure."

"Wh-what? N-no, I'd never … !"

"There have already been too many lost opportunities, and the sandstorm has been coming for a while. I have seen this myself." Mazdek shook his head. "But what I do not understand yet is why I must keep you here."

Ishuna jerked in shock hearing that. "What? B-but you said —"

The Dragon smiled at her as she stopped.

"I am *Sargt*, young Davrin," he said, forked tongue slithering out. "You have made many choices to walk your path. Now those choices have brought you to my Spire, where *I* must now make a choice."

"W-what choice?"

"Whether or not to Guard against the fate of the Davrin which Wruzdiin has seen will happen if you give birth anywhere *except* atop my Hoard."

Now he appeared like a predator. Moved like one. His orange-fire aura became visible as he let her sample just a hint of it.

It made her freeze in fear.

"You may not leave my Spire, Ishuna. Your sire is not happy to have you here, but he will bow to my wishes. I suggest you do the same."

WRUZDIIN WAS STANDING BESIDE THEIR NEST WHEN ISHUNA AWOKE AGAIN, and she began screaming garbled accusations at him, jolting Xala awake.

She was reaching for her sword before she was fully aware, though she took no action against her ancient Uncle while he merely watched Ishuna with arms crossed and eyes narrowed. He didn't answer any one of her words, and he held himself back from lashing out at her, though he clearly wanted to.

"That wasn't real!" her *qu'essan* shouted. "That was a trick! An illusion! You spelled that dream on me to make me run away and leave you alone!"

Wruzdiin tilted his head. "Then test it, Ishuna. Please, try."

They watched as he spun on his heel and stalked back upstairs to wherever he'd been spending his time.

Xala blinked at her, saw the cait shaking, and asked, "What the fuck is going on?"

Ishuna pursed her mouth so hard they were nearly grey. "I'll tell you as we ride out. We're leaving. Tonight."

Xala felt her jaw drop at the unexpected concession. She took a moment to get her feet under her, mentally and physically. "Wait, we need supplies, *qu'essan*."

"Just take what's in the downstairs room. We'll hunt the rest. Hurry!"

At least none of their possessions were missing; everything was there including the horses and all the magical items which helped them survive the Red Desert. They took the single day's worth of food and water that always appeared in the storeroom and quickly led their horses down the shallow steps out into the night.

"Morning's not far off," Xala warned, looking back at her. "We won't be out of the shifting valley before we need shelter from the midday sun."

"That'll not matter nearly as much as proving an illusion."

"What was an illusion? I didn't understand what you were shouting at Wruzdiin."

Ishuna's eyes teared up, but she stubbornly led her horse toward the valley floor. "Jennyn was either wrong, or she lied to me. That 'seeking what I missed most' led me into a trap. And seeing as she was *there* with Lord Rousse, I suspect they plotted together well before Innathi's wedding."

Xala didn't reply, focused on leading them safely to a mounting spot in the fading moonlight. She kept their pace manageable to prevent broken horse legs, despite Ishuna's nerves and clear desire to kick her horse to move faster.

They traveled for several hours as the sun rose along with the temperature, and Xala's gut warned her to be wary. Either something was watching them, or they'd interrupted some magic flow, or crossed a ward.

The direction which was supposed to lead them out of the valley and the distance hadn't seemed to change much, if at all, but all the morning animals she'd seen here on her way in were notably absent. Xala heard only the trickling of the clean stream running down the center of the valley.

When the rushing slither of scales across rock broke the strange stillness, her horse panicked even before Xala could place it.

How fucking big is it . . . ?

"No!" Ishuna began screaming, weeping inarticulately.

There was no way she could control her horse.

"Ishuna, dismount!" she shouted, risking a command just beneath her words often used to nudge reluctant guards. ***"Now!"***

It worked. The pregnant royal was off her horse before her frightened beast bolted. Xala did not control her mount much longer before the gelding squealed in response to a deep, threatening hiss.

Equine eyes rolled as the shadow of the creature above them blocked out the light behind a giant hood and a massive pair of wings.

Oh, my fucking Goddess . . .

Xala barely had time to kick off and away from her own bucking and rearing horse, rolling along the stone, before the beast charged the stampeding horses. A strong pair of forelegs launched the long body straight down the rocks, headfirst, appearing like a liquid stream of orange fire until it hit a cliff. The tucked wings expanded, and the fucking winged serpent dove off the ledge and glided upon the air.

Landing right on top of Xala's horse in a mass of coils. A feral scream ended in the crack of bone, hooved legs jerking before going limp.

Fuck!

The bright-fire beast reared up again without looking their way, tucking in its wings, and slithered impossibly fast after Ishuna's mare. Catching it not ten instants later, the giant serpent dispatched her the same way.

Saddle, supplies, and tackle were deftly removed before it began eating.

"Oh, no . . ." the Seer whimpered. "W-We need to run."

"Run where, *qu'essan*?" Xala asked seriously.

"B-back to the Spire."

"That's four hours' walk uphill. We'll only die tired."

"I'll not just *sit* here," Ishuna shouted hysterically, "and wait for the damned Dragon to drag me to his nest to lay his egg for him!"

What?

Xala rubbed her face, trying to catch up with the *qu'essan* since the moment she woke up.

Alright. The Dragon is awake.

That explained a lot from the last hour.

She crawled over to kneel with her back to the Dragon — entirely against her instincts — and wrap Ishuna close, so at least she wouldn't have to watch him eat both their horses.

"Look at me," she said, taking her jaw in both hands. "Wruzdiin warned us when we got here, didn't he? We can't leave now, and neither of us are ready to die. Let's negotiate."

"With what?!" Ishuna looked horrified. "You'll *not* offer any of our magic items! We need those for the Desert!"

"I won't offer anything until I understand what's going on," Xala replied. "But he's eating our mounts. At the very least, he owes us a trouble-free ride back to shelter and water, plus a meal of equivalent quality."

Ishuna's mouth hung open, her eyes threatening to glaze over. She'd stopped being able to think.

"Very well. Stay here." Xala stood up and faced the Great Serpent, cupping her mouth and projecting as only a Captain could. *"HAI! Tagnik'zur! Hai!"*

Despite the snake-like appearance, the Dragon *did* have rows of teeth now stained with red blood. If he had viper fangs, Xala couldn't tell because he was biting through bone and swallowing whole chunks of the horse without chewing. Any spines or horns on his body were minimal, though he could open his jaw disturbingly wide.

Large enough to swallow me.

The hooded legend seemed ravenous enough to start in on the second helping, so when he spared a glance for her call, Xala's knees almost turned to water.

"When you're done!" she shouted. "I wanna bargain!"

The Captain thought she was seeing things when the beast nodded his head like a normal sentient sitting at a table then went back to his raw meal.

In the meantime, Xala coaxed Ishuna to cross the stream, take a quick drink, and sit to rest beneath a rock overhang whose shadow shrank as the sun climbed higher.

"Anything you want to tell me before he's done?" Xala asked, working to calm her core and breathe despite the constant chewing. They'd been riding hard and the *qu'essan* had panted out some *version* of her dream, but the warrior had made little sense of it.

"H-he will make me stay here to give birth," Ishuna said miserably. "He wants my baby. It's a bua, Xala, not a cait. And these *males* want him more than I do. H-he … may let me go after that."

A son. Well, fuck.

Xala had assumed — she'd hoped — that Ishuna had been talking about her 'daughter' this whole time because she had seen this in a vision. The Captain knew how much the *qu'essan* had been planning around the sex of the baby, but Xala had been concerned about her ability to adjust if that were not the case.

"No room for discussion about keeping you here?" she asked, leaving the level of desire for the child alone for now. The Seer was trying not to show how terrified she was, but her bodyguard could tell.

"I have no choice," she whispered. "Wruzdiin had a vision about me and told the Dragon. That's where your uncle has been. The Dragon believes what he saw!"

Xala nodded, noting the change in identity for the blond mystic as well. *Not sire, not Ilharn. Alright.* "Isn't that the opposite of what he was trying to do when we first got here?"

"Th-they don't agree on it."

"Interesting. Did you get a name for the Dragon?"

Ishuna paused as if surprised she hadn't said it yet. " … Mazdek. The Flame."

Xala nodded, weighing some ideas in her head, working on an opening gambit before Ishuna said something else surprising.

"You could negotiate to leave, Xala," her Seer said morosely. "You are able. The Dragon told me Wruzdiin was lying when we first got here. I believe he would let you go."

"To go where?" she asked, arching her brow at the younger female. She waved her hand. "The first problem is that he ate my horse. The second is even bigger, because I can't solve it by getting another."

"W-what problem."

"I have nowhere to be." Ishuna gave her a look, to which she shrugged. "I'll stay with you, *qu'essan*, see you out of this next year. Seems we've gotten into bigger stuff than I can defend you from, but …"

But that started long ago. Back at Koorul when I was too busy fucking to see the long trouble coming.

"But I can protect you from having to face this alone."

Ishuna was relieved enough to weaken; she nearly tilted over and fainted again, but Xala caught her.

The *qu'essan* whispered, "They don't understand. No male ever will. Thank you … for not leaving me alone with them, Xala."

The older female put her arm around her, and Ishuna rested her head on her shoulder until Mazdek was finished. Once he was approaching them, Xala got to her feet, partly shielding her from his view.

Xala studied him clearly now. "Great Serpent" described him well from head to the tip of his tail quite far down the line, except for the strong front arms — or forelegs, perhaps — and the wings. His body was at once that of a legless snake and a flying drake, about which Xala felt confused for a moment.

Mazdek could easily rear up to use his clawed hands any time he wished, and with that long, lower body, she did not imagine him flying anything like a bird. Probably a glider most of the time ... unless he could change form anytime, as the stories suggested he could.

The Flame possessed the scaled, flared hood of a cobra rolling off his furrowed brow and connecting farther down on his shoulder blades, either as shade against the sun or possibly absorbing more of its heat. His eyes were pure metallic gold with vertical black slits, a gaze at which she couldn't look for very long.

His mouth was the least snake-like thing about him right now — a strong jaw somewhere between a lizard and a canine filled with teeth — yet his tongue was forked and purely snake. She could bet that he "smelled" with it just like one. He also possessed short, subtle but sharp bits around his muzzle, eyes, and head, rather like modified scales that had risen to form a point. His "horns," she supposed.

Encouraged that no powerful aura had yet swept out to slap hers around, Xala bowed. "Mazdek, the Great Serpent. We've entered your Spire seeking answers, and we have woken you after having found some. Is this true?"

He watched her, too quiet and thoughtful for something which had just wolfed down two horses in large, lightly chewed bites. He gave her a clear, deliberate nod; the large voice she expected didn't come.

Affirmative, then.

Ishuna was biting her lip to keep from saying anything harmful to her bodyguard's efforts.

"You've broken your fast using our possessions, confiscating them, which Wruzdiin said would not happen," Xala continued. "Now we are at your mercy, but I am not a cowering supplicant and will preface any agreement of cooperation with a bargain for compensation for those mounts, even after the fact."

Mazdek listened and did not interrupt her. She could see a small smile of amusement on his face but trusted her gut that he would rather interact than simply dominate.

Her Great Uncle was the best example she had of how this Dragon might treat his guests, even as she was just beginning to sense the sheer magic of the beast. Entertainment might be the best response she could expect by standing her ground.

That was alright. Not the first time she might have to bend the knee to a more powerful male. Better her than Ishuna.

"Shall I state my compensation?" she asked.

He made a very Davrin hand-sign for her to do so.

Very well.

"Give us access to more rooms in the Spire during Ishuna's term, and the luxury of a bath once in a while. Return all our other supplies, all magic items, then take us and our possessions back to the Spire, conscious and without having to walk. Lastly, I'd like a warm meal, enough for both of us to start with. Going forward, something better than the raw food we've found in the storeroom every day."

Mazdek's tongue slipped out just before he exhaled a thoughtful hiss rather than an irritated one. His voice didn't possess the same quality of a snake; in fact, it sounded more like Wruzdiin's manner of speech.

"Seems quite a list of demands for two horses."

"They were royal stock, well-bred and laboriously trained," Xala said seriously, feeling the genuine loss more than she had when the blood had flowed. "They were very valuable. They've carried us for the year we've been away from V'Gedra, we never had to change them out. You've cost us a great deal in losing them, Great Serpent, but all I ask in return is fair trade."

"Fair trade?"

"Yes. Those horses allowed us to go other places, they helped us find better food, they carried us so we could reserve our strength for more sentient matters, as they carried our supplies without complaint. You've taken all that, so you should return it in kind. Allow us to go to other places within the Spire, allow us to find better food and water, then carry us and our things where we need to go next. The fact that we must stay at your tolerance is beyond bargaining, the only questions now are 'how.' "

Mazdek was gradually starting to smile. "You're asking me to become your missing horses?"

"After you digest them, you will be," she remarked.

He laughed, his eyes nearly coaxing her to look at them as they glimmered. Then he considered in silence for a while, his smile remaining, his tongue flicking out in her direction once or twice.

Then he said, "I believe I can respect you, Captain. Granted."

Xala's face warmed, not really expecting that — either the compliment or the agreement — but she straightened her back and nodded once in acknowledgement. "Deal, then."

Mazdek turned around to slither over to the blood stains in the dirt, gathering up the saddles, bags, and tackle and bringing them back to set before her.

"Anything missing, Captain?" he asked.

Xala kneeled and checked things over as Ishuna moved backward in tense silence. It took a bit because she was thorough but ultimately shook her head. "No, it's all here."

"Then I shall carry it, and you two shall ride on my back as we return to the Spire."

"Oh, Goddess," the *qu'essan* whispered in disgust.

Mazdek did not react before continuing. "Then we shall see about a bath in a different room than you've been, and a warm meal. We can work out particulars as we wait for the child's arrival. How does that sound?"

"No choice," Ishuna whispered again, the resentment clear, but Xala kept her attention on the Dragon and nodded.

"Sounds like a start, Great Serpent. Thank you for negotiating."

CHAPTER 3

WRUZDIIN'S ATTITUDE DID NOT GROW ANY WARMER FOR THEIR PRESENCE after the Dragon's decision, though he refrained from starting fights — mostly by avoidance. He left to go elsewhere in the Spire as often as he could be.

Xala began to believe she could never break the armor he'd built against his family no matter how hard she tried.

Once inside the Spire, Mazdek had proven he could shift his form to be less as a giant, winged serpent and choose a shape closer to their own standing form walking on two legs. Sometimes he possessed wings and sometimes he went without, but always he had that shining, flame-scale tail which seemed too long for his height, despite the fact he was taller than the Davrin by a head or more. His proportions favored the Humans over the Elves, that was clear.

Their host provided what they'd agreed without further games and only a little teasing. Ishuna accepted the added amenities with the same bitter silence as her sire, leaving Xala to sigh to herself.

This is going to be a long year.

Over a few weeks, however, Xala noticed Mazdek inquiring about her own comfort more than the other two. Her skin prickled as she realized that he wanted something from her.

"What is it, Snake?" she asked bluntly, better able to look at his face without freezing. "What's on your mind?"

Mazdek offered a slow nod without blinking. "What can I offer the Royal Captain Ja'Prohn to share her body with mine?"

She jumped. "Huh?"

The Dragon smiled a little and continued, calm and frank. "In addition to mutual pleasure. That is assured and requires no negotiation."

Confident bastard, she thought, arching her eyebrow.

Now that she knew what this look meant, she realized that he had been interested in her for weeks. Possibly from the day he woke up.

In hindsight, Mazdek was behaving much like several Zauyrian men she'd known, the ones whose proposals she had accepted. She'd never enjoyed drama to go with her fucking, and ever since Koorul, if both were guaranteed to ride in the same wagon, Xala chose to do without.

Mazdek had apparently figured this out. The Dragon seemed to be randy but restrained, kind of like her, as she took her time to consider.

This also might explain Wruzdiin's recent hostility toward her, if he was aware of the Dragon's desires. *More drama right there.*

"Pretty sure you're not offering Ishuna's freedom for a fuck?" she tested, smirking.

He shook his head. "No. My offer is to you alone. I am certain the Royal Family has received more than enough benefits from the use of your body, Captain."

Ouch.

"Nothing right now, then," she said, standing up from the table. "An idea like that takes getting used to."

Mazdek nodded, accepting.

And waited.

It didn't take long to bring herself around once she started considering it. Her body opened to the idea as soon as her mind did; like with the Zauyrians early on, she grew more curious.

How would it work, to rut with a Dragon?

Xala hadn't gotten laid in … three or five years? Sometime back at the Palace, and apparently that had been mostly forgettable. She recognized the feeling, though, and didn't fight it. She might be giving up a good opportunity to ask for something tangible or politically clever, but …

Fuck it all if I can't ask anything that won't just lead to drama.

She told him later, "I want discretion, privacy, and fair play. No magic with any intent to overpower me. No pregnancy or disease. No leaving the Spire under any circumstance, and ***no*** setting off either Ishuna or Wruzdiin by rubbing it in their faces."

She paused, staring at his golden eyes to show how serious she was. "The *first* time there's any drama about us fucking which is not begun by one of them, we're *done* fucking."

Mazdek raised a ridged, smooth-scaled brow. "You are suggesting more than once, Captain?"

"If you want. If you can keep quiet." She smirked. "I'll wager the first time can be improved upon by both sides."

He lifted one corner of his scaly mouth. "Discretion. Privacy. Fair play. All of those honored will prevent the rest." He nodded his understanding. "Is that all, Captain?"

Xala squashed the temptation to ask for something tangible; she nodded. "All I really want out of it if I'm going to do it at all. Agreed?"

"Agreed."

He watched her, and she could see the respect was genuine. For a long time among her own race, that respect had been largely absent, and the Dragon looked even more Human right then.

"How curious you are, Xala. Will you come with me now?"

Nodding, she stood up, not allowing herself to second guess anything. She reached to take the large, rough hand he'd extended toward her, and the Dragon pulled her close.

They didn't walk anywhere but just *appeared* in another room within the Spire. A clean nest of animal hides lay stacked upon the ground without a bit of treasure to be seen. The room was warded for protection and silence, she could feel it, though it also possessed a small window which drew her to look outside above the valley.

"*Salty shitballs*," she muttered, breathing against the stomach-turning height while Mazdek chuckled behind her. "Are we near the top?"

"Close enough."

The vast spread of red dunes offered her a glimpse like a soaring raptor. Near the horizon, she spotted an abrupt change just before it curved and disappeared from view.

"Is that ... water?" she whispered.

"It is the ocean."

Xala frowned. "South or east? Or west?"

"Yes."

His arms slipped around her as he embraced her from behind. She could feel an erection pressing into her backside, its heat seeping through the backside of her trousers. Given that he never wore any clothing, she wasn't exactly sure where it had come from.

A pleasing size, though.

Dry lips nuzzled her neck and hair, his tongue flicked once against her ear as she attempted one more navigator's.

"Based on our maps, we shouldn't be near the coast."

Mazdek ignored that and began undressing her, his hands a rougher texture than any Human man's. Xala gasped often, shivering despite herself. She *liked* how boldly he explored her shape as he stripped her down.

Once she was naked, she detected a subtle quiver in her partner, in his breath and hands, restrained excitement amplified by the near-constant sliding of his excessively long tail. His touches lingered on her breasts and backside and between her thighs, discovering the texture of her skin and resilience of her muscle.

The Dragon wanted her like a wanderer wanted an oasis. Not knowing what to expect, she allowed him to take the lead, falling easily into the strangest and most memorable coupling she'd ever experienced.

The master of the Spire quickly brought her down onto the nest of furs with him, holding her close and facing him as they lay on their sides. His arms pressed her into him, clawless fingers exploring the scars on her back without triggering the pain.

"Uhm —"

Then, in a rush of scales and incredible flexibility, the Desert Dragon trapped her in his coils from her ribs down.

"Whoa, w — !"

She was surrounded.

He'd left her arms free to grip his shoulders, but she couldn't see anything but flame-scales below her breasts. That didn't mean she couldn't *feel* how his massive tail weaved between her knees and spread them apart.

She tested but couldn't close her legs, holding still as something hot and moist prodded at her slit.

"Mazdek —"

She sucked in air as his coils shifted in sequence along her entire body, squeezing, tightening, and the place she'd call his hips writhing as the Great Snake gently scented her and nuzzled her.

A moment later, the wedge of a near-steaming phallus pressed into her cleft, she could only hold on, the side of her face pressed into the heated scales of his collarbone as he slowly, slowly began to push his prick in.

"Whoa, shit — *Ngh!*"

His coils constricted in a grunt of pleasure, temporarily stopping her breath at the same moment she felt him enter, her cunt stretching wider to take him. Apparently, they did not need any more lubricant than the modest amount she'd already produced from his caresses.

"H-hey ..." she warned when she could suck in another breath. "Need to breathe."

He chuckled, hissing out on a breath of his own as he writhed and sank deeper. "Apologies ... It has been some time."

Xala stared vacantly at a point on the wall, all her attention pinpointed on his gradual penetration as his coils continually felt her up. His cock was wide. Getting wider. She didn't know what it *looked* like but couldn't even see how far they still had to go.

She shivered as his long body adjusted his entire grip on hers. "Same here ..."

"*Mmm?* Decades?"

Xala thought about Akil Safiya, the Head Guard at Koorul. Long dead now, but he had happened before the Queen's Punishment. She had liked him.

She hadn't much enjoyed anyone since.

"S-since the last good one, yeah. Decades ..."

Mazdek rumbled into his chest, breathing deeper with a nod, and tightening his coils and arms to hold her closer still. He took an incredibly long time to push into her snatch, and confused as she was at first, soon realized she didn't mind.

Mutual pleasure, for certain, and unhurried.

Eventually, Xala came to understand that being wrapped in a bundle with him like this *was* his mating. The Great Serpent was already fucking her, making her head swim as every tiny finger-width of his penis slid into her body.

Sensation increased as he did so, her skin becoming ever more sensitive, pleasure spreading out into the rest of her body from all their miniscule movements, until she floated helpless in their constant waves.

"F-fuck," she gasped, sweat dotting her forehead. She constricted her own inner muscles around him to let him know she liked it. He hissed in pure contentment when she did.

Finally, she opened her eyes, only to realize the light and angle of the sun had changed and that she didn't know how long they'd been lying here like this. She lay trembling at what she saw.

His aura was shining. A brilliant orange shot through with gold and red, the perfect balance of their red sands and the sunlight above. His own eyes were closed.

Not asleep, I hope?

"Mazdek — ?"

His response was to slide in just a little more, touching at last the tip of his massively wide cock to the mouth of her womb. A small explosion seemed to go off inside her guts; she grunted and squeezed down on him.

Then he squeezed down on her.

"Sh-shuhh — !"

He showed teeth then, grimacing, his tail tightening as Xala wallowed in a mind-wrenching orgasm while not being able to breathe. She relished as much as she could but soon had to tell him, hands thwapping desperately at his constricting coils.

Mazdek eased his grip just enough …

And then the first, scalding spurt of Dragon jism launched inside her. She froze in place, aware of every cunt-stretching pulse and flex until she remembered she could breathe.

Breathe!

Xala filled her lungs to scream in release, high in the Spire where other residents couldn't hear her.

CHAPTER 4

THE DESERT SPIRE – 188 B.S.E.

ISHUNA AWOKE FROM ANOTHER TERROR IN REVERIE, HER HEART AND HEAD pounding as her heavy belly cramped yet again. Her time wasn't until another two or three months perhaps, yet she wondered for what seemed the hundredth awakening if it was happening. If her fate was coming early.

No. Her own abdomen settled soon enough, replaced with familiar hunger and the need to relieve her bladder. Drudgery by now, nothing she looked forward to or took any comfort in.

She'd finally had the expected dream about him as well. Her sire had been right; she wasn't bearing a daughter. The bua would have gold eyes. Like Wruzdiin.

Since she had the dream, Szoroan's son seemed to grow ever more active, kicking her, and always reminding her of the night in the royal stable where the Blade Singer had tricked her. Breeding her like a mare.

I still can't believe Mazdek wants it.

That he wanted to claim a Davrin infant for his Hoard and would keep her prisoner here until she dropped the baby out of her body.

Just as well that they'll take him. A well-thread path to darker thoughts. *He will never leave the Spire …*

Therefore, he would not share the same fate as Innathi's half-bloods.

And perhaps his grandsire will see the penis and be willing to teach *him something.*

Ishuna's middle turned cold once again to imagine the three together.

Without me.

Two powerful males here already hated her, and she would be forced to give them a third to raise, to teach however they wished.

With no Mother's influence at all.

Ishuna wouldn't be here to tell her side of the tale, to explain … Her sire could tell the bua whatever he wished about the absent mother, and about *her* Mother …

No doubt he will tell only the worst of it.

Her body burned in denial of that inevitable victory, made worse as she knew by now that she was helpless to prevent it! She had tried to leave the Spire's valley again, had attempted the risk of aborting with what little access she had to materials beyond a long fall down the endless stairs … An option she was thus far unable to summon the courage to take.

Mazdek was always there before she could do anything to harm herself or the child. He could put her to sleep with a spoken word, and he'd carried her back to her bed numerous times already, none of them with so much as a harsh or chiding word for her, in spite of how she might scream at him when she saw him next.

Perhaps that was how V'Gedra would fall without female heirs. An outside source the Queen would not see coming, but Ishuna had planted the seed here. A Dragon and two powerful male mystics with clear Visions to guide the Desert Realms.

No …

Her sire had seen her line continue through her son. This had been brought up a time or two, by the over-lording Dragon and his bitter, resentful mystic. They never mentioned Szoroan or his line at all. They focused on her, as if it would placate her to be more cooperative, instead of showing her exactly how her attempt to come to terms with her rape, with raping Szoroan first, would backdraft on her in the worse way.

After relieving herself in the middle of the night and drinking yet more water, eating more food, Ishuna passed Wruzdiin on the way back to her bed.

He sat cross-legged on a small, exterior balcony overlooking the valley. His back was to her, and she felt the impulse to cast something that would push him over the ledge. At least that would take care of one male holding her prisoner—

But nausea swept over her, and she groaned. He heard her but didn't look around.

"You *will* kill me, Daughter," he said, "if you must take comfort in a dream of revenge. Just … not yet."

Ishuna gasped at the red haze which flashed before her eyes as she breathed deep, as she couldn't seem to get enough air.

Fuck you, you old slut!

How *dare* he call her Daughter only now, after refusing to acknowledge her search for him for months? After ignoring her while they shared the Spire. Or, if not ignoring her, looking at her like he was disgusted by her!

"Who is Indrath?" she demanded hoarsely.

Wruzdiin's head lowered some as if he looked at the ground, as if he was giving his answer some thought. She had no idea why he even considered it, given how little he'd spoken with her altogether, but she waited, clenching her fists so hard it hurt.

"The other side of the coin you could have chosen," he said, with almost no derision in his voice for once. Still, he did not look to turn around, and she did not move forward to better see his face. "But the coin itself was tarnished the moment you were born, thanks to your Mother. With no reflection which would have offered you light."

"I am tired of hearing you berate her every chance you get, aged-out Consort," she hissed. "Do not mention her again. You are not worthy to even *speak* of the Thousand Year Queen, you shriveled wastehole."

Such insults had set him off before, garnered his anger and his attention more quickly than anything else.

But it did not work this time.

She wondered if he had finally realized that she couldn't truly do anything to hinder him or control him. *Not here at the Spire*.

Much as it pricked her pride every time she thought about it, Ishuna knew she held only as much power over her sire's attention as he would grant her. *Some* attention was better than utter neglect, even fights more horrid and hurtful than anything she'd had with Innathi.

Fights which sent both Xala and Mazdek to seek peace elsewhere, until the sire and daughter wore themselves out.

That was better than Wruzdiin pretending she didn't exist.

Sssuch a weak fool. Remember what he ssaid. You will *kill him. The pain will end.*

When?

When will it end?

Wruzdiin sighed, slow and careful, as he refused the familiar bait for the first time since her arrival. "What will you do after you have given birth here, Ishuna?"

She ground her teeth. "None of your concern."

The old mystic chuckled with a dark edge. "Ah, but it has been for so long already. And yet, when presented with the test I knew was coming, I failed."

"Poor sire," she sneered. "Once again to tell me the *awful* details you *claim* Mother did to you when you lived with her? You know, seed-giver, I haven't even seen the whip marks which supposedly mark your back. You could be lying, and Mother isn't alive to defend herself against such accusations, is she?"

He tensed again as if he was about to jump up, and they would start into the fight at full speed once again. Instead, he shook as if he might be beginning a seizure …

And then she realized he was weeping, clutching the stone beneath him with his fingertips as if to anchor himself. As if he feared growing dizzy enough to topple over.

"For what you will do to him, Ishuna," he said, broken and angry, "I am glad I will not live to watch the rest."

"You hate me for what I haven't done! For just existing!" she shouted. "How dare you! How dare you judge me like this!"

She left abruptly, taking the last word, grumbling and hissing the vilest things she could think of as she plodded back to her nest to lie down and cry. *Again.*

Eventually the same thoughts would come back around to disturb her rest for the thousandth time.

And how many did you judge on the same kinds of visions, putting the sword in Cris-ri-phon's hands because it was already as good as done?

The amethyst spider pendant was still around her neck, its leather thong replaced many times by now, so dirty and fraying yet again.

Ishuna covered her ears and screamed to drown out her own voice inside her head.

"IT FEELS AS IF I CAN DO NOTHING BUT WATCH."

Xala lifted eyes to the open window and the sandstorm raging outside, though none of it swept in here. She was wrapped up, naked and warm, within Mazdek's coils as he held her from behind.

"I can't reach either of them," she continued. "Ishuna is sliding away from me, much as I've tried to hold on to her. Wruzdiin has already, from all of us, long ago. And somehow, we forgot all about him ..."

Mazdek reached to tuck a strand of white hair behind her long, tapered ear. He seemed to like touching them, as he possessed neither hair nor ears to speak of. And she let him.

"Wruzdiin was broken the last time he left my Spire," the Dragon said. "Neither his mind nor his magic have fully recovered, though I went to retrieve him, so he would not die in the Desert."

Xala turned her head up, looking up and back at him. "Why?"

The Great Serpent shrugged. "In the moment, I did it to spite the Queen of the Davrin for her cruelty. Looking back, I realized it was to aid in keeping more possibilities of your future open."

The Captain lay quietly, thinking about her own punishment at the orders of her former Queen. "What did she do? He ... seems whole ...

?"

"Physically, he is again. He does not even have the scars you carry, Xala. I gave him back what she had disfigured and amputated."

"Amputated?"

"Having a whole body was enough to give him some will to live, but he would not allow me in deeper to mend his aura or soothe the tortured dreams. At the time, I would have killed him to force it. My Sleep had been coming upon me regardless, and Wruzdiin knew it had been a risk to come retrieve him at all. He said he would wait for me."

Mazdek paused. "I did not Awaken again until he called me about Ishuna and yourself arriving at the Spire."

Five hundred years later?

"And Wruzdiin has been alone all that time?" Xala asked, her brow furrowing with concern as her gut felt sick. "After you recovered him like that?"

The Dragon shook his head, his tail sliding and retightening a set of coils looped around her left thigh. "We met frequently in Dreams, Xala. He was not alone, and he had his duties. He has strongly preferred solitude from other Davrin for most of his life."

Xala frowned, trying to imagine how a bua of House Ja'Prohn would manage that. Mazdek grunted a wry laugh.

"Indeed. I believe this is one of the greatest disputes between him and his Mother, made worse when she recommended him as a Royal Consort when he was young. He had no choice, I understand. Wruzdiin had many desirable traits, physical and magical, and Alyarra had decided early he should sire her heirs, though I know she never asked him. She made a public decree of her favor towards him, something his Mother benefited from a great deal."

Xala listened without interrupting, wanting the story to continue. She remembered her Great Uncle's favor, his grace and intelligence. She remembered his beauty when he was young, and how he had made House Ja'Prohn proud. She had been a child at the time, so her uncle had seemed wise and mature to her, but now she realized he'd probably been younger than Ishuna was now.

"Alyarra courted him for longer than was deemed becoming of her own station, or so I heard. And yet this one immutable quality of his, the need to be alone, clashed with all his birthright was supposed to provide, until one day he left V'Gedra without her blessing."

Oh, shit.

"He found himself some years later at my Spire, after a journey of his own, while his visions became stronger and ever more confusing. I gave him refuge." Mazdek paused. "And companionship for which he yearned."

"Hm." Xala wriggled around within his scales. "Like … this kind?"

The Great Serpent smiled. "Among others. Wruzdiin was trustworthy, I knew, but he also had to leave the Spire or there would be deeper consequences for the Desert as a whole. He returned to V'Gedra at the right time, when the Queen sought an heir in truth. His reappearance stunned her, perhaps, but she accepted his gifts and humbleness before her."

Like Cris-riphon …

"It's interesting how time echoes," he remarked. "Alyarra claimed Wruzdiin to perform his duty, pleased he had not forgotten, but … it would seem she had never forgiven him for choosing his own time to leave her. For realizing there was something else more important to him than his Queen."

Mazdek fell silent for a bit. Xala tensed a little as she waited for what he'd already told her.

"Wruzdiin is correct that she lured him back to V'Gedra a second time, to conceive another child, and when it became clear he intended to leave her again afterward … She imprisoned him. And tortured him."

Goddess damn it …

"After Alyarra tossed him far out into the wastelands, she set to work scrubbing his existence from her city's memory, and to continue the manipulation of how your people saw the 'mystics' like him versus the arcane, which had started long before that point. The only reason Wruzdiin lived was that he saw me coming for him one last time. He held out."

The Captain licked her lips, hesitant to suggest what she would say next. "And … he did not 'see' any warning of what would happen to him?"

Mazdek did not reply immediately. He thought about it. "Perhaps he did. Or perhaps he was blind to the signs, as are many things too close for us to see clearly."

Xala let that sink in; to her frustration, her eyes became wet. She blinked as she thought about Ishuna. "And he cannot look at his daughter without remembering?"

"Unfortunately, though I am not certain *he* knows all he feels about Ishuna." Her warm, reptilian companion squeezed her. "Ishuna has been in his visions of late, and I think it is clear to both you and me that he cannot see her as she is in this moment, but as someone who has not yet become."

She paused before speaking again. "How do you see her?"

His tongue flicked gently along her long, pointed ear, halfway between a tickle and sensual play. He sighed, stroking her hair again. "Wruzdiin has a message he wanted me to give you. When you are ready to hear it."

While that seemed like a sharp turn in topic, Xala thought perhaps it wasn't. "Alright. I think I'm ready. Tell me the message."

"Very well. The next time Ishuna leaves V'Gedra and heads into the Desert, do not follow her."

"What?"

"Stand by her as you will in the coming centuries but wait for her to return. Do *not* follow her. You will be needed more in V'Gedra."

Xala's first thought was that she could not imagine how the city would need her more than the Seer — they hadn't needed her in two centuries — but she nodded. "Simple enough."

"Perhaps not so simple. But important all the same."

"Okay. Got it."

Mazdek licked her again, dipping down to caress her shoulder and breast, taking in her scent, clearly still enjoyable to him.

The opportunity was there, so Xala allowed the Dragon to pull her back into a wordless melding of bodies and auras as she opened herself to accept him again.

CHAPTER 5

SHE'D OFTEN STARTLED HERSELF AWAKE IN THE MIDDLE OF THE NIGHT WITHIN the silent Spire, but on the eve of dawn upon which her son was to be born, Ishuna awoke clawing her chest with her fingernails.

It burns!

She sat up quickly, aware that cramps had been roiling her gut for some time, settling deep inside her hips and radiating down her thighs and up her back. Even now, the dark dreams seemed to follow her out, trying to grab hold of her and drag her back under. She wailed at the stars through the window, struggling to keep her head above the surface.

"XALA!"

Her bodyguard wasn't far away, though they each kept a different room to sleep. The older female heard her and came running. The third time Xala had gotten up that night and came to her side, as Ishuna swore it was finally happening, but then they stopped.

This felt different. *Urgent*. She wanted to pass out now, to fall back asleep and not have to suffer through it …

"*Qu'essan*," Xala murmured, comforting, familiar hands checking her over while her tongue asked familiar questions.

Her fingers hovered over the bleeding claw marks on her chest after the former Captain helped her sit up to stuff more bedding behind her back.

"*Qu'essan*, what is this?"

Ishuna whimpered, aware now her spider pendant scraped against the raw flesh, but she just shook her head, heaving to get enough air as she writhed through the next contraction.

"Alright. Alright, breathe. Here. Like we practiced. Mimic me, Ishuna. Come on. Look at me."

Xala stayed with her as the dawn broke, giving the laboring mother water, food if she needed it, although her appetite was gone. The Captain massaged cramps out of her legs and assisted in changing her position as needed.

Xala talked to her, kept her present and aware, so the voices didn't call her back into a trance.

Ishuna was in the Desert Spire. It had been two years since Szoroan had rutted her inside the stable. She had traveled so far, for so long … and she found the valley here. She found her sire!

Her horrid, broken sire.

Innathi was right. The Queen-Mother might as well have been right about him being dead. Damn Jennyn for giving her hope! Damn the Ice Lord for setting her up!

Yesss … They conssspired to sssee you humiliated and broken, but you will shhhow them! Won't you, Ishhhunnna?

Yes. I shall.

As Xala tired from the hours of tending and the sun approached midday, she finally announced that the head was low and in the right place.

"It's time to push, *qu'essan*. Push your baby out …"

The screams from the darkness arose as she tried, so loud she could no longer hear Xala's voice as she kneeled right in front of her. She thrashed upon the edge of a trance, as her body tried to expel what seemed lodged in her cunt.

She couldn't focus, couldn't concentrate.

He iss Ourss! It iss time!

Not now. Not now … ! Oh, Goddess, leave me alone!

Asss your blood mixes at lassst, he will let Uss in! IN as he comess OUT!

Help! Someone help me!

"MAZDEK!"

She jerked at a male voice breaking, as the hisses retreated into shadows. *W-Wruzdiin … ?*

"My *To'vah*, we need you!"

Taller figures gathered close to her.

"Help him!" her sire pleaded. "It's not enough. She is not close enough. Your Hoard cannot protect him from here."

"Hm. Agreed."

Someone tore the spider pendant off from around her neck. Ishuna screamed as more little hands and a multitude of shadowy claws scratched and snatched at her, desperate not to fall back into the void.

"Careful!" Xala cried as the Serpent Man swept Ishuna up into his arms. "She's ready! She must push soon, or he might suffocate — !"

The Dragon carried her off. She knew not where.

Ishuna blacked out, no longer hearing Davrin voices, and yet … she didn't fall back into the screaming void, either. When she blinked her eyes open again, she met a familiar, metallic gold gaze staring intensely at her.

And everything was … quiet.

The Dragon's hood flared wide as if he was on alert, his wings spread open as if he would offer her shade from a hot sun which had vanished. Her face was drenched from tears, her heart pounding desperately to give her strength.

Before she had a chance to say anything, her entire middle clenched up once again, tightening down hard and strong. The contraction lasted so long, continuous, and unyielding, making her moan and hiccup and writhe to sit up as the irresistible urge to bear down overwhelmed her.

She had to get it out. This wouldn't stop otherwise!

"X-Xala!" she whimpered as the clutching finally eased. The last contraction didn't make much progress. "I want Xala!"

"She cannot be here. It shall be only you, me, and your son who is ready to come out."

Strange clinking noises sounded in the distance as the "bed" beneath her shifted as if it was made of hundreds of little beans stuffed into a canvas. Blinking blearily, she saw that he'd laid out a rough blanket for her to rest upon, and itself lay overtop a massive pile of coins and gems.

Enough wealth to conduct trade with the farthest Dwarves at the Great Lake for decades.

Oh, Bra — Ow!

"You may not call out to the shadow goddess here, Ishuna. She will wait outside."

He placed a cool, damp cloth across her forehead and tired, dry eyes. She groaned in relief. When he put a cup to her lips, she drank the water, but he wouldn't give her too much. She didn't *want* his hands touching her but lacked the strength to respond with more than a grimace as he tested her belly.

Then tried to open her legs to see between them.

"Fuck you!" she snapped, kicking out at him, and missing.

Mazdek breathed out through his nostrils and watched her, waiting in silence through the next several contractions. Ishuna writhed on her back, screaming in frustration as it seemed the baby had stopped on the cusp of birth, requiring a slightly stronger push she didn't have in her.

It felt like she was slipping backwards.

"C-can't do this …" she wept, trembling.

The Dragon timed his own movements well, sliding into position behind her when she barely had the awareness to notice.

Lifting her up, he provided something stable she could brace herself against as she followed his silent urging to get up and squat. His enormous tail slid around in front, lying upon his treasure and encircling them completely as Mazdek's arms held her, one hand cradling her hard, distended belly.

Something felt disgusting, lodged in her crotch. She was certain she felt his magic; he was feeding it gently into her.

Healing?

Or just numbing the pain?

"Last one, Ishuna," he murmured. "Deep breaths before this final time. Breathe. Now."

She did so as the impending contraction arrived, yet for once she seemed not on the edge of an abyssal ravine. Mazdek held her steady; she wouldn't fall. She was safe to focus.

Her head cleared a bit.

Momentarily, she forgot to feel sorry for herself; she listened to the deep, rumbling voice coaching her through this last part.

Oh, Goddess, oh Goddess, get it out! Please!

Her entire body quivered with the effort. She put her head down and pushed through the long contraction, feeling things move. The downward pull of the world assisting her in finally … *finally!*

She passed the baby out in a rush of fluid atop the canvas covering Mazdek's treasure. Her eyes swam, a high pitch in her ears. She had no strength left; if Mazdek were to let her go now, she would fall.

She tried to look between her legs, glimpsing a small, white patch of drenched hair plastered down by a bloody membrane. A tiny, black body flinched, seeming as stunned as she was.

Then Mazdek carefully laid her down, helping her to unfold her cramping legs. Once she was resting and without disturbing a coin, the Dragon shifted between her legs to pick up her son.

No … no, leave him alone. He's not yours …

Mazdek cradled the messy newborn with astonishing care, his tongue cleaning the membrane, blood, and body fluids off him — especially his face so he could breathe. The stimulation saw the infant responding, moving his limbs, gasping at the air.

Then the baby Davrin filled his lungs and cried for the first time, loud and healthy. She blinked tears away, unable to raise herself up, hypnotized to watch the odd ritual, so primal in its nature it made her heart ache.

The wail turned to a short shriek of surprised pain when the Dragon made a small cut in the tender chest with his clawed finger.

H-hey … ! Ishuna shouted, her body numb and unresponsive. *No, stop! I'll kill you!*

Blood collected on the claw and the tip of his finger, Mazdek tasted it, paused, and nodded. With another gentle lick directly along the cut, the newborn skin sealed up as though the wound had never been. Her baby quieted into an exhausted sleep, nestled against the Dragon's scaly chest.

"Mazdel," the Dragon whispered.

Mazdel ... she repeated.

A naming.

Mazdel.

The Flame of the Desert had given her son a Name, one which sounded like his own.

A protective ritual so strong that it pushed her out entirely. She was back on the edge of darkness. Ishuna mustered every drop of strength she could to speak.

"D-don't s-send me back out there. It's quiet h-here."

He looked at her, golden eyes seeing her, wary of what he saw. He shook his head with regret.

Then he spoke.

"Sleep, Ishuna."

Losst ... .

We lossst himmm ... !

Not for long. We shhhall wait.

Will find him again ... We know where he isss.

We know he cannot live.

Not like all the ressst.

We shhhall return.

And we know who shhhall pay the price ...

AT LEAST THEY HADN'T BEEN KICKED OUT IMMEDIATELY.

Xala had known the time to leave the Spire was imminent, but Mazdek and her uncle agreed Ishuna had to heal and come out of shock.

Despite very clear hesitation and inner conflict, and always without actually touching her, Wruzdiin cast small, regular spells which helped Ishuna's body return gradually to a pre-pregnancy state. The *qu'essan* was unconscious much of the time, her spider pendant nearby as no one wanted to touch it or throw it out.

She twitched and flinched in her sleep, and the disturbing dreams and visions seemed to continue.

During the mata's aftercare, Xala saw Mazdek in between infant feedings. To her gratitude, the Dragon had allowed her to hold Mazdel a few times under his direct supervision.

The child was already a week old by then, and the bua had clearly been feeding regularly. He was darling, and healthy, and modestly quiet as long as his belly was full and his rump was clean.

"Just *what* are you feeding him?" she'd asked once, studying the tiny face as if she might remember it more than the many other babies she had seen in her lifetime.

She very well might, considering the circumstances.

"I feed him what he needs," Mazdek replied vaguely, looking outside the window as if distracted by something. His long tail weaved a continuous curve along the floor. "He could not drink from his Mother."

"Why not?"

"Her milk was poisoned."

Xala watched him for a moment, trying to decide if that was simple prejudice that might come from her uncle. Mazdek seemed at least to believe it a strong enough metaphor to hold the line against any bonding between the *qu'essan* and the son she didn't want.

Mazdek had quickly become protective of the infant as well. He and Wruzdiin had taken the stance that the Mother should not even hold the baby before she left — lest she harm him, supposedly.

This was something that rankled Xala deeply. She had protested while Ishuna was sleeping and not listening to the argument. That was when she had been told to expect to be back in V'Gedra before another week had passed, once Ishuna's body had recovered.

"What?" she said with an incredulous laugh.

It had taken a year of wandering to find this valley. Getting back out was at least going in a straight shot, and they probably could have ridden home in a quarter the time.

But now Mazdek had suggested they would not need horses to make the long trek back.

Goddess damn it.

No one had talked as much as Xala would have thought necessary for after the birth. *She* had wanted to talk, and though Mazdek only said what was necessary at the time, he might have given more if Ishuna or Wruzdiin had been more willing to communicate.

But they hadn't. They really hadn't.

Now, Mazdek was only concerned about Wruzdiin and the baby — whose name she didn't even know. She'd been a fine companion to him; they'd had some good times and conversations. She respected him, and he respected her.

But now it was time for the Captain to leave, along with the Royal Daughter she'd brought with her.

The baby was left in Wruzdiin's care as Mazdek approached Xala that last time, his golden eyes noting Ishuna sitting with her knees drawn up and touched to her forehead. All the belongings they had brought with them surrounded her.

The Dragon met the gaze of the former Captain from House Ja'-Prohn.

"I thank you for your company, Xala, and for your future strength. Remember the message, but … I apologize that you must remember very little else."

CHAPTER 6

THE OUTSKIRTS OF V'GEDRA – 187 B.S.E.

THEY WERE AMONG A CARAVAN, MET AND BARGAINED WITH, HEADING INTO the Davrin capital city. They'd met Cris-ri-phon's forces long before they saw the pale-stone streets of the Queendom's desert jewel. Xala bribed a lesser official as the inspection was going on.

"Get a message to the General. *Felnuuar* requests his personal assistance in an important matter out at the gate. And give him this. It belongs to him."

Her mundane messenger studied the ring, not knowing its value. "*Felnuuar*?"

Xala nodded. "He'll understand. Go."

As she expected, it took some time to hear back. Patiently, she tended a bundled, disguised Ishuna in the meantime.

The *qu'essan* had given birth in the dunes, much closer to the borders of the Queendom than expected, but the infant had died shortly after. It had turned out to be male, not the daughter they'd thought to nurture in secret.

The shock had been too much for Ishuna.

Her charge was in a lethargic state of deep apathy, which was understandable. She could barely walk or make herself eat, and so Xala had made the decision to abandon their search for the Spire, and return to the capital and her family to mend her body and spirit.

"Xala!" Cris called out. "You've returned!"

He must have ridden out directly from the military offices rather than the Palace. He looked splendid in his armor, and his entourage was an even mix of Human and Davrin.

The Captain bowed as he dismounted, swiftly approaching her. "Sorcerer-General."

The Godblood smiled to cover his worry, looking around and behind her for his wife's sister.

"General, the … uh, the Royal Seer should be taken to the Palace as soon as you can arrange it."

Some of the caravan traders who had been hovering near in their curiosity now shifted nervously. They glanced toward the cloaked figure they had carried here alongside a clear Davrin warrior.

Cris's face was as young as ever, his bronze skin and dark hair striking along with his steel-grey eyes even before one got to the fine armor and distinct uniform honoring both Musanlo and the Queen of V'Gedra.

Most men anywhere near his status would have been willing to simply give orders to see this done. Instead, he moved over to Ishuna himself, kneeling in front of her and trying to lift her chin so she would look at him.

"Ishuna? Are you hurt?"

She jerked away and shouted, "Don't touch me!"

Xala sighed as murmurs spread through the small crowd of traders and soldiers. *Now with the public drama.*

The next moment, however, the *qu'essan* blinked and seemed to recognize the General. Xala was just close enough to hear her whisper.

"I w-want to see my sister …"

"Of course, Seer. Right away. Can you ride? We'll take my horse."

Cris-ri-phon helped her to her feet, allowing no one else by Xala near her as he boosted her up onto his stallion, something she barely tolerated.

Nodding and gesturing to Xala to join him, the Sorcerer-General led his horse without trying to mount up behind his sister-in-law and walked on his own two feet back toward the Palace.

ISHUNA WAS BACK IN HER OWN ROOM, IN HER OWN BED — MAINTAINED AND kept the same for her return. She awaited the Queen when Cris found a private place to ask Xala to speak with him. She couldn't deny the request, even if she could omit anything personal for the *qu'essan*.

Her own chain of command had long been broken, but she was still under him where it came to Palace security, so she joined him in that first, silent interview full of gestures.

⋆What happened on your journey?⋆ he asked. ⋆How was she hurt?⋆

Xala pursed her lips. ⋆I'm curious, General. What do you think happened?⋆

The Queen's Consort was extraordinarily blunt on that matter as he focused intently, to the point she doubted she could outright lie without him detecting it. His magic had grown strong enough and his anger was just starting to show.

⋆I've been around a long time, Xala. I've seen those signs before. I would say she's been raped.⋆

Damn.

In all their talk in the wilderness before the stillbirth, Xala never learned whether Ishuna would want her to name Szoroan or not.

If the Captain did so now, the Blade Singer would likely be apprehended, stripped of all honors, and put to death under Innathi's Soul Blade before Ishuna was even out of bed.

This would happen whether that was part of Ishuna's plan or not. Maybe the Seer could not form a plan at all at this point, or maybe she just needed more time, but Xala truly did not want to make such decisions on behalf of the Seer following a fulfilling journey together, despite the terrible, heart-breaking ending.

And beyond that …

Xala feared that Queen Innathi would want to punish her for such failures, as what had happened in the stable would inevitably come out to explain what had led to such a troubling homecoming. The scars on her back itched, and for the moment, the warrior wanted nothing more than to avoid the wrath of a second Queen, for another similar failure.

You don't belong in V'Gedra anymore, "Captain." You certainly don't belong among the royalty. Yet you'll linger regardless, won't you?

You have nowhere to be.

Xala exhaled, choosing her gestures carefully. ★Royal matters, General. I beg your tolerance to let Ishuna speak for herself and not spread damaging rumors like that in the meantime. Perhaps it is best to let your Wife and Queen handle this. She is coming, isn't she?★

The powerful Sorcerer detected no lie in this, but he narrowed his eyes thoughtfully. He nodded. ★Very well.★

"UGH! YOU NEED A BATH, ISHUNA. COME, IT HAS BEEN PREPARED. I WILL help you, and we shall talk. You must tell me what happened while you've been away."

Innathi had come at last, but she couldn't overlook the road stink. Thus, Ishuna had time to consider, and reconsider, as they waited for privacy. The Seer appraised her older sister's plusher form, as she'd recently had her fourth child with her General-Husband. Her breasts were still full of milk.

At least she didn't bring the baby along and insist I hold it …

Nor were any of the other three siblings pestering their Mother and Aunt for undue attention, no doubt being kept back with their governors.

Ishuna blinked slowly as something did not seem quite right about that memory. *Except Leuren'qo. He is old enough to be serving his sire in the army …*

The first son was an adult now.

Impossible. It's too soon!

The Guardsvrin were outside, of course, and probably Xala, too. The General kept away as he should, and Innathi helped her bathe with a hesitancy and reluctance to get wet which proved she'd never bathed her own children. This show was a deliberate effort to construct the intimacy needed to have a sisterly talk.

Ishuna had asked for Innathi before getting on Cris's horse; she truly meant it at the time. But now, the Seer wasn't sure she wanted to share, and she had trouble remembering the most important parts.

Something is missing …

"I can't believe that spider pendant hasn't gotten lost," Innathi said with a smirk. "So many decades, so many frayed thongs. You really should have gotten a chain for it by now. It's ridiculous the way it is tied at the back. Here, let us take it off."

Ishuna allowed it while gripping the sides of the tub, feeling very odd; she ducked her head as the Queen set it aside on the edge of the tub. Her chest itched, and she had the impulse to scratch where the silver and amethyst had been.

Looking down and surprised to see her skin was perfect, unmarked.

Something is missing.

"So, did you find it?" Innathi asked.

"Hm?"

Find what?

"The Spire. Did you find the Spire?"

Ishuna stared at the surface of the tiny pool of water for a time, unsure how much time passed as she failed to answer. She looked at her breasts, her belly. *Normal. No signs of change.*

Her sister did not notice anything at all amiss, seeing her naked.

Innathi sighed. "I expected not, otherwise you'd have been much happier upon your return. What happened? You are as glum now as you were when you left."

Again, Ishuna failed to answer her sister, her Queen. Her only blood family she could acknowledge …

Something … Is. Missing!

Ishuna shook her head. "A wasted journey. We found nothing. I am still … unable to see, my Queen. The mystics were wrong. I apologize for being useless."

Innathi leaned in, squeezing her bare shoulder firmly. "You are trying *too hard*. Your gift will come back when you are ready." She hesitated. "Would you want to talk to a Deathwalker? That seemed to help you once. What was her name — ?"

Ishuna shook her head urgently. "No. Not one of them. They are *no* help!"

"Very well, be easy, sister." Innathi laughed lightly, rubbing her back with a washcloth. "Don't leave V'Gedra like that again, Ishuna, I worried every day you were away. Promise me you won't leave on such a vague, sun-dream search like that again."

The Royal Seer, when pressed, managed a nod to satisfy her Queen. But again, she failed to answer.

"MY QUEEN, I THINK SOMEONE HARMED ISHUNA ON HER JOURNEY, AND SHE is too ashamed to confess it. Even to you."

"Don't be presumptuous, Cris. Xala was with her, and she says no such thing happened. Ishuna has always been moody, I can hardly tell a difference from when she left, or even the past hundred years for that matter."

Perhaps because you never have time to really look at her, as you rarely do our own children.

The Consort-General closed his eyes and exhaled slowly, guarding against such ungenerousness. "Innathi, I swear to you. I saw her face when she first looked at me. I've seen survival terror of that nature before. She hadn't yet realized she was home."

Innathi set down her quill and narrowed her eyes at him. "And yet she tells me all is well, and the search was fruitless."

"She had time to build some walls before you arrived."

"And say that is so, what do you propose we do, dear Husband? Tear them down with destructive spells like you do in your war games?"

He frowned at her mocking expression. "Xala brought them back early. She made a command decision to do so, I'm sure of it, but she wouldn't answer me."

"Oh, she wouldn't?" Innathi turned a scroll slightly. "Because she said it was a royal matter outside your security duties, wasn't it?"

"Yes, but I am not certain that is true. I think you should ask more questions, my Queen."

"I shall add it to my interrogation list," she commented dismissively. "Despite Ishuna's protest that I leave her bodyguard with her. I *did* give my sister complete authority over Xala Ja'Prohn, if you recall, and yes, that is something I might regret a bit now."

"If you suspect she is hiding anything, it is in the best interest of your Queendom and your children that one so close to you is transparent in any trouble they may have encountered —"

Innathi slammed down her palm, scowling at him; she'd nearly made him jump. "I suspect nothing, you do! Yet *you* were the one who convinced me to let her go in the first place, Cris. You said it would do her good, and it didn't. She is *worse* than before!

"And now you wish to accuse my own sister *and* my childhood guardian of being a security threat because they won't describe their pointless ventures and embarrassing failures to you in detail?! You try to use our children as leverage to make me alter my understanding with my sister's personal guard, but in that, you overstep your bounds, *Consort.*"

The Sorcerer bit his tongue against a sharp retort, fist clenched hard as he silently looked to the side. It would do no good to push her further.

"Forgive me, my Queen. Then, if you'll grant me leave, I'd like to see our new daughter in the nursery before I head out to the walls again."

"Leave granted, General."

CHAPTER 7

V'GEDRA – 187-163 B.S.E.

ISHUNA WATCHED THE CAPITAL CITY IN THE TWO DECADES TO FOLLOW.

She was always listening.

Another half-breed child was added to the royal nursery. And then another. The sight she'd seen before — of Innathi holding Cris at knife-point with that cursed dagger as he bred her — continued. The Queen seemed to relish each pregnancy, her magic and powerful presence at their pinnacle as her belly swelled.

Soul Drinker was always at her side, reminding the people of the consequences in being caught weakening the Queendom in the face of the increasingly aggressive Naulor or their allies.

The blatant fertility was something no Davrin matron had ever matched before. It placed the Queen of V'Gedra head and shoulders above any large House of note.

Yet the children were all half-Human.

This seemed to encourage the Zauyrians to presume more influence than they really had, prompting silent sneers and private slurs among the counselors and administrators alike.

The main source of distrust, it seemed, was that Innathi didn't seem to know when to stop. They said the General had asked for heirs — just a couple heirs — to become her faithful champion. Maybe the first three would have been enough. Three was more than most Zauyrian women could bear before they died.

And yet now … Innathi had just conceived her seventh child with the Godblood.

All the while, the Royal Seer's influence waned as she bore her nightmares in the evening and saw shadows in the daylight with numbing regularity. None of it was specific enough to mention, only a sense of dread and foreboding which lingered in the corners.

Through it all, there remained a sense of something … missing.

What is it? What can't I remember?

The people were growing concerned, according to Xala. War and battle were on the incline, and their Queen grew more ruthless on account. Astounding that the General of the Army was the one trying to caution against using undue shows of force.

"Undue?!" Innathi shrieked, once Ishuna figured out this most recent ward and listened in one evening. "They decimate our borders year over year! They capture Zauyrians for prisoner exchange yet *kill* my Wilder on sight! They bring *walking trees* that do not bleed and resist fire! And still Yivon officially denies aggression. She refuses to meet! This is *our* Desert, our heritage, and for what we offer in precious metals and magic, she has no right to cut us off from the rest of the continent!"

Innathi growled in her fury, and Ishuna could well imagine her sister drawing the black dagger as her comfort.

"I shall see all of them trapped inside Soul Drinker and send a message, Cris. You will bring back as many prisoners as you can, *especially* the Pale Ones! Let our people see for themselves what we are doing to keep them safe, so they may be grateful for all I have given them!"

Such displays happened. They were satisfying. Horrifying. It felt like they had won something, and yet … it also seemed like control was slipping.

The seventh child was a cait. Four males, and now three females. The relief that Innathi could still have daughters was short-lived when all remembered they weren't true heirs of V'Gedra, and most of them seemed to want to get out of their Queen-Mother's Palace and run to their father in the field as soon as they were old enough.

The children grew far too quickly, as if more Human than Elf.

Ishuna hadn't left the Palace or the royal "safe" routes since she'd returned from the deep Desert, much to her sister's satisfaction. She wandered, studied, slept in Reverie, and listened to every bit of gossip she could. She tried to see her visions and mostly failed. She practiced enough magic to remain a mage, but nothing compared to what her sister was.

The three later nieces and nephews did not bother her as often as the early ones did, although she was aware that they whispered about her behind her back. They said she was "mystic."

Which, once again, was being used among the populace to suggest someone unwell. Someone strange.

And always dreaming.

One dream to which she clung lately held a glimpse of a mound of gold crying like a Davrin child. The treasure cried for its Mother, for Mother's milk, and in the dream, her breasts ached as her nipples leaked, begging to feed the hungry child.

It was a strange dream. Like her.

How quickly old prejudices resurfaced when she no longer had the strength or worth to push back at them.

A meeting held one day would sear the edges of the veil surrounding her thoughts, later to set it aflame. Perhaps this was inevitable, as more and more Blade Singers had been coming to the central school in the city. Ishuna had long wandered its libraries as one of the few places she could go outside the Palace that her sister approved.

The bua didn't say a word when he nearly collided with her rounding a corner. He had been talking to a friend, a fellow Blade Singer, and his voice caught in his throat as he halted, stunned and silent.

His friend spoke first, recognizing her. "*Qu'essan!*"

A graceful, purely appropriate bow followed before he pulled his friend to the side, nudging him to follow his lead. The bua did after shaking himself out of his momentary stupor.

"Forgive us for obstructing you. Can we assist you, *qu'essan*?"

She nodded acknowledgement, satisfied with the humility, but then shook her head. "No, Blade Singer. I am finding what I need. Do you keep up with the General's mandate?"

"We do, *qu'essan,*" the one said confidently while the other remained silent. "Coming in from the distant borders for new study shall always have its place, even if we spell-dancers learn better in action!"

Ishuna narrowed her eyes at what seemed a backhanded compliment but shrugged. She hadn't the energy to defend the Zauyrian Sorcerer. She looked at the other one. At his face. His eyes.

Familiar.

"If you'll release us, *qu'essan?*" the first suggested.

The other dared not speak. She never heard his voice.

"Of course," she said mildly. "Dismissed."

She watched them go with the sense that she should know why her heart was beating so loud within her ears.

I almost … remember.

What was missing.

She meditated on this for days, yet never drew close to the answer.

She felt numb here. Deaf to her own song.

For centuries, she had been impaired.

I must stand somewhere outside of V'Gedra to hear the song again.

ISHUNA LEFT XALA BACK IN THE CITY, GRANTING HER LEAVE TO VISIT SOME family among House Ja'Prohn who *didn't* despise her. She didn't tell anyone at all where she was going. Perhaps she wasn't certain herself.

No one cares.

They won't stop me.

A simple concealment spell allowed her to sneak past the sentries and move unnoticed through the wards, entering the old underground tunnel leading from the Palace to the ravines of the Edonil foothills.

Alone and unseen, she walked for the rest of the day and into the

her cunt dripped down her left thigh as she kept her knees wide open and her ass up. Behind her, something lapped at the fluid.

Rrready to try againnn … ?

Through eager hisses and encouraging growls, rasping, stubbled tongues probed around her fingers, encouraging her to remove them from her back hole. Once she did, split tongues immediately replaced them, squirming into her pucker.

**Yesss … Ourrrsss …*

She yelped as tongues fought for space; she remained in place, writhed in need, her thighs quivering, empty sex twitching. Despite the intense and unfamiliar focus, her asshole relaxed beneath their service.

Until they stopped.

Get downnnn … .

Ishuna could not question; she settled down, bracing her weight on her shoulders.

**Shhhow Ussss …*

She reached back to grab both buttocks with her hands. Wordlessly, she spread them wider.

An invitation, though she did not know to what.

Ssszoroan.

She blinked, recognizing the name of the Blade Singer. *Szoroan … ?*

**He cuckolded Usss …*

Whatever clutched her back shifted down slightly. A horn-like tip probed at her winking rear portal.

**Took you … closed you to Usss …*

It penetrated her smoothly, the length soon followed by coarse edges scraping at the inside of this tighter passage.

Until we fffound a new way inssside.

The Seer groaned loudly as the strange phallus rippled on its own, burrowing into her ass, pulling itself inside like an earthworm in freshly tilled soil. Each flex spread her anus wider as the invader sought her depths, its girth stretching her so tight she thought it *must* stop there.

Until it reached even deeper inside, only got thicker.

**Sso many blocksss in Our way …*

And her body yielded again.

★*We shhhall make them pay! Yesss?*★

"Ohhh, pleeease!" she moaned, writhing underneath it, unsure what she begged for.

It tightened its hold on her back and shoved forward, forcing a grunt from her lips. Her strained orifice squeezed partway closed, clamping down tight on a round bulge now clogging her excreter.

She couldn't get it out.

The shadow had secured its anchor to her body before claiming more, latching onto her back, gripping her wrists. It pressed them to the rocky ledge, then began feeding on her aura while a second probe teased her empty cunt open.

Oh, goddess — ! Stop!

★*Hehhhh … Not a goddessss.*★

Th-then what are you?

★*You know. You sssaw Usss. Sssaw thisss joining … in your mirror.*★

Ishuna hesitated to recall that, whimpering as misery warred with want to feel the second phallus slithering its head between her slick petals without entering, without thrusting.

Thisss …

The second cock nipped at her clitoris, making her flinch and scream before it dipped partway inside her body, thrashing and twisting at the entrance of her slit before withdrawing.

***Thisss** is ressserved for a sssire, no? If you call Usss, we shall make of Ourss-selvesss a ssire to you. Jusst call Usss …*

"A-a sire … ?"

★*We shhhall be your Priestesss …* ★

So heavy.

She couldn't get up, couldn't move forward, or hope to separate them. The weight on her back was too much, the anchor locked in her rectum beyond prayer to squeeze it out.

The Priestess could hold her like this for hours, or may have already done so, all the while scratching at the sides of her breasts, clinging to her, supping upon her aura while they became so deeply familiar …

Ishuna climaxed twice while it played with her, without touching her dripping slit. She shuddered as the smaller, prehensile cock ceased nipping her nub and reached forward to find her lax mouth.

It slipped in, gagging her like Szoroan to quiet her noise while the Priestess rode her. Her knees grew sore, but she couldn't close her legs without being fulfilled.

She didn't have the strength.

Weak.

Like her Mother always said.

Priestess! Priestess, please!

Yesss.

H-How do I call … ?

Call for what?

For y-you to … s-service me …

A hiss of pure bliss.

It tugged backward in her ass, pulling hard to remove the turgid knot, stretching her purple ring taut. The moment of relief was snatched away as the Priestess forced the Davrin's gaping netherhole take the bulge again. It relished her mewling as it leaned in, leaned down, claws caressing her breasts.

Lissten for Our True Name, Ishhhunnna. Invite Usss in … and in repayment, We shhall give you a worthy daughter. Unlike that first ssson.

First son.

The creature ripped off the veil of the spell, tore it to shreds. Her head threatened to split in half, and Ishuna gagged, choking around the oozing cock in her mouth.

She remembered.

Rrrrrraaaugh!

She remembered!

They STOLE him!!

The Priestess chuckled, pulling the squirming appendage from the Seer's mouth and sliding it into her cunt. **Would you killll him, Ishhhunnna?**

Ishuna gasped for breath, staring at the ground as she was doubly penetrated, ready to peak from the arching, intelligent tease digging between her netherlips. *K-Kill who?*

★*Kill Ssszoroan. Kill Wruzdiinnn. Kill every male who hasss ever wronged you. Our cocks will ssserve you, to sssee it happen. We will give you what you want. Our power shhhall be bound here, added to yours ... forever.*★

Ishuna orgasmed with a loud cry, hips rolling as she spread her knees wider, as both cocks dripped their filth inside her. It *burned*. In her ass, on her tongue ...

Against her womb.

★*When your ssisster ssslips farther as a man's broodmare, we could help you sssave the Queendom and the Matriarchy. With Usss, you will be powerful, Ishhunnna. You sshall never be weak againnn.*★

Priestess ... ! Augh, gah ... So deep!

The Priestess's cockhead squirmed relentlessly, latching onto her flesh inside. Nestling in like a rock-cleaner ready to feed. Ishuna bucked at the sharp, ethereal pain, a new penetration.

She climaxed from it.

Goddess, it *hurt*.

★*You are rrready to try againnn ... Call Usss. Conceive your First Daughter in ritual with Usss ... the firsst of a new line of powerful daughtersss ...* ★

Ishuna listened.

She heard that True Name, even above her own crooning and moaning, prostrate before her new Priestess. Power flowed in through the thick anchor lodged in her ass, and foreign seed pumped through the writhing phallus in her cunt, filling her womb in advance.

A pool of jism ready the moment their auras merged.

Ishuna wriggled and swayed her hips, whispered the name.

★*Morrre ...* ★

She said it louder.

The air around her began to vibrate. She gripped her fingernails into the stone ledge and filled her lungs.

She shouted the Name.

Invited them in.

★*Perrrfect pronunciation, Ssseer.*★

Boiling shadows rolled around her as multiple prickly hands seized her hips, and she yelped in fear. Before they could start pulling, the anchor suddenly shrank, leaving her pucker loose, clutching weakly at almost nothing.

The cock in her cunt swelled instead, stretching her near to the size of her first infant. The prickly hands withdrew.

Argh, Priestess!!

The Priestess held her down, riding her aura and body, burrowing into every weak spot, every crack in her shields ...

Until they came together. Auras merging into one.

Ishuna drank them in and, the moment after, they both knew.

... pregnant ...

Again.

⋆*To give you powwwerrr, chillld. The means for revenge against the Dragon who ssstole your ssson. Against your sssire for rejecting you like a fffool, for helping to debassse you, ssstrip your memory from you ...* ⋆

"P-promise?" she asked aloud.

"Ohhh, Isshunnaa ..." the Priestess breathed in reverent satisfaction. "We promisssse ..."

They loomed above her. Tangible, and present.

In and on top of her.

She reached a fumbling hand back. This time, she touched something.

Something real.

Ishuna sweated and trembled on her knees, becoming aware of the pain from their coupling vying for her attention.

Ow ... Get ... out ...

A light chuckle. *Too late.*

"Ssstrong Isshunnaaa ..." the demon cooed then, drooling on her back. Licking her. "Ourrr new Valssharresss ... ."

"V-Valsharess," she whispered.

They pulled their double-cock out of her two raw holes, drawing another yelp as mixed fluids spilled down her thighs and onto the dry ground. Her own voice answered back.

You shall be the Savior of the Davrin people.
Thus We have Seen.

CHAPTER 8

V'GEDRA – 162 B.S.E.

THE SERVANTS HAD SEEN ISHUNA ENTER THE PALACE LIBRARY, YET XALA ALmost missed her when she scanned the familiar shelves and seats.

Her posture had changed.

"*Qu'essan?*"

The bodyguard approached with caution, a subtle chill moving up her spine when Ishuna turned around from the scrolls she'd been browsing.

She smiled. "Good morning, Xala. It's good to see you. How was your visit?"

The Captain couldn't remember the last time she had been caught standing with her mouth open. "Um. Good. I guess."

Ishuna looked her up and down; her eyes seemed paler in this light, closer to topaz than the sandy copper of before.

"I have a question for you, Xala," the royal said, straightening her back and looking as elegant as her Mother.

Xala jerked herself out of her stare. "Yes, *qu'essan*? What is it?"

A frown then, disapproving. "You called me Ishuna more often in the Desert."

Had she?

"Yes, you did. I'd like you to do so again when we're alone. Speak frankly, no one can hear us."

Xala swallowed, looking around the library. A few other scholars sat near enough to hear them if there hadn't been some sort of protection. Shifting her senses, she kicked herself for not picking up the sound ward before now.

"Alright. What is your question, Ishuna?"

"Do you remember my sire?"

A sensation like a long needle punching through her skull and into her brain struck, making Xala wince with a hiss.

Ishuna kept staring at her, unblinking, with those strange, light-colored eyes.

Like eyes I've seen before … Gold, but not quite.

"N-no, *qu'essan*. I do not."

"Not true!" Ishuna barked. "I remember! So must you!"

Xala clutched her head at the stabbing pain.

"You knew him! His name was Wruzdiin, your Great Uncle! We are cousins, you and me, but Mother never told us!"

AH! Fucking Goddess!

"Ishuna, please … ." She pressed her palms to her temples as hard as she could, as if she could squeeze the pain out that way. "S-slowly … I-I think I know what you're trying to do, but … slower. Or you'll break me. A-and I'll be no good to you."

The younger female brought her voice down and drew her aura back, giving her bodyguard a chance to take a full breath.

Xala's head throbbed horribly. She groped for a chair to sit down. Gripping the arms, she felt something trickle out of one ear and reached to touch it, unsurprised to see it colored red. She breathed deeply, afraid to move much or look at Ishuna's eyes while she willed herself not to vomit onto the floor of the royal library.

"They stole *your* memories, too," Ishuna whispered bitterly.

They? They, who?

With all her effort, Xala centered herself within the eye of the sandstorm within. She couldn't figure anything out at this moment, so she didn't try controlling the winds. If little else, she at least understood the signs of a powerful spell being challenged by Ishuna's anger.

"Just ..." the Captain began hesitantly. "Just tell me ... two things which should be different, Ishuna. I must go lie down, or you may kill me trying to set those memories free. But I promise, I will meditate on what you say."

Her *qu'essan* followed her advice in this, as she had in the desert when they'd been traveling together. They still needed each other.

"We found the Spire," Ishuna murmured. "We did *not* turn around having failed."

Xala couldn't remember that, but she nodded slowly. "Got it. That's one. Two?"

"My baby *didn't* die in the wilderness," the Seer added, her voice trembling.

Xala's felt her heart clench in her chest as she sensed its truth.

"They kept him at the Spire."

She was struggling to breathe as she still gripped the chair harder, staring at the floor.

"That Dragon — !"

Lifting her palm, Xala wheezed with a desperate nod. "That's enough. N-no more. I-I will return when I can. I promise."

Looking hopeful, Ishuna granted her bodyguard leave to rest as she needed it.

"*Come back to me*," she whispered urgently as Xala made her way out. "You're the only Davrin I can trust."

"ISHUNA, WHERE IS CAPTAIN XALA?" CRIS ASKED. "I HAVEN'T SEEN HER WITH you lately."

Ishuna's back was to him as she poured over a scroll, jotting some detailed notes. "It seems like you wouldn't have much opportunity, General. But if you must know, she is resting. I believe she may have strained her abilities the last time we sparred."

"Sparred?" He tilted his head. "Since when do you spar with other mages, Ishuna?"

His sister-in-law lifted her head slowly and turned on her stool. She watched him with a chilly expression, but also a little smile. "Since we were in the deep Desert together for two years, Cris. I needed practice, and it was necessary. We paused for a time upon our return but have now taken it up again."

The Sorcerer drew in quickly the realization that, after whole *decades*, Ishuna had brought this subject up on her own, one which Innathi had forbidden him from asking about it. He wanted to skim her surface thoughts, detect any untruths, lower her guard with a soothing, simple charm spell ...

She'd put protections in place, however. His own magic could sense them, and she would be aware of the smallest cantrip if he tried to cast any counter. It surprised him that she was paying more attention to this, but perhaps it was a good sign that she was studying her magic again.

Perhaps it meant her confidence and her visions would return.

Interact simply, without magic, and rely on the mundane.

"I remember similar things," he offered, "when I traveled farther from the Realms and V'Gedra than I'd ever been before. One must be open to many different tactics when traveling in small numbers. Is there anything you discovered that made it worth it, Ishuna, even if you did not find the Spire?"

She made a face.

Brief as it was, he pondered how to interpret it,if she simply didn't like him pointing out her failure or if he'd gotten something wrong.

Meanwhile, she prepared her own answer to his question.

"Perhaps only that most Zauyrian men cannot be trusted to behave properly around two lone women," she said snidely. "I cannot tell you how many propositions we had to turn down once outside the Queendom, among villages, caravans, oases, and trading posts. I had not realized how driven by their crotches all men are."

Cris caught the insinuation for it was obvious, but he did not take the bait. He took a slow breath and wetted his mouth before he asked as directly as he dared. "Does any man acting improperly explain how I first saw you?"

She blinked, drawing back a step. "What do you mean?"

"You lashed out at me, told me not to touch you. You looked like you expected to be attacked. Perhaps again."

The Seer straightened her back immediately, narrowing tawny eyes at him. "Perhaps that was strictly because it was *you*, Cris, and not some other man you could offer to arrest on behalf of my 'honor.' "

That surprised him. He stared at her. "Because … of me?"

Ishuna laughed, shaking her head. "Oh. You do not remember. I have wondered if your long life has made your memory more selective. Although perhaps you never acknowledged it even before you met a few ancients to make a show of that blessing you yearn for."

A very, very old feeling began to return, called up from a dark place he'd forgotten existed with the birth of his first son. She was making him waver, not the other way around. He could do nothing but what he'd done before: grip it by the hilt, withdraw what was so cutting and take a long, careful look at it.

"You mean Koorul?" he said. "When I was a boy."

Ishuna's white brows shot up and her purple lips split into a brilliant grin. "Oh! My Goddess, you *do* still remember! Tell me. Does being a 'boy' excuse you? Can you see why I might react to you in such a way? I've never touched you, Cris, though you've presumed a few times to touch *me* because you're with my sister."

This was much deeper than he realized. He wasn't prepared for this; he felt the anger all over again.

He remembered Ishuna's deliberate sabotage of the ritual that was supposed to help them *both*, her taunting and ruthless attack of his doubts, using Innathi's jealousy hovering at the border — always petty as a young *qu'essan* but only growing stronger with her maturity.

Leur needed to step in to finish it.

Houda's disappointment in him cut deep. His older brother's frustration had been clear. His own realization that he *couldn't* be both the Sun Sorcerer and the Deathwalker they'd wanted him to be.

Not if he would have Innathi, too.

He had to choose, and when he'd also had to leave V'Gedra, the price had increased.

I can't be both.

And Ishuna didn't want to be healed anyway.

Leur. God, I miss you, brother. I shouldn't have been away so long, until you grew so old, we couldn't relate anymore.

And Ishuna had mentioned the ancients. What did she know? Or was she bluffing?

"Where do we stand, Ishuna?" he asked, keeping his anger under tight control. She wasn't practiced enough with interpersonal experience to be able to hear it. "Perhaps we can work toward a better place, you and I."

She shrugged. "You have enough children filling the Palace and you remain the Queen's Consort-General until you die, Cris-ri-phon. How will it be other than it has always been? Unless I want to try to rip you apart, which Xala has been good enough to teach will only isolate me from all of you. Even her." She harrumphed, smirking. "We are still family, are we not?"

The Sorcerer watched her warily. She had been about to outright accuse him of violation, he'd known it. If not at Koorul, then at the garden ritual he did not complete to heal her aura.

She was right in that they had almost never touched since then.

Now she was telling him they were family? That they would live with what had been?

"We should talk more," he suggested.

She kept smiling. "Of course. Thank you for all the protections you offered for my journey, though it is overdue. Many nights and days, those gifts saved us much trouble and suffering."

Cris blinked, somewhat mollified. Xala had thanked him for those valuable objects both before and after; Ishuna never had. He nodded. "You're welcome. I needed similar in my travels."

"I guessed." She looked away and down at her open scroll, eyes scanning a few lines. "Perhaps we can spar sometime, Cris, when Xala says I'm ready."

He tried to look down at what she was reading, but her hip shifted just right to hide it from view. Her pose was uncharacteristically sensual. It recalled his failed ritual again in the pavilion, and he backed off.

"Certainly, *qu'essan*. I'll be interested to see what you've learned."

She was finished talking, and Cris left hoping to get another opportunity to speak, though of what he wasn't sure.

Not if how she'd looked at him upon her return from the deep Desert twenty-four years ago was *because* of him, and not something she experienced while seeking the Spire.

Wruzdiin has a message he wanted me to give you. When you were ready to hear it.

"Musanlo grant it," Xala murmured, having made sure she was alone, and no one would hear her as she meditated outside beneath a small sunshade.

Ishuna wouldn't approve of her choice of prayer, but sometimes Musanlo was just there in ways others weren't. The Sun God — favoring Humans mostly, depending on the story, and male in every account — just made more things happen from where she stood. Musanlo's Eye was often there to hear or see when things went awry.

The former Captain had become quite familiar with all the Sun offered in her exile, and she had always respected Cris-ri-phon for the homage he paid to the Red Desert's most prominent deity.

She was just coming out of her most recent efforts now, and she had heard his voice.

Mazdek.

Heard his warning.

He'd set an extremely powerful spell, not Elven in nature, and the Captain was still not sure how Ishuna had broken it by herself.

Since then and over the last year, the two of them had been working to unravel it for Xala without killing her. This had provided a good opportunity for the Seer to practice her magic and study for ways to set Xala "free." This saw the *qu'essan* delving into more of the ancient collections from her Queen-Mother's time and devoting herself to those studies.

They realized it was difficult for Xala to recall anything specific about her great uncle while standing in V'Gedra itself — this thanks to the lingering efforts of Alyarra, they now knew. So, Xala had begun riding out into the wilderness to meditate on what methods Ishuna gave her to try.

It was out here that she made her breakthrough. She was remembering more of Wruzdiin, as she'd done before, but just today, Xala finally recalled the name of the Dragon.

Mazdek.

The massive, orange Serpent Man with whom she'd mated on multiple occasions, out of Ishuna's sight.

Hm. Best not volunteer that any time soon.

Theirs had been a private pleasure, completely lacking in drama, when she most needed it. Xala wanted to keep it that way.

She didn't remember everything even now, but she had that best memory of her time at the Spire, the knowledge her Great Uncle was alive, and that Ishuna was right.

They had found the Spire. Her baby hadn't died but instead had been born on a Dragon's Hoard to fulfill one of the old Seer's visions.

Ishuna's son — Xala couldn't recall a name — would never choose to leave the Spire. If he were taken, Mazdek would be compelled to retrieve him at any cost.

Or so he had told Ishuna in a dream.

Xala still wondered how much Ishuna remembered that she did not, but concerning her even more were *other* details which the Captain was noticing now. Signs which disturbed her.

Ishuna had improved dramatically with her illusions and being careful in her personal habits, not speaking about the possibility at all, but her bodyguard knew her well enough to notice some familiar changes.

Such as that fermented radish juice the pregnant *qu'essan* had taken a liking to in the Desert but was never seen in V'Gedra among the high class, because it was peasant food. Xala had recognized the scent on Ishuna's breath twice now.

She also noticed that Ishuna was excited for each day, as if she had a purpose or a plan. She held her head high, the same way she had when she thought she carried the next Heir to V'Gedra, before learning that it was a bua.

Is she pregnant again? If she is, will she hide it even from me this time?

Later, Xala made her confessions in their private room in the archives.

"I remember enough, Seer. There is more to unravel, but I remember that it is true, what you told me."

To her surprise, Ishuna's eyes filled with tears, something Xala hadn't seen in years, even the *qu'essan* at her most morose. She clasped her hands tightly together in her lap, taking a deep breath to keep her composure.

"You remember my firstborn."

Xala nodded warily. "Yes. A bua with golden eyes." She lowered her voice. "Much like the Dragon's eyes."

Ishuna's hands separated, and she clutched the arms of her chair as if she would turn it to splinters in her grip, her demeanor changing swiftly.

"Yes. Stolen from birth. Pure and unsoiled." She glared; her aura throbbed with a red threat. "I want him back."

The Captain worked to control her expression at the apparent change of heart about the disappointing birth. She wasn't sure what Ishuna thought she would do with him within the Queendom, but perhaps there were more options if they simply acknowledged him publicly.

"What of the magical connection to the Hoard, *qu'essan*? Were they lying about that?"

Ishuna maintained the hateful glare but shook her head and spoke with outward calm. "No, they were not. But there may be something I can do. I have been searching, working for this. I must return to the Spire within the next year. My son is still young. He can still know his Mother."

"Um. You will head into the Desert?"

"Yes."

Though the warning was plain in Xala's mind — *Do not follow her the next time.* — it would be too strange not to say it.

"When do we leave, *qu'essan*? And will you tell me your plan now, or once we are riding, as before?"

Ishuna sat oddly for a long time without answering, staring as though she were looking through her. Xala waited, her tension trying to rise as she continually tamped it down.

"Soon," Ishuna said, her eyes sliding to the side. "It will not take as long as before. I will have spells to help. Do not make any preparations at all. That would alert my sister. You will not need them, anyway. I will take care of everything this time."

Having survived all manner of harsh environments and many conditions through her seven centuries, Xala could not believe that to be true. Not even the Sorcerer-General headed into the desert unprepared.

But she bowed her head and did not argue. She could see this lifted the Seer's confidence immediately, and Ishuna smiled broadly.

"Soon," she repeated.

CHAPTER 9

THE DESERT SPIRE – 162 B.S.E.

WRUZDIIN STOOD OUT ON A BALCONY FACING TRUE NORTH. HE EXHALED slowly, wishing this was the moment when his body would simply … stop. When at last he would have oblivion.

Another quarter century, and already the visions came too soon after the last ones. Scarring his every attempt to rest.

"You weep, *Kiabil,*" Mazdek stated.

The ancient Davrin turned around, looking into the dimmer room of the Spire. His grandson, Mazdel, had been curled up dozing in the Great Serpent's cradling coils, but the child awoke abruptly at the sound of his rumbling voice, blinking innocent, golden eyes.

Wruzdiin wept, this was true, but at least a sight like this could still raise one corner of his mouth.

"She has accepted the outsider bond," he murmured quietly. "Ishuna grows much stronger now. She and her allies *will* pose a threat to you, great To'vah."

The child rarely spoke, for the constant song he heard around him often spoke on his behalf, but his shining eyes widened in response. Mazdel shook his head in denial, whimpering softly. The Flame lifted the bua out of his tail and cradled him close, reassuring him with a gentle squeeze as the two sat in the center of the room in quiet contemplation.

Mazdek never asked Wruzdiin for too many details of these visions, and the elderly Elf knew the Dragon had abundant gifts, knowledge, and insights of his own to weigh against them. Because of that, the Seer tried not to struggle too much when he could not make out a clear outcome, as if it wouldn't change.

The visions within his own lifetime could *always* change and did more often the faster they approached the present. Only the one vision beyond Wruzdiin's own lifetime had never changed, after what they had done to his and Alyarra's daughter.

Its stable familiarity comforted and terrified him.

Mazdek knew this, so he did not ask. The Dragon did not hound him for assurances or "proof" like the Thousand Year Queen had. He did not grow angry with the perceived loss of control and attempt to bargain with fate.

Mazdek'pien the Flame was much, much wiser than that.

"That was what she never understood," Wruzdiin murmured.

Mazdek and his son lifted their chins to listen.

"She thought my visions were meant for her. Another resource for the Queendom. It is no surprise to me that Innathi turned out the same. If the mystics couldn't 'prove their worth,' then we were withholding what was not ours to hide. Accusing us of creating chaos in an otherwise orderly and safe existence. And we should be kept out of the way."

His To'vah watched him, waiting for him to continue. Wruzdiin swallowed before he did.

"She never believed some of us are simply born to observe the forces of chaos becoming order then becoming chaos. She could not believe that it is a random curse of our birth to be able to *see* such things." Wruzdiin wept for a few more moments before he could finish. "My Sight can direct nothing. It can stop *nothing!*"

The Dragon nodded in agreement but offered him a smile. "I have always viewed it that you can suggest many ways we may embrace the storm *when* it comes, Kiabil, for it always will. Born where we have, it is the rarest of Existence, an equilibrium at once in motion and in stasis. Those living and dead all work to remain in it as long as possible. When it works, a world becomes a being … and that is paradise."

The old mystic's hand quivered as he nodded to hear these words again, though his chest still ached for what was yet to be for that world which had *become*.

The *Sargt* knew the storm would arrive because the world still thrived, strong enough to respond. They were *alive*, and Mazdek had chosen not to sleep since Ishuna stepped inside the Spire.

Here, at the end, were some of their best years.

"Thank you, my To'vah," Wruzdiin said, willing his heart to slow down just a little bit as he made his mouth move. "And because … I wish to say it again, though I know the word is not the same to you."

Mazdek smiled. "Say it as you need to, Wruzdiin. I shall thank you for it, each time."

The ancient Elf sighed. "My To'vah, I love you. I shall until my last breath."

Young Mazdel tried to concur with his grandsire, wrapping small arms around the big, smooth-scaled chest and clinging to him.

The *Sargt* once again answered. "And for this, *Kiabil*, you have my truest thanks. For always."

V'GEDRA – 161 BS.E.

ISHUNA'S GLOWING ENERGY DID NOT HOLD OUT. IN THE NINE MONTHS FOLlowing her oath to return for her son, she retreated to her bed more often. "Soon" became "later" for whatever she planned for her firstborn at the Spire.

After a year of studying, meditation, and escaping unseen out of the Palace, Xala spent most of the time *not* thinking too much about it at all, lest either the Queen or her Consort pick up a telling thought in an unwary moment. The Captain waited, guarded, observed everything going around her, as she always had. She made excuses to the Valsharess when Ishuna could not attend some function. She fended off the occasional curious niece or nephew who threatened to be a bother.

Xala did not think Ishuna was eating more, but one time she caught a glimpse of Ishuna's plate on a tray, implying it had either had *more* food on it than when Xala had brought it in — now all consumed — or Ishuna had spread the delicate mash into a thin layer around the entire plate before licking it up with her tongue.

I suppose one is as likely as the other.

Meanwhile, a strange threat out in the city turned much of Cris-ri-phon's attention inward rather than out among the dunes. Innathi barely followed Cris's advice to keep it quiet so it might be coaxed into the open, but Xala had been taken to the side one time and given a hint by the Sorcerer-General.

"Summoned creatures," he told her in private. "Harrying the outskirts of the Elondil and moving around in a circle around V'Gedra. We think there must be an agent *within* the city, whom we must flush out as quickly as possible."

Seeing her nod in understanding, he continued. "If I ask you to guard my children in the Palace alongside Ishuna, should I have such a moment of need, would you do this?"

She blinked in surprise but answered with her gut. "I would, General. No further justification needed. But would our Queen approve? Could she not ask me as well?"

"She'll not ask," he said regretfully, holding her eyes with a warmer gaze than she ever saw on a Davrin. "But she won't stop you if it's informal."

"Ah."

No duty given, no public punishment required in case of failure.

"I thank you for your swift answer," the General said. "I sensed no hesitation, for which I'm grateful."

She sighed to herself after he left, needing to find a safe place to sit and reflect on the churn of unfamiliar emotions following that request.

As a newly realized cousin to Ishuna, so too was Xala cousin to the current Queen, and thus, all of Cris-ri-phon's little half-breeds as well.

The Royal Au'renthia had most recently bred with House Ja'Prohn instead of House D'Shauranti, something that *should* have upset the millennia-long status quo and probably would have given her a second chance with Alyarra.

But only if anyone here remembered Wruzdiin.

Only if the late Queen hadn't stripped the Ja'Prohn sire status and acknowledgement from her Daughter-births entirely.

How had she even gotten away with that?

Rubbing a sore spot at her temple for even thinking to untangle the past, Xala grumbled to herself, drifting to another thought.

Ishuna's son.

His existence made House D'Shauranti the most recent sire to the Royals, though it was by force. Yet if the Seer succeeded in somehow wresting her child from a Dragon, if she made him public, that might only entrench them further in the status quo with Matron Lizabet at the top.

Hmph. Maybe Great Uncle had the right idea. Just say, 'Fuck all politics, and leave.

If Wruzdiin had never come back that second time, Ishuna wouldn't have been born, and he would not have suffered so much to become so bitter. Xala might still not have remembered him, but perhaps …

No. Koorul still could have happened, and Ja'Prohn would still be unacknowledged. I might still be out serving the Sorcerer-Kings of the Realms instead of the Matriarch's sister. Or maybe even that Ice Lord, Rousse.

The Lord of the North seemed like the type to recruit followers in their weakest moment.

With no true answers going down that path, Xala dropped it and let everything be.

NOT TWO WEEKS LATER, CRIS-RI-PHON CALLED ON THE SEER'S BODYGUARD exactly as he had said he might.

"I need you to stay with the younger children, Xala. There's trouble in the capital and Innathi must make an example in public."

Xala nodded. "Watching for the night?"

"At least. If there's trouble, you know where to take them."

Xala nodded, and Cris-ri-phon pulled a plain gold ring off his finger, offering it to her.

"Call me with this if something happens that you and the other Guardsvrin can't handle. I'll be here with our Queen in a breath."

She felt the unspoken pressure that the circumstances must be dire if she called.

"Understood, General."

Ideally, she *wouldn't* have to drag the rulers back before they'd accomplished their goals in making a personal appearance to address whatever trouble festered in V'Gedra.

That same night, Ishuna left her impenetrable quarters, appearing at the nursery with a mocking little smile on her lips. Her voice touched the very surface of her thoughts in a less familiar spell.

Baby tending, my friend?

Xala answered, having to focus on sending as well as receiving. **The Sorcerer-General asked a favor.**

A favor? Interesting. Ishuna paused, frowning. **I was planning to leave for the Spire tonight.**

Xala gaped. ** … Tonight? Why tonight? I cannot leave to go with you, qu'essan!**

Ishuna chuckled, shifting her weight on her feet. It was then Xala noticed that even though the Seer's stomach *appeared* flat, her hips and legs suggested she carried a lot more weight than she did. She was also standing two steps back from her, so they couldn't accidentally brush.

Xala had a sudden urge to reach out and see if she could touch the illusion … .

Don't touch me! Ishuna barked.

The Captain lowered her hand immediately, and the Seer drew herself up, lifting her chin. **Very well, Xala. I'm disappointed that you're stuck here, but I can use this, too.**

Xala frowned. **Use what?**

Tell my sister I'm not feeling well, as you've been doing. Make excuses while I'm gone if you must. Ishuna's mouth twitched. **Though I imagine she will be very busy and may not even notice.**

The Seer strolled down the hallway at a good pace, heading back either to her rooms or beyond that, the archives or library. Xala struggled with the extreme urge to follow her, as she'd always done.

Ishuna heading out alone, tonight. The *qu'essan* had said she would take care of everything to travel. *How?!*

The Spire was far away and obscured on any map; the roads themselves dangerous. Ishuna might not be well enough; she may be pregnant and hiding it in plain sight.

Meanwhile, Xala had promised Cris to stay with his children. Her half-blood cousins. *Tonight, of all nights.*

Mazdek's voice fluttered within the swirl of her thoughts. His memory was very quiet as she snatched at it. She nearly missed.

"Stand by her as you will in the coming centuries but wait for her to return. Do not *follow her. You will be needed more in V'Gedra."*

"Simple enough."

"Perhaps not so simple. But important all the same."

"Okay. Got it."

"Not so simple," she whispered, her lower lip trembling. "But important all the same ..."

That night, Xala Ja'Prohn stood guard at the nursery and allowed her life-long charge to leave her sight.

CHAPTER 10

THE DESERT WILDERNESS – 161 B.S.E.

HER LABOR CRAMPS BEGAN BACK IN V'GEDRA BUT WERE STILL FAR APART. Ishuna *had* been willing to risk the ritual jump, even that distance, or even perform the circle a couple of times, as needed—

Nnnooo! Our Daughter musst be born alive to ssucceeed!

The answer was no, thus, now she must fly.

It's just as well Xala was never going with me.

Ishuna could still use that unexpected bit of trust the Sorcerer-General had shown toward her bodyguard, but only if she didn't squander it by acting too soon.

One step at a time.

Ishuna was certain Braqth still tested her despite all she'd learned and done the last two years. The Spider Queen would be testing her faith and loyalty for years more.

The Priestess who'd impregnated her would fly her as close to the Spire as they could get, knowing roughly where it was. Ishuna would lead the way for the rest. Cooperation required payment, however. A guarantee against the constant impulse to betray when presented with new opportunities on either side.

Ishuna was aware of the humility, the swallowing of her pride, that it required.

The Priestess had changed into a red-eyed, black-maned bat-beast with grey skin, four arms, and large, leathery wings. They were large and strong enough to hold the *qu'essan* to their front, gripping her buttocks and around her back while they flew, her arms and legs wrapped around their waist.

Ishuna had been told she must be naked from the waist down and remain accessible any time the Priestess needed to strengthen their bond. The labor pains had only begun, but they could not afford to have them *stop*, just as they could not afford to be delayed. Even the small, burning leaking would help increase the contractions.

And continue the preparation.

Therefore, Ishuna flew most of the way there, through the desert night sky, with one of the demon's cocks writhing around between her legs. The Priestess seemed to enjoy the self-torture of leaking but not spurting until after they landed, which was hours later.

Once their feet touched the sandy rocks, the Priestess didn't hold back.

"*Argh!*" Ishuna groaned as they twisted her around, set her down, and put her onto all fours with hips pulled up.

Her legs wouldn't hold herself up from the cramping in belly and thighs, so she could only gripe and squeal as her Priestess-sire reentered her with both cocks, locking them together, and letting loose a scalding spray of sticky webs of seed.

Yesssss!

Despite her aching back, heavy gut, and increasing cramps, Ishuna felt stronger after the rough coupling.

Our bond renewed yet again.

"*Mmmnnn,*" Ishuna groaned, her tawny eyes open as she looked at the horizon. She continued to stare as her Priestess tugged back to withdraw.

What do you sssee? they asked.

Ishuna glanced to her right and her left, catching familiar landmarks and a trickling stream.

Another contraction began.

She gasped and struggled to speak. "T-Take me o-over to that overhhang by the w-water … That … is the border …"

The Priestess picked her up. The stars spun for a moment as Ishuna stared upward. She was carried, her swollen belly painful beyond belief now that the ecstatic rush had faded.

Worth it.

This would be worth all of it.

Because she had all the power and knowledge that she needed to challenge the Dragon of the Desert, the one who had imprisoned her and stole her child still wet from her womb!

Braqth had spoken.

That would be his downfall.

"It's too soon," Wruzdiin whispered helplessly as he followed Mazdek into the hidden lair where he kept his Hoard. "Please, not now."

His heartbeat filled his ears, the sorrow filled his chest, until he felt he might collapse to the floor. Little Mazdel was hiding among the Hoard, peeking warily over a jewel-encrusted chest. The bua knew something was wrong.

He just didn't understand how much so.

"Too soon how?" Mazdek asked with his usual calm, beginning to shift larger pieces of treasure out of the way, searching for something.

"If you try this now, *Jennu'Sargt*, you shall be greatly weakened by the time the biggest trial comes for the Davrin."

The Flame sighed in his search. "Do not be formal now, Wruzdiin. Just what is it I mean to try?"

The ancient Seer studied his To'vah continuing searching his Hoard while Mazdel kept out of the way at first. Soon, the child began digging with both hands through the coins as if he might uncover what his Ilharn was looking for.

Wruzdiin tried not to choke on his next words. "You mean to

destroy your Hoard to free Mazdel. In doing so, you make yourself vulnerable to my Daughter's allies. Enough that they may succeed."

The silent bua stopped digging, looking wide-eyed and horrified. A moment later, glancing at Mazdek and judging no denial, the child began to cry.

Mazdek's hood flared with tension, exhaling on a quiet hiss. An enormous, copper-orange tail curved around the slope of gold, falling still as the To'vah turned his eyes upon two Elves of such disparate ages whom he'd chosen to keep with him.

"I will only do that as a last line of defense. It is not my first choice but could be my last." Mazdek bent and lifted the bua standing upon his treasure. "The Abyss wants *him*, and my assuring that they fail to claim him this day is part of your race's survival, is it not?"

"I ... I-I hope so," the elder Davrin murmured. "Y-you know, I have told you *all* I know, but neither of us can be certain of every step between now and then, and I will not be alive to see it."

Mazdek nodded familiar, blameless acceptance. "Then I will defend my Desert *and* my Hoard, Wruzdiin. I can do nothing else. The challenge will draw Brothers as well. This will not go unnoticed."

"But *which* Brothers?"

Metal slid in chinks and clatters as the Dragon dug deeper with one hand, cradling his Davrin child close with the other arm. Mazdel wept without words, as he'd never formed a habit of using them. The sounds escaping the young son's throat were constant though not escalating as the rest of the Hoard hummed, keeping their shared aura stable and strong for their To'vah.

Finally, Mazdek pulled out a shining, golden shield with a grunt of satisfaction, next stepping over to Wruzdiin, whose soft sandals missed touching the first gold piece by less than a hand-width.

The Dragon held out the shield, but Wruzdiin kept his hands hidden in the sleeves of his robe.

"No," the old mage tried to refuse, grimacing in despair when the To'vah spoke his Words brusquely.

"*Si majak nomeno ekess wux*," Mazdek said.

And it could not be unsaid.

"Please," Wruzdiin whispered, now beyond hope.

"I give this shield to you, Kiabil. Accept my gift. With it, both of you shall escape Ishuna's wrath in the here and now."

"Prompting a hunt by the Abyss," the Davrin replied as intense, golden eyes stared into his own. "I-I have nowhere safe to go with him."

"The Abyss has enemies," Mazdek growled. "You know them. *Find* them. They will help you. They will help Mazdel."

"I would stay here. I would die here by my Daughter's hand, as I've Seen."

The To'vah leaned closer, the force of his and his Hoard's aura growing stronger as young Mazdel quieted, staring between his Ilharn and his grandsire. Wruzdiin trembled but did not step back or blink.

"This is why I saved you, Kiabil," the Dragon said, golden eyes shining. "I cannot do this. *You* must. Come back to the Spire if you will, but *not* before you've hidden your grandson from those who would use him against me. I will do my part for the Davrin. You must do yours. Take these two precious pieces of my Hoard away from the rest."

The golden-haired mage finally blinked out the tears which had been threatening; his mouth quivered but he nodded, reaching with both hands to take the golden shield from his To'vah's briefly reluctant grasp. He did not try to take Mazdel quite yet; the Dragon knew it was because he hadn't yet spoken the same Words for Ishuna's son.

The metal was warm and woven with strong magic; Wruzdiin could taste the enchantment on his tongue. He turned it to study the symbols carved into the front. The sun dead-center and full to bursting, flanked on either side by the Sister Moons in the phase when they looked most like two archers' bows facing off with each other.

He began reading the runes inscribed on the inside edge even before Mazdek pointed them out.

"Wherever the Sun Does Touch," the Dragon said. "If you know a place well, imagine it. Standing in the sunlight, and you will know if that place is open as the anchor point. If not, you can follow the threads of light to the next closest place, even if you have never been there. You will view the sands like a condor soaring above."

Wruzdiin swallowed. "I understand. Wh … when does the sun rise?"

"Soon. Ishuna is still in labor, but we have time to mask our walk to a sun-touched spot."

THE FUTURE VALSHARESS GROWLED IRRITABLY, CRAWLING ACROSS THE ROCKS as her body worked to expel her offspring. She dribbled a trail of tainted birth water, pouring out in unusual abundance; her High Priestess required her to create a circle with it.

Ishuna relished being so active during this birth, unlike her first birth. When she'd lain helpless and pitiful, carried around like a doll as Xala and Mazdek had done all the preparation.

And claimed all the reward.

Gooood, Ishuna. Now fffollow the rrritual as prrracticed.

Much harder now with the distraction of her labor. She dripped sweat and yet could not leave the circle to replenish her loss at the trickling stream, so tauntingly close. Not until afterward.

Ishuna *would not* fail.

Birthing fluid. Blood. Semen. Webbing. Other pieces brought with us …

She began to chant, her voice strangled by each contraction growing more powerful and closer together. This didn't matter. She only had to keep going as she knelt upright with bleeding knees far apart, still naked from the waist down.

Inside, she felt the head drop low and truly began to burrow and force its way out of her womb.

At last!

The sun was rising, and this ever-shifting valley which contained the Dragon's Spire would not be able to hide from their innumerable eyes this time. The birthing circle would be a beacon and an anchor.

A gate.

It would mean no limit to the number who could find this place and tear it down.

One Dragon and one miserable, old wizard will not be able to prevent me from retrieving my son!

★*Yess. Yessss! We shhall sseize him! We will breed his magiccc and create your own Housse. A new lineage through him, breeding with Our Final Daughter …*★

"Final Daughter …" Ishuna blinked, her eyes stinging from the trickling sweat. "Yours and mine."

She'd heard this before now; not a surprise though she had not believed it. She believed it now.

The unborn on the cusp of being born grew more active than Mazdel had ever been. She felt … *claws* … on the inside!

Horns.

Even teeth!

A jealous Daughter. Ready and determined to make her Mother's womb inhospitable to any more natural sibling.

Ishuna screamed as daylight touched her, unable to continue the chant, but her Priestess took it up in her place.

The Gate to the Abyss was almost open.

AFTER THEY'D LEFT THE SPIRE, MAZDEK HELD THEIR CHILD ALL THE WAY through the rocky hills with a hold on Wruzdiin's arm as well. The To'vah aided him to keep his balance, assisting him over multiple boulders and crevices to counter the heavy pack and unfamiliar weight of the shield and maintain speed.

"What is the shield's Name?" the old mage finally thought to ask as the relic seemed to glow even in the weak light of the dawn.

"*Mitneh'thran*," Mazdek answered.

Wruzdiin concentrated on the meaning. He understood the Word for illumination, and for the act of attaining lift, of gliding upon the air.

Light. And Flight.

Plain enough, and yet he shook as if he would soon be asked to throw himself off a high cliff and only then discover the secrets of all the world or smash himself upon the rocks.

At least the pain in his chest might finally stop.

"Do not show me where you plan to go."

Wruzdiin bit his lip to keep from disobeying and maintained the mental image of red sand dunes and nothing else. He also felt his long-time companion withdraw from the edge of his thoughts, where it seemed he had always been.

Both males also tried not to slow down amid young Mazdel's mourning whimpers and occasional struggles to get loose and run back to the Hoard left behind.

"I regret ever asking this of you," Wruzdiin said. "I should not have let you be so compromised ..."

"You did not," Mazdek said. "Not the one or the other. I understand Miurag, Kiabil, and you have only begun to glimpse beyond what the Baenar normally see. The To'vah have been always. An individual Brother is not eternal, but we are close enough to play the games and mitigate the damage, reducing wasteful challenges like these."

Wruzdiin shook his head in denial. "Beyond 'wasteful,' Great Serpent, you are in danger! I have seen it!"

"The Spider Queen does not have the resources or the wisdom to take my place," Mazdek replied. "She will discover that, and it *will* be wasteful. What comes after will not be her choice but mine."

"But the Abyss forces that choice to be made in the first place!" the old Seer cried. "And V'Gedra ... y-you may be unable to Guard against what happens near V'Gedra!"

Mazdek didn't reply to that at first, but Wruzdiin recognized his silence, not doubtful but knowing.

The Dragon had seen so much more than he ever would.

"Yet the cries of your people do not extend forever into the Abyss," Mazdek rumbled. "You have not had that vision again since Mazdel was born."

His heart seemed to interfere with his breath; the Seer could only nod.

"Hold onto that, Wruzdiin. Follow that pattern. I will do the same. It is because of this I can meet the storm even as I cannot prevent it."

As the sun rose to reveal its complete circle, copper-orange scales and the long, blond hair of an elder shone together with *Mitneh'thran*. Ishuna's son appeared like the odd piece of silver and onyx between them.

The auras all around strengthened, for the time had come.

Young Mazdel dug his fingers into the broad, hard chest as he sensed that he was about to be handed away. The child's scream achieved an extraordinarily high pitch, seeking to drown out what his Ilharn was about to say.

The Dragon dragged his claw down the bua's chest again, identical to how he had the first time they'd met.

This time, Mazdek left the wound unhealed.

"*Si majak jacion,*" Mazdek said, handing the bua out to his grandsire, who reluctantly accepted the second gift.

The Baenar child continued to cry, taking this new wound of many still to come. The Dragon refined his Words.

"*Si majak Mazdel ekes shio'Baenar.*"

I gift my son Mazdel to all Baenar yet to be born.

CHAPTER 11

THE DESERT SPIRE – 161 B.S.E.

HER NEWBORN DAUGHTER WAS HORRIBLE.

An ugly snout and curled ears. A white mane instead of real hair, her skin as dark as her Mother's. Terrible little spines jutting off forehead and jaw, elbows, and the bestial reverse-joints of her legs. She had two arms though had room for four, and her thrice-split tongue licked greedily at the blood which covered her.

Ishuna trembled on her side in agony. She believed she was going to die with *this* as her last sight.

Nnnooo, Valssharess. Nnot yet. Good worrk.

Her Priestess reached in to rub her stretched belly and destroyed femininity, chanting in a deep rumble which stopped the bleeding and tightened her up, numbing the pain.

...although this didn't really heal her.

Ishuna knew they would have left her to recover much more slowly, to relish the pain, if time *hadn't* been of the essence.

The result was the same. She was scarred by the Eternal Pit for as long as she lived. Infertile, with flaring marks reaching up her inner thighs. She'd never bear a pure blood cait as the Heir to V'Gedra.

This is where the lineage stops, Ishuna thought.

Wruzdiin had been right. *Again.*

Rage swept through her as she watched her Daughter's Priestess-sire poke and prod at the new abomination, each casting long, creepy shadows in the dawn light. The newborn tried to grasp at their clawed finger in a mockery of affection. The Priestess whispered that she'd be sorry for that.

Then turned to look at her with sickly, yellow eyes.

⋆Arrre you rrready to try again … ?⋆

Ishuna recoiled. "No! It's far too soon. I've endured enough for now."

The Priestess cackled. *⋆Ohhh, that'ss only jusst begun. We are sso very proud of you. We meant … rrready for your revenge?⋆*

To that, she answered with a narrowed glare and a nod. "I am. I have been waiting."

The Priestess of the Spider Queen straightened up, lifting their four arms as if to tear down the sky.

⋆The Gate awaitss, the barrierrr is thin. Pick up Our Daughter and take Uss to the To'vah who took your ssson!⋆

MAZDEK SENSED WHEN MIURAG WAS MADE TO YIELD.

The wounds hardest to heal come from within.

He finished preparations, embracing the vigorous response of his Hoard and its acknowledgment of the defenses and the obstacles which might keep the Desert Spire standing through the attack.

His world would continue to live, though too many unbound demons flooded the borders. Of this, he was not concerned.

The true threat lies somewhere beyond the Eternal War.

As always, the instigators and aggressors were too proud to see it.

Regardless, no true *Sargt* rolled over and allowed his territory to become just another battleground for all to abuse.

"They intend to challenge me for the heart of the Desert," he murmured to his Hoard, fingertips caressing the coins. "We intend to extract a cost so great they shall not realize when I have begun to fall. May they retreat, missing the signs, and believing they lost."

Such a fall would take millennia if done right, granting him the option of slowing it, perhaps turning it. For a while afterward, at least, Mazdek could hold the land, if not the essence of all its people.

He'd seen this path the moment he lifted the *qu'essan* into his arms and took her to give birth atop his Hoard.

Challenge presented. Message sent.

The Flame left his Spire to meet the hordes of the Abyss after calling one Brother to hold the Arena and bear witness.

THE SUN WORKED IN THE DRAGON'S FAVOR AS HE HAD SEEMED TO APPEAR directly out of its blazing eye. He did not speak, threaten, or try to parley with the wave of shadows.

He charged.

Wings open wide, hood flared, claws splayed, all of it blurred together as the speed of the defender accelerated.

Ishuna was yanked back by warty, disfigured hands, clutching her newborn. She barely ducked in time to evade the streak of fire slamming directly into the first wave of smaller creatures spilling into the valley. The Flame cut a swath, setting most of the alight, and cutting the stone deep for the rest to fall in screaming.

The ground trembled beneath her bare feet.

The Davrin stared, her mouth agape, as Mazdek took a new form she'd never seen. One titanic yet too fast for her mortal eyes to witness exactly how he captured and shredded a score of strong beasts at once, somewhere in the center coils of his serpent's body.

The next, the Dragon crushed with the thrashing tail impossible to avoid, slapped them with wings so hard they soared into the air, bit them into pieces, teeth chomping and ripping before he spat them out. Massive, fiery hands slammed them against ground and cliff alike, claws puncturing skulls and bodies freshly attacking out of the gate.

"H-He's enormous!" she squeaked.

Her voice was lost in the cacophony of shrieks and roars as multi-limbed and winged deformities tried to skitter out of the path of Draconic destruction. Few were fast enough.

Next came the storm-strength winds and cutting sand, scouring flesh, and then the spontaneous eruptions of liquid rock and fire from deep in the earth as the ground broke and split asunder, shaking even more violently beneath her.

At first Ishuna thought — *hoped* — this was her Priestess's efforts to drive him back. But watching so many of them tumble into the magma, hearing their raging shrieks, and seeing her allies suffer most, she quickly accepted it was not.

"He's too strong," she whispered, chilled to her bones.

We made a mistake.

"We prrropelled our expennndables firsst," the Priestess assured her with a snarl and a laugh. "He comes out sstrong, but We shhall tire him quickly. Trusst Uss, this is not Our first battle."

"You've won against a To'vah before?" Ishuna clarified.

"Trusst Uss. The Sargt is alone. He has called no one to help."

She must. She must believe.

At his first sign of weakness, Ishuna knew what she must do.

V'GEDRA

"XALA?" ASKED ONE OF HER HALF-BREED COUSINS "DO YOU FEEL WELL?"

No, I don't.

For some reason, sweat had popped out on her bow, and she had grown dizzy. The child had heard her heartbeat racing.

She wasn't feeling well.

"I . . . ." Xala attempted to still the shakes as they began, looking to the curious Guardsvrin who had already been judging her presence all night and into the morning. "I need a quick break. Just going to relieve myself."

One of the others, much younger than her, sniffed at one who couldn't wait, but her elder experience still allowed her to leave the room unchallenged.

Xala stumbled into Ishuna's wing at first, the shakes getting worse. Her heart wouldn't slow; it kept pounding in her ears.

What's wrong? What's happening?

She blinked tears from her eyes and realized …

All her symptoms were those of weeping.

She was crying. The grief welled up from so deep, it was coming out whether she liked it or not.

"Wh-who?" she asked, more to herself.

Who is in danger? Who is being hurt?

"Ishuna?" Her throat closed, and she felt her own denial, as if she had seen it herself to be so certain.

No. Mazdek.

"F-Fuck me," she cursed, clutching her chest as she sank to her knees. "Ohhh, Sisters, no, please, don't ..."

Mazdek!

Long ago, he'd agreed: no drama, no lies, no price greater than mutual pleasure as they lay together. Yet that did not mean the Ja'Prohn mage wouldn't cry once she became aware of his mark left on her aura.

Aware of it now only because the damned Dragon was actively trying to *free* her from it!

Why now?!

"Captain. Help us."

She froze. *Not possible.*

She turned her head toward the open patio on her right, stunned to see Wruzdiin had returned to V'Gedra. Somehow, he'd had gotten *into* the Palace and close enough to find her without anyone seeing.

"What the fuck ... ?" she whispered, blinking her eyes against the morning light.

Her elder uncle stood tensely, heavily weighed down with a pack of supplies, a shield made of gold—

And a Davrin child she hadn't seen in over twenty years.

"I thought he couldn't leave," she rasped.

"Please, Captain," he begged. "I must find his sire."

THE QUEEN'S CENTRAL CITY HAD CHANGED ENOUGH SINCE HIS TIME THAT Wruzdiin absolutely needed Xala as a guide. However, he did *not* need her to remain unseen and unheard anywhere in V'Gedra.

It turned out the old hermit was the one keeping *her* safe from unwelcome witnesses, obstacles, and eavesdroppers.

Xala had accepted this, leaving her post at the nursery despite her promise to Cris-ri-phon. She was still cursing herself for it.

"This is what you fucking meant, isn't it, Uncle?" she fumed. "About that message, and me being 'needed more' here she left again?"

"I did not know this would happen," Wruzdiin replied bitterly, clutching a clinging, comatose child to his chest. The large shield fought for room on his shoulder next to the pack. "That he would send me away, send us *here* to find you. I also saw you giving Ishuna the chance to turn on you, but you must have sensed the danger yourself, did you not? Something was off about her. She was not well."

"Shut up," the Captain snapped, rejecting the question.

Young Mazdel's bright white hair was covered from view, for he'd been wrapped in a blanket despite the increasing warmth of the day. The illusions and mirages helped, but Wruzdiin told her that a *physical* shield from the open world would keep the bua calmer and less likely to struggle.

"Not that I blame him for his reactions," Wruzdiin added, eyes flicking nervously about the streets.

"Well, he's the quietest broodling I've been around lately. Does he talk at all?"

The old mage rubbed the child's back in comfort. "Not really."

"Huh. Then what's with the blood?" Xala had noticed a relatively small amount dotting the rough blanket. "Is the bua hurt?"

"Deeply." She saw clear mourning in her elder's eyes, taking a deep breath before he continued. "But the blood comes from a claw mark on his chest. A small one. A necessary step to give us time to hide him before …"

"Before?"

"Before the bua's guardian may be compelled to come search for him. If the *Sargt* leaves the Spire now, we *all* lose this battle."

Xala scowled ferociously enough that her face hurt. "And you think Szoroan can do any fucking thing *at all* to hide you from something I've never even been able to see?"

"No, I do not," Wruzdiin replied firmly. "But we must find him all the same. We listened to Ishuna's dreams for months. It is not who Mazdel's blood sire *is* but who he *knows* which will help us now."

They'd reached the brightest part of the day before Xala managed to learn where Szoroan was posted, playing herself off as a messenger to some unimportant official at House D'Shauranti. It still wasn't easy, for news had spread about the Queen and her Sorcerer-General presence and activities on the other side of the city. All major Houses were on alert and outside of their routines.

Wruzdiin had ruthlessly erased those short intervals of time from the conscious memory of those they questioned. He worked to leave no trace of their inquiries, nor would they leave any physical signs to track once Wruzdiin explained to her how he'd gotten here so fast — and how they would reach Mazdel's blood sire within the same afternoon.

"Szoroan's not stationed in the capital," Xala told him, aware of the constant stress as Mazdek defended his Desert far away — a magical bond all three of them felt, though her less keenly than the other two. "We have to go to Kelni'ga."

"I have never been there, my niece. Show me in your thoughts where we must go."

KELNI'GA

THE WAY IN HER MIND HAD BEEN CLEAR ENOUGH, FOR AFTER WRUZDIIN USED his golden shield, Xala found herself standing in a familiar outpost a good three days away on horseback. She tried to describe even to herself how that long "sun leap" had even felt …

Not nearly the nausea I would have expected moving at the speed of light …

Almost certainly not an accurate description of the process, she didn't think. Wruzdiin had said something about sunlight being the major "component," but they weren't literally riding the sun rays even though unbroken sunlight was required to control the direction.

Kind of like a highly competent gateway that's surprisingly easy to walk through … Except the gateway closed around them as the light did, and they hadn't needed to take one step.

While Wruzdiin's control was impressive, there was the artifact itself to consider.

"Where the fuck did you get that shield?" Xala murmured, looking around Kelni'ga after rubbing her eyes and attempting to "see" through any mirage — and failing.

"Mazdek's Hoard. He sacrificed it to help us succeed, so let us not fail him. Where is the Guardsvrin Post?"

Few of the younger Davrin and none of the Humans recognized

Xala when she needed to show herself to gain information, but her uniform from V'Gedra was enough to get some cooperation, if only for them to say they hadn't seen Szoroan, but he was here "somewhere."

They each suffered just a little amnesia in their daily duties.

The mood was much calmer here than it was in the capital; they hadn't yet gotten the news about the "purging" going on, or if they had, it wasn't relevant until there were stories available to speculate and gossip about.

The Sun had moved another hour closer to setting as the day reached its hottest. Mazdel mewled in sweaty misery beneath his blanket as Xala found them water and some dried fruit from a military vendor. She hadn't brought a lot to barter with since they'd left the Palace so damned fast, and she noticed Mazdek hadn't "sacrificed" any of his coins to help feed them.

By now, most sensible soldiers required to be on duty had long ago found shade in which to stand or crouch. They were moving as little as possible, while the search trio covered nearly the entire outpost, unseen unless there was need to be seen, searching for one Blade Singer who remained elusive.

Szoroan was nowhere in public or any of the places Xala could go and ask. They could be missing him if they trailed each other at all, and then there were the closed barracks and the offices, but ...

"Are we going to check each by foot and keep spelling them all? There must be a better way. You found me on the first try."

"*I* did not. Mazdek did. I'm certain you felt it, based on your state when we found you."

Xala kept quiet while Wruzdiin panted softly, thinking of their dilemma. Her uncle was approaching such exhaustion that he finally took her advice to claim an available bench beneath a thin-limbed tree. The old mage rested his arms after settling Ishuna's son on his lap. The bua remained essentially in shock and unable to walk himself.

Wruzdiin hadn't complained at all about the child's weight, and Xala could only presume he was using a lot of magic not only to keep them hidden but to increase his endurance. From the way he slouched now, it was probably wearing off.

Or the rush of fleeing the Spire is finally catching up to him.

Xala watched as Wruzdiin gently pressed his lips to the top of the blanket covering Mazdel's white head. She frowned as a few unpleasant memories finally caught up to her. "So, you actually care about him now?"

The golden-eyed Kiabil sighed. "I wouldn't be here if I didn't, Xala."

"Sure, you would. Mazdek only has to command you, right?"

Her uncle didn't reply.

"You didn't seem eager to have him even after he was born," she commented. "The Dragon was the only one tending him."

Wruzdiin shrugged irritably. "My mind was here, on this day. Now that my body has caught up to it, I find I care a great deal what happens to him. Take it how you will, Captain."

No sense in badgering him further. Xala let it be, and they pondered the time passing even now, numbed somewhat to whatever was happening at the Spire, though the three of them trembled.

The battle was still going on. They knew but didn't say it aloud.

Mazdek was still fighting whoever Ishuna called.

Soon, Wruzdiin tensed, and Xala looked around. Her uncle might not have recognized the face but the fact that someone, a young soldier, seemed to see through his spell.

The bua moved to approach them.

"That's him," she said, and got to her feet while the To'vah's mage remained seated with his grandson.

Szoroan was extremely wary of her yet closed distance all the same. She wagered he had something ready if they attacked him, even though his blades were still sheathed and crossed on his back.

The Captain's first thought was that someone must have commanded him to come here. *Because he clearly doesn't want to.*

And whoever sent him would be someone who knew they'd arrived in Kelni'ga, too.

"Hey, Szoroan," Xala said, hands on her hips and closer to her weapons. "Who sent you?"

Szoroan smirked then, shaking his head. "Pity your instincts weren't that sharp a quarter century ago, Captain."

"Shove the sand fox boast and answer me, Blade Singer."

He straightened his back, refusing to cower. He stared cooly at her before indicating Wruzdiin. "The old one already knows. I'm supposed to take you to him."

The ancient mage probably recognized resemblance of the sire in the child he held but chose not react except to stand up. Murmuring another spell of strength, Wruzdiin left the bench still holding his precious burden, his shield, and his pack and took a step forward.

"Lead us to your Lord, Szoroan. Enough time has already been wasted."

His 'Lord.' Fuck.

She'd guessed but would have gladly been wrong. Even in the high heat, a chill ran down Xala's spine as she realized that Szoroan didn't consider Queen Innathi his true ruler. That was trouble well-buried within the ranks.

Who else thinks that? How far does it go?

Szoroan led them to a bright blue tent on the edge of Kelni'ga. Observing the lack of footprints or sign of either a recent set-up or lingering residence, Xala worried this tent hadn't been present when they arrived. She glanced at Wruzdiin, met his eyes, but he kept moving toward the entrance when Szoroan opened the flap for them.

"Wruzdiin," she said in warning.

"I know, Xala," he replied, holding his grandson close. "I am aware."

Once they all got inside, Szoroan closed the flap behind them, and it took time for their eyes to adjust to the dimness out of direct sunlight. Wruzdiin took the opportunity to peel the damp blanket from Mazdel, giving the bua a chance to cool down. His eyes were open, irises metallic gold like his grandsire's, and he clung to his caretaker's robes.

Szoroan shifted as if he was curious to see Mazdel, and Xala blocked his view just for spite. She heard a chuckle on one side, surprised to feel a cool, welcome breeze within the tent itself.

"He is a beautiful child, Wruzdiin," said a charismatic voice Xala had heard before. "Congratulations, Szoroan. Come closer so you may take your view."

Shit.

Xala knew what to expect as her eyes finally focused. She hadn't seen this "guest" since the Queen's wedding almost eighty years ago, but the Lord of the North looked the same: naked from the waist up with that signature, leather sarong covering his legs and feet, flawless bronze skin, and long, auburn hair about his shoulders, and that regal, steady poise.

Then the Captain blinked, spying a crown of ivory horns reaching up through his hair. His eyes no longer had green irises; they were blank, a clear and warm ivory matching his horns. He turned his head to smile at her in particular as her heart picked up.

What the — ?

"Lord Indrath Rousse," Wruzdiin said with absolute certainty whom he addressed. "You are an enemy of the Abyss."

The Ice Lord bowed his head. "I am, *Kiabil'bekil*."

The old mage shifted his stance as if needing to stand his ground. He kept his focus. "And you fashion yourself a guardian of Miurag."

Wruzdiin received a very beautiful smile in response.

"I am that, as well. Two things in common with your To'vah, I see."

Mazdel's grandsire shook his head. "No. He *wasn't* an enemy of the Void until he adopted the son *you* staged to be born on the very cusp of it. My To'vah chose *this* conflict rather than see the blameless fall with his Mother and doom every Baenar in his territory. You owe him a favor for that, Lord Father."

Indrath Rousse tilted his head at the title. "Oh? Do I?"

Wruzdiin nodded without a flick of doubt. "Yes. For that, and for coming to you for help rather than going to one of your Mothers."

Mothers?

The horned Lord's attention flickered toward her briefly, and Xala bit her lip, keeping her mouth shut and her thoughts clean. She watched alongside Szoroan.

Finally, the ivory-crowned Elf smiled again, his chuckle alluring and hypnotic. "Point taken, Wruzdiin." His gaze briefly landed upon Mazdel, noting his drooping eyelids and leaking tears. "Such a beautiful child. I am curious, I admit, how your Sight has compared to mine in this realm, but ... perhaps that is less important now than what is happening at the Spire."

"Agreed," her uncle said through closed teeth.

"What do you need from me on behalf of this precious boy you hold so jealously in your arms?"

Wruzdiin began at the opposite end of where Xala expected him to. "I need you to return with me to the Spire, Indrath. I need you to help Mazdek close the Gate since he hasn't done it by now."

If the Ice Lord was surprised, he didn't show it, though Xala thought he was oddly still as he contemplated this.

"And this is your 'favor'?"

"No, I will negotiate with you to help us close the gate," the old Davrin said bluntly, lifting his shoulder to cause the shield to swing. The Ice Lord didn't hide his interest in the relic, seeming intrigued as Wruzdiin continued.

"The favor to Mazdek is simply to leave Mazdel in the Red Desert among other Baenar, and do *not* interfere with his becoming. Do not remove him from the Desert or from the Baenar at any time, by any means. That is non-negotiable."

Lord Rousse grinned with amusement, revealing a sharp set of fangs. Szoroan and Xala stared. "I will consider this 'favor' without modification if you tell me what you have *Seen*, Great Grandsire."

"No condition is to be added," Wruzdiin replied. "These are the Words of a To'vah, Lord-Father, not mine. I am the messenger."

"But you have authority to negotiate with that shield for additional resource."

"My To'vah has given it to me. I own it. I may do with it as I wish, including trading it."

The ruler crooned with interest. "And what of protection for poor

Mazdel while he 'becomes'? You will not negotiate for that?"

"I do not need to," Wruzdiin replied. "You revealed your intention the moment you arrived to marry Innathi to Cris-ri-phon. You will not allow either demon or sovereign to get far in their plans without usurping them. You shall continue to do so."

The Ice Lord exhaled in cool delight, looking up at the ceiling of his blue tent, closing his eyes as if he had heard exactly what he wished to hear. A moment later, he lowered his chin and settled that warm, empty gaze upon the *Kiabil* once again. His tone was almost affectionate.

"I rarely have the opportunity to fence with one as well-informed as you seem to be, Wruzdiin. Though usurping the plans of enemies with poor impulse control is not as difficult as all that."

"I care not. My To'vah held the only line you are *unable* to cross. Your plans would mean nothing without that. So, what say you about protecting his son from your enemies?"

Lord Rousse's face brightened. "Our son, is it? Hmm. So be it, *Kiabil'bekil*. I shall grant that favor to Mazdek'pien the Flame, in return for what he's given us. Mazdel shall live among his own within the Desert for the whole of his life, and I shall not interfere with his coming of age."

The words seemed to settle firm in the air, something tangible, not the least bit slippery or tinged with doubt. Xala looked at Szoroan only to see him staring at his small, terrified offspring. The Blade Singer had tears in his eyes and his arms were crossed.

"What?" she barked at him. "Regretting something, *Qobor*? There's plenty of that to go around."

"Fuck you, Captain," the lower male murmured, the tears still visible but scowling at her.

Neither Wruzdiin nor the Ice Lord interfered when Xala caught Szoroan off guard. She slammed a hard fist into his jaw, making him stumble back.

"That was for Ishuna," she growled.

Szoroan snarled, contemplating drawing his blades on her, she could see it, and the Ice Lord laughed with joy before lifting one hand to him.

"Not in my tent, if you please," he said. "We've been generous letting you two linger, but now the first punch is thrown, and it is time to see the fight truly begin."

The crowned Elf waved his arm.

"Sleep well, my beloved children."

Wait!

... Fuck.

Fuck ... !

Two of the royal half-breeds dozed with their heads in her lap. Her hands rested upon each one, occasionally rubbing their warm backs. They cuddled her back. One had his thumb in his mouth.

What happened? Had she fallen asleep at her post?

What the fuck happened?

"Xala?"

She scrambled to her feet at the voice of the Sorcerer-General, upsetting and jolting the children as they protested, her heart pounding in her ears.

"Y-Yes, General, I apologize, I-I shouldn't have —"

Cris was smiling warmly at her, though he looked exhausted. "Nothing bad happened, Xala. At ease, please. It was a *very* long night and day, and you look as though you've been awake as long as I have."

He wasn't angry. As if she hadn't failed to protect.

If that was so ...

When am I? What happened?

"Is Queen Innathi returned to Court, then?" Xala asked, and Cris nodded.

"We've accomplished what we set out to do. Please prepare Ishuna for a debriefing with the counselors and the Deathwalker. There is much she must know of what happened in the capital just now."

Uhhh ... .

"She is in her quarters," Xala said, the same excuses filling her head again. "I will check on her."

"Thank you, Xala. And thank you again, for staying. Even if Innathi will never say it, you've done well by us and our children."

CHAPTER 12

THE DESERT SPIRE

THE SPINNING VALLEY WAS BEING DESTROYED, AND YET THE SPIRE STILL STOOD against all reason.

Creatures flew to smash their bodies into it, and if they did not meet Mazdek's massive tail and be batted back like buzzing beetles, then they careened off an unseen barrier protecting the red stone reaching for the sky.

Nothing which struggled upon the ground had reached it yet, after hours of a frontal assault. The earth kept cracking and heaving, spewing up magma from underground or directly from the Dragon's mouth, to sear and smoke Braqth's forces as they charged. For all the hills and mountains and rock formations forever altered within the otherworldly space, the Spire itself did not succumb to the quakes called by the To'vah.

Yet the Abyss kept trying to bring down the Guardian. Assured that their numbers could overwhelm him.

"Your sson is his weakness," said the Priestess, "and your Daughter iss the exploiter of that weakness. What this land rememberss of your aura through your childrrren, Ssseer, shall let Usss in ... given enough time." They cackled. "Well done, Our future Queen, for no Elf on Miurag has ever tricked a Dragon such that We usurp the Guardian's Hoard!"

Is ... Is that true?

Ishuna frowned as her Daughter chewed greedily on her nipple, lapping blood and milk. Her fingers dug painfully into the newborn, and she quivered. "Mazdek knew what would happen. He explained it to me. He *allowed* it. I told you."

"Then he has underesstimated the dangerrr."

"What if he didn't?"

"As long as he is alone ..." The Priestess twisted to sneer closer to her face. "He did."

Maybe.

"What is thisss doubt, Isshuna?" the demon snarled. "Rejoice in your vengeance over him! We shall recover ALL which he ssstole from you and take **more!**"

The Seer stood in her bloody, white shift near the Gate, holding her baby as tiny claws pricked her breasts. She was well-protected by countless defenders who would sacrifice themselves for her, simply for the opportunity she'd given them in this valley. Although none of them had yet reached the Spire, neither had Mazdek managed to charge the Seer standing at the portal.

Though he knows I'm here.

Through the morning, it had seemed to her that Mazdek suffered no injuries. And yet, the Abyss kept pushing and pushing regardless of loss.

Now Ishuna felt the Priestess grip the back of her neck tightly. "Yesss! Sssee!" They bellowed in terrible joy. "They've drawn blood!"

That was true. One or two large gashes showed in the Dragon's copper-fire hide. Shimmering, red blood.

Clearly his.

The spider-demons attacked in the thousands. Most of them would be destroyed, but only a few of them needed to land a bite and inject their venom.

"Victorrry is innnevitable!"

Ishuna wasn't listening. For once, she heard no voice inside her head. She was caught in a trance, gazing down the skeins of webbing toward her future.

And the future of all Davrin.

WRUZDIIN RETURNED TO THE SPIRE, APPEARING ON A BALCONY.

He was alone.

He still carried *Mitneh'thran*, though he'd dropped his pack back at the Ice Lord's tent. His joints ached. His back, shoulders, and arms all protested the heft of the heavy sun shield in spite of having alleviated the strain of carrying his grandson as well.

He just didn't have the strength to put into the endurance spells anymore.

The earth far underneath his feet trembled, and the Spire sang in alarm. Listening, the old mage felt it as though his heart began to bleed.

The pain he'd kept at bay long enough to travel, to do what he must, returned ten-fold. He choked and moaned in horror as he collapsed onto the plain stone just inside the circular room above the battleground. The golden shield clattered to the ground and skidded away from him.

He'd meditated in this room many times. Threaded within its makeup was a Ley Line which allowed him to communicate with Mazdek's Hoard.

Wruzdiin meditated now, focusing on his success so they could *all* feel it. He wouldn't drag the Great Serpent down by his fear, though afraid he was.

I have not failed you, my To'vah! Hear me!

The Hoard bid him speak; they were listening.

**Mazdel is safe. He will remain so for years yet to come. Szoroan has his duties and will not escape the consequences of his actions.*

**Xala is in V'Gedra and will not remember anything that will give our To'vah-son away to the Abyss, even if she will still grieve for us without understanding why. My great niece is the most loyal Ja'Prohn to all Davrin that ever existed, and she will remain at Ishuna's side every step of the way after this day.*

★Your strength will always be with her, for my daughter will need her.★

His head aching from the intensity of his predictions, the ancient Kiabil smirked a little.

★And lastly, Indrath will catch up with me shortly. He's just outside the Arena. Just a little longer, I promise.★

Mazdek's waning strength saw a much-needed resurgence. Wruzdiin wept to feel it.

Slowly, he climbed to his knees, his ears numb to the atrocious screams and shrieks, to the clashes and explosions of the battle outside, to which he faced the other way. Occasionally a winged demon would come into his view, try to smash itself against the Spire which repelled it before it even got close.

The Hoard's strength was holding for now, protecting the Spire first but trying to shore up its Master as well. Wruzdiin opened his aura and willingly added what pitiful strength remained to both Master and Hoard.

He didn't care if it consumed him, if it broke his aura entirely. His Queen had broken his body and his will centuries ago, and if she had understood how to break auras, she would have.

This, at least, he could give with his entire heart to those who needed it most. Whatever would remain of Wruzdiin the Seer had only to wait for Ishuna.

THE LARGEST BAG OF PUS AT THE REAR WAS FORCING THE HIVEMINDS THROUGH the battle grinder when, suddenly, it reared back as its flesh began to melt.

"Hhhhow are YOU hheerrre?!" it howled.

"I was invited, of course."

Broad, scarlet-red wings extended full to catch the air as the Lord of Ice Heart hovered face-to-face with the so-called "Lieutenant" Barrgrah.

"I'm unimpressed with the lack of finesse in your apparent strategy,"

Indrath said. "On a singular target it *might* work, but …"

The Infernal grinned, leaving the rest unspoken.

Clearly, not even Barrgrah's boss had a back-up plan if anyone from the Hells arrived. *Typical horde.*

Mazdek had thrown multiple sources of the fire element at his enemies, including super-heated rock and open flame, though the demons with that resistance were finally overtaking the field. The *Sargt* had a great deal of fight left in him, but he was going to need the Infernal Son.

Shall I? he offered.

While they're watching, the Flame managed, barely affording the distraction from defending his Spire.

Indrath *felt* the moment when Mazdek allowed the Ice Lord to seize control over his raging fires. The Infernal Elf was only too delighted to turn it on its head.

Lava cooled instantly through the entire length of the valley, trapping hundreds of fire-eating demons in cold, pitted, black rock. Orange flames turned into cold, green Hellrime, dimming the light and turning the air poisonous to any demon trying to breathe. Corpses dropped in place.

The air "commander" failed to exchange more than three blasts with Indrath before the brute fell out of the sky. Landing upon frosted lava, the commander was seized and torn limb from limb by his own minions which had appeared through a surprise portal.

The Ice Lord grinned as thick streams of webs and a thousand poisonous darts struck his magical shield in front of him, followed by a strike of every element attempting to break it … most canceling the other out. He burned off the lingering webs and vaporized the darts of venom, sending the ashes down upon the peons. He lifted his voice toward the Gate.

"A bit concerned, are we, Priestess?"

They had every reason to be. The Infernal Lord had something Braqth's Servant did not: a birth-link with Miurag.

Children of my blood still walk the lands and swim the seas.

Indrath and Mazdek even shared a son now. They were two Guardians of Miurag against the Hordes of the Void, with home-ground advantage. The battle would shift in their favor.

It already is.

Indrath laughed, relishing their display of power, thinking to taunt the High Priestess again. He held his tongue to see that Ishuna had abandoned her protection by the Gate.

And the Priestess was gone.

ISHUNA HAD BEGUN RUNNING ON BARE, BLEEDING FEET THE MOMENT INDRATH had shown up.

Her Priestess had compelled her, an urge impossible to resist as endless strength flooded her. She suppressed her aura so Rousse couldn't see her, chanting breathless words for impenetrable, invisible protection. She enclosed her and her writhing Daughter, who was strong enough already to cling to her chest like a leech, while she carried the essence of her Priestess inside.

We abandoned the Gate, she fretted. *They will destroy it, the Dragon and Rousse!*

★In time, yess. Neverr mind that. Reach the Ssspire! You may enter, Baenar-blood. You may bring Uss with you, as you did before! Claim your sson, and through him We shall make the To'vah Hoard hear Usss! Sset Our Daughter among his gold and he will be corrupted! Brroken! The To'vah has been bitten a score of timess! He holdss back Our Venom only because of that gold!★

Cooled lava had scabbed over crevices which would have been impassable, allowing her to run across the raw wounds of the valley. Where one path had been blocked, another had opened up.

The on-going chaos covered her path as well; nothing glimpsed her or so much as pushed her while demons of all shapes missed her being there. Her Priestess protected her from random magic or a stray, Abyssal weapon, hardening her personal shield as she passed underneath the bat-winged Elf and skirted the enormous, serpentine To'vah whose attacks now aimed directly at the Gate.

They were going to close it, perhaps break the back of the army, before hunting for her.

Not much time.

Once Ishuna reached the curve of steps at the base of the Spire, she surged even faster, sprinting up to the first platform. Her dark-skinned feet left red footprints nearly invisible upon the smooth, crimson stairway.

When she entered, she caught scents which brought every moment, every memory flooding her thoughts. In an instant, everything they had tried to bury when they sent her away from here, she reclaimed.

Inside was calm and quiet compared to outside.

My sire waits for me.

Ishuna ran past the crude stable which had once contained Xala's horses. She rushed past the room where she had first woken up, lying in a primitive nest with her ankle turned from fainting out of the saddle. She ignored both the water room and the balcony where Wruzdiin had wept beneath moonlight with his back turned to her.

I should have pushed him off the ledge then.

Ahhh, but We ssensse it! We sssmell it! Dragon magic closse!

Using her shoulder together with her aura, Ishuna pushed open the final, slender, stone door of a room about mid-way up the Spire. She breathed in, blackened soot and dust crusting her wounded feet, and saw nothing much different about it except for what it contained.

Bare and circular like so many others in this accursed place, a large, golden shield lay upon the floor not far from her sire. The room had an open balcony as well, overlooking the sand dunes rather than the valley. The battle was fought behind them.

Near the center, Wruzdiin pushed himself up to his knees, trembling like the broken Davrin he was. The golden-haired wizard leaned forward only enough to plant his palms flat upon the stone, his scraped fingers gripping it as if he might fall off a cliff. The too-old male somehow sported an erection beneath his neutral-colored robes.

Disgusting.

**Sssacrifice him to Uss … **

Ishuna shook her head as if to clear it. "Wruzdiin. I've come for my son. Where is he? Upon the Hoard?"

The servant of the Spire shuddered and grimaced, blinking dry, blood-shot eyes and looked up, vaguely focusing on her. As it had always been between them, he didn't mince words or leave her any doubt of his opinion of her.

"Gone," Wruzdiin said. "Long ago. Cut off from the Hoard. Y-you could have saved a great deal of waste, Ishuna. You'll never find him here, at the Spire, *ever* again."

Ishuna stood in shock — no lies in those golden eyes — as her Priestess shrieked inside her head.

Imposssible!! He would not sssurive the loss!

"Oh, but it is," the old servant murmured, still kneeling, trembling, yet he'd heard the outsider clearly. "No Ilharn will fight harder than when you've given him no choice but to do so, Daughter. Even if he has wounds he cannot ignore forever."

"And you think it is not the same for the Mother?!" she shouted, clutching her wailing demonblood harder, barely noticing how the tiny hind legs shredded at her shift. "*You* were the ones who forced me to stay here! *You* were the ones who made me push him out onto that greedy, consuming treasure! You stole him *and* my memories and sent me back to mourn and grieve for what I never knew! You think there will *not be a price to pay for that?!*"

"Of course, there is," he whispered as he nearly toppled over, barely focused on her. "But it will be the … lesser of those costs we chose to pay. Do what you will, Ishuna. I have earned all your hatred, and my path has vanished beneath my feet. Yours, however, is clear, and it is a lengthy one. It begins now."

The hard jab at her drowning soul recognized that they — her sire and her — had had the same vision at last.

Hers, only just now. Standing by the Gate before she ran here.

He had seen his decades ago.

He knows.

The metallic, red-rimmed gaze stared into tawny eyes now writhing with building webs. Without looking away, her sire reached for the gold shield and dragged it to him—

Ssstop him, Isshuna.

He struggled to his feet, his erection still visible before he covered it with the artifact, and took a few steps backward toward.

Ssstop him! He iss Ourss!

The balcony —

Ishuna yanked her daughter to one arm and raised her other, releasing the pent-up rage from herself *and* the one who would empower her in the future. A mighty, purple blast erupted from her palm, striking the golden shield dead-center.

Wruzdiin did not have the strength to hold on to it. Her magic wrenched his arm out of its socket as the valuable piece went soaring over the ledge, spinning and wobbling above the ever-shifting valley where it landed somewhere far out of sight.

Red haze swallowed her vision as she blasted her sire one more time, striking his chest and stopping his heart—

ISSHUNA! NO!

Dead before the force sent him backward to flip head-over-feet over the edge.

Gasping, she rushed forward to catch the end of his long fall. Mazdek roared out, as if to fill the entire valley with his voice, even before the old Elf's body broke upon the sharp rocks below. Her entire body quivered; she could not seem to get enough air and for a moment she felt like dropping her daughter to follow him over the ledge.

Maybe she would jump.

Both of us together —

NO!

The sharp stab of pain brought her to her knees, increasing until she crawled back inside the room. Still, Ishuna chuckled aloud, carefully pulling her demon-child back with her, far enough until she knelt inside the Ley Room.

Almost precisely where her sire had been lying, draining himself to the point his aura would never heal.

Of course, I wouldn't, my Priestess, she crooned. *Such an impulse would be as wasteful as this battle. My sire had nothing left to give us. He was worthless, a shell of a male, as he's been since my Mother broke him.*

⋆We wanted him ssstill!⋆

Well, I did not.

⋆You dare rebel — ?!⋆

After seeing what I have, I must.

⋆Seeing what?! When?!⋆

Ishuna winced at the pain but growled. *Enough, Priestess. You missed it.*

⋆Shhoww the visionn to Usss!⋆

I will not! I have let you use me quite lewdly over the last two years, while I learned and grew stronger, but the festivities are over.

⋆You cannot get rid of Usss. You are bound.⋆

How true. Like my sister and her Human abominations, our marriage is complete, Priestess, and with this child cannot be annulled. But if you think I will submit to such gross violations like I am nothing more than your puppet, just know I can deny you my visions, and the one I've seen means I ***shall*** *remain one step ahead of you. My gifts are not — and will* ***never*** *be — yours to feast upon. You'll have to cling and hope to catch a glimpse of scraps when you aren't distracted by your appetites.*

⋆Yyyou Cunnnt … ⋆

Ishuna smirked at the bare wall, staring at nothing. *You destroyed that. You cannot make anymore, yet you still need me. If you wish to stay, if you wish me not to kill myself …* Her thoughts paused. *If you still wish me to hunt down my own son … we shall have to cooperate. I felt your fear when Indrath Rousse appeared, and I know Cris-ri-phon and Soul Drinker are different traps laid by him, waiting to be sprung at V'Gedra. Will this be our greatest opportunity, or will he be our mutual defeat?*

The Abyssal Priestess hissed, her protest muted from the thunder of before. *⋆The Spider Queen will not be pleasssed.⋆*

Yes, She will be. Already she is laughing at you, that you did not see this coming. Now you are trapped here. Ishuna grinned as she heard the hiss of doubt. *I have come to understand what she likes, Priestess, and I have such games to show her. Such intrigue. Cris-ri-phon and Rousse will not see it coming any more than you did.*

The clinging creature shifted within her — making it painful as possible — but considered. The battle outside was slowing; the number of demons no longer climbing or constant but diminishing. The Gate was blocked, and soon it would crumble from the force being pressed on both sides …

We've lost the Spire, Ishuna said. *But I can give us V'Gedra. I can have all the Davrin worshipping Braqth. Gaining power from Her, strengthening our link to her. There will be another chance to challenge the Dragons. They cannot attack us first. We have time.*

★Hssss. True. The Dragonss … or ssomething Greater … . Yesss. But one more thinning … ★

Yes?

★Give Usss Mazdel as well. Do not repeat what you have done with Wruzdiin. Tithe him, and We will cooperate. We will accept V'Gedra insstead.★

Ishuna trembled, glancing down at her daughter's ugly face and wincing. *Agreed. Oh! And one more thing?*

The High Priestess growled. ★*Yesss?*★

Ishuna kneeled with her baby right in the middle of the room, pressing the small, naked back to the stone. She held the newborn by the throat, and her fist flared to life with Abyssal power as the High Priestess shrieked in alarm.

The Royal Seer plunged her hand through the fragile ribcage and gripped the heart, crushing it before the infant had a chance to cry out. She felt her daughter's essence flow into her, up her arm and into her chest, strengthening her forever.

And the tears came quickly.

My first tithe, Priestess. In time there may be another, by a womb not mine.

The High Priestess didn't answer; they gargled and supped upon the decadent essence, mollified despite her removing a crucial piece from the game.

Going forward, the Davrin will bear no female demon-children, ever again.

Whyyy? her rider sneered.

We are a vain people, this will not work among us. They will rebel against me first, and then you. If these beasts are to be necessary for Her power, yet are born that ugly, then make them sons. Any daughters I see won't live to emerge from between her Mothers' legs.

Pain coursed through their link, a burst of fury and punishment, and Ishuna suffered it gladly. Her teeth gritted, she denied that her insides were truly melting; she would withstand it. These tricks would not work; she wouldn't succumb to this again!

At once, it stopped.

Hrmmm. We are pleassed you are no longer sso pitiful, Isshuna. Resspect is yet to be givennn, however. We look forrrward to the Gamess, young Ssseer.

A four-winged demon had abandoned the battle and came within her view. Ishuna sprinted forward with enough magic and insight at her fingertips to leap off the balcony and out from the Spire, much farther than any Davrin should have been able to jump.

"Catch me!" she commanded.

The creature curved his path and came to her immediately, reaching out four limbs separate from his wings to snag her mid-air and pull her up against his bumpy, hairy torso. She clung to him as he held her close, flying her out and away from the broken Gate and the thousands of bodies.

A massive loss to the Abyss filling the desert valley.

Ishuna and the Spider Queen's Priestess ceded the battlefield to the Hells this time.

And left the Dragon's Spire still standing.

Mazdek had chased the outsiders to the Gate where nine out of ten attempting to return to the Abyss were crushed and burned.

The portal itself was cracking thanks to Indrath's more precise, focused attacks on key anchors which dug deep into the Dragon's territory.

Defiling chains he had tried for hours to claw away but to no avail.

Wruzdiin's bargain would be well worth the loss of his shield.

When the gateway to the Infinite Pit closed at last with a sucking, sundering rip of air and space, Mazdek spun around and began hunting every last creature whose smell assaulted his nostrils and his tongue within his own home.

Indrath would observe with amusement, and none of them would escape; their bodies would be shredded, and their essence diluted, eventually to drift out unclaimed into space.

Out! OUT!

Indrath had to use his wings *and* his magic to catch up to him. "Slower, To'vah, slow down. I think you have uncovered them all. There is just that one little one I see scampering up the mountain." He chuckled. "I will get him."

Exhausted beyond ability to speak, even to thank the Infernal Elf once the stragglers had been dealt with, Mazdek at least managed to nod with respect. He then slithered over the bodies filling his valley, his huge, serpent's body grinding them against the fresh igneous rock as if he was a Human man scraping his boots at the doorstep.

The wounded Dragon made his way back to the base of the Spire, locating Wruzdiin's body. Indrath paused in the air to watch curiously as Mazdek ate it without lingering on the taste.

The Infernal said nothing and went after the last imp in the valley.

The elderly Seer was the only one today the Dragon would deign to swallow and digest, though he was tempted to think the gesture was almost meaningless. The same result would occur if he simply let the body rot with the others.

No. Wruzdiin would want to aid in my healing.

What mattered much more to the To'vah was knowing for certain that Wruzdiin's Daughter — still Mazdel's Mother — had *not* chosen to wrap her sire's essence in those razor webs, as she'd done herself.

She did not force him to join her.

Mazdek had felt it mid-battle. The death of his *Kiabil* had been too sudden for Braqth to have gotten a grip on him. The Spider Queen left at the end of the battle with her web empty and her belly growling, being denied the new sup.

This was a sign that Mazdek might endure what was coming, that it might be worth it, because Ishuna's first true sacrifice hadn't been her Dragon-touched sire or her cousin, Xala.

But her tainted, unnamed daughter.

Yet even taking that alternate path, Ishuna had caused him more harm than she realized.

Mazdek sniffed around the base of his Spire briefly, feeling ill from the spider venom flowing in his blood but unwilling to show it. He left Indrath behind as he struggled to shrink down, to change form and shift back among his Hoard in its hidden cave below, still intact despite the earthquakes.

What he saw, smelled, and tasted was just as he feared.

With Mazdel missing as a crucial piece, and Mazdel's demonic half-sister sacrificed in Wruzdiin's room, with which the Hoard had been connected, the Abyssal taint was spreading into a raw, gaping wound in his Guardian magic.

The venom in his blood couldn't be expunged or neutralized while his Hoard remained like this.

I have to destroy it. I must start again.

The welcome part was that it would free Mazdel, truly. The To'vah would not come searching for him, would not put the child at the risk of being found. Destroying his Hoard would settle the bua's dreams and give him the chance to learn how to be a Davrin Elf.

A true Baenar Not a piece of treasure.

The unwelcome part, however …

"If you try this now, Jennu' Sargt, you shall be greatly weakened by the time the biggest trial comes for the Davrin."

Mazdek breathed out. Slow. *I know, Kiabil. I know.*

Still, the To'vah began by crouching down, placing his hands upon his Hoard, and heating it up.

One piece at a time.

Each piece would be counted, one more time, each Name spoken as it grew so hot as to lose coherence. Each piece would give back to the world the spark he had given it, and the rest which reentered the earth was no longer his to Hoard.

The Flame would melt it down. All of it, except the shield and the son he'd given away. He would return everything to the realm of the Dark Sister, until it could be found again by the Tundar and the Yungar.

And made once again into an offering for the To'vah.

The Abyss had come at dawn. Musanlo's Eye now sank behind the horizon for another night. Although Mazdek could not see it, he knew the Brother God of the Sky would have to wait until the next dawn to see who had survived.

If Mazdek saw the next sunrise at all, then the next million or so would be a long, long bleeding out.

A SMALL, COWARDLY THING RAN ACROSS THE ROCKS, NOT TALL ENOUGH TO reach up to a horse's belly even if he could stand up straight. He was scrawny, his ribs showing and arms like green, warty sticks. His tail flicked nervously as he scrambled over the broken rock.

The tether had been severed, and he was marooned. Lost.

The glint of metal captured his eye in the red-gold light of the setting sun. A compulsion struck him as he greedily darted straight toward it before any of his brothers. Nothing followed behind him, but he seemed to imagine they were.

When he came upon the glittering shield with carvings on its face, the Abyssal imp chittered happily and seized it with both hands. The shield itself struck out then; the imp couldn't drop it quickly enough.

"*EEEEEE!*"

The shield landed with a clatter while the imp hopped around, flapping blackened and blistered hands. "*Damnshitfucktwittycunty ow! bitchmotherfucker — !*"

"There we are. I shall take that."

Indrath revealed himself, stepping forward to retrieve the shield from where it had been dropped, relishing how big the creature's eyes grew before he froze in fright.

With a chuckle, the Ice Lord showed the imp how *he* could hold the artifact with his bare, unprotected hand. "What matter, beastie? Too much serenity for you?"

The creature of chaos spat at him. It was the last thing he would ever do.

"That is all of them," Indrath said, mostly to himself, although he wasn't surprised to look over his shoulder and see a Tilabil standing somewhat above him on the rocky slope. "Ah. You're a bit late."

When there wasn't a response, Indrath lifted the shield to where she could see it as well. "What do you think, 'Jennyn'? A fair trade for a black dagger after all?"

The Tilabil had been surveying the damage to the valley but blinked at him and the shield, standing tall in her drab robe, arms gently folded. The bald head and overly long ears were exposed, her strange skin shifting the colors of fire and language as beautifully as ever.

Her blank, multi-colored eyes were damp though she did not audibly weep.

"I still love you, my son," she said.

"I know this." Indrath offered his most disarming smile. He already knew the answer as he asked, "But are you proud of me?"

"The Spire stands, and Mazdek'pien still breathes," she said.

The Tilabil left it there as if to suggest that this was good enough. Not she nor any of the others could agree with his methods, but even she could not argue with the results.

"What of Mazdel?" the Tilabil asked.

"Mazdek'pien does not want him to leave the Baenar at any point," Indrath told her with genuine satisfaction. "In fact, I have promised, as a favor to the To'vah, to see this done. Should you try to take him, even for his own 'protection,' I have the authority to retrieve him from wherever you would try to hide him and return him to the Desert where he belongs."

His Mother frowned, and he was impressed with himself that he had gotten that much response.

She asked, "And how shall he be hidden right beneath the expanding gaze of the Abyss?"

"The Hells have some skill in such things, Mother, leave it to us."

The Ice Lord smiled, settling the shield on his shoulder, resting it carefully against his wings. He reveled in the afterglow of this victory yet also thought of home.

"One other thing," he said, watching her face and neck. "I plan to begin a family of my own. Innathi has been something of an inspiration and I have been ready to try for some time."

He smirked, glimpsing the concerned swirls within the bald Elf's skin. In the end, she bowed her head slowly in acknowledgment but did not show joy. "Congratulations, my son. We wish you contentment wherever it may be found."

"Such a thing is unlikely, but I'll take the congratulations all the same." He bowed his head with its crown of ivory horns. "Until we next meet on Miurag."

EPILOGUE

THE DESERT QUEENDOM – 161 B.S.E

FOR MORE THAN THREE YEARS, SZOROAN'S SON COULDN'T SPEAK WORDS. THE bua's original name, whatever his mother had called him, had been lost.

An orphan only two-and-a-half decades old had stumbled into the Guardsvrin barracks at Kelni'ga, mute, thirsty, and disheveled, He bore a certain resemblance, and they at least made out something in his garbled, fumbling hand-sign which had Szoroan's officers looking for him.

Apparently, Szoroan unknowingly impregnated a cait somewhere, and she'd gone farther out among the General's forces.

"Killed in action," they said.

She probably wasn't a Blade Singer, or he'd have heard about it.

Or remembered her.

"Never give up the opportunity to be a parent, Szoroan," said a shadowed voice to him some time ago. "At least once. Especially when such resilient innocence has no one else but you."

Probably his commanding officer too deep into her wine.

"How are you going to call him?" they'd asked.

Good question.

Szoroan realized he was tired of the fighting as soon as he held Avel that evening. Something inside him was content to let this harsher time go. For a while, he could exchange it for something … quieter.

So, the Blade Singer had taken leave to care for his child.

At first, he'd struggled with the challenge of tending a strange, distant bua whose Reverie was disturbed by frightful things most times and often stared into space with deep garnet eyes when he was a wake.

Yet, Szoroan was determined not to depend on his Matron for advice, for tutors or whatever rigid plan she'd push on them if he ran to her and lived under her roof again.

He had plenty of connections and friends who would aid him and the motherless bua without telling the Matron of House D'Shauranti.

I'll find another way.

His patience and desire for privacy would prove worth it.

And the first word Avel spoke to him was, "Ilharn."

Yes. I am your Ilharn. And I'll stay with you until you've grown up.

THE OUTER QUEENDOM - 75 B.S.E.

THE CAIT NIPPED HIS EAR, WRAPPING HER ARMS TIGHTLY AROUND HIM AS HE leveraged the mattress to give her what she cried out for.

"Harder. Ohhh, harder, Avel! I-I'm ... oh, *yes!*"

She climaxed just before him, setting loose his release as if she was the archer holding the bow. Immediately afterward, she allowed him to kiss her. Soft and long. While his cock softened inside her slit.

Those were his favorites.

He managed one more, lingering kiss before she was ready to leave.

"I'll be back when I get paid again," she said, smiling impishly.

"I'll be waiting."

A bit later, Szoroan returned home for the eve. His Ilharn always gave him some time to clean up the house.

That night, Avel asked, "Is that normal for a consort-for-hire?"

Szoroan shook his head with an indulgent smile. "Is what normal?"

Avel was wiping down his chest and shoulders, studying one of her scratch marks which had broken his dark skin. "That I always want a kiss afterward. Or ... more than one."

"Ah." Ilharn shrugged. "I imagine each consort has his specialties. Otherwise, why expect returning clients?"

He wrinkled his nose. "Kissing doesn't seem specialized."

His sire smirked back. "Depends on the overall performance."

Avel huffed with dry amusement first but then smiled with a bit of satisfaction.

"Anyway, I don't know what's 'normal,' " the Blade Singer added. "I wasn't ever doing the work you are. I got most of my caits with my uniform or sword technique."

"Well, that worked, too." He opened his arms slightly. "Here I am."

Szoroan chuckled briefly but then tilted his head curiously. "What concerns you, Avel?"

Briefly chewing on his lip, he told him. "Nearly all of them lately want me to finish in their slits. What if … what a bua shows up at our door one day."

Like I did.

Szoroan pressed his lips but shrugged again. "It's rare, son. The caits make the decision whether to continue at all. If she does *and* if she gives birth to a spark you started, she's usually chosen somewhere safe by then." He paused, looking at his hands. "Caits shoulder the responsibility for who makes up their family. Trust me, they have more resources and structure to make numerous decisions on a child's behalf *long* before they show up alone on someone's doorstep. Try not to worry."

The consort exhaled slowly. They'd had this discussion before, but he'd needed to hear it again. "Why do you suppose why … take the risk with me? Not just once, but the same ones, many times, in every place we've ever settled in."

Szoroan shrugged. "Maybe more of them are taking preventatives granted by the General's Army? I haven't been out in the field in a while. Or … maybe it's something you're doing to their aura."

Avel frowned a little. "What do you mean? I'm not doing anything. I'm not even a mage!"

His Ilharn's lips twisted wryly. "You have something about you, son. All Davrin have at least a little magic in them. We're not like the Zauyrians where it's present or not."

"Yes, I know, but I'm still not … forcing them, or tricking them, or anything."

Szoroan frowned, and something dark seemed to pass across his face but he shook it away. "Of course not. That's not your nature, you're far too kind. And you're interested in someone's pleasure besides your own. You do good work, Avel."

He blinked in surprise. "Ah. Thank you, Ilharn."

Avel decided now was the time to push this out of his mind. Again. His sire was right, it wasn't in his hands what any of the caits did after they left him. He was hired to help them feel better for a while, to give pleasure as needed, even to heal some part of them as their people fought against the Naulor and their allies.

His thoughts jumped to another tangent, only barely related. "Oh. And you were right."

Szoroan squinted. "Right about what?"

"Our House is huge. I might be cutting out a fifth of my business worrying too much about pleasuring a distant cousin."

His Ilharn tilted his head back to laugh. "Oh, it took you that long? Had to see for yourself?"

Avel flushed. "Well … I wanted to count them."

"*Heh!* I'm sure you'll enjoy that. It'll take a while." Szoroan winked. "D'Shauranti *is* the most extensive House in the Desert, with only Ja'-Prohn as near competition. The others just sort of bicker amongst each other, but the Palace and those two Houses make up the backbone of the Queendom."

Szoroan took a drink of spiced taze he'd prepared this cool eve, pondering a little more. "Although even still, however many babies our Matrons have, that's still nothing compared to the Zauyrians. We're lucky that they don't live *nearly* as long."

Avel nodded, adding his thoughts even though usually didn't ask much about politics. "Except for the Sorcerer-General, right?"

"Right. Except for him."

"Why is he still alive? Isn't he … I don't know how old he is."

Szoroan shrugged. "He showed up around four centuries ago, I've heard."

"How?"

"No one really knows. A gift from the Queen, some say, or some artifact he found when he left the Queendom some centuries back."

Avel rubbed his palms against his clean waist wrap as he finished up his cloth bath. "A gift … because she wanted him as consort as well? I mean, he is giving her children …"

"Still. Yes." Szoroan nodded, seeming to grow uneasy with the topic. "I've heard they're expecting their eleventh child soon."

"The half-Elves of V'Gedra."

"Or half-Humans, depending who you ask. Yeah. I see one now and then in the army near their Father. They look … stranger than the Wilder mixed-breeds."

Avel frowned, trying to imagine but soon distracted from it. "Why do you have that look on your face, sire?"

The Blade Singer shook his head. "I just don't like going to the capital anymore. I'd never go back again if my Mother didn't summon me every so often. It's only grown more and more divided. You can't be sure who you're talking to, a Royalist or an Alyarrist or the insane fringe saying the mystics will be the ones leading the way. We should stay out as long as we can and keep our heads down. Until something changes."

The young male nodded in agreement but said nothing. This had never changed; his sire had been saying this all his life.

THE PAIR MOVED THREE MORE TIMES OVER THE NEXT HALF-CENTURY, AVEL plying his trade with increasing skill and success, leaving contented caits in each location who recommended him such that both new clients and old even traveled to see him.

He'd saved enough in a relatively short time that his sire had teased him about leaving the military. Avel felt panic, protesting that their income would then be smaller than their expenses.

"The gold will drain away!"

Szoroan chuckled indulgently. "You hoard those coins enough already, you know that? To live after I'm gone, you must trade them sometime. You realize that, right? And you can't take them with you everywhere."

"Don't say that," he replied, feeling so much more than the tease. "I-I know, but I … I *hate* spending them." He hesitated before adding, "It feels like I know them."

Again, his father would shake his head, part in exasperation, part in amazement, muttering again about his strange bua before chuckling. "At least I've never had to worry about you being taken in by a grifter."

That was true. Avel had never even been pickpocketed.

He hadn't parted with a single coin without his consent.

THE OUTER QUEENDOM - 25 B.S.E.

ONE EVENING, A FEMALE CAME KNOCKING LATER THAN THEY WERE EXPECTING anyone. In these times Szoroan was wary of opening the door.

Besides if they bent their "business hours" one time for one cait, it would happen again. Before he knew it, Szoroan would be outside all night, or he'd have to put up a blanket and pretend he wasn't hearing anything. In the latter case, he might be presured to join as well, and ...

I don't want to.

Caits couldn't demand anything of him anymore. Not if he never gave them the opportunity.

He'd worked too hard to be independent of them.

"Come back tomorrow," the Blade Singer called through the door. "No earlier than two hours after sunrise."

No response, he didn't think, although there might have been some whispering.

The unworldly way that it layered itself crept over his skin, and the white hairs on the back of his neck stood up as he stepped back from the barred door.

Was there more than one or two? Had he just made a big mistake letting them know they were home?

"Szoroan." A strangely familiar voice. "Open the door."

Avel was up in an instant, quietly handing him his blades then reaching for the ice spear he'd taught him how to use. These were the right choices, the right training …

Except Szoroan wondered if drawing blades now would only make things worse.

"Ilharn!" his bua cried with alarm.

He spun around.

Something dark and oily had slipped down their cooking column and landed on the small fire in the hearth, chittering with blazing yellow eyes before vaulting — still aflame — toward the front door.

Where it swiftly knocked the metal pole aside and allowed those behind it to force the door open.

He drew his blades.

What followed grew much, much worse.

AVEL JUMPED OUT OF THE WAY AS HIS SIRE TURNED HIS BLADES AND CAST A concussion sphere at the home invaders. Somehow, it turned and pitched straight back at him without being set off. The deep shudder could be felt throughout the dwelling as it struck the Blade Singer.

Szoroan began to bleed from his ears and nose as he collapsed.

"No!" he cried, fumbling for a healing potion in the kit beneath the bed, gripping his spear tightly with one hand.

The young Davrin froze as the fearsome, tawny-eyed sorceress strode into the room with black cloak flowing. She lunged directly at his sire, reaching down to grip him by his throat. She *shouldn't* have been able to pull him up to his feet with one arm like that but, the next moment, his feet were dangling when she pressed him to the wall.

"What's the matter, Szoroan? You don't remember me?" She slapped him. "Hey! Wake up! Off with that incompetent mask!"

"I-I … ."

"Yes? Think *harder*, Blade Singer."

He blinked at her. "I-Ishuna … ?"

"Here we are," she cooed. "Yes, old lover. I have found you at last. You've been running from your place in the Web long enough. Now you'll serve as a message for Indrath."

Avel jerked in shock as black and purple flames erupted around the fist of her free hand. Before he could speak, she jammed it straight beneath Szoroan's rib cage, seizing his heart.

Red blood poured down onto the stone floor, and the younger male started screaming uncontrollably.

Someone knocked the spear from his shaking hands, and he dropped the healing potion as well. Next, he was jerked to his feet by strong hands, his arms seized and locked behind him in an expert move.

"Quiet," an older female murmured behind him. "Stop screaming, Mazdel."

Something clamped down inside his chest, as if to stop his heartbeat the same as his sire. Avel nearly blacked out in the warrior's grip. She held him on his feet and roused him with a couple hard shakes.

"Wake up! Not the time to faint! This is your Mother. Show some respect."

He shook his head, first in denial, then in fear as the sorceress dropped the corpse of his sire and turned around to look at him with mad, tawny eyes. He froze.

"Mazdel," she said, smiling, her arm coated in gore.

N-no …

"I-I'm not … I'm not who you think I am!" he babbled as she grew closer, filling his vision. "Y-you've made a mistake!"

The sorceress was smirking at him, and after a beat she flicked a few spatters of Szoroan's blood onto his face, whispering a command word. For a moment, he felt like something had been ripped off the bottom of his brainpan, turned over so she could examine what was underneath.

Avel screamed harshly as his voice broke on a sob.

Then she gripped his chin in her clean hand and forced him to meet her eyes. Her smile was beautiful, soft, clashing with all the violence and horror in the room.

"I knew it was you. Mazdel."

"I-I don't know who you are …" he whispered.

"We shall fix that. You! Hand me that mirror over on the dresser."

Once she had it in her bloody grip, the sorceress held it up in front of him.

"Look. *This* is your real eye color."

Avel blinked through his tears, despairing to see just how terrified he looked … He could not help but also see the gold specks and soon, they weren't just specks anymore.

His irises filled in as he watched, metallic gold overtaking the familiar, garnet red, until his gaze mimicked the pure gold coins he hated to spend.

Avel looked down and away from the sight, only to stare at the body of the one who had raised him. He wanted to puke.

"My son had gold eyes," the sorceress murmured in disturbing awe, "He was taken from me almost two centuries ago. I do not know how your sire hid you so long, Mazdel, but I am at least glad to see he kept you healthy."

"I am Avel!" he shouted.

She slapped him. "Do not shout at me. You know better."

The tawny-eyed sorceress took him by both sides of his face then, stroking him, not seeming to realize she was smearing Szoroan's blood all over half his face. He trembled in the warrior's grip, wanting to run. To disappear. To hide from this bad dream …

If only they'd let him go.

"You are royalty, my son," she said. "You cannot have known, I see, living here like this, earning your grain as a whore to line your sire's pockets." She scoffed. "There will be no more of that humiliation. Your Mother promises you. Only someone worthy of you may ask me for your favors. You shall be protected. You don't have to worry anymore."

When had he ever worried until now?

Avel lifted his head slowly, gold eyes locking onto ones like smoke-tinted topaz. He didn't know who she was, but figured this must be one of those "insane fringe" that his sire had gone on about from the capital.

Just because she said she was royalty didn't mean it was true, and right now, that didn't mean anything to him. To be involved with the Royalty was the gateway to a worse, sleepless existence.

If the stories he'd been hearing about the capital lately were even half true.

"You are *not* my Mother," he whispered, hitting back harder for it not having been a shout.

The sorceress stepped back, obviously shocked. He didn't know what she was about to do.

"Ishuna, give him time," said the warrior behind him, strong and soft, but with a thread of desperation in her voice. "He'll come around."

The sorceress did not acknowledge her, only glared directly at him.

Finally, she commanded, "Bring him."

Then stalked out of the commoner's home as if it stank.

The warrior obeyed, and Avel took one last, horrid look at his sire's body.

Ilharn.

Taken away from his father.

Not again.

THE DESERT SPIRE – 5 B.S.E.

THE DRAGON SLEPT FOLLOWING THE BATTLE IN HIS VALLEY.

His rest was fitful, his body lying upon a bare floor underground, beneath the protection of a vigilant Spire, as magic worked constantly to excrete toxins and venom out from between his scales.

This Sleep would be shorter than others, for he grew too hungry to keep Dreaming much longer. The catalyst for his Awakening had been set the moment Mazdel heard his Name for the first time since leaving the Spire.

The bua had tried to deny it, at first. He *had* been free, after all, up until the moment his Mother had taken him prisoner. Mazdel became a captive of utmost secrecy, discovering who he was in the dark.

The Desert To'vah Dreamed it all, saw the suffering intended for them both, his essence keening for the youth who could not tolerate the same razor-web chains which held his Mother.

Mazdek'pien was in pain still, years later, when Ishuna broke his heart and finally gave their son to the Abyss.

The To'vah erupted out his Sleep, his roar shaking the earth around him. Drawing another breath, he expelled the air from his lungs in a long call of mourning which lasted so long, no living creature nearby had the courage to wait until its end. Then Mazdek collapsed, tail lashing at the empty walls, slapping against the floor until he could know for certain he was Awake.

The dark Dream had ended for now.

Eventually, the Dragon crawled out to sit underneath an open sky, glad for the company of the stars and the night breeze which helped him to breathe and dried out the sweat on his wings, cooling the flare of his hood.

Next, he went hunting because he must, but returned not recalling what had filled his belly.

What did I eat?

"Some good, Miurag-born food," said a darkly jovial voice. "Not to worry. It should help."

Very few in this world could approach him unseen long enough to speak, but this one could. Especially when he was wearing a smaller form and standing in the shadows.

"Lethrix," Mazdek growled, seeking the familiar glint of his eyes, even when he chose to wear his blackest form. "Why are you here, Brother? Why leave the Deepearth again so soon?"

The golden gaze appeared within the shadow, as did the stark white of a wide smile in a black face. A curious likeness to the Desert Baenar.

"I come up here more often than you realize, when the voices get to be a little … *much*." Lethrix stepped closer, allowing Mazdek to see that his face and wings were relaxed, his sleek, dexterous tail not hostile. "I thought things had gotten easier up here, even with the Sisters missing. The Sun Brother and the Grave Mother seemed enough to keep the young races anchored in the Red Desert. Or wasn't it?"

"They weaken," Mazdek admitted. "The Deathwalkers are being hunted … by Sun Worshippers."

"Oh, dear. That's not good." His Shadow Brother breathed in through his teeth as he scented the air in thought. "Impressive battle, by the way, fending off the Abyss alone. I'd forgotten you could fight like that when the cuffs came off."

Mazdek shook his head. "You've forgotten because I no longer crave it, Brother. If this happens too often, we shall never know Balance again.

We will know only the Eternal War."

"Indeed. I suppose the Four must be all sniffing around here now, or will be soon, and their lords and mistresses probing for weak spots among us." He sighed, scaled lips curled with black humor. "Speaking of weak spots, perhaps it was a *bad* idea adopting a son not of your own rod?"

The Flame snapped his jaws at the Shadow, the burst of pain uncontrollable as he hissed a warning, his hood flaring open. The Black responded with white spines rising on his back, sharp teeth still exposed. They stared, each waiting to see if the other would attack first. The abrupt, false strength left him a moment later.

Mazdek looked away. "May you never lose a son to Outsiders, and know what this is like."

Something rattled in the Black's throat. "Short memory, Brother. You mean 'again,' don't you?"

"*Shuiblith*," he cursed, tail coiling. "That … was so long ago … you still had —"

"*Heh!* I know what I still had. But never mind that." An overly blithe shrug, even though his white smile vanished. "You only harken back to my point."

"Speak your point."

"You know it. When our blood flows in a Dragon Son's veins, at least he has what he needs to defend himself from those threats." The Shadow paused. "Most of the time, anyway. Yet neither of us knows how long this Treasure Son of yours can last before he becomes corrupted as well. You may need a *real* Dragon Son to help defend your Territory *against* him, should he change *too* much."

Mazdek turned away, gazing out at the valley he had rarely left for centuries. The land recovered slowly; a few trees grew here now, and some of the water was flowing, bringing with it the insects, brush birds, snakes, and mice, but the battle with the Abyss poured fresh into his memory, as if it happened the previous day.

Every claw mark and molten ripple of the rocks. No matter how the valley had changed since.

"It is too late for your point, Lethrix. I haven't the will to create another son so soon. Not until this grief stops ... But I do not know when that will be."

Lethrix circled around, moving deliberately to his periphery. "Indeed? That's an interesting change. Hm!" The smile returned. "Perhaps you and I will get along better than we have recently."

The Flame squinted at him. "How so?"

"Well, first bear in mind that I held your Arena. I kept the battle clean, messy as it turned for you."

"I owe nothing for that, Brother. You answered the call."

"Of course, but that wasn't where I was headed."

"Then where *are* you headed?"

Lethrix hummed. "Your Desert is often a quiet place, Mazdek, yet I heard your call even *that* far down."

"And you arrived first."

"And observed the whole thing. Yet, I remain curious."

"About?"

"About why no Brother arrived to ask me to let him in. Only one Infernal, sent by your Kiabil. Not you."

Mazdek's hood constricted. "I did not ask our Brothers to fight with me. That is why none came."

"Why not ask?"

The Shadow's tone suggested he'd guessed the answer. The Flame exhaled slowly. "My Hoard was injured before the battle began. There was a strong chance I would lose it. If I did, any Brother present would divide my Territory."

"Hm! True." Lethrix harrumphed. "Better *that* than something worse setting down its roots. Isn't that what you've said before?"

Mazdel paused. "Yes, but ..."

"Buuuut?"

His Brother was a sly one.

"A territory shift now might make it worse."

"Do tell."

"The Baenar have deep roots of their own. I do not know what would happen to them amidst a Ley-break if the Red Desert was split up among my Brothers. Tell me yourself, which among the younger To'vah would not shrug as the Baenar were divided, carved up like the Orcs, and realize too late what we've lost too quickly between them?"

"I suspected. But nor would you call the eldest. Also a good decision."

Mazdek narrowed his eyes skeptically.

Lethrix blinked and shrugged. "What? I have been Awake ever since Guarding your Arena, piecing it together as you Slept. I dare say you were wise *not* to call upon any Brother, young or ancient, for we're about to witness the worst of it." The Shadow grinned unpleasantly. "Aren't we?"

Mazdek sat mutely.

"The treasure-bua's death just triggered a royal coup in V'Gedra," the Black pushed. "This very evening. Surely you know."

"I know."

The Flame looked in that direction, toward the heart of the Queendom, this thick tail slithering along the ground. Although numb from the blow to his own essence, a trickle of cold still made its way in as he spied something green which hadn't been there until this evening.

Wruzdiin had been right again.

The Black Dragon followed Mazdek's gaze and grunted. "Not a trick of the light."

"Miurag doesn't play such games." Mazdek shook his head. "I had a Kiabil who could see some of the most intense skeins of Chaos and *still* recognize patterns within them."

"Impressive," Lethrix remarked. "Did that drive him insane?"

"No more than it did you."

The Shadow laughed. Soberly, Mazdek continued.

"My Kiabil was right in what is coming, and … I believe he was also correct in a possible path back out of the darkness. He was why I claimed the Treasure Son and then gave him away."

His Brother hummed. "Not sure I'd have the will to do the same. Tell me more, Brother, you hold me rapt. What is the path?"

Mazdek cocked a brow ridge at his tone but answered. "His essence will help anchor his Mother, the daughter of my Kiabil, and possibly *all* Baenar as well. Given enough time. This shall offer the Spider Queen much distraction, with plenty of space for survivors to hide in between the threads of her web."

Lethrix hummed again. "Bold. Very bold. I love it."

The Flame grunted. "For now, we must allow Ishuna to continue to have her visions, albeit with an Abyssal slant."

His Brother tilted his head then nodded agreement. "Alas, no ignorant bliss before the next cataclysm, hm?"

For once, Mazdek shared a morbid laugh with his Shadow Brother. "Not this time. The Hells and the Celestials are about to clash as they attempt to seize V'Gedra and drive the Abyss out at our expense. It is possible that Wruzdiin's daughter claiming her people in the name of the Void will balance that instead, at least for a time, so *none* of them get a permanent foothold."

"Indrath may be a little irritated with you," the Shadow snickered.

"Undoubtedly, but the son he once was may also be glad for it. This chance may give the Sun Brother and the Grave Mother more time to seek the Sisters."

Lethrix grinned. "Risky, but clever. Let all the Outsiders rise to be completely blinded by each other and miss the target, rather than fight them individually? Why not! Perhaps you are the first up here to speak *sense* in the last ten grand or so."

The Desert Dragon dismissed the warped compliment for the tragedy they must embrace. Lethrix waited for a few moments, and when nothing else was forthcoming, he spoke again.

"You might be interested in what I found in the house the morning after Ishuna captured the bua."

The Flame hissed. "I do not want to know what sadist's dagger you found to twist, Lethrix."

"Oh, come, Mazdek. I am convinced he was your son, in truth, even if you didn't swell the female's belly. He took after you in the way that mattered. Look. Look at what I found."

The Serpent Man rumbled deeply, a sound he normally did not make, but he felt on the cusp of charging the irreverent Guardian of the Deepearth. He had only to say one more back-handed thing about Mazdel—

Lethrix tossed a hefty bag toward him. Mazdek heard coins clink together when it landed neatly nearby. The harmony of the metals was almost perfect. The metallic scent reaching his nose made his mouth water, and the Elf-scent attached to the bag made his eyes sting.

"Yours," the Black Dragon said.

The grieving Dragon snorted, his hood rising again. "*You* looted it. Held onto it all this time. Why don't you claim it?"

"I tried," the other answered, straight-backed, arms crossed in amusement. "But this treasure doesn't play nice with mine. Almost as if it was gathered specifically for you, '*Ilharn*.' This is *your* Offering."

Lethrix chuckled at his expression while Mazdek sat stunned, then he cleared his throat. "I shall add that it has been imbued with a *great* deal of Baenar fertility magic, with clear memory. Apparently, the bua found *much* fun and satisfaction in his hoarding."

The Shadow paused, tail flicking playfully. When the Flame did not react, he sighed. "In case I am not being clear, Brother, your son's treasure will help you *and* your valley to heal faster."

Mute still, his hood settling down again, Mazdek slowly pulled the large bag closer to him. It was filled with many smaller bags, but all of them chimed together.

It felt right.

The pain in his chest eased, just a little.

"Faster, yes," he murmured thoughtfully. "But … I may not heal in time, Lethrix."

"In time for what?"

"The cataclysm."

"Ah, yes. Probably not."

"You stand here now, and I have a favor to ask."

"A bargain?"

"No. No bargain, Lethrix. I cannot guarantee I will be of sound mind later to fulfill one of *your* slippery bargains."

"Ohh, I'm flattered."

The Flame raised a sardonic brow then just shook his head, waiting until the Shadow was finished preening.

"Very well," Lethrix said. "What 'favor,' Brother?"

Mazdek met his golden gaze, neither blinking as he clutched Mazdel's treasure closer to his side. "It is up to you if you accept."

"I know. Speak it."

Very well.

"Should the Baenar flee my Desert one day soon, and should they arrive at your borders, allow them in. Give them refuge in your Territory."

Lethrix's eyes turned to slits. "How *oddly* specific. Another 'possible path' from your Kiabil?"

"Perhaps. That one is not certain."

"Hm. And if I *don't* give then refuge?"

"Then ..." Mazdek hesitated. "Their race shall pass. Probably in a manner worse than the Orcs."

"Worse?"

"They will be surrounded by the Hells and Celestials, hunted as the Deathwalkers are being hunted now, but by enemies they cannot stand against. You *know* the Naulor will get involved."

Lethrix exhaled, eyes rolling as he nodded in agreement.

"When they do," Mazdek finished, "the fighting will never pause on the Surface until the Baenar are destroyed. After that, the Territories *will* change again, and in a short time."

The Black Dragon rumbled deep in his chest. "That would keep us all *very* busy for a long time, wouldn't it?"

The Flame started to smirk. "Say farewell to your 'quiet trips' up top, Brother."

"*Hmph*." Lethrix smiled back, slowly. "I *suppose* I can stay Awake a while longer. To wait and see if this 'path' comes my way."

Mazdek could see his curiosity and enjoyment in being asked and felt relieved, accepting some small hope for his Desert's soul. He would even accept the snide comments which followed from the Tomb Guardian.

"And if the chaos is getting a bit much for you up here," Lethrix continued, "be sure to call me again. That *is* one talent I've mastered over most of you."

Mazdek dipped his chin. "You have learned to relish it."

"Not really." He grinned. "I've just learned to be incredibly flexible. One must be when half of the smartest creatures in my Territory think thoughts which eventually become reality."

Mazdek shuddered, hearing that about the Tomb; he couldn't help it. He nodded acceptance. "Then if you are so talented at managing ever-shifting states, Shadow Brother, tell me. Will you give the Baenar refuge if they come to you?"

"Gladly, Sun Brother."

"Thank you."

"Though, they *are* accustomed to their creature comforts, aren't they? And I haven't nearly the open range you have. *Heh!* I might have to offer them my largest room."

Before the baffled Mazdek could respond, Lethrix turned around, making as if to leave. Then he paused to peer over his shoulder, a white grin spreading in blackness like a crescent moon.

"I want to know what 'not of sound mind' means to the Flame, should he begin to dim," the Shadow said. "I look forward to our next talk."

The Tomb Guardian disappeared from the Red Desert in a silent fold of space and time.

Curious how **the Black Dragon** gets involved with the **Davrin Elves** in their place of refuge? Snatch some insight into the magic and bloodlines in the centuries following *The Desert*.

Pick up Tales of Miurag #1: The Deepearth at https://etaski.com/tales-of-miurag/, and read about secrets lost and tangled web of the Great Cavern underground.

The stories also have fantasy maps, timelines, and a glossary! Read extra tidbits about the characters and places in the story when you visit Etaski's series lore at World Anvil! at https://miurag.etaski.com

The Sister Seekers Prequel is available for free!

A century ago, one Priestess left for the Surface. She vanished. This is her story.

Irrwaer is an acolyte serving the Priestesses.

She would rather stay small, quiet, and avoid the bottomless appetites of her matriarchy.

As the healer works among meek males, rowdy Red Sisters, and the sinister sons of demons, she asks a troubling question.

In a place where power passes through daughters, why are the Priestesses only competing for sons?

But even the asking is dangerous.

Sooner or later, everyone disturbs the Spider Queen's web.

In *Sons to Keep*, Etaski introduces the political sphere of Sivaraus through the eyes of the least ambitious. These events occur one hundred years before the birth of the protagonist Sirana in *No Demons But Us,* yet their effects still ripple out from the center of a tightly woven tapestry.

Read *Sons to Keep: a Sister Seekers Prequel* FREE when you join Etaski's newsletter. Subscribe here! at https://etaski.com/about/

Begin *Sister Seekers* with *No Demons But Us,* a polyamorous dark epic fantasy! at https://etaski.com/sister-seekers/

My name is Sirana of House Thalluen. My sister is dead, but I didn't kill her. The infamous Sisterhood couldn't care less if I did.

I am a young Noble trapped in a most wretched spot: accused of assassinating my sister, the Matron's heir. If I take the blame, I am next on the sacrificial altar.

Dark Elves live for intrigue in our underground matriarchy. We bend the rules for the cunning and the bold. To survive, I must play the game.

Court intrigue, demonic rituals, and mind-rending trials against deadly foes - these pervasive webs surround me, spun by our sadistic priesthood and the Queen's brutal enforcers.

Through it all, the Red Sisters delight in watching me. I must prove myself beneath their ravenous gazes, or I will become the next meal for our goddess.

A.S. Etaski spins the first threads of an intense and epic tale with *No Demons But Us*, in which the trials of a young Davrin test her resolve to rise from the depths of fear and hatred tearing her down.

Sister Seekers is a mature, dark epic fantasy with an ever-broadening scope. *Found family* is a core theme throughout, and fans of *Dungeons & Dragons* will find familiar homebrew grounds. Perfect for fans of entwined plots, challenging themes, immersive worldbuilding, and elements of erotic horror. Sexuality and inner conflict play into character growth with nuance, intrigue, action, and magic.

The series begins underground with an isolated race of Dark Elves whose intricate webs first ensnare then catapult us to places a Red Sister can only imagine in her dreams.

ACKNOWLEDGMENTS

To my Hubs, texting family, and online friends who help keep me going,

My greatest appreciation to Doc Kangey, uncovering new skills to improve my books, and who works behind the scenes to improve my tools and options. Check out our hard work and lore yet to come at [Etaski.com] & [Miurag.Etaski.com].

THANK YOU, my Top Patrons who support all my efforts and keep those signed paperbacks comin'!

Sir Cumference, Baelus, Jesse C., Does, John K., Julie S., Paul B., Carla H., Briana R., Josanna, RainbowNight, Lesley PLAY, Kalculys-zero, NotSoWeird, Zenor , Kelly D., Lady Dia Meter, Raymond T., Zeroharas, Johnathon Matlock, Chris R., Daolord, Melwinne, Bradley L., and Roy Meyer, and in loving memory, Stacy Meyer.

ABOUT THE AUTHOR

Etaski has entertained herself with fantasy stories since the first day she sat on a school bus looking out the window. When hand-written letters were disappearing, she scribbled no less than five pages to be worth the postage. Her early stories were written by hand, and she had a writer's callus and three embarrassing novels before graduating high school.

She studied science, archaeology, history, and theater. Frank discussion of sexuality was rare growing up, so she wrote fantasies, theories, and observations within stories for deeper contemplation or just be entertained.

History speaks little on sexuality, yet biology demonstrates how it sways basic choices. Drama reveals our strongest bonds but may fade to black at its most intimate. In the Sister Seekers, the sex and the story are inseparable, and their discoveries will change the journey of Miurag without cutting away.

Etaski's Website: etaski.com
Etaski's Book Page: etaski.com/sister-seekers
Etaski's Series Lore: miurag.etaski.com
Etaski on Patreon: www.patreon.com/etaski
Etaski on GoodReads: www.goodreads.com/etaski
Etaski on BookBub: www.bookbub.com/authors/a-s-etaski
Etaski on Facebook: www.facebook.com/asetaski
Etaski on Mastodon: mastodon.online/@etaski